Mirikai

A PLACE OF PEACE

Anne Sinclair

TheBookStudio

Proudly produced by

TheBookStudio
www.thebookstudio.com.au

To our son Marty.

A caring, kind and loving man.
My love always.

— ACKNOWLEDGEMENTS —

*To friends and family
who've encouraged me along the way.
You know who you are
and I'm very grateful for all your support.*

*My sincere thanks to
Michelle Holyhead at The Book Studio.
Without her encouragement and expertise,
this story would not read as it should.*

ABOUT THE AUTHOR

Anne Sinclair is a New Zealand born Australian with a passion for travel. After residing in Canada for a year, the author returned to Auckland before heading to Australia for a working holiday. Her then partner, Bob, joined her in Surfers Paradise and after a year they went back to their hometown of Auckland where they married before again returning to live on the Gold Coast.

Taking four years out of a forty-year residency, they worked in Lae and Rabaul, New Guinea. Back on the Gold Coast once more, they established businesses, raised their family and involved themselves in Surf Lifesaving and Rugby Union.

Following retirement and the death of her husband, the author moved north to the Sunshine Coast and at the request of family, wrote of her husband's life. This launched Anne into the novel which she describes as 'faction'. Now an octogenarian, her yearning desire to travel and visit more of the world, remains.

CHAPTER ONE

In her comatose state as she gazed out to sea, a resurgence of childhood memories filled Louise's head; her parents, the relationship she shared with her older sister, Julie, and the way in which they incorporated humour into almost everything they did together. This was the beach where Louise happily spent the first eighteen years of her life but now, it was no longer embracing her with the same comfort that it always had.

Though she was a healthy, highly active young woman with many close friends, ever since returning home to New Zealand from North America six months ago, Louise somehow felt unsettled... and she couldn't quite put her finger on the cause.

Sauntering along the sand with the ocean lapping on the shore and the salty breeze blowing through her dark curls, she ruminated that up until this point there had been no romance in her life. Boys from school were always delighted to be her date for social dances and club events but there'd never been anyone she considered a 'romantic interest'.

Truth is, there was never really room for a boyfriend anyway. Working multiple jobs to save travel money was her foremost priority, which left little time for much of a social life. Perhaps a working holiday in Australia could resolve both issues. New adventures, experiences, and challenges were something that drove Louise's spirit.

Her thoughts were rudely interrupted by a cluster of voices anxiously calling her name. When she turned around to scan the open beach, there were only five other people even remotely in her vicinity. The voices continued to summons her and as she opened her mouth in an attempt to reply, no words would manifest.

Within a few seconds, the entire landscape began to spin

uncontrollably. Struggling to retain focus on anything, Louise's eyes closed before crippling pain forced her to her knees. A bolt of pure agony then shot down her right leg while she battled to keep her pulsing head from hitting the sand. As she gasped for breath, visions of soaring high above the clouds filtered through her mind.

The garbled voices kept calling until she could feel her weightless body steadily rise. Unable to move a muscle, Louise succumbed to the surreal forces that were overtaking her entire being.

A gentle touch on the shoulder suddenly jolted her consciousness, terminating the pain instantaneously. One clear voice could be heard coming from directly above Louise's head. Looking up with shock and bewilderment, she saw an elderly gentleman's face smiling down on her.

"Are you alright, young lass?" he asked concerningly, offering his hand.

"I don't know," Louise replied, completely perplexed. "I think I am now. I was hearing strange voices then I experienced incredible pain."

Helping her to her feet, he said, "I'd strongly suggest you go home young lady, drink plenty of water and get some rest. You could be suffering from sunstroke or dehydration. They've been known to cause hallucinations you know."

"Yes, you're probably right," Louise smiled. "That must be it. Thank you for your kindness."

After tipping his cap, the gentleman continued to stroll along the shoreline. Louise couldn't help but stare at him. There was something peculiarly familiar about his mannerism, his smile, and the way in which he walked. It was like she'd known him for years.

CHAPTER TWO

While Louise and Jean were students at Takapuna Grammar, their common sporting interests within the school sparked a thriving friendship. Although Jean was two classes ahead of her, their age difference was no barrier. A rather attractive girl, Jean was blessed with light-coloured curls, piercing blue eyes and a slim figure.

Jean came from a large family and all her siblings were sport oriented. The three older brothers played Rugby Union and her younger sister enjoyed basketball. By most standards, Jean wasn't considered tall but she certainly managed to dart around any tennis or squash court with speed and agility. She was also fond of a game of golf and like Louise, thoroughly enjoyed hanging out at the beach.

The girls also shared a passion for travel and couldn't wait to explore the globe. One morning early in March, Louise phoned Jean to suggest a working holiday in Australia. As expected, her friend was immediately receptive to the idea.

Only six weeks later, after several planning sessions over numerous cups of coffee, the friends departed New Zealand and flew to Brisbane in Queensland. From there they boarded a bus to the vibrant Gold Coast, arriving around midday, and headed to the nearest Newsagent to purchase a copy of The Bulletin newspaper. In the 'Units for Rent' section of the classifieds, they found a few suitable accommodation options and after making three phone calls, settled on a cheap little flat in the heart of Surfers Paradise.

"Yep…'little' is definitely the operative word for this unit," laughed Louise. "You have to go outside to change your mind!"

"And 'cheap' is the other word," Jean smiled ruefully as she stood examining the space. "It will do us for now. I'm going to start unpacking."

The following day Louise secured employment, washing dishes

in the kitchen of a well-known resort only a short distance from their flat. Thankfully by the next morning she'd already been promoted to a waitressing position. Jean also managed to acquire a job at the same establishment, so both girls waited tables in the main restaurant of the Beachcomber Resort.

Louise eagerly took her first order from the guests seated at table No.7 and promptly returned carrying a large plastic tray with four glasses of pineapple juice. As she carefully placed the third glass down on the table, the fourth one instantly slid off the tray. Before the glass crashed onto the carpet below, its sticky contents splattered all over the balding head of a well-dressed gentleman seated at an adjacent table.

"Oops! I'm so sorry sir," Louise whispered apologetically.

She was absolutely horrified about the incident, though the gentleman quietly chortled and told her not to worry about it.

Within moments the Restaurant Manager appeared and asked Louise, "Are you new to waitressing?"

'You've got that right!' she inwardly ridiculed herself. *'And I'm pretty sure that's the end of your fleeting career as a waitress.'* Very nervously she stared up at him and replied, "Well, yes, actually I am," and swiftly made her way to the kitchen.

When she returned, red-faced, with a damp cloth in hand ready to clean the table, the empathetic manager, a fellow New Zealander, merely shrugged his shoulders and said, "It's okay, it happens." He then slowly turned on his heels and smiled back at her as he made his way to the bar.

On Sunday evenings the restaurant hosted a 'Hawaiian Luau Night'. It was a feast for the senses and patrons were entertained by a local live band. As part of their employment obligations, female workers at the Beachcomber were expected to dress 'Hawaiian style' and perform the hula on Luau nights. Complete with grass skirts, bikini tops, plastic floral leis around their necks and hibiscus flowers in their hair, Louise and Jean felt pretty silly…but it did add an extra ten shillings to their weekly pay packets. At that time, no one was aware that the band who entertained on these evenings would eventually become world famous. They were none other than the 'Brothers Gibb' who would later be known as 'The Bee Gees'.

At that time, the twins, Robin and Maurice, were twelve years old and extremely cheeky while Barry, their older brother by four years, was already a bit of a 'spunk'. Their sister, Lesley, was also part of the entertainment on these nights. She performed with a carpet snake which she kept in a basket at the back of a small dressing room the girls shared. Louise and Jean were terrified of the reptile and always changed clothes as near to the door as possible.

The Gold Coast was perfect for Louise and Jean. Sun, sand and surf made for a very casual, healthy, and friendly lifestyle. They immersed themselves in the busy social lives of the young folk who were lucky enough to call Surfers Paradise home. The unit opposite their flat was tenanted by three young guys who lived in Brisbane during the week and came down to the coast on weekends. They were all members of the Surfers Paradise Surf Life Saving Club and were required to patrol the beach on weekends and public holidays during summertime to keep the beach-going public safe. These three guys were great, as were the girlfriends they recycled frequently.

It didn't take long for Louise and Jean to also befriend two tradies who lived on the bottom floor of their unit complex. Don Evans was an electrician and his mate Ross Green was a bricklayer. They were both from Sydney and like the girls, Don and Ross were enjoying a working, surfing holiday. In the late fifties and early sixties, Surfers Paradise experienced a construction boom like never before, so work for tradesmen was plentiful but if the surf was up, absenteeism was a major problem for employers.

Louise and Jean played squash in the local competition and spent a fair bit of their time on the beach while the boys were out on their surfboards. Don played Rugby Union in the cooler winter months, so Ross and the girls became avid members of his cheer squad. There were loads of parties held at both the Surf Life Saving Club and the Rugby Club, the latter of which consisted mostly of Kiwis. Their Maori players were always up for a sing-along after each game and regularly brought their guitars to matches throughout the season. In the Chevron Hotel each afternoon and evening, 'The Maori Hi-Fi's' band drew a massive crowd to every gig. The locals sang their hearts out and almost danced their feet off at any opportunity.

Maureen and Simon Bishop owned the nearby squash courts.

Louise and Jean often had jovial conversations with Simon and discovered that he was a former Kiwi Rugby League representative. A group of his old team mates had just arrived from across the Tasman for a holiday, providing them all with a good excuse to party. Simon decided to ask the boys from 'The Maori Hi-Fi's' to put down a traditional New Zealand 'hangi' on the vacant land next to the squash courts.

"That'd be good eh, boy," Richie, the lead singer agreed, as did the balance of the band.

On Saturday morning they arrived early, armed with shovels to dig a huge hole in the sandy soil. After the earthmoving was complete, they built a fire underneath a structure of old bricks and some large, hardened rocks. On top of this base, pumpkin, sweet potato, cabbage, chicken and pork were placed and wrapped in a large, wet, bedsheet. More drenched sheets were used for additional layering then the sand that they originally dug up, was shovelled over the top. There was ample food to feed around fifty guests.

While the hangi steamed throughout the day, numerous trestle tables were erected upon which to serve the delectable culinary delights. Later that afternoon, in-between the band's first gig and their evening show, the boys returned to remove the sandy earth and uncover the food. As they gently transferred the feast to the trestle tables, it looked mouth-watering but...

Richie shook his head and looked grimly at his mates. "I don't think we should eat this, eh. It doesn't smell right."

"Yeah bro, smells like shit!" Tui admitted.

Upon closer inspection, the problem was finally revealed. The septic system beneath the squash courts had, over time, leached into the sandy soil of the vacant lot next door. This sewage was responsible for tainting the food as it steamed underground. What a disaster...and a complete waste of time and good food! After a lengthy clean-up and a long haul to the dump everyone gathered at the local pub, bitterly disappointed but they all managed to laugh it off.

• • • • •

Louise and Jean usually double-dated with Ross and Don on their outings but one Friday night, Ross plucked up the courage to ask Louise out on her own. 'The Captain's Table' was a prime venue. It overlooked the beach and the ambience was quite romantic. Over dinner and a bottle of Cabernet Sauvignon, Ross opened up to Louise for the first time about his past.

"I have a sister, Emily, a couple of years younger than me but we don't keep in touch. Sadly, she's legally blind. She lives in Sydney with her two daughters." Ross paused briefly then added, "We lost our parents in a car accident when we were in high school. I think that's why I'm a bit shy, as you've probably noticed. You might have also figured out that I'm blind in one eye. Born that way I'm afraid. It sure made my school years tough, constantly being teased and bullied. Needless to say, I wasn't too fond of school so I opted out early." He took a deep breath and looked up at Louise. "I never talk about those early years but I honestly feel like I can chat with you Lou."

Louise was absolutely stumped. She didn't quite know how to respond, except to say, "I'm so sorry Ross…and I'm glad you can relax enough with me to talk about it. My childhood was quite the opposite, so I can only imagine what it must have been like for you."

Ross became slightly restless. "Enough about me. I don't know much about your background Lou. Tell me your story."

Louise took a sip of wine and gently swallowed. "I grew up in Auckland and I have an older sister, Julie, who's a nurse. She married John Keane who lived across the road from us. He's a doctor now. I left school at fifteen because I wanted to work and save money to travel. All my life I heard Mum talk about Canada, she's from Vancouver, and I wanted to go there. I worked three jobs, saved hard and finally got there. After working in Vancouver for a few months, I visited some of Mum's friends across Canada and made my way down into America. Then I travelled through the southern states by bus, back to the west, and up the coast from Los Angeles back to Vancouver."

"Sounds like a great trip," Ross commented.

"Yes, it certainly was," Louise admitted. "When I got back to New Zealand I lived at home, worked two jobs and then got itchy feet again. I rang Jean to see if she wanted to come to Australia with me and she did, so here we are. Enjoying the sunshine and the Gold Coast lifestyle."

Ross casually leaned back in his chair and asked, "Is your sister like you?"

"She's almost nine years older. I think I was quite a surprise to my parents," Louise gestured. "Julie's a tall, fair-haired, compassionate woman. We're rather similar in appearance and despite the age difference, we're very close. In fact, we all are. Mum came to New Zealand for a working holiday and happened to meet Dad in Auckland, so that was as far as she got. Dad and his brother own butcher shops. We live right on the beach on the North Shore. I went to Takapuna Grammar and I loved sport - track and field, swimming, basketball...pretty much any sport really. I had a stable, happy childhood."

After finishing their conversation and the bottle of wine, they left the restaurant and walked hand in hand back to Louise and Jean's flat for coffee. Upon arrival, they found a note from Jean saying that she was out with Don for a while.

As Louise was busily preparing coffee, Ross came over and hugged her from behind. She slowly turned to him and their lips met. As they kissed, their embraced bodies stumbled towards the lounge. These kisses were something quite new to both of them and as they intensified, Ross fumbled with the buttons on Louise's blouse. She really wanted him and when they finally managed to lay on the lounge, Louise became very aware that he too was aroused. Just as Ross released the final button of her blouse, they heard footsteps ascending the stairs outside.

The couple quickly parted and Louise rushed back to the kitchen counter to complete the coffee making and do up her buttons. They were both flushed, as this was their first foray into romance. Now somewhat embarrassed, Ross promptly consumed his coffee and headed back down to his unit.

• • • • •

Louise strolled past an eclectic art gallery on Cavill Avenue one

Saturday morning and decided to take a peek inside. The assistant looked up from the watercolour painting that she was working on and introduced herself as Jillian Rhodes.

"If there are any pieces that catch your eye, just let me know," Jillian smiled. "Some of the paintings are mine and there are also a number of local artists who sell through this cooperative. I'll leave you to browse. Enjoy!"

The gallery was unusually quiet so Louise and the assistant chatted for a while, discovering that they shared a common love for body surfing and art, although Louise admitted that she wasn't artistic by any means. They bonded immediately and over the subsequent weeks, both women enjoyed catching up to surf many waves together.

Within a couple of months, Jillian, who was a school art teacher during the week, was transferred from the Gold Coast to a new school in Caloundra on the Sunshine Coast, north of Brisbane. "I promise to call you when I get settled," she assured Louise. "I hope you'll come up for a visit and do some surfing."

The promised call came from Jillian some six weeks later. "Come up and visit on the May Day weekend Louise," she suggested. "I only live one block back from Dicky Beach and I surf every day. Can you get that long weekend off?"

"I sure can and I'd love to do that," Louise replied. "I now have an office job so no more shift-work for me anymore. And my weekends are my own. I'll ask to take a half-day off and catch the Greyhound bus up on the Friday afternoon. Is that okay with you?"

"That's great. Let me know what time you're due in Caloundra and I'll pick you up at the bus depot. Finally bought myself a little car last week!" Jillian announced excitedly.

• • • • • •

True to her word, Jillian was at the depot when Louise's bus pulled in. "So good to see you Louise! I don't know many people up here yet, so it's great to see a familiar face." She squeezed her friend tightly.

Jillian's small two-bedroom flat was only a short drive from the depot and as soon as they opened the front door, the women changed into their bikinis, grabbed their towels and headed over to Dicky Beach for a swim. The water was cool but the waves were perfect for body surfing.

Back in Jillian's flat, following a hot shower, the women relaxed with a glass of chilled white wine and caught up on their respective pieces of news. Jillian confided in Louise and told her that she'd met an engineer who was working on a dam just outside Caloundra in the hinterland. "It's becoming quite serious," she admitted.

In return, Louise told her friend that she was still seeing Ross and they were getting along really well. "I don't know where it's headed. Time will tell, I suppose," she smiled.

Jillian had already painted a couple of local scenes since she moved. One particularly stood out to Louise. It depicted the wreck of the ship '*Dicky*', after which the beach was named. Louise truly admired her friend's work and said, "I'm telling you Jill, when I finally settle down in my own place, I'll buy one of your paintings; probably this one of the Dicky Beach wreck. I just love it."

When Louise returned to Surfers Paradise, and her new bookkeeping job with a TV repair company, she and Jean were chatting over coffee. "I'm tired of being a waitress," Jean blurted, slumping in her seat. "I want to move to Brisbane and look for a 'real' job Lou. One of Don's friends in Brisbane is an electrical contractor and he's about to launch into a big project. Don phoned to see if he had work for him and he has, so we want to move north together. Would you mind?"

"No, not at all. I guess it's time to move on and see more of Australia. We've been on the Gold Coast for almost a year now," Louise sincerely assured her friend.

That evening, Louise told Ross about Jean and Don's plans. Ross confessed that he too felt like a change of scenery and suggested that perhaps now was the perfect time, especially since their two pals would be moving north on their own.

"What do you think about us moving to the West Coast for a while Lou? Get some work. Have a look around?" Ross prompted.

Louise thought about his proposal for a few moments. "Why not. I like the idea. A new adventure...and I love new adventures.

Western Australia sounds terrific. There's just one thing before we go. I want to head home and visit my family back in Auckland. Mum and Dad sold the shops a few months ago and they're retiring."

"Okay. Sounds like a plan," Ross declared. "I haven't been to New Zealand. You can show me around your home town."

• • • • • •

They departed Brisbane and flew across the Tasman for a scheduled two-week holiday. Louise introduced Ross to her friends and family, telling them of their future plans.

A week into their trip, Julie quietly took her sister aside. "Ross seems to be a decent guy, Lou, but I noticed that Mum and Dad haven't taken to him at all."

William and Elizabeth were attempting to dissuade their daughter from returning to Australia. "Why don't you stay home for a while Louise? Your mother and I would love that," her father persisted.

Louise reasoned that their reluctance was due to the fact that they didn't want her to be eight hours flying time from Auckland. She was touched by their concern but being young and adventurous, Louise knew that she would follow through with the plans that she and Ross had made together.

CHAPTER THREE

At first, Western Australia's capital seemed to be a very long way from anywhere. Ross quickly found work in the construction industry on the outskirts of Perth but it took Louise a little longer to find a job. Eventually she sourced some secretarial work with a mining company. Renting a mediocre two-bedroom unit close to their workplaces and the beach, Ross and Louise began saving for a car. They wanted to leave the city on long weekends and discover places like Cape Leeuwin and Margaret River, a fledgling wine producing area to the south, also renowned for its surf beaches.

Their relationship flourished and they grew ever closer. Even though Louise didn't find sex very exciting, or understand what some of her friends raved about, she felt that it was the dutiful thing to do and endured the intimacy whilst enjoying the affectionate aspect of the bond they shared. From time to time, she'd reflect on their sexual liaisons and think, *'Surely there's more to it than that!'* But in the end, Louise accepted the fact that perhaps there wasn't any more to the experience.

Over coffee one evening Ross assertively said, "There's so much to see in this State Lou. Monkey Mia to the north, where people feed dolphins by hand at the water's edge; Kalgoorlie to the east is a gold mining town that looks really interesting too. Covering the distances between them is pretty vast, across long, straight roads that aren't always in good condition, so we'll need a sturdy vehicle that's capable of holding together over sand and corrugation."

"Yes," Louise agreed. "And it would be extremely helpful if it was big enough to sleep in, should the weather turn nasty. Living in a tent in the soaking wet isn't for me, I have to say."

Ross had always demonstrated an excellent work ethic and began entering bricklaying competitions. The winner was determined by the tradie who could lay a thousand bricks in the quickest time. Ross attained a number of awards for his efforts and he was a proudly skilled tradesman. In turn, Louise was achieving success in the mining company, graduating from a pool of secretaries to become the Office Manager and within a short period of time, she was promoted as Personal Assistant to one of the Directors.

Internet technology and computer skills were becoming a necessity in the commerce sector and although Louise found this challenging, it captured her interest and she embraced the new techniques while absorbing as much knowledge as she could.

"Ross, eventually, as a side-line to my job with the company, I wouldn't mind starting up a small business teaching others the skills I've learned on the job," Louise explained. "My idea would be to first run evening classes from home and see where that leads. If it turns out to be a success, I could resign and pursue the teaching instead. What do you think? Would it be okay with you if I taught here at home in the evenings?"

"Of course. I'm fine with that," Ross replied, showing great interest in Louise's initiative. "I know you like challenges and with your happy disposition and ability to get along with people, I think you'd enjoy something like that. It wouldn't require much capital if everyone brought their own computer to the classes."

Louise's mind was suddenly consumed with planning and ideas for her business. Within days, placing an advertisement in the local newspaper resulted in four replies; three from women who were all keen to embrace the new technology.

As the business grew rapidly, it wasn't long before Louise's name became known. Her ability to clearly and patiently impart her knowledge to others spread around the city of Perth and before she knew it, working on Saturdays even became necessary. As Ross also worked most Saturdays, this caused little disruption to their time spent together.

Through their respective jobs, Ross and Louise gathered around them a number of friends and acquaintances. Some shared the same recreational interests and when the couple purchased a suitable vehicle for their excursions, whenever time allowed, they would take off on camping trips with like-minded friends in tow.

Their lives were extremely busy and in time, as Louise's business continued to thrive, Ross commented over dinner one evening, "You know what Lou? Our weekend trips seem to be falling by the wayside. Work commitments are interfering with our leisure time. When are you finally going to resign from the company and make your side-line business a full-time career? Instead of working weekends myself, I can take on little cash jobs that come up and we can get our weekends back."

Louise knew he was right. Within a week she resigned and rented a quiet boardroom-type office space in the city, placed another advertisement in the newspaper and set upon what she hoped would develop into a full-time career teaching Internet Technology and Computer Skills.

Again, word of mouth and advertising proved to be beneficial and within six months the business had already expanded. She was now teaching classes of 8-10 students at a time. It seemed that everyone in class knew someone who could benefit from her knowledge.

"This is really fun Ross. I'm so glad that I bit the bullet and expanded. It's very satisfying to see my students achieve their goals and graduate," Louise proudly said as she hugged him.

•••••

On a particularly calm Sunday, Ross and Louise hired a small launch, packed a scrumptious picnic lunch and headed out to Rottnest Island. After a leisurely swim and some snorkelling, they found a picnic table and set about devouring the prawns and sipping their perfectly-chilled white Riesling. Tiny quokkas were playing within a short distance of the table.

"They're so cute…just like miniature kangaroos," smiled Louise.

While she was admiring the tiny critters, Ross had already refilled their glasses. He turned and stood in front of her. Slowly bending down on one knee, he gently took Louise's hand in his own and candidly looked up into her face. "Lou," he softly said, "we've been together for a while now and I want it to last forever. Will you marry me?"

Louise was absolutely dumbfounded. Yes, she did love him, but they'd never discussed marriage before. This came right out of left field. She occasionally wondered if one day marriage might be a possibility but had never given it serious thought. Ultimately, she knew that she wanted a family and would like to be married before having children.

"Well...what a surprise this is!" Louise responded cautiously. "Have you been thinking about this for a while, or is this proposal as spontaneous as it seems?"

Ross smiled as his eyes widened. "Yes, for a while now. We get along so well and I love you. I'm just hoping that you love me enough to say 'yes'?"

Louise lovingly threw her arms around Ross and whispered, "Yes, yes, yes!"

With a huge sigh of relief, Ross affectionately kissed her and said, "I thought we could select your engagement ring together. Don't think I'd be too good at choosing the right one. Besides, you have to really like it because you'll be wearing it for the rest of your life."

CHAPTER FOUR

Over the course of the next few days, Ross and Louise realised that planning the nuptials would be difficult. They only wanted a small, intimate celebration. Louise would love to have her family attend but with sister Julie pregnant again, her husband working long hours at the hospital and their two-year-old daughter to manage, she knew that they would be reluctant to travel the distance to Perth. As would her elderly parents. Ross and his sister Emily grew apart many years ago, so he has never even met his teenage nieces.

"I don't mind that my family won't be at the wedding, but I know that you would really like your family to celebrate with us," Ross remarked as he sat down.

"What a dilemma!" Louise returned. "I'd be reluctant to spend our hard-earned savings on returning to New Zealand, especially when I know that Mum and Dad - particularly Mum - would want to take over everything. They'd expect us to be married in a local church with all the usual trappings of a big wedding. That's not at all what we want."

Ross agreed. They briefly sat in silence, each trying to resolve the issue in their own mind.

"Okay, how about this" Louise started. "Why don't we get married here in Perth with just a few close friends and advise the family later. Let's arrange a casual, barefoot event on the beach at Scarborough with a celebrant to conduct a simple service. We can then all head over to our favourite 'Sea Shells' Restaurant opposite the beach for lunch afterwards. What do you think of that idea?"

"I reckon that would be perfect," smiled Ross. "We'll make a list of invitees and keep it short. And, let's not tell our guests that we're getting married. We don't need gifts because we already have everything we need, so keeping it a secret would be the way to go.

That way it'll be a surprise for everyone." He then hesitated for a moment. "On the other hand, you may want to ask Jean to be your bridesmaid. If that's the case, I'd ask Don to be my Best Man. But… do we really want or need attendants at our 'no fuss' celebration?"

Louise quickly pondered the idea. "Look, I'd really love Jean and Don to be here but I don't think I want a 'bridal party' as such. It's too complicated."

"I agree," Ross said, slowly nodding his head.

"Don and Jean were talking about visiting Perth for their next holiday. Why don't we try to get them to settle on a date for their visit, and not say anything about us getting married?" Louise suggested.

Ross, completely in favour of Louise's idea, decided to call Don and sound him out. "How about you two firming up those holiday dates," Ross encouraged. "When we spoke to you in January you were talking about coming over here at Easter. Do it mate!" Don quickly signalled for Jean to pick up the other phone so that she too could hear their conversation. She nodded enthusiastically and grabbed the receiver. "We have plenty of room for you to stay with us," Ross added, "and we'll meet you at the airport. We might even take some time off while you're here to show you around. You know, do some camping and surfing. Go down to Margaret River and taste some of their fabulous wines. It'll be like old times."

"Bloody good suggestion mate," Don concurred. "Tomorrow Jean and I will apply for two weeks leave. If it's approved, we'll book the flights and let you know."

• • • • •

Louise's face lit up with excitement when Don phoned Ross to say that their holiday leave had been accepted. "We can't wait!" he shouted. "We've booked the red-eye flight for Thursday afternoon and arrive just after midnight on Good Friday morning. With the public holidays included, we'll be there for two weeks. Hope this suits you both because the flights are non-refundable. Oh, and one more thing…I'm not bringing my board either, so wax up your spare one for me and let's hope the surf's up."

"That's great news Don," Ross replied. "Make sure you pack something other than boardshorts and thongs because we're having a posh lunch with friends of ours on Easter Saturday. We're looking so forward to seeing you both mate."

When Ross hung up the phone, Louise's broad, cheeky smile beamed back at him. "Now we can arrange our wedding," he proclaimed. "We've got six weeks to get it organised."

"What a surprise in store for everyone. Especially my family," Louise said, tongue in cheek. "It will be a fait accompli by the time they're told. We can expect plenty of flack and criticism but they'll get over it."

• • • • • •

Sifting through the Yellow Pages directory, Louise found three Marriage Celebrants to contact within their area. Fortunately, Dianne Sutton was available at short notice thanks to a previous cancellation.

The next phone call was to 'Sea Shells' where Louise and Ross were well known. Without alluding to the fact that it was for a wedding celebration, Louise reserved a small, private area of the venue for sixteen people, advising that guest numbers may change slightly. The receptionist explained, "We have concertina doors to make the room smaller or larger, so that won't be a problem."

With a view to the informality and secrecy of the upcoming occasion, rather than tipping off their friends by sending out invitations, Ross and Louise phoned each of them. This was their overall spiel. "We have good friends coming over from Brisbane and we want you to meet them, so we're organising a posh lunch at 'Sea Shells' for noon on Easter Saturday. Hope you won't be going away and that you can join us. We thought we'd all meet for drinks in the shade overlooking the beach opposite the restaurant at about 11am. We'll arrange an esky of grog for pre-lunch drinks. Our shout!" One couple had already planned a holiday to Esperance but all the others said that they would be available and were looking forward to it.

Her wedding dress was next on Louise's list. Again, it had to be simple. A cream-coloured, slimline, full-length dress with shoe-lace straps. She'd also need closely-matching sandals. Jewellery was easy; Louise wanted to wear the pearl earrings and single pearl pendant that Julie gave her for her 21st birthday. A plain, gold bangle that belonged to her grandmother would complete the look. In keeping with tradition, this took care of something 'old' and something 'new'. As for something 'borrowed', perhaps the dress-maker could think about that while she was also making something 'blue', which Louise decided should be a blue garter.

Close to Louise's office there was a wedding outfitters store. The following day she popped in to discuss her ideas with the owner. A statuesque woman, perhaps in her late forties, introduced herself as Rita Marsh. She attentively listened to Louise's every word.

"So…you don't want any beading?" Rita asked. Louise shook her head. "Then may I suggest a cream shot-silk fabric. It would fall very nicely and take away the starkness of a plain silk, providing more 'interest' if you will. I think it would be a marvellous choice. I'll show you a sample of the fabric I have in mind."

Rita stepped into the back area of the store and returned with some samples. At first glance, Louise pounced on what she considered would be perfect.

Smiling gracefully, Rita said, "I thought that one would catch your eye." From behind the counter, she produced a pad of paper and a pencil, and began sketching. Within one minute Rita came up with exactly what Louise had envisaged.

Louise informed Rita of her jewellery choices and added, "I'm a bit concerned about my something 'borrowed' item. I can't think of anything. Would you be able to help me with that?"

"Leave it with me Louise. I'll give it some considerable thought and get back to you," Rita assured her. "For now, please allow me to take some measurements and your contact details. "When you come in for your first fitting, I will run my ideas past you."

Being the consummate professional that Rita was, Louise's measurements were recorded in no time and she made it back to work just as the first of her students were filing into the office.

At home that night while preparing dinner, Louise gasped. "Gosh Ross! We almost forgot about wedding rings."

"True," Ross blurted, almost spilling his beer. "I tell you what…I could meet you in town tomorrow after work. I'm pretty sure the jewellers don't close before 5:30pm. Should give us plenty of time, don't you think?" Louise agreed. The sooner the better.

A week after Ross proposed, Louise chose a plain but stunning solitaire engagement ring with the idea that her wedding ring could slot securely on either side of it. After trying on several gold bands, one was perfectly contoured to match her engagement ring.

"What a confusing array to choose from," Ross commented. It took him a while but eventually they settled on a simple, flat, wide band of white gold.

A week later, Rita phoned Louise. "The first fitting is ready if you'd like to come in during your lunch hour one day this week. I'll be here Monday to Friday. Please bring in the shoes you'll be wearing with your gown, if you already have them."

On her way home from work that day, Louise stopped at her favourite shoe shop and found a nice pair of strappy cream sandals. They were understated but elegant just the same.

With excited anticipation, Louise couldn't wait to see the makings of her wedding dress. She rushed to the shop the following day and Rita happily greeted her at the counter. In the fitting room, once the gown was gently positioned on Louise's frame, she faced the mirror and sheer pleasure showed in her eyes.

"Now I gave some thought to your 'borrowed' item and I ran this up for you," Rita said, handing Louise a long piece of the same fabric used for her gown. "Even though you seem to have all the wedding arrangements covered, there's one other thing you can count on…and that's Perth's unpredictable weather, particularly around late morning at the time you've planned the ceremony. The 'Fremantle Doctor' is sure to blow in from the Indian Ocean and it can be a little chilly, so you may need a stole for warmth. I know you didn't order it, but I'm going to loan it to you if you'd like it to be your something 'borrowed'. I've securely weighted the ends so that it can't fly away if the wind does get up."

"What a brilliant idea and certainly a practicality that I hadn't considered," Louise replied. "Thank you, Rita. I'd love to borrow it. You've solved my problem beautifully."

Rita demonstrated several different ways that the stole could be worn. The outfit remained simple, elegant and practical, just like Louise herself. "Oh, and for the final touch," Rita added, "you'd better try on the garter for size." It was delicately laced with a pale blue ribbon braided through the centre. A perfect fit, positioned just above the knee.

Admiring her handiwork, Rita smiled and said, "I think only one more fitting will be required Louise, and as most brides-to-be tend to lose a little weight before the big day, we'll leave the fitting until about a week before the scheduled date. Any minor adjustments to the gown can be made then. Now lastly, do you want a headpiece or veil of any type?"

Louise hadn't considered that. She intended to get her hair cut quite short just before the wedding and opted out of carrying a bouquet, but that's all she knew. "I think I'll just put a small hibiscus or frangipani behind my ear, and I'll pick that on the day. What do you think Rita? It's in keeping with my 'KISS' plan - 'Keep it Simple Stupid'."

"I think that would be delightful!" Rita admitted.

"After the ceremony, instead of throwing a bouquet that I won't have, perhaps I could throw the garter?" questioned Louise.

"Good idea," Rita agreed. "In that case, how about I make another garter, one for you to throw and one to keep?"

"Love it!" Louise concurred with elation.

•••••••

Over a crispy-cold beer on the deck, ten days before their wedding, Ross suddenly exclaimed, "What about the wedding cake?" In all the planning and excitement, they'd neglected this important element. "Gotta say, I don't care too much for fruitcake Lou, but you know I'm rather partial to chocolate cake topped with rich chocolate icing."

"Me too darling," Louise returned, licking her lips at the very thought of it. "Everything else we're doing is pretty unconventional, so let's pass on the fruitcake tradition and run with the chocolate cake. I'll call 'Sea Shells' and ask if they could make one for us.

After we cut the cake, the staff can serve it up for dessert."

"Ah yes, I'm marrying a very sensible girl," Ross grinned. "And what about the night before the wedding Lou? I've heard that the groom shouldn't see the bride before she walks down the aisle or in our case, down the beach."

Placing her pointer finger to her lips, Louise thought about Ross's question and answered momentarily. "Mmmm…that's true. Well, Jean and Don will be staying here with us, so on Friday morning, why don't you boys take off on an overnight camping/ surfing junket? It would just mean that you both have to shower and change and get to Scarborough before I do. Obviously, you'll need to take dressy clothes with you and just tell Don that you're both going straight to the restaurant. He knows that we've organised a luncheon with friends." Louise scanned her eyes over the long skirt she was wearing and added, "As for Jean and I, we'll take my car to the beach. I know she'll question why I'm so over-dressed but I'll just tell her that as I'm the hostess and it's a special lunch, I thought why not go all out!"

Ross slowly got out of his chair and said, "Sounds like an excellent plan my love." Collecting their empty beer bottles, he then continued. "At least I don't have to wear a suit. Cream slacks, a white linen shirt, pair of deck-shoes, a shower and a clean shave… shouldn't look too suspicious." He ambled inside and placed the bottles on the kitchen counter. Returning to the deck, Louise rose from her chair and Ross placed his arms around her waist. "I think we've got everything covered. I'm really looking forward to seeing our friends' faces when they watch you walk down the beach to join me. And I'm pretty sure when they see the celebrant, it will be the first hint that we're getting married. Are you excited my beautiful bride-to-be?"

Louise kissed him and held his cheeks firmly in the palms of her hands. Tears of joy began to well in her eyes. "I can't wait to be Louise Green," she said softly. "Six months ago, I hadn't even thought of being someone's wife…and now look what we're doing!"

• • • • • •

The week of the wedding swiftly arrived and on Tuesday, in her lunch hour, Louise went for her final gown fitting. It was perfect and no adjustments were required. Rita meticulously placed the gown into a garment bag, together with the stole and both garters. After the two women shared a polite hug, Rita wished Louise all the very best for her impending marriage. Now, Louise and Ross were finding it more difficult than ever to maintain their secret.

On the Wednesday after work, Louise had her dark hair cut and styled just as she had envisaged it. Above the shoulders, soft and feminine with plenty of layering and texture. Her husband-to-be was equally as pleased with the result.

They'd discussed the issue of a photographer but Ross was very reluctant. With no sight at all in his left eye, Ross's eyelid was slightly drooped and he'd been self-conscious of it ever since childhood. As an adult, he largely overcame being embarrassed about his appearance but still remained hesitant to have photographs taken. In this instance though, he knew that Louise would want to mark their special occasion and send pictures home to her family.

"Instead of a commercial photographer Ross, how do you feel about giving Don and Jean our cameras before the ceremony and they can record the event for us? I'm sure it wouldn't be an imposition for them and that way we can get some candid, relaxed shots, instead of 'purposefully posed' photos. They can also take photos of our guests and in turn have the guests take photos of them."

"I'd feel a lot more comfortable with that," Ross admitted. "Yep, let's do it that way." He smiled to himself and slowly felt the tension ease from his neck and shoulders. *'That's my girl. Always so thoughtful and considerate.'*

CHAPTER FIVE

Louise and Ross casually chatted and discussed final wedding arrangements as they drove to the airport to meet up with their friends. Two years had passed since they'd seen one another and the couples were looking so forward to catching up. Departing the terminal at around 12:30am they arrived home some twenty minutes later, all very tired and more than happy to flop straight into bed.

The following morning over their Good Friday breakfast in the unit, Ross suggested to Don, "How about you and I drive a little way south to Dunsborough and catch some waves? The surf and weather reports are great for the entire Easter weekend. If we leave shortly, we could have half a day on the waves then knock back a few beers and watch the sun set over the Indian Ocean. It's a full moon too."

"Sounds fine with me mate," Don eagerly replied.

Ross finished his second slice of toast and added, "We'll stay the night and on Saturday morning we can catch an early morning wave, then shower and spruce up into our good rags and be back in Perth by 11am. That's when we've planned to meet everyone at the beach across from the restaurant. It's my shout mate. And I already have beer in the esky…knew you wouldn't say no. Just have to pick up some ice on our way down."

After the men left, Louise and Jean lingered over coffee with plenty of 'girl chat'. Louise was very cautious not to let any secrets accidentally slip out. "We've got the whole day and night together Jean. What do you want to do first?"

"Well, being a public holiday, I presume most of the shops are closed. So, I'd really love to go and see a 'chick flick' at the cinema while the guys are gone. Been a long time since we watched a movie together. Are you up for that?" asked Jean.

"You're a mind-reader my friend! I'm totally in," Louise grinned.

Very late that afternoon when the friends arrived home, Louise quickly whipped up a tossed chicken salad for dinner, which they enjoyed on the deck over a couple of wines. At around 9pm Jean began to weary from her long-haul flight the day before and both women decided to call an early night.

Sleep didn't come easily for the bride-to-be. There was so much to contemplate and ponder over. Excitement was mounting and the enormity of the following day was absorbing her with stark clarity.

• • • • • •

Saturday morning unfolded and beckoned Louise through clear skies. *'Nothing can go wrong from here,'* she cheerfully convinced herself. "Jean. Are you awake?"

"I sure am…been up for an hour," came Jean's response from the spare bedroom. "I'm still trying to finish this stupid crossword puzzle that I started weeks ago. Seriously, it's doing my head in!"

Louise laughed and sat bolt upright in bed. "That means you need a good, strong coffee…come on, I'll make you one."

"The 'Sea Shells' restaurant is a ten-minute drive from here," Louise told her friend over breakfast. "We'll meet the guys at Scarborough Beach around 11:15am."

"Sounds good", Jean replied.

Both women casually showered and dressed. Jean stood open-mouthed when Louise emerged from her bedroom. "Oh, you look absolutely stunning," Jean commented. "Am I under-dressed?"

"Not at all. You look lovely Jean. I just felt like glamming up as the host of this luncheon," Louise answered.

Ross was well organised and thoughtful enough to quickly phone Louise before she left the unit. "We just stopped at the bottleshop and grabbed the drinks and some more ice. Now we're making our way to Scarborough, so everything's going to plan. Should be there in about five minutes."

Louise let out a gentle sigh of relief. In order to be fashionably late for her wedding, she wanted to arrive ten minutes after the scheduled time. This ensured that guests would already have drinks in hand and she certainly didn't want to arrive before the groom.

Ross and Don pulled up at the park and hauled the esky from the back of the ute. Restaurant staff, as requested, had set up a table with drinking glasses under the trees opposite the venue and another smaller table down on the sparkling shore of the Indian Ocean.

One of their perceptive friends noticed the small table arrangement at the water's edge. "What do you suppose is going on there?" he asked Ross, pointing in its direction.

"Don't know," Ross responded. "I'll wander down and check it out." Setting his empty beer glass down, he then removed his shoes and casually strolled down to speak with Dianne, their celebrant.

Within a few minutes Louise and Jean arrived. At that point, Ross beckoned their friends down onto the sand to join him.

The guests chatted while making their way to the shoreline, looking at one another questioningly. Meanwhile, Louise had asked Jean to wait on the grass while she swiftly returned to the car. On her way, she picked a frangipani flower from a nearby tree and whilst at the car, skewered a toothpick through the base of it and placed the bloom behind her ear. She then grabbed two cameras from the back seat, locked the door and returned to Jean.

Handing the cameras to her friend she said, "Would you and Don mind taking a few pictures please?"

Suddenly, Jean twigged. "Oh my God! You two are getting married!"

"Yep, we are," grinned Louise. Her eyes lit up. "You make your way down and I'll follow in a moment. I just need to take off my sandals."

The excitement was palpable. Smiles of approval radiated from the faces of their guests as they turned to watch the striking barefoot bride glide her way down the beach towards her groom. This scene drew the attention of many onlookers and as the guests cheered, whistled and laughed, so too did the gathering crowd.

Facing each other, holding hands and looking deeply into one another's eyes, Ross and Louise proclaimed the vows they'd memorised and zealously exchanged wedding rings. Finally declaring them "Man and Wife," Dianne then smiled at Ross and added, "you may now kiss your bride."

As soon as the register was signed their guests let loose with further cheers, offering kisses and hugs of congratulations. The group then followed 'Mr and Mrs Green' over to the 'Sea Shells' restaurant where celebrations began in earnest.

After a delicious lunch was devoured by all, including the chocolate wedding cake/dessert, Ross knelt down on the floor and Louise placed her foot up on his raised knee. He leaned forward and kissed her leg before slowly removing the garter. Louise then acquired it from his hand and turning her back on their guests, threw it over her shoulder. Amid the laughter, one of their single friends caught it and waved it in the air with delight.

Much to Ross's great surprise, Louise had secretly organised a local Maori couple who were very well known in Perth, to sing and play guitar after lunch. The musical treat was Louise's wedding gift to her husband. Everyone danced and joined in the entertainment until it was close to 7pm, when the reception came to an end.

The day had gone just as they planned. Ross and Louise couldn't be happier. Preparing to leave the venue and bid their farewells, a rather tipsy friend asked the couple, "Where are you going on your honeymoon? When do you leave?"

Ross affectionately placed his arms around his wife and said, "We want to visit the Dampier Peninsula but it's too hot there until mid-year, so we'll wait a while. Besides, it allows us to spend quality time with Don and Jean while they're over here."

●　●　●　●　●　●

By Sunday afternoon Louise knew that she had to inform her family of the news. They couldn't delay the inevitable any longer. With the phone on loud speaker, she called her parents in New Zealand.

"Hello, William Parris speaking," her father answered.

"Hi Dad, it's Louise and Ross calling you from Perth."

"This is a lovely surprise. Are you calling for Easter? Just a moment, I'll ask your mother to pick up the other phone so we can both talk to you," he suggested. William then called out to his wife downstairs. "Liz, it's Louise. Grab the other phone!"

"Hi my darling Louise," her mother announced. "We were just talking about you yesterday when Julie and the family were over for lunch. We were wondering what you had planned for the holiday weekend."

"Well," Louise began. "Ross and I have been pretty busy over the last month or so Mum. Are you and Dad both sitting down?"

"No, but we can if you want us to. What's news? Are you coming home?" William probed with optimism.

"No Dad, not for a while anyway," his daughter confessed rather nervously. "We're calling to tell you that there was a quiet little beach wedding yesterday."

"Oh, how lovely," her mother commented. "Anyone we know?"

"Ah, yes…in fact, Ross and I got married." Louise quickly placed her hand on her heart and glanced over at Ross. "Isn't that an exciting surprise?" she added.

Louise heard two intermittent gasps then complete silence on the other end of the line. "Are you still there? Mum? Dad?"

"Yes, we're here," William quietly replied. "I think we're both in a bit of a shock. I mean…we would have liked you to have it here…at home with your family."

"I know Dad…and I'm sorry about that. It was sort of a spur of the moment decision. Jean and Don are here from Brisbane for Easter, so we just thought it would be a good time. It was a long way for you two to travel and with Julie pregnant, it just felt right having a small, informal wedding with our friends in Perth," Louise explained. "I hope that you and Mum are happy for us? We'll send you some photos when we get them developed."

William gathered himself and sighed heavily. "Of course! Yes, we're happy for you sweetie, but as I said, we just wish you could have been here with your family." Her mother didn't utter a single word. "Mum's only quiet because she's trying to process this unexpected news," William assured her, "but of course we wish you every happiness. Will you phone Julie and tell her, or do you want us to do that?"

"I'll call her right now Dad," Louise told him. "We wanted you to know first. And thanks for your good wishes, Mum and Dad. We'll talk soon. Love you. Bye."

Louise and Ross hung up and looked at each other. "Oh gosh, that was more awful than I expected Ross. And now we have to do it all over again. Oh well. Here goes," Louise grumbled as she dialled her sister's number.

"John Keane speaking."

"Hi John, it's Louise and Ross calling from Perth. Happy Easter. Are you all well over there?"

"We're in great shape, thanks Lou. Well, Julie's getting a bit out of shape…but she's happy, and now that Lucy's into the 'terrible twos' she's really keeping us on our toes. How about you?"

"Yes, we're good thanks John," Louise responded. "Is Julie nearby at all? If she is, can you stay on the line and put her on the other phone so we can talk to you both at once?"

"Sure thing. Here she comes now." John gestured for Julie to pick up the other receiver.

"Hi little sister. Happy Easter to you. What's up?" Julie asked.

"Well, Ross and I got married yesterday. Just a small ceremony on the beach at Scarborough."

"Wow! Really? That's awesome news. Have you told Mum and Dad yet?"

Louise and Ross smiled at her response. "We just got off the phone to them. I think they're in shock." The newlyweds then went on to tell the Keanes all about their big day. Louise explained, "We were scared of a take-over if we returned to New Zealand to get married. You know Mum, she would have wanted the whole church and reception bit, and neither of us wanted that."

"Ah yes, John and I had to endure all of that, so I get where you're coming from," her sister confessed. "Still, I would like to have at least help arrange it, but I totally understand."

Their planned honeymoon later in the year was discussed, as was the impending birth of Julie's baby by that time. Half an hour later, both sisters said their goodbyes and hung up.

"Gees whiz," Louise remarked, sinking into her chair. "I think we should open a bottle of champagne now that's over."

Ross, Don and Jean couldn't agree more.

●●●●●●●

After spending a week holidaying with their friends down in the Margaret River and Cape Leeuwin regions, it was back to work as usual for Mr and Mrs Green. Their lives returned to normal until about a month later, when Ross arrived home from work one evening.

"A work mate of mine and his wife are moving to the East Coast and they're selling their two-bedroom house. It's pretty close to here. We should take a look Lou. It hasn't been listed yet but he wants a quick sale and on the surface the price seems reasonable for this part of Perth."

"Does it?" Louise enquired.

Ross added, "It's on a quarter acre block of land in a quiet side street, about half a kilometre from the beach one way, and shops the other. I've arranged for us to go over there on Saturday afternoon to have a look at it."

• • • • • •

Tom Hamilton and his wife, Marguerite, met Ross and Louise at the bright yellow front door of their home and showed the couple around. The Greens were impressed with the street appeal and the inside of the house was painted in neutral tones with Tasmanian oak flooring. Some recent renovations had been very tastefully carried out: a new kitchen, a second bathroom, and a walk-in robe had been added to the master bedroom. The back garden still required some work but Ross felt that with his brick-laying skills, he could make something appealing of it.

Ross and Louise sat down at a table on the large back veranda overlooking the yard where two established trees grew. Tom brought out a bottle of wine in an ice bucket for the women and opened beers for Ross and himself. Marguerite soon joined them with crackers and dip and negotiations began. Tom stated the figure that he and his wife hoped to receive.

"We'd like to go back and think about it overnight Tom," Louise said. "This has come a little sooner than we had planned financially, so we need to consider our options if that's okay with you both."

"Yes, of course it is," Tom concurred.

On the drive home, Louise announced, "What a nice couple Tom and Marguerite are."

"Yes," Ross agreed. "I've enjoyed working with Tom. He's a good, honest bloke. I wish he wasn't moving but I sure like that house. Has a good feel about it and at a glance I'd say the second-hand furniture we already have would fit in it. That being said, you might want new stuff for our new place. So, what do you think about making them an offer, say $5,000 less than their asking price and perhaps we can negotiate from there? Recently I've been looking in the real estate magazines around here and given the size of the land and central location, I think what they're asking is pretty much on the mark. If the transaction took place directly through the bank, there wouldn't be any agent commission for Tom to pay…and that would be a further negotiating factor. What are your thoughts Lou?"

Louise gazed at each home as it passed her view and replied, "Unlike you, I haven't been taking much notice of the housing market but we could drop by a real estate office and speak to someone about the values around here."

Parking within the vicinity of a shopping complex where a major real estate office was located, Ross and Louise browsed the advertisements in the front window and entered to make some inquiries and comparisons. Around twenty minutes later they returned to their car feeling comfortable that their offer was within the median range.

Monday of the following week, Ross took half a day off work. He'd booked an afternoon appointment with their Bank Manager, Mark Reynolds, to discuss the matter. Both he and Louise had saved well since living in Perth, so they wouldn't require a large loan and interest rates were currently below six percent.

Mark informed Ross, "I know the area well. Our family home is in the adjacent street. There would need to be a building inspection if your offer is accepted and if that proves to be okay, I see no reason why a loan of this size wouldn't be approved."

That evening the Hamiltons accepted the Green's offer, the building inspection was carried out the next day, and its approval enabled the loan to be authorised two days later. With a thirty-day contract signed, all that was left to do was to pack up and move. Ross and Louise were euphoric. Their future now set.

"Life has been too easy," Ross smiled as he reclined on the couch.

"And we still have our honeymoon to the Dampier Peninsular in August to look forward to. That'll be a really nice break from the winter chills of south Western Australia."

CHAPTER SIX

Louise's business continued to prosper and Ross was happy in his bricklaying contract work. Together they redesigned the back garden of their new home and planned to make a start on it after returning from their honeymoon. By that time the weather would have warmed up, encouraging their new plants to thrive.

As August fast approached, they compiled a list of items to load into the back of their 4WD. They intended to camp the majority of the time and had already purchased most of the camping necessities.

• • • • • •

"There's no need to rush Lou," Ross insisted. "We have three weeks to see it all."

Louise was so excited that she could hardly contain her child-like emotions. They were finally on their honeymoon, ready to explore the many wonders that Western Australia had to offer.

Taking six days to drive to Broome, they stopped at Geraldton and then Monkey Mia to hand-feed the dolphins. "What an amazing experience! Their mouths seem to smile and their eyes are so gentle. Such beautiful creatures," Louise deduced.

"Yes, my love…just like you. A smiling, gentle-eyed, beautiful creature," Ross teased as he washed his hands in the salty water.

Ross's highlight definitely had to be swimming with the whale sharks off the coast of Exmouth. "That was incredible," he declared to Louise. "The exhilaration of being right alongside those huge mammals and to touch their spotted bodies was thrilling. I was really emotional. A once in a lifetime opportunity that I'll remember forever." His wife agreed, even though she was slightly intimidated by their enormous size.

There was much to be seen and so much to learn. Ross and Louise quickly became avid photographers, capturing every possible aspect of their new adventures on film.

Port Headland was another scheduled stopover. In this busy port, iron ore was its main export. They took a detour to Tom Price Mine and spent three days in Broome where under a full moon, they witnessed a visual spectacle - the 'Stairway to the Moon'. Magnificent Cable Beach at sunset incorporated a camel ride along the sand, followed by Margarita cocktails at the Cable Beach Hotel whilst watching the sun sink into the Indian Ocean.

North of Broome all the land and its associated businesses were owned by the community, that being the local Aboriginal population. The two-hundred-kilometer road remained unsealed and at the halfway point, the Greens veered west towards the coast to Banana Well. 'Rustic' was an understated word for this small fishing town, and the mosquitoes were savage. They only spent one night here.

Back on the main road once again, they were forced to negotiate the soft and powdery red sand all the way to Cape Leveque. "Thank goodness for the 4WD," Ross grinned. "I can't imagine tackling this in any other vehicle."

"Absolutely!" Louise agreed, struggling to keep her body weight centred in the passenger seat.

Arriving at Kooljaman Resort Caravan Park around lunchtime, they checked-in and set up their tent before walking down for a swim in the ocean. It was so refreshing and extremely remote. The cliff faces mirrored a dark rust-red colour in total contrast with the miles of fine white sand and clear, aqua-turquoise waters. Humpback whales migrating north from the Antarctic to their breeding grounds were clearly visible offshore. In abundant numbers they breached and slapped their huge fins and tails as they frolicked.

By late afternoon fellow campers were either booking-in or returning from a day of sightseeing. Their vehicles, just like the Green's 4WD, were veiled in fine red dust. Everyone happily gathered together to discuss the experiences of their day. From this information, other travellers could glean sound advice on what to see next, and when.

Before bed that evening, hand in hand, Ross and Louise walked down to the deserted beach. The moon had not yet risen and the sky was a mass of stars. The great Milky Way and the Southern Cross stood out brilliantly. Together they lay on the sand studying the heavens and marvelled at the occasional falling star.

"It's so peaceful. The only thing I can hear is the lapping of tiny waves along the shoreline," Louise said as she rubbed her weary eyes.

Ross too was feeling pretty exhausted after their long day. "Tomorrow we'll venture over to Swan Point, Cygnet Bay, and Bardi, on the other side of the Dampier Peninsular. I'm looking forward to learning more about the pearling industry. I've read quite a lot about it, and for years it's flourished here in the north west, in the hands of the local Chinese populace," he explained. "We'll need an early start, so Mrs Green…let's get you to bed before we both fall asleep here."

Very early the following morning Ross and Louise carried out their plans from the previous evening. At Swan Point, dolphins played in the currents between the mainland and nearby islands. Along its rocky edges, the water was so clear that turtles and fish could easily be observed from Ross and Louise's position on the rock wall overlooking the estuary.

They lunched at Cygnet Bay and chose pearl meat from the menu. It was ridiculously expensive but also very delicious. As they looked out to sea, Louise remarked, "The colour of the southern Indian Ocean is so different to the Pacific Ocean on the east coast, and here in the north, it's different again."

"So true," Ross agreed. "It almost feels like we're in another country altogether."

Having just purchased a new home, buying pearls certainly wasn't on the Green's agenda. But they were beautiful to look at, and learning about the pearling industry and its processes was highly educational. There were also some truly unique and fascinating pieces of pearl jewellery on display.

Louise asked Ross to stop at a roadside market-type stall where they were selling arts and crafts produced by local community folk. Here she purchased an intricately carved boab pod. This tree seed was about the size of a man's fist and the carving depicted an emu, a kangaroo and local flora in dream-time style, similar to indigenous rock art painting. Louise knew that she had the perfect place at home to display it.

Returning to camp, the couple spoke with a small group of backpackers whilst making their way up to the amenities block. The group highly recommended a great half-day Mudnumm discovery tour ran by a local indigenous man by the name of Bolo. Ross and Louise decided to make a reservation for the next day.

When they woke to yet another glorious morning, the Greens were enthused about their upcoming adventure. Joining them were two other couples. One couple were staff members at Kooljaman and the other, middle aged, had heard about Bolo's tour from fellow grey nomads they met while travelling the top end.

Swamp-like terrain often saw the group up to their knees in tacky mud and whilst keeping a sharp eye out for lurking crocodiles, they conscientiously searched for mud crabs and bombs (shellfish containing snails or crabs). All tourists were required to wear reef waders to guard against sharp mangrove roots but Bolo was barefoot. He even managed to trap and catch a spotty cod with his feet.

"Unbelievable!" Ross remarked, shaking his head in disbelief. "His feet must be made of leather!" Louise was equally dumbfounded by Bolo's incredible reflexes.

During the trek their tour guide sought out examples of bush tucker, bush medicine, demonstrated how to draw water from a paperbark tree and built a shelter whilst explaining why it was built in that particular way. He also pointed out the type of thin, straight trees from which they made their spears.

"Before we cross this mangrove swamp, you need to be aware of the huge tidal variance here," Bolo warned the group. "Please be careful and keep your eyes peeled."

As they slowly waded through the estuary towards Bolo's shelter, the ocean rushed in revealing masses of swimmer crabs just asking to be caught. Once at the shelter, everyone took a dip to cool off and rid themselves of the murky mud. As they did so, Bolo came down to the shore carrying a fish's head. He then made a peculiar squawking sound while throwing it high into the air. The seafood snack was swooped upon by a large osprey responding to his call.

Whilst Bolo conducted the tour, his nephew spent the morning scouring for oysters and set a fire to cook them up for lunch. Bolo's mother made a superb damper to accompany them. The four-hour scheduled tour ended up stretching out to more than five hours, thanks to their extremely knowledgeable tour guide and the enthusiasm of his group of 'whities'.

"Today will be recounted and recommended to everyone we come across on our respective journeys Bolo. A wonderful tour. And please thank your mother for her amazing damper too," affirmed Louise.

Bolo responded with a huge smile, revealing his endearing dimples and brilliant white teeth. "That's what I like to hear Louise. My aim is to spread as much knowledge about our culture as possible."

The deep sandy track leading to the main road was slow going but the Greens finally made it back to their campsite at Kooljaman by mid-afternoon. When they pulled up, Ross noticed a note pinned to the front of their tent awning. It read: *'Please visit reception and ask for Rama'*.

The couple dawdled up to the foyer and were asked to promptly enter the Resort Manager's office. As they did so, Rama briefly introduced herself and requested that they be seated.

"Mr and Mrs Green," she started. "This morning I received a call from the Perth Police Department and they need you to call them urgently. I'm very sorry to inform you that apparently your home has been completely destroyed by fire." She paused for a brief moment, studying the two baffled faces opposite her. "Please feel free to use my office phone to make that call. Again, I'm so sorry to be the one to deliver this awful news." Rama then quickly left the office and closed the door behind her.

Louise and Ross remained glued to their chairs in total shock. Within seconds, Louise began sobbing. "Our house!" she cried. "Destroyed?" Her shaking body slumped onto the desk.

Ross leaned forward and placed his hand firmly in the centre of her back as his eyes began to fill with tears. "I have to talk to the police and find out what on earth happened."

Sergeant Burrows at Scarborough precinct answered his call. "It occurred in the very early hours of this morning Mr Green. Authorities are trying to find the cause and so far, there's no evidence to suggest any suspicious activity. The damage to the house is extensive I'm afraid but the separate garage and the vehicle inside it appears to have dodged the flames. When will you be back in Perth?"

Clearing his husky throat, Ross replied, "We'll be there as soon as we can catch a flight out of here...but I'm guessing that'll be tomorrow at the earliest." He then abruptly hung up the phone.

On leaving the office, a receptionist at the front counter offered to help the distraught couple make arrangements for a flight out of Broome. The only available departure to Perth was at 1pm the following afternoon, so she booked them two seats.

The Greens didn't get an ounce of sleep that night. Not only was their honeymoon over, their world was in tatters.

Packing up camp early the next morning, they then drove three hours south to Broome. Ross arranged to garage their 4WD at a small parking facility and by 12:15pm they were at the airport, nervously waiting to board their flight.

Ross phoned his friend, Ken Wilson. "Hey mate," Ross started, "don't have much time to chat right now but I'm calling to let you know that we lost our house in a fire. Only found out about it yesterday afternoon..."

"Yeah, I know, bloody hell!" Ken interrupted. "Really sorry about that mate. Janet and I saw it on the news yesterday morning but we had no way of getting in touch with you. How are you coping? How's Louise? Was it insured?" he probed.

"We're okay...still in shock I think," Ross admitted. "We took out building insurance for the mortgage but didn't get around to the contents before we left. At least it wasn't new furniture I suppose. Anyway...we're about to fly out of Broome and I was wondering if one of you could possibly pick us up at the airport and accommodate us for a couple of nights?"

Ken was happy to help in whatever way he could. "For sure my friend. I'll bring Janet with me. I know she'll want to come too."

In Perth, the Wilsons picked up Ross and Louise from the airport and drove them straight to Scarborough Police Station.

"The investigation hasn't turned up any evidence of arson

and the firies are pretty certain that the source was located in the laundry, most likely an electrical fault," Detective Parsons advised. "They've passed their findings onto the investigators and all seem to be in agreement." With shoulders drooped, the body language of the Greens said it all.

Returning to the car, Ross asked Ken to drive them over to the charred remains of their home. Blackened timber and shattered glass littered the immediate area surrounding its foundations. Nothing could be salvaged. Ross and Louise gently wept and tried to fathom the devastation before them.

Louise scrounged through her handbag for the car keys then unlocked and opened the garage door. "I don't know why I took the keys away," she solemnly uttered, "but it's just as well I did." Retrieving her car, the distressed couple then followed the Wilsons to their nearby home.

The Greens still had five days remaining before they were due back at work. And there were a lot of decisions to be made within that time. First on the agenda was to fly Ross back to Broome to collect their 4WD.

"I want to be back in Perth as soon as possible," he told Louise. "I reckon three and a half days should do it. Meanwhile honey, you have to find us an interim place to live while we get our lives sorted."

CHAPTER SEVEN

Mid-flight Ross scanned the cabin, astutely observing the other passengers onboard. Their relatively happy demeanours were annoying him and he could feel small beads of perspiration appearing on his forehead. Turning his thoughts to Louise only elevated his emotions. He was stewing over their misfortune.

Landing in Broome, Ross retrieved the 4WD from the parking precinct and began the long, lonely drive south. With their happy lives turned to custard, he sensed the black dog creeping over him once again…a disturbed state of mind that he knew all too well.

● ● ● ● ● ●

His early days at primary school is when the teasing and bullying over his undeveloped left eye first began. Being different, other kids were quick to find fault. As the brunt of their ridicule, Ross learned to defend himself whenever a fight broke out.

During high school, Ross's unhappiness increased exponentially when his parents passed away. He was fourteen and playing truant on a regular basis came as no surprise to anyone, least of all the school's counsellor. Ross's manner was sullen and rebellious, aided by the fact that he knew he was old enough to legally finish school.

Family friends took in the siblings and Emily's blindness meant that she required full-time care. Ross became increasingly difficult, ill-mannered and almost non-communicative. The family were at a loss as to how to manage the situation.

Child Services took on his case and sourced a mentor in an effort to guide him in the right direction. Selwyn Beasley adopted that role. He was a self-employed bricklayer from Bankstown, looking to employ an apprentice. Ross was placed on trial for three months and told that if he liked the work and behaved himself, Selwyn would consider offering him an apprenticeship. The troubled teen really enjoyed the physicality of the trade and the bond between student and mentor developed into a solid friendship.

Ross needed Selwyn in his life at that time and was forever thankful to him. He had managed to haul Ross from the abyss to which he'd become so accustomed. Not only was Selwyn a father figure, he was also a confidant, able to impart in Ross a measure of self-esteem that had been knocked out of him over the course of many years.

It was a seriously tragic day when, shortly after the completion of Ross's apprenticeship, Selwyn got caught in a rip and drowned while swimming at Cronulla beach. Ross lost the only friend he'd ever had in his life up to that point. Grieving exhausted him and depression yet again returned to the fore.

At eighteen, now legally allowed to drink alcohol, Ross looked forward to a few beers with work mates on Friday afternoons and Saturday nights. Before too long he was buying a carton of beer to take home and drink alone. Consuming a couple of 'tallies' each evening inadvertently morphed into three a night. By this stage, cooking a decent meal became too much of an effort so Ross opted for takeaway instead, which he'd collect on his way home from work.

Driving home one Saturday night after a drinking session that started around lunchtime at the local pub, Ross lost control of his old car and slammed into a power pole. He crawled out of the severely damaged vehicle and staggered home in the pitch black, nursing what he suspected was a broken arm.

After sleeping off the harrowing night, Ross deduced that he required medical attention and caught a cab to the nearest hospital. X-rays revealed a badly broken wrist which nursing staff set in plaster. He phoned his new boss to advise that he was unable to work for six weeks. This news wasn't well received at all.

Bored, lonely and miserable, Ross would stroll Maroubra beach each morning. Watching surfers meld with the ocean soothed his soul, giving him the clarity to reassess his life. He often thought about Selwyn too, and the lessons his mentor instilled in him.

When the plaster finally came off, Ross purchased a second-hand surfboard and after closely observing other surfers for weeks on end, taught himself to surf. Catching waves was exhilarating and the peace of witnessing sunrises from the offshore break allowed him complete freedom.

Out here on a balmy November morning is when he and Don first met. As tradies, they both enjoyed catching an early morning wave before work and as their friendship grew, they ventured off on surfing safaris to the northern beaches. On long weekends they were willing to trek further afield in search of the elusive, perfect break.

Meeting one afternoon for a beer, they discussed the viability of chasing some waves up north. "Why don't we pool our resources and buy a wagon or something? Travel up the coast for a surfing/working holiday?" Don proposed.

Ross couldn't respond quickly enough. "Mate…you're a genius! Sounds awesome to me."

Together they found an old VW Camper, already fitted out with the necessities. Resigning from their respective jobs within a week, they threw their tools and sleeping bags in the back of the Camper, strapped their boards to the roof-rack and set off from Sydney. Heading up the East Coast, they surfed the breaks at Nambucca Heads, Sawtell, Coffs Harbour, Ballina, Byron Bay, Tweed Heads and finally arrived at their chosen destination: Kirra Beach on the southern end of the Gold Coast.

Making their way up to Main Beach at Southport, they rented a site for the Camper only fifty yards from the surf. Now it was time to look for work and stay put until the bitter southern winter was over.

• • • • • •

Reaching an isolated town just on dusk, Ross refuelled at the Roadhouse and wandered over to the tiny pub. The 'pins and needles' sensation in his legs began to ease as the blood circulated freely. He enjoyed a counter meal and a crisply-cold ale before purchasing a carton of beer and some ice for the esky.

Knowing it was unwise to drive at night when native wildlife become drawn to the highway's dazzling headlights, Ross bunkered down. Out the back of the Roadhouse he pitched his tent in a desolate paddock, guzzled another beer and grabbed a few hours of restless sleep.

In the piccaninny dawn he packed up and hauled the esky onto the passenger side floor. Ross had heard that the Roadhouse was well known for its enormous bacon and egg burgers, so he indulged himself. Breakfast on the go and a few ales consumed whilst underway would suffice until the next stop. Before leaving he phoned the Wilsons but there was no answer, so he left a message on their answering machine.

The seemingly endless kilometres south continued to taunt him and the further he drove, the more his depression festered. Unable to find a radio channel to distract him, he focused on his own voice. "What in the hell did we do to deserve this? That's what I want to know!" he shouted, shaking his head all the while. "And on our bloody honeymoon for God's sake! What are the chances? Seriously, you couldn't even make this shit up!" Adrenalin coursed through his veins as he slapped his hands hard on the steering wheel. "Jesus, I need a beer, or maybe five," he convinced himself. Awkwardly leaning over, he retrieved a bottle from the esky.

Yet another remote pitstop and a few more beers later he ate, refuelled and replenished the esky's ice. The bangers and mash went down a treat, as did a huge stretch to alleviate his aching back. It was the short break that he desperately needed. With a fresh beer at the ready, he departed the Roadhouse and quickly settled into the monotonous trek once again.

Disillusioned whenever he thought about Louise and their circumstances, Ross was beginning to seriously consider a change. Weighing up his options, he mulled over numerous possibilities and in the end, his mind was set. He knew exactly what he needed to do. Smiling at himself in the rear vision mirror, he declared, "Good one Mr Green…you've earned another coldie!"

●●●●●

Ardently searching through second-hand furniture stores, Louise was surprised at the cost of most goods. They were quite expensive. Even though she was extremely grateful to Ken and Janet for their hospitality, staying with them for much longer wasn't an option. Heaven knows how long the insurance company would take to process their claim.

When she arrived back at the Wilson's, the phone rang and Ken answered.

"Hey buddy, how are ya?" Ross enquired. They briefly spoke then with a puzzled expression on his face, Ken handed the phone to Louise.

"There's my girl," Ross laughed. "I'm in...where am I? Oh yeah, I'm in Geraldton. Just got here. I'll camp tonight. Should be back late tomorrow. How's it goin' Lou?"

"Well, I miss you and I wish you were here," Louise answered apprehensively. It almost sounded as though Ross was drunk. *'Surely not! He wouldn't drink and drive. He's obviously just extremely tired,'* she assured herself. Continuing on she added, "The police called and confirmed that the fire was caused by an electrical fault in the laundry, so I submitted the insurance claim together with the Police Report. They said it shouldn't take more than ten days to finalise. Oh...and I found an unfurnished unit that might be suitable," she added. "I just want you to approve it before we make any commitments."

"Okie dokie," Ross slurred.

"Try to get a good night's rest Ross. Look forward to seeing you tomorrow. Drive safely," his wife advised him.

They both hung up and immediately turning to Ken, Louise asked, "Did Ross seem really tired to you?"

"Honestly, to me it sounded more like he was drunk," Ross commented offhandedly.

Louise didn't reply. She ambled into the kitchen to help Janet prepare their evening meal. Immediately following dinner, she excused herself from the table. "Think I need an early night if you don't mind," she announced.

"By all means," Janet smiled.

Reading for a while without absorbing anything, Louise's thoughts kept returning to Ross's slurred dialogue. It was really out of character for her husband to drink and drive at any time, let alone during a long trip. Eventually she fell into a fitful doze.

• • • • •

Towards mid-afternoon, with Ken and Janet at work, Louise found herself regularly peering through the front window awaiting her husband's return. Around 4pm she heard his 4WD coming down the road and ran outside just as Ross pulled up in the driveway. He half stumbled out of the driver's seat and weaved his way towards her, bleary-eyed and sporting a stubbly beard. They tightly hugged and Louise could smell beer on him. Ken was right. He had been drinking...and driving.

With arms around one another they entered the house and Ross flopped onto the lounge. "Don't suppose there'd be a cold beer in the fridge, would there Lou? I could really use one right now," he said.

Louise brought over two stubbies of beer and Ross downed his bottle quickly. "Ah, just what the doctor ordered. Thanks Lou. I'm buggered."

"I bet you could use a shower after that long haul," his wife commented while slowly sipping her beer.

"You sure have that right," Ross agreed. "I'm probably more than a bit on the nose. I'll bring the gear in from the car first."

Showered, shaved and still bloodshot-eyed, Ross emerged from the bathroom with a towel around his waist and went straight to the fridge for another beer. "Want another one?" he asked.

"No thanks," came Louise's reply.

"God...I still can't believe this has happened to us. We were going so well and then bang! All up in flames. I've been thinking we should move on for a while," Ross suggested. "Go somewhere that offers good money and a change of scenery. You could sell the business and I can lend my hand to just about anything. We need to recoup some losses I reckon."

Totally astounded, Louise had no words.

"Well? Say something Lou! I want to know what you think of the idea."

"Give me a second, Ross. This has come from nowhere. I'm pretty much speechless. I know the fire's been a massive blow but the insurance payout should be enough to rebuild. I thought you were happy here in Perth?"

"Yeah, I was, but now it's time for a change. At least for me it is," Ross admitted.

"And what's that supposed to mean exactly?" Louise retorted.

"It means that if you don't want to come with me, I'll go on my own," he replied. "You can keep running your business and I'll go and isolate myself somewhere for maybe six months or a year. Earn some real bucks."

Louise raised her voice in retaliation. "But Ross, we've only been married for six months! Are you saying that you want to end our marriage?"

"No, not at all. I'm the one who's pissed off so I need to get away for a while. Not from you my love, but if you don't want to come with me, honestly that's okay. Depending on where I end up, we could probably get together when you close the office over the school holidays. You could meet me somewhere or come to where I'm working."

Tears surged in Louise's eyes and a compelling need to escape consumed her. As she quietly made her way to the bedroom, she heard Ken's vehicle drive into the garage. Busying herself sorting through Ross's dirty clothes, she then took them to the laundry and loaded the washing machine. All the while, her head was spinning over the conversation they'd just had.

Janet arrived home twenty minutes later and the couples gathered on the veranda to catch the last of the afternoon sun. Ross's tongue was loose as he openly voiced his thoughts to the Wilsons. Louise remained completely silent.

Clearly noticing that her friend was upset, Janet suggested, "Let's go inside and figure out what we'll do for dinner tonight, Lou. It's getting fairly cool."

Out of sight in the kitchen, Janet placed her arms around Louise and hugged her closely. "This has come as quite a shock, hasn't it Lou?"

"It certainly has...and I don't know how to handle it. If I did go, I'd have to sell the business or put on a manager and that would have to be someone I completely trust. The latter wouldn't really be an option because the whole teaching thing is so personalised. And would the business be saleable? I just don't know."

●●●●●●

Up at the crack of dawn, Ross donned his wetsuit, grabbed his board and drove the short distance down to Scarborough beach. The waves were pretty average but he needed to get out beyond the break for the peace and tranquillity it afforded him. After a while, looking ashore he noticed that the newsagency was opening its doors.

Emerging from the ocean, he took a cold shower at the amenities block, washed the sand and salt water off his board and placed it in the back of the 4WD. After grabbing some loose change from the console, he entered the shop and purchased the 'Weekend Australian' newspaper.

Seated on the veranda with a cup of coffee in hand and pen at the ready, Ross glanced at the headlines before retrieving the Employment section. He meticulously perused the columns, circling positions of interest.

By the time the others surfaced, he'd circled a myriad of advertisements in Australia and overseas. A New Guinea position was the one that stood out for him. Bricklayers were required in Lae for a six-month contract to build a glass manufacturing factory. The construction company provided mess accommodation for single expats but for couples, off-site married accommodation was also available and partially subsidised by the employer. Ross's airfare would be covered and his wages paid in Australian dollars. Tradesmen were required to commence work within three weeks.

While Louise wandered out onto the sunny veranda, the Wilsons remained inside, allowing the couple space to sort out their immediate future.

"This sounds really good Lou." Enthusiastically Ross read out the New Guinea advertisement and pointed out the potential for Louise to work in the township of Lae. "You could set up a business just like you have here; teaching computer and internet operations," he encouraged.

Louise scanned her eyes over the yard and replied, "Sounds like it's just as well I kept our important paperwork in a file in my office. You know, passports, birth certificates, mortgage documents. At lease they didn't get lost in the fire."

"Clever girl. Now tell me what you think about all of this Lou? I'm supposed to go and inspect that unit this afternoon but if we did decide to do this, we'll have to let the agent know that we're no longer pursuing a rental."

"I'm concerned about my business Ross. I can't just walk away and leave my students stranded. I'd have to stay on until it sold, if it's worth selling. And if I did decide to leave, I would definitely teach until the end of the semester then close it altogether. I'm very reluctant to have a total stranger manage it. Perhaps I could talk to the real estate and enquire if a sale would even be feasible."

From the kitchen, the Wilsons were intently listening to their conversation and it quickly became apparent that Louise wasn't dismissing any new possibilities. Janet looked at her husband and said, "Ken, come out the front with me. I want to discuss something with you."

Settled on the front step, Janet looked at Ken and with some excitement in her voice said, "I've been a little disenchanted with my own job lately, Ken. Being Brian's secretary isn't very stimulating and a change wouldn't do me any harm. Louise and I worked together in a similar capacity so my knowledge of what she teaches is fairly substantial. I wonder if she'd consider offering me the opportunity to run the business in her absence?"

"I know you haven't enjoyed your job for a while now, so this sounds like a good idea to me," Ken agreed. "Ask Lou and see what she thinks."

"I'll wait until she mentions the business again then put the proposition to her. She can only say 'no' and if she does, I won't be the slightest bit offended," Janet concluded.

Over breakfast the Greens discussed their options with the Wilsons and asked for their opinion whilst voicing their concerns. The timing was right, so Janet put forward her suggestion to manage Louise's business.

Louise's eyes lit up. "Oh, Janet! That would be perfect! You know as much about I.T. as I do. You have good rapport with people, the patience of a saint, and you've always been able to explain yourself well. You are obviously someone I can trust and that's so important to me. We can work out a salary that we're both comfortable with."

"Problem solved!" both men voiced in unison.

Ross was very animated. "I just have to secure this job. I really want to give the New Guinea contract a shot. It's short, just six months, which will allow us time to decide if we want to remain up there and source other work. It's so exciting. A whole new adventure and a fresh start."

Turning to the Wilsons, Louise asked if she and Ross could possibly stay a bit longer, until Ross's job was secured.

"Absolutely! We're more than happy to have you both, so don't worry about that," Ken replied. "Janet will need to familiarise herself with the business operations anyway and this will give you both time to accomplish that."

"Thank you both so much. You've been really good to us. I'd better call the real estate and let them know that we no longer require the unit," Louise reminded herself. "And Ross, you'd better get moving on that job application," she implored him. "Now, to conclude our mammoth morning of decision making, I think we should all go out to lunch and celebrate."

Two hours later the couples alighted from a taxi and shortly thereafter were happily ensconced on the first floor of a seaside restaurant. Seated beside a window overlooking Cottesloe beach, the view was stunning. Both women sipped champagne and discussed the business whilst the men settled for rum and coke. They all chose the house specialty from the menu: seafood marinara linguine. Fresh, perfectly seasoned and extremely tasty.

As the afternoon wore on, and the rums started to take their toll on Ross, he became rather aggressive towards a fellow who accidentally spilled beer down his arm. Ken hauled Ross outside and the couples quickly hailed a passing cab. They left the scene before any further trouble could ensue.

Once at home, Ross lay on the bed and snored himself to sleep.

Meanwhile, Louise explained the business procedures that she'd established and the teaching methods that were implemented. Janet was all ears. "Up until now there's been no need to market the business as my students refer the course to their friends. If it does become necessary to advertise, we can discuss that at the time. We'll be in contact regularly so if any problems arise, they can be resolved over the phone."

• • • • •

"I'm calling to advise that your application for the position in Lae has been successful, Mr Green. It has been approved," a representative from the Australian-based employment agency informed him.

Ross explained that his wife would be accompanying him and enquired about employment for Louise.

"I'd wait and get settled first," the Rep suggested. Most of the businesses in town are small-scale and don't require assistance from large employment agencies in Australia."

The Rep also told him that within the next week he would receive two airline tickets, one for himself and the other for Louise, the latter of which Ross would be required to pay. The Rep then requested personal details for their working visas, which the company would manage. Ross was provided with instructions regarding Customs and Immigration procedures in Port Moresby, their first port of call. "It will be an hour or so wait-over for your connecting flight to Lae," the Rep added. There you'll be met by a company representative and escorted to the married quarters reserved for you."

'This sounds like a very well organised and efficient organisation,' Ross thought to himself. Finally, the Rep provided Ross with a phone number in Lae, which he was welcome to call with any further questions that he may have.

Ross thanked the Rep wholeheartedly and hung up. *'Wow! We're actually doing this,'* he acknowledged.

• • • • • •

The Greens went shopping for work clothes for Ross and some light summery clothing for both of them. Unless they ended up in the highlands, cool weather gear wouldn't be necessary.

Ross arranged for a local dealership to sell their vehicles and hired a contractor to clear the rubble from their block. The building insurance cheque, which they received much faster than anticipated, arrived two days before their scheduled departure. This was a huge weight lifted from their shoulders. They paid out their mortgage and banked the balance of the insurance payout, transferring some to a branch in Lae. Packing was easy, just their clothing, a few of Ross's tools and their cameras of course!

The evening before they flew out, their friends, most of whom had attended the wedding, surprised Louise and Ross by arriving at the Wilsons with armfuls of food and drinks. They felt that a good old-fashioned send-off was in order.

Ken fired up the barbecue and one of the guys had brought along his ukulele, so shortly after dinner the party was in full swing with a sing-along continuing into the late hours. Again, Ross drank far too much rum and exited the party early, strongly encouraged by his wife. Louise was disappointed with her husband's behaviour and becoming increasingly concerned about his drinking habits. More often than not, Ross was obnoxious on the rum and she didn't want to deal with that tonight.

CHAPTER EIGHT

Other than a toddler suffering from severe airsickness, the Green's flight from Perth to Port Moresby was relatively uneventful. As they disembarked and made their way across the sweltering tarmac, fierce heat and humidity smacked them in the face like a sauna.

"Oh my God!" Louise groaned. "I don't know how I'll ever get accustomed to this climate." Struggling with their carry-on bags, Ross lent a helping hand and relieved his wife of the cumbersome load.

After Customs clearance and a brief wait time, the couple then boarded a small Twin Otter for the two-hour journey to Lae. Below them, vast expanses of dense jungle stretched as far as the eye could see. They were greeted at the tiny airport by Ross's foreman, Allan Mathews.

Loading their luggage into the tray of his twin-cab utility, they were then driven to the company's married quarters. The accommodation consisted of four modest dongas, all exactly the same, positioned side by side. Unlocking the door to their compact one-bedroom home, Ross and Louise found it sparsely furnished but thankfully, there were ceiling fans. The kitchen/lounge which opened out to a small covered deck, had a bed located at one end.

Allan informed them, "There's an elevated water tank that gravity feeds to the house. Linen, kitchen utensils, cookware, fridge and washing machine are all supplied. Across the lawn, hidden behind that hedge are the 'boi hauses' where the domestic staff reside. I've already spoken to one of the bois and I'll interview him for you tomorrow."

Ross and Louise looked at each other, perplexed. "Everyone hires a domestic here," Allan explained. "It's too hot to do all the chores yourself and they're cheap to hire." He then went on to advise the Greens to keep their valuable belongings secure.

Sweat was accumulating on Ross and Louise's clothing as Allan spoke. "Just dump your stuff and we'll lock up and go. I'll take you over to the single quarters beside the workshop, show you the office and introduce you to the three blokes that arrived on Saturday. You can have a nice cold beer and some dinner with them and I'll drive you home afterwards." Allan smiled at Ross and added, "I'll help you gather some supplies tomorrow morning and let you settle in while I collect the other two guys, Leon and Bruce, who are flying in from Brisbane tomorrow afternoon. Then you can start Wednesday at eight. All good?"

"Sure thing, no problem," Ross replied.

Whilst Allan chauffeured the couple through the township of Lae, they studied their surroundings from the back seat. Allan pointed out the two supermarkets: Burns Philp, and Steamship Co. Both stores sold groceries and domestic supplies. "There are two banks, a pharmacy, newsagent, butcher shop, bakery, hairdresser and a second-hand car yard," he told them. "And there's even a Jeweller, would you believe it? We've got two hotels: 'The Melanesian' which is a bit up-market and 'The Cecil', it's down on the water. That one's got a pool and some barbecues...great hangout on weekends."

"Terrific. Ross and I love a good barbecue," Louise admitted.

Allan continued with his informative tips. "There's a good market called a 'bung', where fresh produce is sold on Saturdays. It's preferable to buy these items here in comparison to the supermarket. Freezer cargo ships deliver meat, butter, cheese and all that kind of stuff from Australia, but the fruit and veggies aren't too fresh by the time they hit the shelves."

Turning left into a small yard, the office building out the front displayed a 'Davis and Turner' sign. Behind that office was another yard that housed bricks on pallets, a number of vehicles and a front-end loader. Even further down, a long building with a row of numbered doors also backed onto this yard. Allan parked the utility and announced, "These are the single quarters and down the end is the Mess. Come and take a look."

Inside the Mess were a number of tables and chairs, a small lounge area with side tables and at the back of the room, a food servery behind which was the kitchen. There seemed to be plenty of action going on. In a corner to the right was a large, glass-doored fridge containing bottles of soft drink and beer. Alongside it were shelves filled with drinking glasses and a solitary timber 'honesty box'.

Three men were seated in the lounge area, beers in hand, chatting amiably. Allan introduced the Greens to the trio as Ross's work colleagues. "Joe, Bob, Ian…meet Ross and his wife Louise." He then informed the couple that the men arrived from Australia a few days ago and commenced work yesterday. "I'll grab you both a beer, they're icy-cold," he announced.

When he returned to the group, their conversation revolved around new experiences, many of which were cause for amusement, particularly in regards to misinterpreting the native language.

Allan laughed and went on to explain, "The language is pretty simple but new people tend to over-complicate things. Personally, I love it…then again, I've been here fifteen years. The best time to learn it is when you're really tired or half-tanked. There's an excellent program on ABC radio following the 6am news each weekday morning. It's a five-minute session hosted by a Port Moresby cop named Mike Thomas. Well worth a listen, I'm telling you. There's also a publication called 'Introduction to New Guinea Pidgin' which the newsagent in town sells. It's written by a Catholic Missionary, Father Mihalic and it's a great reference book. I strongly suggest you all grab a copy because it'll make your lives easier. The labourers, we call them line-boys, try all sorts of tricks on the new fellas…so I'm here to inform you that you've all been officially warned."

A voice boomed from the kitchen. It was the bos boi announcing that dinner was served. With the group now seated at a table, Allan introduced 'Speedy'. The Chimbu man, like most highlander men, was stocky in build. Not the most handsome of men but his smile oozed kindness and his sharp, black eyes sparkled.

"Apinun ol gera," he greeted the group, before rushing back to the kitchen.

"Speedy's been with us many Christmases," Allan smiled and nodded. "He's a much loved and respected staff member. By the way, locals count years in Christmases, and months in moons."

The group enjoyed their smorgasbord-style meal of sausages, sweet mashed potato (kaukau), cabbage and beans, followed by ice cream and chocolate syrup for dessert.

With dinner finished, Allan drove a weary Ross and Louise back to their donga. On the way he joked around, amusing the couple no end, while they made plans for the following morning. "I'll pick you up at 7:30am," he instructed. "You can both have some brekkie in the Mess before we go into town and stock you up a bit. I know you must be pretty exhausted but if you could make a list of essentials before you crash, that'd be great. It'll save us some time."

Waking early the next morning refreshed from a sound sleep, Ross and Louise unpacked their suitcases and had a good look around the area before Allan arrived.

"Morning lovebirds. Manage to get some shut-eye?" he enquired.

"We sure did mate. Slept like logs I reckon," Ross replied.

After breakfast in the Mess, the Greens asked Allan if he'd mind taking them straight to the used car yard in town. "If we purchase a vehicle that'll give us our independence and eliminate the need for you to drive us around everywhere. Is that okay by you, Allan?"

"Absolutely," he responded. "Jump in and we'll go take a gander."

They pulled up out the front of the yard and Allan introduced Ross and Louise to salesman Graeme Donnelly. He showed the couple what was available and explained, "The roads outside the immediate township leave much to be desired. You're going to need something pretty robust if you plan to get out and about."

The Greens appraised a small Toyota 4WD that would be perfect for their needs. The price was reasonable so they signed the ownership and registration documents and wrote Graeme a cheque.

"Now that you've got your own wheels, how about you follow me back to your place and we'll organise your haus boi now. That way you can shop later at your own leisure," Allan suggested.

Meeting back at the donga, the Greens prepared coffee while Allan walked over to the boi haus. Within a few minutes he returned with their potential haus boi, dressed in a pure white cotton shirt and shorts, long white socks and jet-black, highly polished, pointed-toe shoes. The man's footwear was obviously far too big for him, as he had to lift his knees much higher than necessary in order to walk properly.

"This is Yobe," Allan announced as they walked in the door, introducing him to his prospective employers. "Please meet Mr and Mrs Green."

"Nice to meet you, Yobe," Ross said.

Louise gently gave him a single welcoming nod, along with a beaming smile.

Allan faced Yobe and in pidgin, set out the following details of his employment agreement. Yobe was to commence work at 7:30am in the mornings and end at noon, three days a week. "Mande, Trinde and Fraide," Allan instructed him. Yobe would do the dishes, wash the floors, clean the house and attend to the washing and ironing. His wage of $7 a week would be paid each Fraide, and he'd be provided with his own coffee, sugar and milk. He was told not to steal from the Greens and that they would not steal from him. "Do not chew buai during working hours," Allan insisted, "and when you finish for the day, make sure that you lock the donga securely."

Yobe listened to Allan's instruction earnestly, nodded frequently throughout, and when Allan concluded, the boi grinned widely, presenting his pearly white teeth.

After repeating their conversation for the Greens in perfect English, Allan asked Ross and Louise, "Are you happy with this agreement? Would you like to add anything?

"It all sounds fine to me," Ross replied. "Are you happy with that Lou?"

"Ah, yes. That's wonderful. Thank you Yobe. So, I guess we'll see you on Monday morning."

"Tenkyu Misus na Masta," Yobe grinned as he swiftly left the donga to advise his 'wontoks' that he had 'wok'.

Before leaving, Allan felt obliged to offer the Greens some firm advice. "There are many highlanders in Lae and for some of them, relocating to the 'big smoke' means that they've never seen a white woman before." He looked at Louise seriously and added, "It's not advisable to wear shorts or bikinis around the house or when you go shopping, and don't go the botanical gardens alone. If you're driving and you hit a native, don't stop, just keep driving and go straight to the police station."

Ross and Louise were intrigued by Allen's pointers and continued to pay careful attention to his every word.

"You'll notice many of the men around town carrying long-bladed bush knives. Now there's no need to be alarmed," Allan assured them. "They're only used for cutting overgrown grass or taro roots for food. The women carry 'bilum' bags which are string-knitted with long handles. In them they cart everything from market produce to empty bottles they've collected, even their babies. These bags hang on their heads and down their backs. It's quite astonishing how much weight they can carry in them."

"Please, take a seat Allan," Louise suggested, sensing that far more valuable information was yet to be divulged.

He went on to tell them about the 'betel nut' known locally as buai or belinat. "The nuts from areca palm trees are ground together with crushed coral or lime to create a powerful and highly addictive stimulant that produces a similar effect to alcohol. When mixed with saliva it turns red and stains teeth, lips and pretty much anything else it comes into contact with. If it gets onto fabric, it will never come out. That's why I told Yobe never to chew it at work. When swallowed it rots the stomach and over time, it has the same effect on teeth. The natives have an amazing ability to squirt it through their teeth, a fair distance, and with considerable accuracy. Others splatter it, so you'll notice globs of it on the roads, footpaths and even in the grass. What they spit out, they call 'buai pek pek'. 'Pek pek' is basically pidgin for 'shit'. If buai is mixed with alcohol it quite often leads to violence. On Fridays, the locals all head to the bung and fights usually erupt. You might hear bush calls and shouting as a chase breaks out. The natives frequently fight to the death too. Europeans aren't permitted to hit a local but believe me, it's often tempting," Allan admitted.

Redistributing his weight in the saggy chair, Allan remembered another crucial point. "You also need to make sure that you take a regular dose of quinine tablets, so put them on your shopping list. Malaria's prevalent up here, as is Dengue Fever…and they can be debilitating. Believe me, I've had them both. Thought I was going to die from Dengue! Both diseases are carried by mosquitoes and we have no shortage of those. One of the ingredients in tonic water is quinine, so get onto the Gin and Tonic Louise," he proposed.

Slowly rising from his chair, Ross and Louise did the same. "You've provided us with a wealth of knowledge Allan, thank you so much for taking the time to do that," Louise said gratefully.

"And one last thing…" Allan began. "The beaches around here aren't too flash. The Markham River which flows down from the highlands carries some rather undesirable objects at times. Things like animal carcasses, sewerage, you name it. The villagers wash in the rivers so you never know what you might find. Like I said yesterday, The Cecil's your best bet to cool off."

"Oh dear, that's just charming!" Louise grimaced.

"Well, I'd best be off and I'll see you at work tomorrow, Ross," Allan said, firmly shaking his hand. "By the way, because it's so hot here, everyone takes an hour and a half for lunch. Siesta time: noon to 1:30pm."

"I like it…a nap in the middle of the day sounds great," Ross admitted.

● ● ● ● ● ●

Stepping out of the 4WD at Burns Philp, known as 'B.P.'s' to the locals, the Greens then entered the store and purchased two medium-sized eskies, some beer, cleaning products, groceries, and a few very sad-looking vegetables to tide them over until Saturday. The store also carried a small selection of furniture and appliances so they snapped up a radio, along with a small table setting for their outside deck.

Given that the freezer cargo ship unloaded yesterday, the selection of items seemed fairly meagre. Fortunately, the butcher shop displayed chops, chicken and steak, so it's here that they also acquired cheese, milk and butter. The bakery next door held very little variety in the way of bread. At the newsagency across the street they bought yesterday's edition of 'The Sydney Morning Herald', the New Guinea newspaper known as 'The Post Courier', and Allan's 'suggested reading' publication: 'Introduction to New Guinea Pidgin'.

After arriving home, unpacking and stowing away all of their purchases, Louise prepared sandwiches and took them out on the deck where they sat reading the papers. The Post Courier's 'Positions Vacant' section advertised an office position in Lae for a ledger machine operator. It also provided an address for the establishment.

"This could be a good opportunity for me," Louise commented, passing the paper to Ross. Knowing that he was due to commence work in the morning, she was as keen as mustard to find out more. "I'm not doing much now, so I thought I might go back into town and see what I can find out. Is that okay with you?"

Ross looked at her absent-mindedly. "Sorry love…my answer is yes, and no. I mean yes, by all means find out about the job, but being brand new here, I'd much prefer to come with you. I can just dawdle around town or find a shady spot to read, no problem at all."

Driving to the end of the town's main street, they located the I.P.I. building and it appeared to be relatively modern. Ross leaned over and kissed his wife on the cheek.

"Here goes," Louise smiled as she stepped out of the 4WD. "Sure you don't mind waiting?"

"I'll keep myself busy, don't you worry darling," Ross replied.

Upon entering the building, a huge sigh left Louise's lips. *'Yes, it's air-conditioned!'* was her immediate thought. Climbing the stairs to the first level, a door marked 'Co-operative Wholesale Society' was clearly visible. She knocked and entered before being greeted by a middle-aged gentleman who introduced himself as Edgar Bennett.

"How can I help you, young lady?" he asked.

Louise explained that she was responding to the ledger machine operator advertisement in the newspaper.

Edgar's face lit up. "Oh, that's wonderful. The ad's been running for two weeks now, so I thought I'd never find anyone. We've fallen so far behind because our previous operator urgently resigned to return to an ill family member in Australia."

Louise handed Edgar her references. He merely glanced over them before handing the folder back to her. "Tell me about yourself and your experience, Louise. Please, take a seat."

She obliged and proceeded to fill him in on some brief details.

"Let me explain the purpose of the Co-operative Wholesale Society," Edgar started. "We purchase in bulk to supply village trade stores throughout Papua and New Guinea. This enables the village-owned stores to on-sell the goods at very reasonable prices. The majority of their customers have little money and rely largely on what they produce from their own gardens for personal consumption as well as for producing income. Many of these villages are extremely remote. Sometimes it can take days to travel from a main thoroughfare to jungle villages, carrying the stock by hand, canoe, or donkey which they call 'hos bilong Jesus,'" he smiled.

Noting Louise's enthusiastic attention, Edgar continued. "The position requires the ledger machine operator to be proficient in recording our office staff's wages, along with debtor and creditor ledgers. Currently the machine's located in a different room because as you'd be well aware, they're noisy beasts. Ultimately, I'd like to see a small, workable, sound-proofed room constructed here in a corner of this central office. I was hoping that the new person who fills this position would be able to design a functional space that we could have purpose built. How do you feel about all of that, Louise?"

"I know I can handle the work you describe," Louise responded honestly, "and I think it would be fun to design a small sound-reducing space. Could you possibly show me the area you have in mind for this 'cubicle' and perhaps provide me with the measurements?"

"Follow me," Edgar responded as he made his way through the large office space. Along the way, Louise was introduced to Barbara, Boniface, and Polong. Barbara, an Australian woman, was the wife of an Army Colonel at the nearby barracks. Boniface and Polong were both young Papuan men, immaculately attired in white shirts and dark trousers with highly-polished black shoes. They each had in their shirt pockets distinctive red, white and blue-edged air-mail envelopes. Louise later learned that this was a 'status symbol' indicating they'd received mail from an overseas friend. Invariably, the envelope was empty.

The corner where the cubicle would be constructed was filled with boxes of stock. Edgar promised that they'd be relocated that very day, should Louise accept the position offered. And she did, much to Edgar's delight.

Returning to his desk they discussed her monthly salary and she was advised that employment could commence the following day if she so wished. All was agreed upon and Louise officially had a job. She skipped down the steps with a sense of contented anticipation and discovered Ross at the base of the stairs.

"Thought I'd enjoy the aircon while I can," he smiled. "How'd it go Lou?"

"I can start tomorrow," she chuffed.

Ross was genuinely happy for her and glad to know that she had something productive to occupy her time. On the drive home, with measurements in hand, she began designing a functional little office in which to work.

"I think I'm going to enjoy working there," she told her husband. "It's air-conditioned, so that's a big plus, and we get siesta time too. It should work well with just the one car, as long as you don't mind dropping me off and collecting me. I start at 8am in the morning, so can you drop me off on your way to work?"

"Definitely. I don't mind working my schedule in with yours at all. I think it's great that you've found employment," he proudly declared.

• • • • • •

"You've done a great job on this design, Louise. It's contemporary, practical and in keeping with the simplicity of the entire office space. I'll call a cabinetmaker and see when he can do it," Edgar smiled.

Within fifteen minutes James, the cabinetmaker, arrived at the office. He studied Louise's drawing and said, "Yep. Shouldn't be a problem. I'll get it drawn to scale and write up a quote. Soon as you accept it, I can make a start."

Edgar looked surprisingly at Louise then immediately back at James. "Are you new in town, James?" he queried. "The usual response to a job like this is 'won't be long', and that means it takes forever."

James laughed. "Yeah, haven't been here very long but no, seriously, I can get to it straight away. I know an electrician too, so

I can organise that side of things if you like. Just say the word."

Edgar thanked James sincerely and he left with the sketches safely housed in a folder under his arm.

It felt like Louise had only been at work for a few hours when siesta time came around. She hurried across the road to meet Ross and slithered into the passenger seat of their 4WD.

"No need to rush, Lou," he laughed. "I'm learning that this is the 'land of wait-a-while'."

Back at the donga they ate lunch, accompanied by an icy-cold ale and set the alarm. Despite the heat, or perhaps as a result of it, nodding-off came easily.

Returning to their respective jobs, the Greens settled into a routine over the course of the following day and Friday afternoon saw their short working week come to an end. Driving home, Ross said to his wife, "It seems customary on Fridays to head for the pool at The Cecil after work. Have a swim, a few drinks and apparently the hotel puts on a mean barbeque. Just about all the expats in town gather there. I think we should go. It will give us a chance to meet some of them. Besides, I'm stinking hot…could sure do with a swim."

"I won't say no to a dip either," Louise agreed. "In that case, from now on we'll remember to take our swimmers and towels to work on Fridays, so we can go straight from there."

The Cecil Hotel was a hive of activity as the Greens joined Ross's five colleagues and his foreman, who were settled around a large table constructed from logs. Louise was introduced to Leon and Bruce, their latest recruits, then the group unanimously decided to jump in the pool. Sadly, the water was lukewarm, far from the temperature that Ross and Louise were expecting. Thanks to a light south-easterly sea breeze, at least there was some form of cooling reprieve. Afterwards, all members of the group threw money into a kitty and imbibed a few glasses of South Pacific brew.

During the course of the evening Allan said, "If any of you don't have plans for Sunday, I have a suggestion. In the jungle about half an hour out of town, there's a waterhole and a cleared area where you can spread out and have a picnic. The water's clear and fresh to say the least. Great spot to go while you're acclimatising to these temperatures. I could ask Speedy to put a picnic together and you can just bring along what you want to drink, your swimming gear and a rug if you have one." He then looked at Louise and added, "You'd be the only girl but I reckon you can handle it if the boys watch their manners."

Louise laughed. "I think I'll cope, Allan. It sounds idyllic and it would be lovely to actually feel cold again. Even the water in the shower's warm."

The following morning, the Greens ventured over to the Saturday 'bung' market. Every expat in town seemed to be there, along with hundreds of locals; both vendors and buyers. Some of the women 'meris' and haus bois trailed behind their European employers carrying large woven baskets and bilum bags.

Some vendors had laid woven kunai mats on the ground where they exhibited their produce, others had long tables displaying fresh fruit and vegetables. All items were bunched in small piles for 20c each. Some of the produce Louise and Ross had never seen before. The meris looked beautiful in their colourful blouses and many had their cute little babies 'pikininis' with them, all seemingly well behaved but many with snotty noses. Most of the locals were chewing buai and many of the elderly 'lapun' folk either had rotten teeth or none at all.

There were also stall holders displaying numerous wooden artefacts including elaborately-carved crocodiles, turtles, masks and spears. Larger, smoother carvings of dolphins, sharks, sail fish and herons were superbly crafted by the people of Talasea, in the West New Britain District, an island off the eastern shores of the mainland. There were also fish traps made from strips of bamboo which the Greens later saw imaginatively turned into hanging lights. A huge variety of necklaces and bracelets made from seeds, coloured beads and shells, assembled by the meris, were also for sale. Ross and Louise thoroughly enjoyed their first bung experience.

On Sunday morning they woke to yet another glorious day. Meeting at the Mess around the scheduled time, the group then packed the two vehicles and Allan led the way. The terrain was extremely rough and dusty but the jolting drive was immediately forgotten upon sighting the tropical wonderland before them.

From the picnic site, they were welcomed to a kaleidoscope of shapes and colour. Surrounding them, bright red and yellow parrot-beak and heliconia blooms, banana palms, crotons in every colour imaginable, canna lilies and several varieties of ginger grew in abundance. Prolific delicately-fronded ferns tightly hugged the perimeter of the watercourse and a burbling stream meandered through the rocks to complete the nirvana.

They all entered the water inch by inch, its temperature was extremely bracing. At only waist deep, the chill was more than enough to cool down their entire bodies.

"This river originates from way up in the highlands," Allan informed them. "You'll be surprised to know that it sometimes snows up there. And given that the water has seen little sunshine through the jungle canopy, that probably explains why it's so cold."

Twenty minutes later, withstanding the water temperature for as long as they could, the group retreated to the clearing to catch some sun and enjoy one another's company. Everyone had a story to tell: where they came from, why they came to New Guinea, and their aspirations for the future. Financial goals were a common denominator. Speedy had provided an interesting lunch to say the least, which the group followed up with a peaceful siesta on the lushly blanketed grass.

• • • • •

Ross and Louise's lives continued without much change in the pattern. Their jobs were keeping them busy and on weekends they tried to get out and explore as much of the Territory as possible.

A good golf course in Lae attracted the couple and they'd often hire clubs from the Pro Shop and play a few rounds on Sunday afternoons. There was no shortage of young bois begging to be their caddie for a few hours and given the oppressive heat, the Greens were grateful to have them at their disposal.

In the end, one caddie named 'Sevenup' became Ross's regular boi. He was the seventh child amongst his siblings and Sevenup's eldest brother's name was 'Oneup'. Away from prying eyes at the clubhouse, Ross would sometimes allow Sevenup to hit a ball with his own self-crafted club made from a tree branch. In the local language it was fashioned from 'arm bilong' tree. It was incredible how accurately and how far Sevenup could direct a golf ball with this implement.

The Greens also discovered some other strange names of local people. One child, born on the night of the census was named 'Census', a set of twins were known as 'Somehow' and 'Somewhere', and another child was blessed with the name 'Jesus'.

Ross got a real kick out of water skiing behind Allan's boat. Louise was reluctant to try it, much preferring to watch from the observer's seat while Allan drove. Ross had never skied before now but with his surfer's balance, sheer will and determination, he managed to stay up and thoroughly enjoyed the thrill of the sport. They launched the boat in the filthy Markham River and crossed over to the much cleaner Labu Lake. After skiing, they headed down the coastline to Salamaua, an area of great wartime significance. While picnicking there, Allan casually mentioned, "It's just as well you could stay up Ross. There are a few 'puk puks' that call Labu home." After the Greens curiously looked to him for further explanation, Allan laughed and said, "Crocodiles!" Ross and Louise were left gaping in horror.

● ● ● ● ●

Christmas was fast approaching which meant that the planning for a celebratory dinner had to be organised. Being mid-contract, none of the boys were opting to leave Lae. Two of the men's wives were coming over from Australia and Allan was arranging for the couples to stay in vacant dongas alongside the Greens. Louise was very much looking forward to some female company for a while.

Everyone was receptive to Louise's idea of booking a large table at The Melanesian Hotel for something a little sophisticated, so she reserved a table for dinner. Allan wouldn't be attending as Speedy had already invited him to stay at his village for Christmas. Allan apprehensively accepted but he was always up for new experiences and there were plenty of those on offer in New Guinea.

"Long we liklik or liklik long we, Speedy?" Allan asked him. One phrase had quite the opposite meaning to the other but ultimately the answer was that they'd travel on foot through the jungle from the Lae/Goroka Road to the village.

"Em e long we liklik tasol, Masta," Speedy answered.

Allan wondered about that reply but committed regardless. The others were excited for him and couldn't wait to hear all about his journey when he returned. If he returned. There were still cannibals up there in the jungle!

On Friday, two days before Christmas, the visiting wives arrived for a ten-day holiday with their husbands. Olivia and Lesley were the wives of Joe and Bob. The two Brisbane couples were already close friends back in Australia.

They moved into the dongas as planned and once settled, Joe and Bob took their wives over to meet the Greens. Louise had arranged a platter of nibblies and all three couples sat outside on the small, shaded deck, chatting away and getting familiar with one another. The heat was stifling.

"Would you like me to take you into The Cecil for a swim?" Louise asked the women.

Lesley answered instantaneously. "Oh my God...yes please! Anything with the word 'water' in it sounds amazing. What about the guys?"

"The boys want to set up a portable barbecue area for us all to use while you're here," Louise told them. "Far more preferable to do that now, in the afternoon shade, compared to doing it in the morning."

The women completely agreed. "We'll just grab our togs and be back in a jiffy," Olivia called out as they headed to their dongas.

Driving into town, Lesley commented, "It's so ridiculously hot Louise! How do you stand it here?"

"Well, surprisingly you get used to it," she replied. "Mind you, it's not like we have a choice. At least my office is air-conditioned. I don't know how the boys cope outside all day but they seem to manage. Thankfully they're in more of an advisory position and not just laying bricks all day like the poor labourers. The Mess and the dongas have fans too, so that's a bonus. We always find a way to cool off somehow. A few nights ago, the rain bucketed down, so Ross and

I went outside and got drenched. It felt fabulous," Louise laughed. "As you can imagine, in this climate the consumption of local beer is fairly high. In fact, the building that our guys are working on will be a glass factory. Not sure if you knew that," she added. "Its main production will be making bottles for 'South Pacific Lager'."

• • • • •

The Melanesian Hotel put on a Christmas spread that well exceeded Louise's expectations. A scrumptious buffet of seafood, chicken dishes, pork specialties and every tasty salad combination that one could possibly wish for. The busy chefs had really outdone themselves. Sitting in an air-conditioned dining room topped off the special occasion, especially for Olivia and Lesley who were suffering from the high humidity.

With the group's meals devoured and some wine and beer under their belts, Ian quietly slipped off to the bar and bought a round of drinks. "Gin and tonic for the ladies and rum and coke for the men," he announced on returning to the table.

On hearing the word 'rum', Louise immediately felt nervous. Pushing her emotions aside, she continued to enjoy her gin and the women merrily chatted between themselves. It was when Ross ordered another round that Louise realised the likelihood of them leaving the hotel before all the guys had shouted a round each, was pretty slim. At this point she abstained from drinking and assumed the role of designated driver.

Ross had been very 'hail-fellow-well-met' all evening but suddenly, after three rums, he became far less so.

"Do you think you need any more to drink?" Louise secretly whispered to her husband.

He looked at her bluntly and in an unnecessarily loud voice exclaimed, "Don't tell me what to do, Louise!"

This triggered a pause in the group's conversation which Ross didn't notice, but Louise most certainly did. She was totally embarrassed and became withdrawn for the remainder of the evening.

Assessing the situation and sensing Louise's uneasiness, Bob made moves to finally wrap up the celebration. "Gosh…it's almost midnight!" he remarked. "What a great Christmas Day! I know it's my shout but I couldn't handle another drop. I owe you guys one. Let's go. In the morning we can meet up for breakfast at the Mess."

Everyone agreed and Louise let out a sigh of relief. This was the first time that her husband had personally snapped at her after a rum session and she was shocked and saddened by his outburst. To be perfectly honest, his wrathful eyes frightened the heck out of her.

• • • • •

Allan and his faithful companion Speedy returned from the jungle unscathed. Although Allan looked slightly thinner than when he left, he was still beaming his fabulous smile. Joining the group for a barbecue at the Green's donga to celebrate New Year's Eve, he recounted his experience.

"As expected, I knew the village would be further away than Speedy let on," he laughed. "We had to fell some trees just to be able to cross the rivers and at the first small village we came across, the natives provided us with a canoe. From here we paddled upstream for about two kilometers until we reached Speedy's village. Bloody hell! It was hard yakka," he muttered, shaking his head. "Thankfully, paddling back was so much easier because we were going with the flow. Speedy's family were so welcoming. Honestly…lovely people. They all slept on woven kunai mats on the ground, that was their way, but one of the meris had made me a hammock to sleep in. Christmas morning, they all attended the mission church service and afterwards Speedy's father and uncle caught and slaughtered a much-coveted pig and roasted it over the fire for dinner. It was so tender and juicy."

Allan then went on to say that his fluent pidgin English was invaluable but when the family conversed in 'plestok', their own village dialect, he was completely lost. "Overall, I'm grateful to Speedy for the experience but it's highly unlikely I'll repeat it anytime soon. It was tough."

Two days later, after having shown Olivia and Lesley all there was to see around the immediate township of Lae, including the pristine waterhole, it was time for them to return to Australia. Louise felt that she'd made new friends in the boys' wives and as they departed, all promised to remain in touch. The glass factory site and Louise's office reopened the following day so work resumed and life rolled on.

CHAPTER NINE

An advertisement appeared on the town's noticeboard, inviting interest in a charter flight to Rabaul for the long weekend at the end of the month. The Greens knew that the township, located on the island of New Britain in the Gazelle Peninsular, held a great deal of WWII history. Ross and Louise jumped at the opportunity to add their names to the list.

The fully booked charter included flights in a DC3 from Lae on the Friday afternoon, returning Monday in the early evening. It was up to individual guests to organise their own transport and accommodation after arrival in Rabaul, so Louise arranged a hire car through Avis-Rent-a-Car. She also reserved accommodation at the Ascot Hotel in Mango Avenue for three nights.

On the afternoon of departure, upon boarding the aircraft, the Greens were rather surprised by the small canvas seats set out in side-saddle formation, facing either side of the fuselage. The couple recognised a number of their fellow passengers.

As the DC3 took to the sky, it suddenly became obvious why they were told to bring warm clothing. Daylight was clearly visible through the numerous gaps in the bulkhead and there was no insulation whatsoever, making the cabin freezing and conversation virtually impossible due to the noise.

Landing in Rabaul, passengers couldn't wait to alight from the deafening plane. The Greens were met by an Avis representative who introduced herself as Lyn Collins. They signed the documents for their vehicle, an Isuzu Bellete, then Lyn handed them a small folder containing maps of the area, tourist brochures and her business card. "You'll find my home phone number on the back of the card, should you have any problems. Where are you staying?"

"The Ascot," Louise replied excitedly.

"Excellent. That's very central. Well, enjoy your stay and here are the keys. Your car's parked just over there," Lyn instructed, pointing in its direction. "I'll be here at the airport when you leave."

Quickly perusing the map before they drove off, Louise could see that all the hotels were clearly marked. They left the airport, driving past the golf club, squash courts, the edge of Chinatown and then into the main street. Beyond the yacht club, the Travelodge and the Kaivuna Hotel, they then entered what appeared to be a fairly sizeable shopping precinct. It's here that they located the Ascot Hotel, on the corner of Mango Avenue and the tree-lined Malaguna Road.

Registering their arrival at reception, Ross and Louise received their room key and carried their luggage up to a pleasantly appointed room overlooking Mango Avenue. Dinner was being served in the dining room so they ventured down, armed with the paraphernalia they received from Lyn.

The couple had previously read-up and acquired some knowledge of the war-time history of Rabaul, so they selected a number of historical sites that they knew they'd like to visit. "A drive around the harbour's edge to Kokopo would be a picturesque start," Louise suggested. "Then just outside Kokopo is the Bitapaka War Cemetery which was established and is still maintained by both Australia and New Zealand Returned Services Associations." She scanned the map more closely while partaking of a delicious chicken and mushroom schnitzel. "It looks like Pila Pila Beach is the closest place for a swim. That could be refreshing."

"I'm happy to be directed by you my love," Ross commented. "And with so much to see and do tomorrow, I think we should finish up and have an early night."

In bed only a short time, the Greens suddenly heard yelling and shouting in the street. Looking down from their window they could see a man being chased up Malaguna Road by several other men, all bush calling and yelling in pidgin. As the chasers hollered, more men joined the scuttle, gathering up stones in their haste and launching them at the poor victim.

At breakfast the next morning Ross and Louise were told, "The bung's nearby, so that's pretty normal for a Friday night. The man being chased is probably in a bad way…or dead by now."

"Wow!" Louise exclaimed. "I'm glad we decided to stay in last night."

After donning swimwear and light clothing the couple gathered up their hats, cameras and a few other bits and pieces. They then headed down to the car. As Ross turned the key in the ignition, its engine slowly whirred but refused to start. He tried again, several times. A quick inspection under the bonnet didn't reveal any obvious issue. "Could be the starter motor," he told Louise. "Battery's fine, spark plugs look okay and she's got plenty of fuel. We'll have to call Lyn."

The Greens entered the hotel's reception area and phoned to inform her of their plight.

"Oh dear, I'm sorry to hear that," Lyn acknowledged sincerely. "Unfortunately, our mechanic's off for the long weekend…and all of the other hire cars are booked out." She hesitated for a brief time and added, "Could you please just hold for one moment."

Returning to the phone Lyn said, "Thanks for waiting. Okay…I had a quick chat to my husband and I think we can resolve this issue. We have no plans for the weekend, except for tonight, we're having dinner with friends. If you know what you want to do today, we can certainly escort you around. Just give us about an hour and we'll come and pick you up."

"Gosh!" Ross replied, rather astounded. "That's a big ask. Are you sure you have nothing better to do?"

Lyn laughed. "We love this place Mr Green and we enjoy sharing it with our visitors."

Accepting her very generous offer, the Greens then grabbed themselves a coffee and patiently waited under the fans in the lounge area, studying their maps and familiarising themselves with the area.

When Lyn and her husband Neville arrived, Louise told them about the places they'd like to visit. Neville said, "All good. We've got our beach gear and Lyn packed some food in the esky. So, let's get you out and about."

Ross and Louise transferred their belongings into the Collins' vehicle and they were underway. The morning was still young and the weather, absolutely perfect. Driving along the harbourside road, Neville and Lyn revealed some of the history behind the town and its villages as they passed by. They stopped at several sites to view wartime relics. Japanese landing barges in tunnels carved from the cliff-faces were excavated by locals under forced labour to hide the barges and their personnel from the enemy. Hauled in on rail tracks from the sea, they were completely hidden from aerial view. Lyn pointed out a small island known as 'The Beehive' which had literally popped up overnight as a result of an earthquake. A small hill known as 'Vulcan' had also risen from the sea floor in 1878, once an active volcano but now considered dormant.

Driving through Kokopo, Neville directed the Green's attention to the site of Queen Emma's steps. They were the only remains of 'Ralem', the original plantation home of Queen Emma of the South Seas. She was said to be a flamboyant, colourful Polynesian woman who owned trading ships throughout the West Coast of America and the South Seas during the latter part of the nineteenth century. She died in 1913 under very mysterious circumstances.

They travelled on to Bitapaka and the beautifully manicured War Cemetery before heading further along the coast road bordering Blanche Bay, past plantations of copra, coffee and cocoa. Turning left, they drove along the hibiscus-bordered driveway of Tovarua Plantation to a beach lined with coconut palms. The reef, only a hundred yards offshore, saw the white water break over crushed coral sand and propel towards the beach.

"This is a favourite spot for local expats," Lyn smiled. "The Watson family own this land. They encourage visitors to the beach and we're quick to take advantage of their generosity."

Unloading the car, they erected beach umbrellas, laid their towels on the bleached sand and entered the tepid pristine water.

"In Lae we need a boat to get well away from town to enjoy anything like this," Ross commented.

Laughingly, Louise spread her arms wide open and said, "This is what you imagine a tropical paradise should be. It's close to heaven, I imagine. How privileged we are to be here. Lyn, I'm so glad our car wouldn't start."

The couples indulged in Lyn's superb hamper of salad rolls,

tropical fruit and chilled orange juice. After lunch, the gentle sea breeze swept away the sultry air and they lay back on their towels for a siesta. Dozing off to the rhythm of the tiny waves lapping against the shoreline and the sound of rustling palm fronds was sheer bliss.

After another dip, the Collins' and the Greens reluctantly packed up and ventured back to the Ascot. We'll pick you up at nine in the morning," Neville advised, as he and Lyn waved the couple off.

Left to their own devices for the evening, Ross and Louise walked a short distance along Mango Avenue to the Travelodge for a light dinner. The setting was romantic and after their idyllic day, the couple felt contented and relaxed.

"I really like the Collins'," Ross smiled. "They've proven to be the ultimate hosts. Perhaps they can recommend somewhere to take them out for lunch or dinner. I suspect they'll credit us for the hire car, so we can spend that money treating them for their goodwill."

Walking back to the hotel by way of the waterfront, Louise remarked on the beauty and cleanliness of Rabaul. "Sure, there are still globs of dried buai on the pavement…but that's par for the course in the Territory."

• • • • •

Next morning, drawing up near the bunker, Neville explained, "This is where Admiral Isoroku Yamamoto planned the Japanese operations in the South Pacific during WWII." The top and turret of the concrete structure was covered in grass. Eight steps led down to the entrance.

"It's a bit claustrophobic inside and there's no lighting at all," Neville warned. "At the end we climb a few steps up to the turret. It's a small space but I think we can all fit in there at once. I've got the torch so I'll lead the way…and if you feel the need to get out, just let me know."

Following the torchlight down a narrow passage, the bunker became increasingly airless. The couples arrived at five stairs which they slowly ascended and accessed the small, round turret. Neville directed the torchlight across the ceiling and surrounding walls to reveal a hand-drawn map of the South Pacific.

"This was the hub of Japanese Command," Neville expounded. "The bunker couldn't be seen from the air and it was relatively obscure from the land as well. Amazing hey?"

"Fascinating," Louise remarked. "Such a significant historical site."

Making their way back to the entrance, everyone was relieved to gasp fresh air. As they took in their surroundings, Neville pointed and said, "Across the road is the Rabaul Club where you can see mortar marks in the walls and further along is the Returned Services Leagues Club. They're talking about turning the Rabaul Club into a museum and I think that's a great idea. I'm constantly in awe of the fact that we're living so peacefully here on what, not so long ago, was a bloody battleground. In the bush, armoury, unexploded mines and large brass bomb casings are still being found."

Wiping the sweat from her forehead, Lyn said, "Time for a swim, that's for sure. Let's head over to Pila Pila, it's a plantation beach not far from here."

When they arrived, a very red-lipped, toothless lapun man wearing only a lap lap with a cloth bag tied around his waist, approached them as they walked through the coconut palms. He grinned at the group and Neville gave the man 40c.

As they moved on, Louise asked Neville, "What was the money for?"

"The Tolai man and his family are the owners of this plantation and there's a 10c per head charge to use their beach. In return, they keep it spotlessly clean," he told her. "The Gazelle Peninsular, Bismark and many other parts of the South Pacific were settled years ago by the German and Dutch, which you probably know. They developed these coconut and copra plantations in 1914 during WWI. They then fought the Japanese and in 1922, following the Treaty of Versailles, Germany no longer controlled these Territories. Residents were expatriated, leaving their assets to the local people. In the case of the Gazelle Peninsular, the Tolai Tribe are now extremely wealthy. They just sit back, watch the coconuts fall from the trees, dry them out, and sell the copra. A charmed life you might say."

Bathing in the temperate sea, the Greens were so impressed with the pristine beauty of this location. Neville surfaced after holding his breath underwater for quite some time and panted, "We manage to get a surf here at Pila Pila for about a month each year. Expats flock in droves around that time but as you can see, it's a fairly popular spot on any given day."

Soaking up the shade in-between swimming, Ross turned to Neville and said, "We could easily live here. Lou and I have been wondering what to do at the end of my contract, but there doesn't seem to be much construction going on in Rabaul."

Neville threw his wife a strange look and Lyn returned a slow nod. "No, not too much work for a brickie but plenty for painters," he smiled. As a contractor, I've got more than I can cope with on my own. I do have a line boi but I need a tradesman. So…if you were willing to take direction and learn how to paint properly, I'd take you on. When does your Lae contract finish?"

"Supposedly, early March. But you know how these things are, it could run a further couple of weeks," Ross admitted.

Rubbing his chin whilst gazing at Ross, Neville elaborated on his offer. "If you're serious about moving to New Britain and working with me, I can keep an eye out for accommodation and a car for you. Places come up all the time with expats completing contracts and moving elsewhere within the Territory. They often want to sell their cars and the houses they've been renting are vacant again. Anyway, you two can talk it over and let me know your thoughts."

"We'll certainly do that. Thanks for the offer, Neville," Ross smiled.

Driving back into town they stopped at the Coffee Hut attached to the Travelodge for a bite of lunch before heading high up above sea level to the Seismological Centre, known locally as 'haus guria'. The view down the full length of Simpson Harbour to Blanche Bay was spectacular. Frangipani, hibiscus and crotons thrived in the grassed surrounds of the small building where earthquakes and volcanoes in the volatile Pacific Region were measured.

Guided by a Tolai seismologist, the couples were enthralled by what they learned. "We haven't had a serious eruption from the active volcanoes surrounding Rabaul in a long time, but Matupi continues to emit sulphur-smelling steam from its crater," he explained. "We go down into it weekly, on foot, to measure the temperature and composition of these gases. Earthquakes are fairly constant here as well, though most are so small that residents seldom feel them. Nothing larger than about 5.5 on the Richter scale has occurred for quite a while."

The group watched the needles move on the graph as he spoke, making the experience all the more real. "Captivating stuff," Ross remarked. "Where would we be without science?"

Descending back down the mountain mid-afternoon, Lyn said, "We thought we'd have a barbecue at home this evening. Would you like to join us? I know you'll want to freshen up, so we can drop you back to the hotel now and pick you up at say…5pm, if that sounds okay?"

"Of course, we'd love to Lyn," Louise replied, knowing that Ross would feel the same way. "We'll bring the drinks. What's your poison?"

"A bottle of white wine would be nice, if that's what you enjoy," Lyn responded. "Thank you."

"I'll bring some beer as well," Ross added, winking at Neville who smiled in return.

• • • • • •

From the expansive timber deck of the Collins' home on Namanula Hill, a spectacular ocean vista to the east captured the Duke of York Islands and New Ireland in the distance. The stylish two-bedroom, open plan interior was tastefully furnished with cane furniture and bright cushions which seemed to be the signature of New Guinea décor. Framed photographs depicting local scenes hung on the walls throughout the residence. It radiated a delightfully casual, tropical feel.

In their spacious kitchen, while Neville opened the wine, Lyn said, "We're originally from Auckland but we've lived in Rabaul for three years now. The boi house is just behind the hedge at the back, and next to that, we have a large shed with a huge workbench. That's where Neville keeps all of his ladders and work materials, plus our two cars. We also have an office set up in the spare bedroom, perfect for our requirements."

"I'm from Auckland as well," Louise smiled. "The North Shore; Milford area."

"That's amazing. We both lived about eight miles away, in Northcote. Neville and I met at Northcote College."

Louise paused for a brief moment then studied the Collins' closely. "You know what? Your faces actually look vaguely familiar to me. Did you play basketball on the North Shore or belong to the North Shore Youth Club?"

Lyn's smile grew wide. "We belonged to the Youth Club. Were you a member too?"

"Well, in fact," Louise began, "I was the club's first secretary. Just after I left school, Detective O'Shea from the Takapuna Police Department contacted me. He felt there was need for a Youth Club in the area and asked if I would be willing to help him establish one. I've no idea why he asked me because at the time, I was only fifteen. I can only assume that as I was Registrar of the Basketball Association, knew a lot of people and played a lot of sport, it made sense to him. As you know, the club was hugely successful."

"Yes, it certainly was," Lyn agreed. "We joined at the very beginning just after they acquired the sailing club hall for Sunday nights. I remember 'The Buccaneers', our resident band, and the pop-up coffee shop on Friday nights in Takapuna for late night shopping. That was a great place to hang out. Some of the parents used to supervise and the shop owners sponsored it. The police always kept a good eye out for us and I do remember Detective O'Shea, not that we had anything to do with him other than at the Youth Club," she added with a smile.

"I remember all of that too," Neville added. "And I recall the day before the Auckland Harbour Bridge opened to vehicles. The foot traffic and a parade started from the city side of the bridge and ended up in Devonport. We rock 'n' rolled all the way behind that band while they played on the tray of a truck."

"You're kidding!" Louise was flabbergasted. "I was also there! What a small world we live in."

Neville glanced at Ross and said, "Enough chit chat for now, time to fire-up the barbecue. Let's grab one of those beers and get cooking mate."

Marinated scotch fillet steaks and a cracking Caesar salad were the perfect accompaniment to the couples' jovial conversation. As the evening wore on Ross asked the Collins', "Is there somewhere special we can shout you lunch tomorrow? You've been so wonderful to us, and our Charter doesn't leave until 4pm."

"That's very kind," Neville answered, "but Lyn and I have already made a booking at the Kulau Lodge. We're taking 'you' out for lunch! We'll pick you up at around 11:30am after you've checked-out, load your luggage into the car then we can take you straight from the Lodge to the airport."

• • • • • •

"Doesn't it ever rain in Rabaul?" Ross queried Lyn as the couples gazed out across the pristine water from a prime table within Kulau Lodge.

"The weather has been superb this weekend, I'll grant you that, but the tropical downpours are never too far away. If you've noticed the height of the gutters along the roadside, that will give you some indication as to how much water we receive when the heavens do open up. Otherwise, it's beautiful one day and perfect the next."

Louise examined the Lodge's authentic interior. A woven kunai roof, supported by massive timber poles and beams. Suspended fish traps framing globes adorned the ceiling throughout. The entire floor space was covered in a layer of finely-ground coral. Elegant décor consistent with an island theme incorporated cane furniture displaying brightly-coloured upholstered cushions. This was a decorating style that really appealed to Louise's senses. She loved the 'tropical' feel of it.

Adding to the establishment's originality, all restaurant staff wore thongs with a hibiscus placed behind one ear. They were dressed in vividly-coloured fabrics: the meris in floral blouses and the bois in shirts of the identical fabric. Both genders wore them over dark lap-laps.

As an entrée, both couples ordered the famous 'amat pis'; Kulau

Lodge's signature dish. Served in small clam shells, Ross and Louise thoroughly enjoyed their first taste of 'raw fish' marinated in kulau (coconut) milk and lemon.

For main course they chose baked kingfish with fresh local prawns. Centred in the room was a long table covered in banana leaves. It showcased a smorgasbord of tantalising salads made from fresh, local ingredients for guests to serve themselves. The Collins' and the Greens indulged in numerous varieties. Tropical fruit salad with cream made for a refreshing final course.

Realising that time was fast slipping away, Neville and Ross briefly disputed who was going to pick up the bill. In the end, Ross insisted upon paying then the couples made their way to the carpark and left, albeit reluctantly for Lakunai Airport.

"Thank you both so, so much for all you've done for us," Louise said appreciatively. "We've seen and experienced far more than we ever could have on our own."

"Honestly, it was our absolute pleasure," Lyn smiled, glancing at her husband. "We've enjoyed it just as much. And I'm truly sorry about the car business too. I'll refund that payment for you tomorrow."

Neville concurred and handed Ross his business card. "Keep in touch. Let us know when you think you'll be back. I'll hold off employing anyone until I hear from you."

"Yeah, end of March or first week in April I reckon…but I'll confirm as soon as I know the exact date. It'd be terrific if you could hold that job for me, please Neville. We will be back."

Louise laughed. "I still can't believe Ross and I are planning on living here, all because our car wouldn't start. Has to be fate!"

• • • • •

The Greens felt restless until mid-March when Ross's contract expired. They were missing the Gazelle Peninsular already. Friday would be the boy's last shift at the glass factory and Allan planned a send-off at the Cecil Hotel.

Joe and Bob were investigating a contract in Port Moresby because despite the heat, their wives were receptive to coming to the Territory. Leon and Ian planned to return home to Australia while Bruce wanted to remain in Lae. This worked out well for the Greens, as he purchased their Toyota 4WD.

Gathering under a Poinciana tree, their favourite spot in the grounds of the Cecil Hotel, there was much chatter amongst the group. Again, Louise found herself to be the only woman present. There was certainly a shortage of single women in Lae which is why most of Ross's single work colleagues were keen to go elsewhere.

Beer flowed, meals were enjoyed…and then came the rounds of rum. Louise was concerned right from the outset. By the time the hotel closed at 10pm, Ross had directed some sarcastic remarks towards her, most within earshot of others in the group. Every time he opened his mouth, he seemed to be deliberately putting her down. She tried to distance herself from him but as she spoke with Allan and Joe, he still cast cynical looks her way.

Finally, it was closing time and they all wished one another good luck in their chosen endeavours. Allan drove the Greens home with Louise firmly settled in the passenger seat.

Outside the donga all three alighted from his 4WD and said their goodbyes. Allan shook Ross's hand, wished him well and then hugged Louise. "I've really enjoyed your company over the past six months. All the very best in Rabaul," he said. The Greens waved as Allan drove away.

Louise then unlocked the front door and felt around in the dark for the light switch. From behind, Ross slammed her in the back with both hands, forcing her to lose balance and crash into the dining table. "Bloody hell! Hurry up woman," he shouted. "I gotta go to the toilet."

Upon impact, Louise immediately felt the wind expel from her lungs and severe pain in her ribs.

Moments later, Ross returned from the bathroom and switched on the light to find Louise sitting on the floor. "What in the hell are you doin' sittin' down there in the dark? Get up stupid!"

Gasping for air and cradling her ribs, Louise didn't move. Tears flowed down her cheeks, angered by her husband's violence and her excruciating pain.

"What's the matter with ya woman?" Ross grabbed his wife by

one arm and attempted to lift her to her feet.

She shrieked in pain. Slowly regaining her breath, she whimpered, "I can't believe you shoved me in the back! I hit the table really hard and my ribs are so sore."

"Did not!" Ross protested loudly. "You prob'ly tripped on somethin' cause ya drunk. Get up and go to bed."

Alarmed, saddened and very sore, Louise stayed put until she heard Ross snoring. Slowly creeping into the bedroom and changing into her pyjamas she then painfully crawled into bed, desperately trying not to disturb her husband. Lying awake, staring into the blackness, thoughts of their whirlwind first year of marriage filled her head.

Morning came all too soon and when Ross woke, he rolled over to hug his sleeping wife. Just before he kissed her, Louise let out a yelp. Her ribs ached with the slightest movement.

"What's wrong?" he asked abruptly.

"I think my ribs are bruised from the fall last night," she answered.

Ross looked at her curiously. "When did this happen? Where? Why didn't you tell me about it?"

Louise quickly concluded that he was too drunk to recall the incident so there was little point in raising the issue. "Never mind," Louise bluffed. "I'm sure it'll settle down."

Undressing in the bathroom, she examined the bruising around her ribs before stepping into the shower. It was very obvious. Washing herself was a struggle but Louise was determined not to divulge the extent of her pain. After taking a couple of Panadol, she dressed and finished packing.

Bruce had kindly offered to drop the Greens at the airport, so he pulled up outside the donga at 9am sharp. "A bit hungover this morning mate?" he asked Ross as they loaded the luggage into the back of the 4WD.

"Not at all. Fresh as a daisy thanks Bruce," he laughed.

Yobe swiftly appeared from the boi haus and farewelled the Greens just before they drove out. He was very shy but still managed a cheeky grin.

After giving them both a floppy handshake, typical of local

people, Ross handed Yobe an envelope containing two weeks wages. Yobe's grin widened then in a flash, he was gone.

CHAPTER TEN

Exiting the arrival gate at Lakunai Airport, the Greens were thrilled to see Neville and Lyn again. For Louise, this was exactly what she needed right now; new friends and yet another fresh start.

The Collins' drove Ross and Louise straight to their new harbourside home which shared its back boundary with the Cosmopolitan Hotel. A month ago, Neville heard that the former expat tenants were returning to Australia within two weeks, so he arranged for the Greens to take over the place and purchase their old vehicle.

Inside the modest abode only essential furniture items were scattered throughout; a table with some chairs in the living room and four single lounge chairs. The main bedroom contained a double bed with built-in robes and except for a single wardrobe, the second bedroom was otherwise empty. Kitchen cupboards were bare and an aged fridge had certainly seen better days. A dilapidated Hoover twin-rub washing machine stood solitary on the veranda.

A haus meri and her family lived in a small concrete block building at the end of the backyard. Maria had four pikininis to feed and keep a roof over their heads, so she was desperately hoping that the Greens would employ her.

From the back door, Neville called out to Maria and as she made her way up to the house, the children trailed behind. He introduced the family to the Greens. Maria, a Manus Island meri of very slight build, was blessed with fine facial features and a lovely shy smile. Joseph was twelve and in what he hoped would be his final year at the Catholic Primary School. Peter, aged nine, and Veronica aged six, both attended the same school and little Leo was just two years old.

Maria didn't speak English so Ross attempted to communicate in pidgin. With a bit of help from Neville, Ross told her exactly what he and his wife required, along with what was expected of her. Joseph and Peter were learning English at school so they helped interpret for their mother wherever necessary. Ross had managed to pick up some passable pidgin from the line bois onsite in Lae and every morning the Greens religiously listened to the ABC radio's five-minute pidgin lessons. Combined with their introductory language book, the couple could muddle their way through well enough.

With hired help now sorted, Ross and Louise's next task was to stock up the fridge. The couple headed into Steamies and purchased grocery items together with linen, crockery, cutlery, glassware and liquor. Returning home via Anderson's they also bought some meat, milk and butter.

Their busy afternoon was spent setting up the house and unpacking suitcases which Louise found particularly exhausting, given the persistent pain in her ribs. She did her utmost to hide the fact. As Ross stacked groceries in the kitchen cupboard he said, "Joining a club's a good way to meet new people Lou."

"Yes, I'd like to get back to playing squash," Louise remarked. "Not sure if it's something you'd enjoy though…could be a bit challenging with your eye. We should keep up with a few rounds of golf as well, I really enjoy that."

The following morning after dropping her husband off for his first day of work, Louise then drove to the squash courts which were located next to the golf club. She completed a membership application form and handed it to the young boi behind the counter. He said, "Misus Sandra will be here at lunchtime so she'll contact you this afternoon."

While driving back through town, Louise picked up a copy of the Post Courier newspaper and took it home to read whilst enjoying a coffee on the veranda. Finding a job was fairly high on her list of priorities, given the fact that Maria would be taking care of all the housework. Besides, the vast majority of expat women worked, so Louise knew that she'd be bored within no time. There weren't any suitable positions on offer but she was optimistic that something would transpire.

Organising the kitchen into a practical working space wasn't easy in Louise's condition but it managed to occupy the balance of her morning. After Neville dropped Ross home for siesta, the Greens shared some lunch, briefly discussed the job that Ross was undertaking then put their heads down for a much-needed snooze.

Louise didn't plan on going out for the afternoon so Ross returned to work in their car. Just as he left, there was a gentle knock on the front door.

"Hello. I'm Sandra from the squash club. Are you Louise?"

"Yes, Sandra, I am," she smiled. "Your manager said that you'd be in touch. This is a lovely surprise. Thank you. Please, come in."

Sandra entered and announced, "We'd love to have you! Welcome to Rabaul. I hope you're wanting to play in the competition because we're always looking for team members. With expats coming and going all the time it's a bit tricky to make up numbers. Would you like to have a hit with me this afternoon at around 4:30pm?"

"Actually, I've got pretty sore ribs at the moment Sandra," Louise confessed, "but I'd really like to have a game in about a week or so, if that suits you?"

"Oh, that's a shame…never mind. When you feel up to it, you can come out any day after 4:30pm. I should be there but if not, my husband Tyler will be."

Louise smiled. "Excellent. Thanks Sandra. Looking forward to it."

● ● ● ● ● ●

By Thursday the pain in Louise's ribs had subsided substantially, so she ventured down to the squash courts that afternoon and met up with Sandra.

"I haven't played for about four years, so I'm very rusty," Louise admitted.

Sandra slowly nodded. "That's not a problem at all, we'll knock you into shape."

The women played a gentle game and felt an instant rapport with one another. They knew that they'd become extremely good friends.

As Louise was preparing to leave, two men arrived with squash rackets in hand. Sandra introduced her to Robert Higgins and Barry

Davis. "Hello boys. I'd like you to meet Louise. She has just arrived from Lae and we're hoping to find her a job."

Both men were accountants, employed by the same company. Robert was due to leave Rabaul shortly and return to Australia but Barry intended to stay on with his wife Helena and their two sons, Stu and Andy. The family were very fond of the township.

"What kind of work are you seeking Louise?" Barry smiled and asked.

"I'm a ledger machine operator but I can lay my hand to pretty much anything in an office. I ran my own business in Perth, teaching computer and internet technology."

Barry glanced at Robert then his eyes instantly returned to Louise. "Ah, well that's certainly convenient. We have an opening for a machine operator but the position hasn't been advertised yet. How about you come in and see the boss tomorrow morning. His name's Harold Jenson. Let's say around 10am. Does that work?"

"Yes, that would be great Barry. I'll be there. Thank you," Louise replied.

After she received the company's address and contact phone number, Robert and Barry hit the court while Sandra and Louise chatted for a brief time. "Looks like you're in luck," Sandra commented, pleased that she had made the connection.

• • • • •

Louise's interview with Harold Jenson went so well that by 10:30am she officially had the job. Taking a liking to her boss immediately, Louise was more than excited to commence work the next day.

One of the first of many colleagues that Louise met in the office was Bernadette Tanner, a spirited woman with an infectious zest for life. She was a fellow Kiwi. "My husband Steve and I flew to Sydney eighteen months ago and bought a yacht," she told Louise. "We sailed her up the Queensland Coast then circumnavigated Papua and New Guinea. Now we live onboard. She's moored near the yacht club, so it's an easy stroll to the office."

Over the course of the next month or so, Louise and Bernadette's friendship grew and their husbands also became good mates.

Occasionally on weekends the couples would sail 'Ocean Maid' out of Simpson Harbour, through Blanche Bay and over to the Duke of York Islands. The underwater visibility was incredible so naturally, swimming and snorkelling over the coral reefs filled their leisure time. Curious, playful dolphins swam in close proximity while turtles, stingrays, reef sharks and an abundance of tropical fish provided them with great viewing opportunities…not to mention the brilliant array of coral species. Steve was a keen free-dive spear fisherman so he caught food to cook aboard the yacht or prepare ashore on the coral sands. It was truly idyllic.

Just as the couples were closely observing a pod of dolphins at the stern of the yacht one Saturday afternoon, it prompted Bernie to tell the Greens about an unusual encounter they had with the creatures. "While we were sailing up the Queensland Coast on a clear, starry evening, I was keeping watch while Steve slept. Around midnight a zephyr was propelling us along nicely and I felt great. Steve will tell you that I'm an awful singer but I really wanted to sing, and as I did, four dolphins came right up alongside the hull and cruised along with us. After about three minutes I stopped singing and they swam away. Five minutes later, I started again and they returned. Steve came up on deck to see what all the noise was about. Yes…that's what he calls my singing…'noise'. We watched the dolphins come and go for ages, so they must have liked my voice."

"Give Ross and Louise a demo Bern. Sing them a tune," her husband teased.

"No, I'm too embarrassed Steve. Besides, the Greens aren't dolphins," she giggled.

Having spent a fair amount of time underwater around the Duke of York islands, Ross decided to enrol in a scuba diving course. The lure of the reef and the prospect of being able to explore its deeper recesses really appealed to him. An introductory course was being offered at the Travelodge Hotel.

Classes were conducted by former Navy diver, Trevor Longmore, and Dr Joe Fong who was later to become the Green's general practitioner. Horrie Cocks, the Powerhouse Manager, also expressed interest so he and Ross both attended their first two lessons on Saturday mornings in the hotel's grand pool. Here, the group were taught how to operate, maintain and use all of the required equipment; from tanks, lines and regulators, right through to mouthpieces, masks and fins.

When their second lesson was over, the group were taken to a nearby beach known as the 'Submarine Base'. While they explored the shoreline and surrounding area, Trevor explained its significance. "During WWII Chinese and Kanaka labourers were forced to tunnel into the pumice of this sheer cliff-face rising out of the sea. A submerged Japanese sub would then sail directly into the tunnel, surface, and release its troops from the bow, thus avoiding detection from the air."

Ross and Horrie could hardly comprehend the number of labourers that would have been required to achieve such a mammoth task.

Trevor continued. "In fact, Rabaul is riddled with tunnels, many of them running hundreds of yards into the hillsides. One such tunnel, which had been blocked-off by a landslide for goodness knows how long, was eventually excavated and found to be concealing racks upon racks of Japanese military uniforms; completely preserved in immaculate condition."

Returning home from each dive at the Submarine Base, Ross was almost jumping out of his skin. "I can't wait until next Saturday Lou! We're going to be diving alongside a sunken Japanese wreck in the harbour. I wish you could see it too." He paused to guzzle down the remaining mouthful of beer in the bottle then added, "You know what? How great would it be if you did the course as well? I can't dive anywhere without a buddy and this is something that we could really enjoy together. Please give it some thought, hey? It's only a six-week course and Joe hinted that if there's enough interest, they'll back-up and run another one straight after this."

"I'll certainly think about it Ross," she replied. "I have to admit, I am feeling far more comfortable in a mask, snorkel and fins than I ever have before.

Louise counted Ross's empty beer bottles on the kitchen countertop while her husband opened a fresh one. It was a continuing concern to her that he was imbibing an excessive amount, considering Neville drank very moderately and Bernadette and Steve only indulged in a couple of ales on the weekends that they sailed together.

•••••

Another dive course commenced within a month of Ross receiving his Open Water Dive Certificate. Louise and her work colleague, Barry, decided to enrol. There were eight students in total, a manageably-sized group.

Five weeks passed quickly and before she knew it, Louise was preparing for her final qualifying dive. At the Submarine Base site, adrenalin pumped through her veins. She was nervous and excited all at the same time. Focusing on her breathing alleviated the emotional tension and allowed her heart rate to return to a steady rhythm.

The group were required to descend to a depth of one hundred feet then after intaking a final breath of air through their regulators, very slowly ascend to the surface. Dr Joe informed his students, "Trevor will remain at this depth with you until everyone has made their ascent. If you experience any problems while you're down there, you all know exactly what to do. I'll be assisting each of you to the surface, one by one. As soon as I know you're safely above water, I'll return to bring up the next student. Any final questions?" All members of the group shook their heads, confirming they were ready. "Okay," he said. "We'll start with Louise first and Trevor can decide on the order from there."

Underwater at the required depth, Louise fixed her eyes firmly on Dr Joe then inhaled a large gulp of air through the regulator. He gave a signal and they slowly commenced their ascent. Louise gradually exhaled air from her lungs, ensuring that her ascension rate was slower than that of her own exhaled bubbles. Showing no panic at any stage, Louise finally surfaced with a beaming grin.

"Congratulations," Dr Joe announced. "You've done it! Unload your gear if you like and I'll see you when we're done."

Ross helped his wife remove her diving equipment and they stood together on the shallow reef, watching and commending each diver as they rose to the surface. Some students chose to remain in the water and paddle around for a while. "Great job, Lou," Ross smiled, hugging her shoulders affectionately. The couple high-fived and Louise had to admit, she felt pretty proud of herself.

While chatting with a local, Louise spotted a fellow student whose body appeared limp in the water. Grabbing Ross's arm, she immediately pointed. "That guy hasn't moved a muscle since I first noticed him."

"Are you sure?" her husband queried, without taking his eyes off the man.

"Yes, I'm positive. He's in trouble Ross," Louise frowned, quickly making her way to the edge of the reef.

Ross flashed past her, dived into the water and swam out as fast as he could. The man was indeed unconscious. As Ross struggled to roll the body over, he discovered that the guy was severely frothing from the mouth. Battling the outgoing tide, Ross clenched his arms around the man's torso and dragged him to the edge of the reef with every ounce of strength he could muster. "Help me drag him up," he shouted to onlookers.

Meanwhile, Louise was desperately trying to attract Dr Joe's attention when he finally surfaced.

Once in the shallows, Ross wasted no time performing mouth-to-mouth resuscitation. Dr Joe rushed to the scene but didn't interfere in the procedure. Despite the fact that Ross seemed to be gagging, his technique was thorough and he was totally committed to a positive outcome. After several exhausting minutes, the man regained consciousness and was taken directly to Nonga Base Hospital for observation.

Exhausted, Ross slumped beside Dr Joe. "That froth he was bringing up was bloody beer," Ross exclaimed. "And that's what made me gag while I was working on him. What an idiot!"

Dr Joe was absolutely furious. "Pulling a stunt like that could have killed him! Then there's the fact that Trevor and I, as his instructors, would have been held accountable. The guy knew that aerated fluids can't be consumed within twelve hours prior to a dive. You all know that."

Within a few short weeks of the serious incident, Ross and Louise purchased their own dive gear and all the necessary equipment. Dr Joe owned an expensive scuba air compressor which was located under his house. He was more than happy to top-up and refill the Green's dive tanks, so he told Ross to bring them over.

"That guy I resuscitated…how's he doing Joe? All good now?" Ross asked.

"Dead!" Joe bluntly returned. "Put a gun in his mouth last week and pulled the trigger. So, I'm guessing that dive was a suicide mission gone wrong. Apparently, his wife flew his body back to Australia yesterday.

• • • • •

Day trips out to the Duke of York Islands with Steve and Bernadette now took on a whole new meaning for the Greens. Scuba diving the depths of the clear blue heaven on earth was magical and encounters with the fascinating sea life captivating. While they dived, Bernie and Steve snorkelled high above them, exploring the shallow reefs and coral bommies.

For Ross and Louise, their lives were anything but dull and their marriage continued to follow a carefree pattern. They'd formed friendships easily and engaged in numerous social activities. Louise played competition squash one evening a week which Ross sometimes watched and they joined the Rabaul Golf Club. Louise would drop him off after lunch on a Saturday afternoon to compete in the men's competition. While he was playing golf, invariably Louise would round up Maria and the pikininis, bundle them into the car and head to Pila Pila for a swim.

Every second Sunday morning they rose early to play nine holes of golf, hopefully winding up before the sun rose high over 'The Mother' volcano, making the heat and humidity rather unpleasant. After golf they'd return home, pack a small picnic then drive to their favourite spot for an hour's dive. On some occasions Sandra and Tyler would accompany them and although not divers themselves, the couple loved to snorkel and share in the picnic on the beach.

Editions of 'The Australian' newspaper always arrived in Rabaul on a late Sunday afternoon flight and they were distributed from the R.S.L. at about 7pm that evening. Around the same time, freshly baked bread was ready, straight from ovens at the Bakery. It was a dinner treat for the Greens once in a while to devour their warm bread, smothered in lashings of butter and Vegemite, all whilst catching up on the news in Australia.

They were making good money in jobs they both enjoyed and Louise's business in Perth was continuing to grow nicely. There hadn't been any cries for help from Janet, in fact, in a recent letter she indicated that she'd be happy to purchase the business, should Louise ever decide to sell.

CHAPTER ELEVEN

Briefly looking up from the ledger machine, Louise peeped out the window of her first-floor room. Across the road, the R.S.L. Club's vibrantly green lawns seemed to shimmer in the heat of the midday sun. Her colleague, Valda, who was also a machine operator, shared the sound-proofed space located behind the main office.

Regaining a comfortable position in her chair, Louise returned to feeding information into the system. Within moments she could feel the building moving but thought very little of it. Small gurias (earthquakes) were rather common in New Guinea. Often, in the quiet of the evening the Greens would hear glasses jingle in the kitchen cupboard as their home shook. It was an occurrence that didn't concern them and something they learned to live with.

Today, this tremor felt oddly different. Whilst gaining strength it quickly became apparent that an earthquake of sizeable magnitude was rocking Rabaul. Trusting her instincts, Louise turned to Valda and said, "We need to get out of here."

As they left their room, they walked towards the outer office. Standing in the doorway, at first glance it appeared the usual staff of five had already gone. While navigating their way through Barry's office towards the first-floor landing, shelving behind his desk crashed, cascading heavy files across the desk which just missed them by inches. The shaking grossly intensified and the surging floor beneath their feet made walking virtually impossible. Dodging a few heavily-laden cabinets, they continued making their way towards the landing.

Finally reaching the top of the stairs, Louise carefully assisted Valda down to the grass below where their colleagues were already safely gathered. Louise was a bit annoyed that no-one attempted to check on them before vacating the building, especially considering

Valda was seven months pregnant.

The ground continued to rock beneath them and Mango Avenue progressively rolled like an ocean swell. From the group's position seated on the front lawn they could clearly see four retail shops. Long pendant lights inside the Travel Agency swung from the ceiling like a pendulum, threatening to crash against the walls. Adjacent to their office, water from the Travelodge Hotel's huge pool violently sloshed into its accommodation, restaurant and reception areas on the ground floor.

Within five minutes, even though it felt more like an hour to Louise, the ground settled. Deciding to head to higher ground, the group stood looking out over Simpson Harbour and they were shocked at what they saw. The sparkling crystal waters of the horse-shoe shaped bay had been completely sucked out to sea. A vast mudflat revealed submerged shipwrecks; relics of WWII, which were exposed for the first time since they were originally bombed and sunk. Pleasure-craft anchored off the Yacht Club wallowed in the sludge like abandoned toys. The majority of the larger yachts, including Steve and Bernadette's 'Ocean Maid', managed to hold their mooring buoys and remain upright, their keels firmly wedged within the muddy landscape.

Locals observing the phenomenon from the shoreline were even more astonished when the harbour slowly began to fill. Suddenly there were people scattering everywhere. Within a short time the water surged and flowed through waterfront premises and retail shops, the Travelodge Hotel, and into the main shopping precinct along Mango Avenue. Untethered dinghies sprawled around the Yacht Club were set afloat by the tidal torrent and littered the low-lying areas of town. The remainder floated out to the Pacific on the retreating tide, many never to be seen again.

Harold closed the office for the remainder of the day. Employees returned to their respective homes in order to assess any damage and ensure their domestic staff were safe. The Green's residence was fairly close to the harbour but fortunately the tidal surge only reached the bottom step of their front entrance.

Ross was already home when Louise arrived. "Are you okay Lou? How's the office?"

She hugged him and replied, "Yes, I'm fine and I think the office is alright. There's stuff everywhere but I'm sure we can handle the clean-up. How's Maria?"

"I found her and the children clustered together in the middle of the lawn when I got here…but they're all good," he assured his wife. "Neville and I were painting a fascia board when the first tremor started. I told the line-boi to stop shaking the bloody ladder but then I saw him running for the hills. All I could see was the pink soles of his feet. That's when I knew it was going to be a big one!"

The following morning news broke that the guria measured 8.3 on the Richter Scale. This was much larger than the 1906 earthquake measuring 7.9 which devastated San Francisco. In New Guinea however, buildings were constructed to modern earthquake standards, therefore little structural damage was incurred. The area of Rabaul was also built entirely on pumice; a porous and thus resilient igneous rock. Even after torrential rain the pumice would rise to the surface and float down the deep gutters of the township.

● ● ● ● ●

Late on Friday afternoon, only two weeks later, another guria hit. This time it measured 8.4 and came from a completely different direction. Steve was aboard his yacht carrying out some routine maintenance at the time, so as the tide receded, he released the mooring line and drifted out of the harbour. When he knew it was safe to do so and the surges diminished, he motored 'Ocean Maid' back onto her mooring.

Meanwhile, Bernadette and Louise were enjoying a coffee after work at the Yacht Club. They rushed outside to tie dinghies up to anything they could find and in their haste the pair became separated. The sea rushed in and with nowhere to secure the final dinghy, Louise went with the flow, wading up Mango Avenue towing the boat behind her.

The Greens had planned a barbecue that evening. Edgar Bennett, Louise's boss in Lae, happened to be in Rabaul meeting with an Indian merchant and they were staying at the Travelodge. Fortunately, their room was on the second floor. Ross collected the men from their hotel at around 6pm and brought them home for dinner. As the group sat on the veranda savouring their barbecued seafood, random aftershocks continued. Each time the ground shook, Edgar's associate would grip his chair while his face turned horribly pale. The poor man was terrified and everyone could see that he was battling to keep dinner down. Calling an early night, Ross returned the men to their hotel and bid them farewell.

Waking to a glorious Saturday morning, Ross went down the street to buy some milk and the Post Courier newspaper. On his return he broadly grinned at Louise and placed the newspaper down on the kitchen table beside her. "Who's this beautiful woman?" he asked.

Louise was shocked to see a photo of herself on the front page. It was taken as she towed the small dinghy up Mango Avenue, her shoes and handbag clearly visible on the boat's seat. The headline read, 'This is how they do their shopping in Rabaul.' "Not exactly a glamorous shot, that's for sure," Louise giggled.

As the Greens prepared breakfast, Ross perused the finance section of the paper. It quickly reminded him that they were yet to do their banking and there was a rather large sum of money bundled in their deposit book. The couple were paid monthly, in cash, and with all the drama of the past fortnight, neither of them had found time to do it. Their valuable documents; insurance papers, passports, bank books and the like, were kept hidden under some old clothing in their wardrobe. While Ross searched for the stash, he shouted out to Louise, "Have you got the deposit book?"

"No," she replied. "It's in the usual spot." Assuming her husband wasn't having a thorough look for it, Louise entered the bedroom and began rummaging through the wardrobe. She too was unable to find any of the documents. This was very concerning. "I'll ask Maria if she moved them."

From the back veranda, Louise called out to Maria and asked her to come up to the house. "Where's the paperwork we keep in our bedroom wardrobe?" Louise questioned her in pidgin.

"Oooh, Misus Louise, mi gat," Maria promptly answered. With a big grin, she lifted her Meri blouse and handed Louise a large, sealed plastic bag containing all of the Greens important documents.

Maria explained she was worried that the water surge from the last guria might enter the house, so she kept the items safely stowed away.

"Thank you so much, Maria. That was very thoughtful of you," Louise sighed with relief.

Maria smiled and made her way back across the yard. As she did so, Louise sat down at the dining table and checked the contents of the bag. Nothing was missing. All the money was there. *'Bless her kind heart,'* she concluded.

The Greens had grown very fond of Maria. She had such a lovely personality and a terrific sense of humour. They could all communicate in pidgin quite well now. One evening while Maria sat in their lounge room chatting, Louise and Ross attempted to figure out her age. She told them that she had small breasts when the Japanese invaded Manus Island but that's all she knew. The Greens deduced that would make her around thirty-eight or forty Christmases, though she looked slightly older.

She also described Leo's birth in her own language. Maria was asleep in a kunai house on Manus Island with other family members when her waters broke. Without waking anyone she walked down to the water's edge and gave birth to her son. After cutting the umbilical cord between two rocks, she tied it off, washed herself and the pikinini, fed him then went back to her sleeping mat on the floor.

Louise and Ross were stunned. "All the gynaecologists, paediatricians and midwives in hospitals back home attend to patients and make a fortune," Louise commented. "And here's Maria, giving birth alone on a beach. Amazing!"

Maria's children were adorable too. Ross paid them to carry out some odd jobs around the yard; raking up leaves, sweeping paths, pulling weeds etc. Louise bought each child a money box and wrote their names on the front. Every Saturday morning she'd call out from the back veranda, "Ole kam," and the four smiling children would come running up to receive their monetary reward. Naturally, naked little Leo was always the last to arrive, his cute legs pumping hard to keep up with his older siblings. Half their earnings went into the money boxes to save for something special and the other half could be spent as they wished. After school, Joseph also worked in the kitchen of the Community Hostel across the street.

Following receipt of their reward money, the children would then sit on the back steps, one behind the other and go through their tightly-curled hair, picking out mites and squashing them. Leo didn't have any hair yet so he was off the hook. The other siblings worked on each other until Maria, on the top step, moved down one step into Joe's spot. Joe would then sit behind his mother and work on her head while the others played on the lawn.

Looking on from the kitchen window, Louise quietly said to her husband, "I struggle not to laugh when they do their nit picking."

"Yeah, me too," he nodded. "Their personal hygiene's pretty good but those tight curls are a worry. Just watching them makes my head itchy!"

The Greens were delighted to be able to help Maria and her children in any way they could. This often meant handing over items that would otherwise be thrown away. In climates such as New Guinea, perspiration causes clothing, particularly underwear, to fall apart very quickly. Dear skinny Maria was always grateful to receive Louise's used bras. Having breastfed children and the much-coveted pigs over many, many years, her eight inch long 'susus' (breasts) hung straight down like old fashioned razor straps. Maria would roll them up and tuck them into a bra, leaving one strap hanging from her shoulder to show the other meris that she was 'sophisticated'.

Last weekend Maria came to inform Ross and Louise that their washing had been stolen from the clothes line overnight. Maria immediately suspected the 'pek-pek' man because he was scheduled to empty the boi haus toilet that same evening.

In order to access the boi haus it was necessary to traverse the gravel driveway, past the main bedroom wall, carport, and low hedge to one side of it, before crossing the backyard. Down the side of the property a fairly high hedge concealed the private lawn area.

Asleep the following night, the Greens were woken by heavy footsteps outside in the gravel progressing past their bedhead towards the boi haus. Ross crept down the hallway and quietly exited the back door. In the carport area a low hedge masked him from view of the boi haus. A few minutes later he heard the footsteps returning. Louise observed from the bedroom window.

Lunging from his hiding place towards the dark figure, Ross yelled in pidgin, "What's your name?"

The man received the fright of his life and stopped dead in his tracks. "Masta, mi man bilong pek-pek tasol!!" he stammered. Man bilong pek-pek was shaking and clutching a long poll on his shoulder, on the ends of which were two drums full of pek-pek.

If Ross had barrelled the man into the hedge, both men would have been entirely covered in the stinky excrement. This was a thought that Louise couldn't delete. She laughed so hard as the image played out in her mind like a comic strip.

Back in bed, Ross sighed. "Well, the pek-pek man didn't steal the washing. He wasn't even here last night. Maria can do her own detective work from now on." He shook his head and chuckled. Fortunately, he too could see the funny side.

• • • • •

During Queensland's school holidays, Louise's friend Jillian came to visit for seven days. The women were excited to see one another again for the first time in well over a year. Maria was informed of her arrival time when Louise left to collect 'Misus Jill' from the airport.

Jillian's flight was on schedule and the friends warmly embraced within moments of spotting each other. "You look fabulous," Louise complimented her.

"I know," Jillian laughed, "and you're more beautiful than ever Mrs Green. I've really, really missed you."

Driving back to the house, Louise neared the corner of her street and found Maria and her four pikininies gathered on the corner, neatly attired in their very best European clothes. Louise stopped the car and the family clambered in to travel the hundred yards home.

Jillian was slightly overwhelmed and had no idea what Maria was saying. She left it to Louise to interpret. "I told Maria that you're a devout catholic," Louise announced, smiling at Jillian. "She wants to take you to Haus Lotu (church) with her on Friday.

"Oh, I see," Jillian replied. "On a Friday? Sure, why not. I won't understand a word but that doesn't matter. It'll be a great cultural experience."

When Friday rolled around Maria proudly took her new-found Australian friend to their native service. The heat was almost unbearable in the crowded space and Jillian found herself wedged between tiny Maria and a huge, unwashed Tolai man wearing only his lap lap. He smelled pretty grim and Jillian later admitted to Louise, "It wasn't quite the 'experience' I was hoping for but at least I'll never forget it."

The following morning while the friends were chatting on the veranda, young Peter came up to the house and told Louise, "Mamma, she got guria na skin i hot!" Maria was trembling with a fever.

Peter and Louise walked to the boi haus to check on her. There was no doubt that Maria's temperature was extremely high but she seemed to be in good spirits. Louise went up to the house and came back with twenty cents. "Here Peter. This is the doctor's fee. Take your mum up to the clinic."

Before long an ambulance arrived and drove into the backyard. Peter filled a small black bag under the direction of his mother and with Leo cradled in her arms, Maria happily waved to her family and told William, her new live-in boyfriend, "Yu do wok!"

That evening after dinner Louise phoned the hospital to get an update on Maria's condition. They were closely monitoring her and she was receiving intravenous fluids and antibiotics. "We'll drop in and visit her before I take you to the Yacht Club for lunch tomorrow," Louise told Jillian.

As Ross and the women conversed over a few beverages, the hot topic of New Britain's unrest finally came to the fore. Just a few months before Jillian arrived, the District Commissioner, Jack Emanuel, an Australian, was assassinated. A number of Tolai men had formed the Mautungan Association, their purpose, to ensure local land rights were adhered to. There were frequent disputes and when the Commissioner visited the Binings area, a group of vigilantes surrounded him, one fatally stabbing Jack with a rusty bayonet. The subsequent trial was due to commence on Monday.

Enormous amounts of publicity in both Australian and local newspapers advised that on trial day there'd be a march on the courthouse by members of the Tolai community. Part of their chosen route was to cross the top of the street near the Green's residence.

"I'm quite concerned about this march," Jillian admitted.

"Honestly, it's mostly media hype Jill," Ross affirmed. "Nothing more than desperate reporters sensationalising for power and profit. And all it really does is cause unnecessary alarm for expats' families and friends back home. I know that Lou and I have to work on Monday but I tell you what…I'll come home just before the march is scheduled to start and we can walk up to the corner and watch it together."

"Really?" Jillian questioned with an anxious tone. "Do you think that's wise?"

Ross smiled at her and replied, "Yes, of course. I wouldn't do it if I thought I was placing you in any danger." Louise also reassured her friend that it would be a peaceful rally but Jillian still wasn't convinced.

Waking at the crack of dawn next morning, Ross quietly loaded scuba gear into the car and drove out to his favourite spot for a dive. He intended to be back home by 9:30am so Louise could have the car for the remainder of the day. When Ross arrived at the beach Horrie was eagerly gearing-up.

"Fingers crossed we don't have another big earthquake this morning mate," Horrie remarked offhandedly. "Don't much feel like getting swept out to sea today."

Ross laughed, even though he knew the odds were pretty high. "Let's explore, shall we?" he suggested as both men eased themselves into the water. There wasn't a breath of wind, the ocean as flat as a sheet of glass. Perfect conditions for diving.

On the drive home, Ross pulled over and stopped the car when he saw Joseph and William. They were trying to hitch a ride into town and William was carrying something large in a paper bag. Ross called them over and enquired, "Where are you going? Can I give you a lift?"

Whilst making their way to the Haus Sik (hospital) to deliver Maria a treat, William explained to Ross that he and Joe had boiled her a chicken and took it to the hospital last night for dinner. Apparently, Maria wasn't at all impressed by the bird and told them in no uncertain terms, "Mi no like kakaruk, me like pik tasol!"

Chastened by their efforts and Maria's reaction, William and Joe then went in search of a much-coveted pig. A nearby local was willing to sell them a piece of pig leftover from the previous day's celebratory feast, so the deal was done.

This morning William and Joe were delivering it to Maria. Now Ross knew exactly what the bag contained. Yes…a huge lump of pig! Parking outside the hospital he said, "I'll wait here for you both, please don't be long." Watching them dash into the hospital's entrance, Ross shook his head. He couldn't believe the lengths they had gone to, in order to keep Maria happy.

●●●●●

"The trial starts at 11am so I'll try to be home about an hour before," Ross told Jillian as he and Louise left for work on Monday morning. Louise felt bad having to work while her friend visited but as half the office staff were struck down with the flu, she had little choice.

Jillian kept herself busy after breakfast, continuing to mark her students' end of term art assignments. By 9:45am Ross arrived home and they walked up to the corner of Attar Street.

Dozens of local protesters walked down the centre of the road, laughing and chattering, many chewing buai. The marching group consisted mostly of lapun men, meris and dozens of children. The astute Australian proprietor of Joe's Steakhouse on the foreshore had handed the elderly male leader of the group a banner which read, 'Eat at Joe's'. Another advertised, 'Rugby League, Queen's Park, this Saturday'. Clearly the marching party had no idea what was written on the banners. The procession was very orderly and at the end of the day, the group gathered for a joyous 'sing sing' in the park.

Ross returned to work and the balance of the afternoon flew by. That evening the Greens took Jillian to Joe's Steakhouse for a meal. Their tender cuts of thick, juicy oyster blade steak, cooked to perfection, were second to none. Accompanied by a vegetable medley drizzled in creamy mushroom sauce, it enhanced the flavour of the meat to a whole new level.

Jillian gently dabbed a serviette over the corners of her mouth and said, "There's no way I'll be eating breakfast in the morning. That was three meals all rolled into one." The Greens completely agreed, relaxing back in their chairs with overly-full stomachs. "I think I might stroll down to the foreshore tomorrow and do some more shopping. Heaven knows I need the exercise," Jillian confessed.

The trio were prematurely woken the next morning by a noisy excavator operating in the street behind them. With plenty of time before the Greens' work day commenced, Ross decided to make Maria some Vegemite sandwiches, which she loved, and take them to the hospital for her.

The women's ward was relatively quiet as Ross made his way towards Maria's bed. On sighting him with the sandwiches, she looked up sullenly and blurted, "Me no like bread, me like chicken that's all!"

Seeing the anger in Maria's eyes made Ross realise that he was receiving the same treatment as William and Joe. She then smugly told him that she'd taken the bus into town yesterday to look for William because she wanted to kill him. She heard that he was seeing another meri. Unable to locate her victim, Maria simply returned to the hospital.

Ross was hurt by Maria's outburst. He immediately turned on his heels and walked away. Driving home he found himself becoming more and more furious with each passing kilometre. "Who does she think she is, lording it over everyone like that, including me!" he snidely vented. "And if she's well enough to go looking for William, she's bloody well enough to be at home!"

The slamming of a car door alerted Louise and Jillian to the fact that Ross was back. He stormed into the house and said, "Lou, seriously, you need to go and tell her off. Maria has way overstepped the mark."

"What are you talking about? What has she done?" Louise asked.

Ross frowned and replied, "She totally rejected my sandwiches and would hardly even look at me. I don't know what's going on with her."

Knowing that Harold was always in the office early, Louise phoned him to say that she'd be very late for work this morning. She then rang Neville and asked him to pick Ross up. Jillian suggested she accompany Louise and the two women left for Nonga Base Hospital within fifteen minutes.

Passing through the men's ward to reach the women's ward, Louise and Jillian witnessed men in all manner of undress. Some wore lap laps and others were completely naked. Jillian was quite horrified by the scene but as soon as they entered the women's ward, she spied a cute little pikinini sitting at the foot of her mother's bed. The baby smiled at Jillian and her heart instantly melted.

Louise located Maria. She was sitting on the floor with three other women, holding court. Leo was lying on a bed happily playing with his toes. As Louise and Jillian entered, Maria's face lit up… until registering the annoyance in Louise's eyes.

Heaving little Leo off the bed and placing him on the floor, Louise then told Maria to sit down. In pidgin she informed Maria that she was cross with her for insisting that her family hike all over Rabaul in search of her chosen food. She then added, "Being unwell doesn't excuse your behaviour and I'm bitterly disappointed that you could be so rude to Ross. He's nothing but wonderful to you and your family, we both are. Furthermore, if you go into town searching for William again, you can consider yourself sacked. No money. No haus."

As Jillian watched on, she cradled Leo tightly on her hip. Louise's angry tirade and finger pointing shocked her, given that Jillian had no idea what was being said.

Maria suddenly bent down to her locker and hauled out a black bag. Furiously burrowing into it, she then extracted a sharp, long-bladed bush knife.

Jillian took one look at the vicious weapon, placed the baby on another bed and bolted down the hallway.

Maria stared at Louise and railed on, ending with "I kill William! He die! Finish!"

"Stop!" Louise demanded. "Put it away!" She then explained that William was always lending the pikininies a hand to do their work around the house, helping them off to school and still managing to hold down his job at the sawmill. There was no way he had time to go chasing other meris.

Maria's mood shifted immediately and as she sobbed, sincerely apologised to Louise for hurting the people she loved.

"Now remember what I said Maria. Stay here in Haus Sik until you're released, otherwise you will have no job to come home to." Louise was unwavering in her delivery as she left the room.

When Louise reached the carpark Jillian was extremely relieved to see her friend in one piece. "Oh, thank heavens," she sighed, throwing her arms around Louise. "A native brandishing a knife scares the absolute heck out of me."

"Yes, I noticed," Louise laughed. "I think a week here is more than enough for you Jill. Just as well you're flying home tomorrow, you'll need another full week to recover."

"Gosh you're a tease Lou!" Jillian chuckled.

"I know," she proudly returned.

CHAPTER TWELVE

Within a few weeks of Jillian retuning to Brisbane, Australia's Prime Minister, Gough Whitlam, visited New Guinea. Via an interpreter, he addressed an audience of hundreds and promised them 'Independence'. Most of those present were locals uneducated in English. They had no understanding of the word itself, let alone its connotations. Expats knew there was very little depth amongst the educated citizens of the country to form a successful, independent government.

This impending shift in the political landscape prompted the Greens to reassess their future. "Do you think we should return to Perth or maybe start afresh in Sydney?" pondered Ross.

Louise always assumed that they'd go back to the West Coast but Sydney was a great alternative. "Well, given that Mum and Dad are experiencing a few health issues now, if we needed to get to New Zealand in a hurry, the East Coast would be far more accessible. Yes, I think Sydney's a sensible decision."

"Real estate's pretty expensive though Lou," he commented. "That may mean selling our block in Perth and probably your business as well."

"Yes, that's true Ross but it honestly wouldn't bother me too much. Janet has offered to buy the business if we did decide to go that way and I think we'd be able to offload the land fairly easily."

"Okay," her husband nodded slowly. "Looks like we're on the same page, so I guess Sydney it is. Let's give Rabaul another six months I reckon. That will take us a bit closer to Independence and give us both plenty of time to get organised and make all the necessary arrangements.

• • • • •

Maria and her family's close relationship with the Greens continued to flourish after she emphatically apologised for her insolent behaviour during Jillian's visit. They all settled back into routine and life was traveling along smoothly.

Jillian would often send Louise copies of various Australian newspapers that weren't available in New Guinea. It was a treat for Joseph to be invited up to the Green's house to read them. On one particular night, Louise noticed that while he was reading, Joseph held the newspaper very close to his face.

She asked him, "Can you see the blackboard at school, Joe?"

"Yes, misus," he answered, "if I sit up the front."

Louise knew there were minimal placements for local children at the high school and a solid 'pass' mark was required. Joseph failed his first attempt in Grade 7 at the Catholic Mission School he attended and was therefore repeating the year. Examinations were to take place in October.

One stifling Saturday morning in late September, Ross was enjoying a cold beer on the front veranda when Maria shyly approached him. She asked, "Masta Ross. Mi laikem ten dollar?"

"What for, Maria?" he questioned quizzically.

She explained that last year she'd visited her young catholic priest to pray for Joe to pass his exams. The priest requested $10 for his services but Maria couldn't pay him. Needless to say, Joseph failed. This year Maria was hoping to borrow the money so that her son would pass his exams and be accepted into high school.

Ross was rather angry that Maria blamed her lack of funds for the outcome but thought, *'Who am I to interfere? She has her own beliefs.'* He retrieved his wallet and gave her a $10 note. "All the best Maria. Joseph's a fine boy, so I certainly hope it helps him."

Maria thanked Ross and just as she left, Louise pulled up in the driveway. Her husband helped unload the groceries from the back seat and said, "I've been thinking Lou…we should buy a new car before we leave. The shipping cost would be minimal and they're so much cheaper here. I've had my eye on a Toyota Crown Hardtop for a while now. There's one on display down at Ela Motors. What do you think? Are you happy to go for a sticky-beak and maybe take it for a test drive?"

"Sure. We need a car either way so if it's financially beneficial, why not? I'm catching up with Lyn at the salon later this afternoon but other than that, I'm free. Let's pack this stuff away now then we can go and check it out."

At the dealership Roy, the salesman, informed the Greens, "This model isn't available for sale in Australia but spare parts wouldn't be a problem at all."

Blue was a colour that had always appealed to Ross and this one happened to be a light, metallic shade. Air-conditioning as a standard inclusion scored a huge plus for the Greens, as did its comfortably spacious, practical interior.

Test driving the Toyota excited them both and within the hour Ross and Louise were the proud owners of a shiny new car. Offloading their existing vehicle was already a done deal because Horrie had recruited new Power House staff who were desperately seeking used cars.

• • • • •

October rolled around and it was finally time for Joseph to sit his school exams. Even though he admitted some questions were slightly difficult, his conscientious attitude allowed him to focus and do his very best. He felt fairly confident that he'd done well.

Neville and Ross were contracted to repaint the ceiling of the Optometry wing at the Nonga Base hospital after many years of neglect. One afternoon a young boy wearing reading glasses entered the clinic with his mother. He looked up at Ross, waved and beamed a broad smile.

At home that night whilst enjoying a beer with Louise, his pleasant encounter with the child urged Ross to suggest, "We should arrange an eye test for Joseph."

Louise was surprised by her husband's caring, almost father-like concern for the boy. "I think that's an excellent idea my love and I totally agree," she replied, hugging him tightly.

The next morning Ross arranged an appointment with the eye specialist and when he returned home from work, called Joseph up to the house. "After school tomorrow, Joe, you need to go to the

Nonga Hospital," Ross told him. "Misus Louise and I have booked you in for an eye test with the doctor. Here's some money for your PMV fare."

Joseph was extremely grateful. "Thank you Masta Ross. Yes, yes, I will be there," he shouted while briskly exiting the back door.

Cleaning up after dinner the following night, Maria was unusually quiet and sombre. Louise asked if something was bothering her and Maria confessed that she was worried. Joseph hadn't returned from the hospital that afternoon. Ross assured Maria that he'd locate her son as soon as he arrived at Nonga Base the next morning.

Neville and Ross pulled into the carpark at 7am and Joe immediately came running up to them. "Why didn't you come home last night, Joe? Ross asked. "Your mother is very concerned."

"They wouldn't let me Masta Ross," Joseph mumbled, refusing to make eye contact. "They say I have Leprosy."

Clearly shocked, Ross hastily tracked down the doctor who assessed him. Sure enough, the diagnosis was confirmed. The Greens had noticed sores on Joseph's knees and elbows but assumed it was either impetigo or as a result of playing sport with the other boys at school.

The doctor went on to explain, "Poor eyesight is a symptom of Leprosy Mr Green, as are scabby sores and pale patches on the skin. In order to test for the disease, I blindfold the patient and pin-prick some patches of skin that have lost pigment. If the patient reacts, it's considered a negative test but in Joseph's case, if the patient fails to react, the nerves are dead and the test may well return a positive result for Leprosy. Last night I took scrapings from the spots for analysis and they were definitively positive, therefore Joseph will require intravenous treatment. Now I'm afraid that isn't a procedure we carry out here, he'll have to be transferred to Vunapope Catholic Mission Hospital some 35 miles away. They provide specialist care for Tuberculosis and Leprosy patients."

"I see," Ross declared, still perplexed by the diagnosis.

"You need not worry for yourself Mr Green," the doctor added. "There have only been two reported cases of white Europeans contracting the disease, though I'd strongly suggest you bring in Joseph's other family members for testing."

"Yes, of course. I'll bring them in tomorrow after school," Ross pledged. Turning to Joseph, he then knelt down and looked up into the boy's sad eyes. "Everything will be alright Joe, there's no need to worry. We will all see you tomorrow afternoon, okay?"

Joseph's glazed eyes stared back at him. "Yes…Masta Ross."

At noon Ross, Louise and Neville went down to the boi haus to deliver the news to Maria. Neville's pidgin was far more fluent than the Greens so he explained the situation, along with the doctor's advice and direction.

Maria wailed, her hands covering her face as the tears flowed. Ross promised her that he'd take them all to Vunapope to visit Joseph every second weekend. She then hugged each of them and with shoulders slumped, slowly entered the boi haus and closed the door behind her.

Tests the following day revealed that Peter had a small patch on his shoulder and Maria had one on her face. They both required ongoing oral treatment to prevent a rapid spread of the disease. William, Veronica and Leo were clear.

"Do you know how this manifested doctor?" Louise asked curiously.

"Well, it hasn't been proven but one theory is that it's spread by body fluids. Joseph informed me that he and his brother still share the sleeping mat that belonged to their deceased father. Perhaps it was contracted through nasal mucus. We really don't know."

The Greens quickly realised that it would be up to them and subsequent employers to ensure that Maria and Peter's tablets were taken regularly, as directed. After saying their goodbyes to Joseph and vowing to see him next weekend, the group sadly returned home in complete silence.

Thankfully, Thursday brought some very welcome news. Joseph had passed his Grade 7 exams and was now eligible for high school. Maria was delighted with her son's achievement, as were the Greens. Louise set the certificate in a lavish gold-gilded frame for the family to present to him.

On Sunday Joseph was thrilled to see everyone together. They spent a few hours in the Mission gardens where Maria proudly handed her son his school certificate. Joseph was stunned by his achievement. While the family celebrated, Louise sought out the head nurse to enquire about Joseph's ongoing treatment.

Meredith explained, "We're doing our best to get Joseph onto oral medication. This is always our preferred treatment option and we're working towards that. The new school year is still some time away so there's every possibility that we'll have him on tablets by then. With continuing treatment, the disease will not be contagious, nor will it worsen."

"So…we can proceed with his high school application now?" Louise queried her.

"I'd suggest the earlier the better, yes," Meredith replied.

Through the Squash Club, Louise had previously met the headmaster of Rabaul High School. Seeking him out the following week, she asked for a quiet chat after concluding their games. The headmaster happily obliged and while Louise enquired about the student application procedure, she also explained Joseph's dilemma. She related the conversation that she'd had with the Mission nurse and the goals they hoped to achieve in order to get Joseph well enough to begin the new school year. If, of course, he was accepted.

The headmaster appeared unfazed by Joseph's story and said, "I have a few application forms in my briefcase. If you'd like to escort me to the car now, I'll give you one to take home."

"Oh, that's very kind of you," Louise returned. "Yes, that would be great, thank you."

Passing her the documents he advised, "Once you've completed them, best to deliver the paperwork straight to the school office whenever you can."

In her lunch break the next day, Louise submitted the forms to school and only two days later, she received a call from the headmaster to notify her that Joseph's application was successful.

"That's wonderful news, thank you so much," Louise graciously replied. "I know you're a very busy man but I do have one question if I may. My husband and I are going back to Australia shortly and we were wondering if it would be possible for Joseph's teachers to ensure that he takes his tablets each morning at school? We've been told that if he stops taking them, the disease will run rampant and may become contagious."

"Ah, Mrs Green, there's absolutely no need to worry about that," he assured her. "I will personally administer Joseph's medication at school every day."

• • • • •

Through the diligence of the Mission Hospital, Joseph was finally permitted to return home and duly commenced high school with a spring in his step. It seemed like February had just appeared from nowhere.

The Greens reluctantly gave a month's leave notice to their respective employers and put the word out that there was a forthcoming house available for rent. Saturday morning of that week, they called into the travel agency and booked one-way cruise tickets to Sydney, including car freight. Now Ross and Louise were all set to sail back to Australia aboard the 'Chitral' in March.

A local letting agent came to the Green's house within a few weeks of their departure date. "I've just rented out a house down near Chinatown to an English couple with two children," he told Ross and Louise. "They have a boi haus and were wanting to chat with your meri."

"That's fantastic," Ross replied. "Maria's a good, honest woman and a great housekeeper. If you give me the address, I'll take her over to meet them tomorrow. Let's say around 10am?"

"Wonderful. I'll let them know to expect you Mr Green," the agent smiled.

The house was very centrally located, close to schools and all major facilities. Ross knew that this would be very helpful for Maria and her family. After introducing her to the prospective employers, they all wandered through the property and Ross was delighted to see that the boi haus would be more than adequate for Maria and the children.

"Now, let's go into the laundry, shall we?" the Englishman gestured. "I'll show you the washing machine."

They followed him into the small room and he handed Maria a booklet. "Here are the operating instructions," he smiled.

Maria immediately turned to Ross, raised her eyebrows and

shrugged her shoulders. In turn, Ross chuckled quietly, quickly perused the manual and showed Maria how to use the machine.

"So, I take it she can't read?" the Englishman commented. "Mr Green, perhaps you could be so kind as to write out the instructions in pidgin for her?"

"Well, I certainly could do that but Maria can't read pidgin either, she can only speak it."

With a rather blank expression on his face, he then continued dishing out employment expectations while Ross interpreted for Maria. When the topic of chewing betel nut arose, she looked at the Englishman and nodded her head.

"Me savvy," she smiled.

When he requested that his children be collected from school at 3pm each day, Ross told him, "Maria can't read the time but if you mark the clock for her, when the hands show 3pm she will leave to pick them up."

"Jolly good," the Englishman returned. His wife pouted and remained deftly silent. "I am happy to hire her on the proviso that she can commence the day after you depart New Guinea."

'Geez whiz! Maria's really got her work cut out for her with this family,' Ross inwardly snickered. *'I'd love to be a fly on the wall when she starts.'*

The following morning back at the Green's house, a hungry kitten waltzed through the front door while Ross and Louise were preparing to leave for work. Once inside, Louise attempted to pat the tiny creature but it swiftly darted into the bedroom upon hearing Maria enter the back door.

Ross and Louise watched on as Maria crept into the bedroom singing, "Pussy kat, pussy kat, yu stap we? Yu go lukim numba wan misus em sindaun long Englan? (Pussy cat, Pussy cat, where have you been? Have you been to London to see the Queen?)

The Green's burst out laughing. It was one of funniest things they'd ever heard…and so unexpected. Frightened by all the racket, the kitten flew out from under the bed, straight into Maria's arms.

"How on earth do you know that nursery rhyme Maria?" Louise giggled.

She explained that a former employer used to regularly recite the story to her children in pidgin. After hearing it at least twenty times over, Maria said the words just stuck in her head.

• • • • •

Mixed emotions engulfed the Greens as they woke on the morning of their departure. They were despondent about leaving New Guinea, their friends, Maria, and her children but also exhilarated to be returning to home soil.

Having never been on a ship before, Louise pre-arranged with the children's respective teachers for them to have half a day off school to board and inspect the 'Chitral'.

When they all arrived at the foreshore, the mammoth passenger liner glistened like a beacon on its mooring in the Simpson Harbour. Due to the gurias, ships weren't permitted to berth at the wharf so passengers were ferried back and forth to the jetty by tender. The Green's Toyota was transported out to the liner by barge and loaded into its hull, along with numerous other cargo items.

Dressed in their very best attire William, Maria and the four children boarded a large tender with the Greens and motored out to the ship. Everyone was so excited to be onboard, particularly the children.

In order to reach the accommodation quarters, guests were required to take the elevator up to their cabins. Other than the Greens, no-one else in the group had ever been in an elevator before so while Louise headed to the bathroom, Ross kept them entertained. They couldn't comprehend how they saw a painting on the opposite wall when the doors closed but when the doors reopened, there was a statue of a white lion in its place. They were absolutely astonished, given the fact that they hadn't even slightly moved their feet!

Louise rejoined the group and they made their way to the bar where Ross purchased a beer for William and soft drink for Maria and the children. The beverages were quickly consumed then the Greens showed them around the ship. Its luxuriously appointed interior was overwhelming. Finally reaching Ross and Louise's cabin, the children bounced on the bed, laughing and playing games amongst themselves.

A call came over the loudspeaker advising passengers that the final tender would depart in fifteen minutes. The Greens slowly escorted Maria, William and the children to the holding bay where they warmly hugged and thanked each of them.

Making their way to the upper viewing deck, Louise cried as she held her husband's hand and waved the family back to shore. She knew that it was unlikely they would ever see their beautiful New Guinea family again.

Weighing anchor, the 'Chitral' began to slowly sail out of the harbour. Ross and Louise remained on deck for what would probably be their last vision of Rabaul. The couple had immensely enjoyed their two years in the fascinating town. They'd formed many friendships during that time and some of them would continue as more expats returned to Australia with the advent of Independence.

● ● ● ● ●

"What a spectacle!" marvelled Louise as the Sydney Harbour Bridge came into view, the sun reflecting brilliantly from the iconic structure. Ross felt like he was almost home. Louise on the other hand was looking forward to meeting her magnificent new city of residence.

During their voyage south, the couple had discussed where they'd like to live. "I'm pretty keen to be near the beach so I can have a surf whenever the waves are up; probably on the northern side of the harbour," Ross suggested. "And work shouldn't be an issue because there are so many major construction projects underway all over Sydney."

The Greens had been advised by the freight company handling their car that it would be approximately 24 hours before they could take delivery of it. The vehicle contained a few household goods and numerous artefacts that they'd purchased during their time in New Guinea, so with only their suitcases to consider the couple opted to stay overnight in a hotel. It was very close to the shipping agent's offices which eased the process of collecting their car the following day. After that...the world would be their oyster.

CHAPTER THIRTEEN

Wednesday dawned and by 8am the hotel was a hive of activity. Suitcase wheels clunked and echoed down narrow corridors amidst the prattling of noisy patrons. After some freshly brewed coffee and mouthwatering croissants the Greens made their way to the customs office.

Ross had managed to snaffle a copy of the Sydney Morning Herald from the hotel, so as the couple patiently waited for their clearance papers to be released, he scoured through the property section. There was a multitude of rental properties available on the north shore.

"I think we should head to Manly," he suggested to his wife, who was absorbed in rearranging the contents of her handbag. "It's close enough to the city by road or ferry, and the beach is only a stone's throw away."

"Do they have a transport department there?" Louise enquired. "We'll have to re-register the car before we do anything else."

After considering her question for a moment Ross replied, "Yeah, they do. We'll attend to that first and then we can chat with a few real estate agents in the area."

By 10:30am with customs cleared, the Greens nervously negotiated the heavy city traffic over the Harbour Bridge. Louise was trying to take in the view of the Opera House and Port Jackson but struggled to take her eyes off the road.

"Wow! The volume of traffic's daunting, Ross," she muttered. "Been a while since we've driven in the city but Perth has nothing on this! We're almost at a standstill."

"I know…welcome to Sydney Lou. And sometimes at peak hour it's in total gridlock."

Re-registering the car was a quicker process than expected and within an hour they were glancing over a huge street map on the wall inside a real estate office. An agent appeared and asked the couple what they were seeking.

With numerous properties in mind, he then proposed, "Would you like to see what we have on offer? I can drive you around. My car's just out the back of the office."

"Ah, yes, that would be terrific," Ross and Louise thanked him.

The first apartment they inspected was airless, pokey and slightly shabby. It held no interest for the Greens whatsoever. The interior of the second property wasn't too bad but it looked out over a vast industrial estate…hardly the view they were hoping for. Ten minutes later the agent drew up beside a far more modern-looking apartment block.

Entering the lift, he selected the third floor. When the doors opened to the exquisitely tiled foyer, they could see four units. Turning left as they exited the lift, Ross and Louise watched the agent unlock the door to Unit 12.

Inside, the unfurnished apartment was open-plan with a view east over the top of the building in front, out to the Pacific Ocean. It was freshly painted and carpeted. The living room opened onto a wide balcony through fold-back doors. On the northern end of this room a large window was designed to catch the sun in winter. The kitchen was clean and contemporary with a new up-right stove and large pantry. Both bedrooms had built-in robes and like the living area, they were fitted with neutrally-coloured drapes.

"What do you think of this one, Lou?" queried Ross.

"Well, the rent's a bit more than we wanted to spend but that includes electricity. The view's great, the space is ideal for us…so yes, I'm very happy with it."

Returning to the real estate office, the Greens signed a one-year lease and walked out with the keys to their new north shore apartment.

• • • • •

Gravity-fed showers in New Guinea were frustrating to say the least, so it was a real treat for Ross and Louise to return to having constant water pressure from their taps. They also welcomed feeling 'refreshed' after showering, instead of dripping in perspiration before they'd even dried off.

By the end of the week the Greens were totally exhausted but their new home was fully furnished, including an office desk for Louise. They opted for second-hand furniture knowing that possibly only a year from now, they may want to purchase a house. The day after they moved in, Louise applied to have the phone connected and come Friday afternoon, the technician arrived to install and activate the service.

Having depleted their minimal food supply, neither of them felt like grocery shopping for dinner. At Ross's suggestion, the corner pub was a great alternative and only a short walk to the end of the next block.

Inside, the old building was pleasantly modern, bright and teeming with patrons...a good sign of quality food at affordable prices. Ross and Louise were hankering for a thick cut of superb Aussie beef. Other than Joe's Steakhouse, the majority of meat in New Guinea left a lot to be desired. They relished in their slabs of char-grilled Porterhouse steak, followed by two rounds of Foster's lager.

Before they left Ross purchased a carton of beer, a couple of bottles of wine and a bottle of Bundaberg Rum. It's just as well they didn't have far to walk home because the alcohol load was heavy. A few more beverages imbibed in the apartment then the couple flopped into bed, though they could have slept on a plank that night.

On Saturday they woke to heavy rain which they'd heard would intensify later in the day. This was good reason to head down to Woolworths, purchase the daily newspaper and stock-up on enough groceries to last them the week. That afternoon while Louise prepared a late lunch, Ross hooked up the TV set and adjusted the reception until it was picture-perfect. They would have much preferred to be sitting on their lovely balcony but as it was sopping wet, the couple were forced to eat and peruse the paper at the dining table.

"They need bricklayers for a block of luxury apartments being built here in Manly," Ross told Louise. "Nice and close to home, so I'd have hardly any commuting to do. You never know, depending on the hours I might even be able to fit in a surf after work."

"Yep, seems ideal for you Ross," she replied.

He read out the end of the advertisement. "...applications onsite Monday to Friday. Qualified tradesmen only need apply." '*Sounds good*,' he thought. "I'll go and see them on Monday morning Lou."

Licking some mayonnaise from his bottom lip, he added, "There's also an ad here for a Bookkeeper to manage an office in Manly. They're switching over to a computerised system. That sounds right up your alley Mrs Green.

"It does," Louise grinned while snatching the paper in jest. "...electrical wholesale company. Head Office in Manly. Tuition provided for the successful applicant. Telephone to arrange an interview." She slowly nodded her head. "You're right. That could be a great fit Ross. I'll contact them for sure."

As the afternoon wore on, showers eased, negating the imminent weather forecast. In the classifieds Ross had found a second-hand twin-fin surfboard for sale at the local Manly Surf Shop. He went to check it out while Louise stayed at home to do some baking, much to her husband's delight.

On his return to the apartment, with board and leg-rope under one arm, clutching a handful of wax, Ross was beaming from ear to ear. "I'm all set love. Got it for a great price too! I can't wait to hit the waves tomorrow...don't care what the weather brings, I'll be out there."

"Good for you. I'll be sleeping in. Then I can't wait to relax on the balcony and hit a good book. I don't know where you get all your energy from. I'm frazzled after this week," Louise admitted.

• • • • •

Ross drove a very short distance to the job site and realised that he could easily have walked. Within ten minutes of meeting the foreman, he was asked to commence work the following day. Fortunately, as this left him little time to prepare, all bricklaying equipment would be provided.

Meanwhile, Louise phoned to apply for the Bookkeeper/ Managerial position. The receptionist advised that they'd received numerous applications and all interviews were scheduled to take place in half-hour intervals on Wednesday. Louise was allocated the 11am timeslot.

Taking advantage of the glorious autumn weather, by mid-morning the Greens headed off for a drive around the northern beaches to familiarise themselves with the area. Manly beach itself was pristine and famous for holding the world's first surfing contest in 1964. To the north, a string of other popular surf beaches and ribbons of golden sand separated by picturesque, rocky headlands extended all the way to the tip of Barrenjoey Peninsula. After stopping for a bite to eat at the North Steyne Surf Club they ventured home, passing by the building where Louise's interview was to be conducted.

Next morning, with his small lunch esky packed, Ross left the apartment at 6:30am and walked to work. Onsite were a crew of five other brickies, including the boss. When the introductions and a brief rundown on the job was complete, the team set about labouring on the exterior of the ground floor apartment. The luxury complex would eventually comprise six storeys with only two spacious apartments per floor.

Dressed smartly for her interview the following morning, Louise met with the General Manager. He introduced himself as Carl Hoffman and proceeded to explain that the company had four other branches in Sydney.

"We've been working with a computer programmer and require someone to install the system here at Head Office and ultimately link the five branches. We're a very progressive enterprise and intend to expand our horizons into Queensland then possibly Victoria." He then sat silently perusing Louise's references, nodding to himself from time to time.

Looking up at Louise Carl added, "Your responsibilities would entail all staff payrolls. Invoicing's handled by each branch but then they'd need to be downloaded to HO. All creditor payments are dealt with here, so settling those debts would also be a requirement. A monthly profit and loss statement and a balance sheet reflecting each store's operation within ten days of the end of the month, needs to be presented at the monthly Board of Director's meeting."

Smiling, he declared, "You certainly possess the experience and qualifications we're looking for Louise. From what I've mentioned, with personal training, could you install this new system and then train staff at the other branches?"

Louise considered the information he'd imparted and asked, "Will the staff training be done here at HO or at the various branch offices?"

"Good question," Carl acknowledged. "At this stage, either is possible. In the case of interstate branches in the future, I suppose it would be desirable for the Branch Manager and a bookkeeper to fully understand the operations, in which case it may be better for you to travel to the branches. How would you feel about that? Do you have family?"

"Only my husband," Louise answered. "He's working locally at the moment so I can't see a problem there. And I really enjoy traveling. Being a Kiwi, I'd love to see more of Australia."

"Well, Louise, I can safely say that as you're the last interview on my schedule, the position is yours," Carl assured her. "Your salary will be reviewed after the three-month provisional period then there are six monthly assessments and an annual bonus based on the success of your teaching ability and all-round efficiency."

"Sounds fine to me, thank you Carl. I revel in challenges and I know this job will offer them. When would you like me to start?"

"I'll advise the programming company tutors who'll be training you and with Tuesday being the end of our pay week, can you possibly start next Wednesday at 9am?"

"Certainly can," Louise replied. "Thanks again Carl, I'll see you then."

Louise arrived home, changed into some comfortable clothing and walked down to the beach. Strolling along the foreshore, breathing in the salty sea air, she considered her newfound job. A couple of young girls were enjoying a bodysurf in the shallow waves and Louise's pleasant thoughts immediately turned to Jillian.

After a small family wedding last year, Jillian and her engineer husband announced they were four months pregnant. Louise was so excited that her close friend was expecting a baby by the end of April.

Suddenly, a realisation abruptly presented itself. Louise and her husband had never discussed having children. She thought about that for a while and concluded, *'We haven't really settled anywhere yet. Maybe when we buy a house, we'll start a family of our own. Besides, there's no rush…we're still only in our twenties.'*

As the afternoon drew on and the southerly breeze began to stiffen, Louise was thankful that she remembered to bring a jacket. Ross would be home within the hour so she slowly started to make her way back to the apartment.

Unlocking the front door, Ross could hear Louise happily humming a tune in the kitchen. She turned and smiled. "How was your day, darling?"

"Bloody hard," he returned. "Painting's a lot less strenuous than bricklaying and I'm way out of practice. Give me another week and I'll be back on track I reckon. Want a beer, Lou?"

"Love one, thanks. I got that job and they want me to start next Wednesday."

"Oh, that's great love. Sorry, I totally forgot that your interview was today. Come and tell me all about it."

They sat out on the balcony and Louise covered the details. Ross seemed unperturbed when she mentioned the possibility of interstate travel and he agreed that the salary structure was more than reasonable.

Returning to the kitchen Louise finished preparing dinner as Ross went for a shower. When he emerged, the couple watched some news on TV while their lasagna baked in the oven.

"We should celebrate our new jobs, Lou. Let's have a wine."

With the Italian dish devoured and a bottle of wine guzzled, Louise began making coffee.

"Slosh a bit of rum into mine will you please, Lou?"

Hesitantly she poured a small amount into his mug. After carrying both cups over to the lounge, she placed Ross's down on the side table and held her own coffee as she sat to watch the ABC 'Current Affairs' program with him.

Ross picked up his coffee, took a sip, looked into the mug then immediately across at his wife. "Did you put any rum in here, Lou?"

"Yes, Ross, I did."

"Can't even taste it," he commented. Taking a large gulp he then got up, took the cup back to the kitchen, grabbed the rum bottle and filled his mug to the top before returning to his chair.

Louise said nothing.

A short time later Ross smiled at her and said, "I enjoyed that. Might have a rum on the rocks." Returning to the kitchen, he retrieved a drinking glass from the overhead cupboard, threw a few ice cubes into it and filled the glass with rum.

"I'm going to have a shower then go to bed and read for a while," Louise said, leaving Ross with his rum.

By the time she dried herself off she could hear her husband loudly laughing in the living room. The book could wait until morning. Wanting to avoid any unpleasantness Louise quickly turned off the light and lay in bed pretending to be asleep.

•••••

Wednesday brought new challenges for Louise. Her first day in the office with tutor, Graham, kicked off a whole new learning curve and whilst the basic principles of the procedures were familiar, the operational idiosyncrasies were foreign to her.

Receptionist, Martha Dean, seemed like a lovely woman. She was married to an insurance broker who commuted into the city by ferry each day. Martha appeared to be about the same age as Louise.

On Thursday afternoon, Carl said, "Graham, Martha, her husband and I are meeting after work tomorrow at the Manly Surf Club for a drink. Would you like to join us, Louise?"

"Thank you, Carl. That's very kind. I'll chat to Ross tonight and let you know."

At home that evening, she passed it by Ross and he was receptive to the idea. "I'll drive home and then we'll walk down together at about 5:30pm," she said.

The following day literally flew by and when the Greens arrived at the club, Carl was ready to order the first round of drinks. Louise introduced Ross to her colleagues and they met Martha's husband, Peter, who'd also just turned up. Everyone chose to have a beer and the group seated themselves at a table overlooking the beach.

Ross was talking to Peter about insurance and informed him of their house fire in Perth. The Green's vehicle was yet to be comprehensively insured and they still hadn't arranged cover for the contents of their apartment.

Overhearing the conversation, Louise remarked to Martha, "I feel guilty that I haven't already arranged contents insurance. Given our previous history, I should have been on top of that by now."

"Don't worry. Peter will fix it up. You should drop into our place over the weekend so he can get the details sorted then finalise everything for you at the office on Monday."

Politely interrupting the men's conversation, Martha put forward her suggestion and the Greens agreed to visit the following afternoon.

Conversation within the group flowed easily and before another two rounds of drinks, Peter offered to be designated driver for those who'd prefer to leave their vehicles in the carpark. Two hours passed quickly and by 7:30pm everyone agreed that it was time to go their separate ways. Peter handed Ross a coaster with his address and phone number written on the back.

Walking home hand-in-hand, Ross remarked, "I enjoyed that, Lou. They all seem like very nice people. I particularly like Peter and Martha. There's the possibility of a good friendship there I reckon. Glad we're seeing them tomorrow and it's a bonus that we can sort out our insurances at the same time."

Mid-afternoon the following day, Ross and Louise strolled only a few blocks to the Dean's residence. It was surrounded by a high, white rendered wall, so they rang the buzzer at the gate. Martha remotely unlocked it and the Greens entered a neat, enclosed garden surrounding a magnificent lawn. The house was also rendered in white with black window frames and guttering. Admiring the garden as they slowly walked up the path, a smiling Martha opened the grand timber door in front of them.

"Welcome. Come on in," she smiled. "Peter's just out the back putting the mower away. He loves the garden and Saturday's his maintenance day."

From the entry Ross and Louise could see right through the middle of the home to the back deck and garden. Off the hallway were doors to bedrooms and an office, then they were welcomed into a huge open plan living/dining and kitchen area. Bi-fold glass doors led onto the deck at the end of which was an outdoor kitchen, bar and barbecue area that flowed out into yet another immaculately colourful garden with a number of fruit trees.

"What a peaceful haven you've created here," Louise remarked as Peter walked across the lawn towards the deck. "I absolutely love it!"

"Thanks Louise, so do we," he smiled. "When we bought the place four years ago it was just a rundown shack but it had good bones and the location was perfect for us. Much of the original design remains but the living area of the house has changed markedly. We knocked out walls, extended others then added the deck. The old kitchen had to be gutted and replaced. Yep, we're pretty pleased with the end result. What can I offer you to drink?"

Ross had brought some beer with him in a small esky, so he handed it to Peter. The women agreed to join them for a cold ale on the back deck.

"Do you want to get business over with before we settle in?" Peter asked after a few sips. "You said that you wanted to insure your house contents and your vehicle, so I drew up the paperwork early this morning. It's in my office. Bring your drink with you, we'll polish them off while we go through it."

Whilst the men attended to insurance matters, Martha retrieved a fancy plate of interesting delicatessen nibblies with some dip and crackers that she'd prepared earlier.

Peter and Ross's work was completed within ten minutes; papers signed and ready for submission. They then rejoined their wives back out on the deck.

Louise was savouring some salami slices when she said, "It's so nice to have access to all these beautiful deli foods again, Martha. In New Guinea we couldn't get anything that even closely resembled what you've arranged on this lovely platter."

"Ah yes, you mentioned living there. We've only visited Fiji. Tell us about New Guinea."

The ebb and flow of conversation came naturally for both couples. Recalling some of the more memorable incidents that occurred during their travels, the Greens brought laughter to the table and time passed rapidly.

"Gee, Ross. It's time we left these lovely people alone," Louise encouraged after looking at her watch. She was amazed to see that it was already 6pm.

"Oh, please stay for dinner," Martha urged, "unless you have to leave of course. I cooked a mild korma curry this morning so it only needs to be reheated. Do stay and share it with us?"

The Greens looked at one another, smiled and agreed to join them. Louise then followed Martha into her state-of-the-art kitchen to gather some table setting items while Peter and Ross talked cars, boats and surfing. They discovered that both of them enjoyed the latter and arranged to hit the beach the next morning, if the surf was up.

"We catch glimpses of the swell from our unit so if it's looking good, I'll give you a call," Ross assured Peter.

Just as Louise walked out onto the deck with placemats and cutlery, she overheard Peter say, "I'll open a bottle of wine for the girls and I think I'll move on to rum and Coke myself. What would you like Ross?"

"I'll have the same thanks mate," he smiled and replied.

Louise's heart rate increased and suddenly her palms became clammy. She'd never once asked her husband to restrict his rum intake, so she knew that he was unaware of how disappointed she became whenever he overindulged. She was dreading the thought of that occurring tonight.

Over dinner Ross told the Dean's that he and Louise had taken out a twelve-month lease on their apartment, providing them with plenty of time to look around and decide where they might want to live, and whether they'd like to buy or build a home. "I'm inspired by what you've done here," he told the couple. "I'd love to sink my teeth into a renovation. Did you live here while you undertook the project?"

Peter glanced at his wife and replied, "In the latter stages we did. Once the bedrooms were painted and we finished the bathrooms, we then moved our stuff out of storage and put it all into the spare rooms. As far as a kitchen went, the microwave and the barbecue were all we needed short-term. Being here allowed me to start on some of the landscaping as well." Again, he looked over at Martha. "It took about two months from the time we moved in, to having the place ship-shape didn't it love?"

Martha nodded. "Yes, give or take a few weeks…but that sounds about right. We managed fairly easily because we were at work during the day, so that helped. On weekends we did some of it ourselves. Painting mostly."

By the end of the evening the two couples had learned a lot about one another. Louise and Martha shared common interests in reading, going to the movies, walking the beach, dabbling in craft projects and entertaining friends. Peter mentioned that he also liked riding his push-bike and bush walking with a bunch of like-minded friends in winter.

"I'd enjoy that too I think," Ross piped up. "I'm not too keen on surfing in the colder months. We scuba-dived a fair bit in New Guinea and played golf as well. Louise is a good squash player so she might get back into that when time permits."

Peter poured another glass of wine for the girls and asked Ross, "Will you join me for one last rum mate?"

Ross obliged and upon hearing the word 'one', Louise's sheer relief settled her.

• • • • •

Out on her balcony with the Sunday newspapers at hand, Louise would occasionally catch a glimpse of Ross and Peter surfing the waves. It was easy to spot her husband's bright yellow board and distinctive royal blue wetsuit.

Watching on, she realised that Ross had never mentioned any friends from his past. Considering they were now in his home city, she thought it was rather unusual that he didn't want to catch up with anyone. Selwyn and Ken were two names that he briefly raised a long time ago and Louise was aware that Ross was devastated by Selwyn's death. Other than that, he was a closed book. Even when she broached the topic of his sister, her husband vehemently refused any discussion whatsoever.

Just after 10am Ross returned to the apartment on a high and couldn't wait for a cup of coffee followed by a few Arnott's biscuits. "That was such a good surf Lou!"

"Glad you enjoyed it," she smiled as he kissed her.

"I was thinking…" Ross said as he took his beach towel to the laundry, "we should go for a drive this afternoon and try to get an idea of where we'd like to live. I reckon we have enough money saved to buy an old place and do it up when we can afford to. What do you think about putting our land on the market Lou? I'd really love to get cracking on a big project."

"Mmm…owning a place is certainly preferable to paying rent. It feels like wasted money. I was actually looking through the real estate section of the paper this morning and there are some charming homes for sale. Wouldn't hurt to go and have a look. My Dad always said that buying the worst house in the best street and doing it up is a good way to make a quick buck. And he'd know because he did it a couple of times before Mum and Dad settled in the home that they're in now. Is this what you were thinking?"

Moving his head from side to side he answered, "Well yes… and no. Peter said you have to actually live in the place for more than a year to avoid some type of tax. We'd need to get clarification on the tax laws but I suppose the real estate agents would have that information."

A load of washing and a few roast beef sandwiches later, Louise grabbed the newspapers and her camera then the couple set off. Driving north to Dee Why they drove past two advertised properties but they had no views and the land was very low lying. Inland to Brookfield, the third house was on a busy main road. Heading back towards the ocean, Narrabeen held far more interest for them.

"Being so close to the beach, this would probably be well out of our price range," Ross deduced.

Louise swung her husband a curious look. "You were telling Peter that you'd only be surfing in the summer, so do we really need to be this close to the coastline? What about somewhere further inland? There's an older residence here described as a 'renovators dream' and it backs onto a national park just west of here. I'd like to have a look at that."

Taking the Wakehurst Parkway the Greens travelled south with Narrabeen Lakes on their left and Carigal National Park on the right. They found the address and were fortunate to arrive just in time for a 2pm 'Open House'.

Two other families were already inspecting the property when they arrived. It was elevated about half a meter off the ground at the front and yes, it was certainly 'old'. There was little paint remaining on the exterior timber, the garden was somewhat overgrown but there was an established tree to one side of the front yard and in the large backyard garden, beautiful fruit trees grew in abundance.

"I really like the established fruit trees, Ross. They sure need some attention but they're reasonably healthy. Looks like they have plums, peaches, limes and a few apple trees."

"It's a great sized yard too," Ross added. "That's a good selling point for future buyers because there's ample room to add a swimming pool. The boundary backs right onto the national park so that ensures privacy and it could never be built out. A big plus!"

The front of the house offered glimpses of the lake and with only one neighbour a reasonable distance away on its northern side, the location was quiet. Other homes across the road sloped downward towards the east.

Ross inspected the perimeter of the dwelling and crouched down to assess its foundations. "The house appears quite sound," he reported to Louise.

The exterior proved to be a good indication of what they'd find inside. Vertical timber panels lined the long hallway and like the Dean's residence, four bedrooms branched off it. Ceilings and cornices were in good shape, a common feature in post-war family homes.

"New kitchen, extended living area, new guttering and the iron roof needs to be replaced," Ross surmised. "Some of the lead-light windows could be restored or sold and replaced with plain glass. A few of the load-bearing walls would have to go which means re-supporting the roof beams. That's not a problem. It'd be great to install a fireplace for the winter as well."

Louise agreed with her husband's foresight and they discussed the tax implications of reselling the property with the agent onsite.

To avoid paying Capital Gains Tax the Greens would only be required to live in the house for a minimum of one year.

Returning to the car with printed details provided by the agent and numerous photos on Louise's camera, the Greens began making their way back to the apartment. They made a brief stop at the newsagency to purchase a pad of graph paper.

At the dining table that evening Ross drew up some rough renovation plans of what he envisioned in his mind's eye. Louise was impressed and only suggested some minor adjustments. Other than that, each room's size was very generous; particularly the bedrooms.

Reaching for her husband's hand, Louise looked at him and said, "I can really see this working Ross. The property's great and I think the asking price is pretty reasonable."

"I agree," he nodded. "Let's leave it until Tuesday then we'll make a ridiculous offer and go from there. We don't want to appear too keen to buy. That way if further negotiations don't come off, we can look elsewhere."

•••••

"You little ripper!" Louise heard her husband excitedly declare as she unlocked the apartment door. "You're timing's perfect love. How was work?"

"My brain's still doing somersaults but it was a productive day. What am I just in time for?" she asked.

Ross looked at his wife and with a beaming smile and raised eyebrows announced, "I just got off the phone to the agent and guess what? We got the house!"

Louise was stumped. "Oh, my gosh! Really? How did you..."

Immediately interrupting her, Ross explained, "I called the agent about half an hour ago and offered $15,000 less than the listed price. We strongly doubted that the sellers would accept it but he just called me back and said he'll have the contracts drawn up first thing in the morning. We need to put down a 10% deposit and settlement is sixty days from tomorrow."

"Wow! That's fantastic news darling. I'm so excited!" Louise finally placed her handbag and keys on the table then threw her arms around him. At that moment the phone rang again.

"Ross Green," he answered.

"Sorry to bother you again Ross," the agent apologised. "I neglected to ask if there are any special provisions you'd like to include in the contract?"

"Ah, yes please Kevin, we'd like to see a building report and have a pest inspection carried out, plus all of the usual searches. Oh…and could you include a 'pending finance' clause?"

"Of course, no problem at all. Who's your solicitor?" Kevin enquired.

Explaining that they were new in town Ross told the agent that he and Louise would arrange legal representation and it was agreed that they'd see Kevin in his office at 3:30pm the following afternoon to sign the contract.

"Terrific, I'll see you then," the agent confirmed before ending the call.

Hanging up the receiver, the Greens hugged and danced around the room like animated children. They couldn't contain their joy.

"With the insurance money we've invested, together with our savings, at this price we won't require much finance for the purchase. We'll only need it for renovations," Ross stated. "And if push came to shove, we could sell our land and your business."

The couple suddenly had so much on their plate, they decided to call their respective bosses, advise them of the situation and request the following day off. Given the circumstances, both bosses were happy to afford them the courtesy.

At 10am the Greens entered the ANZ bank in Manly and applied for a loan. They were informed that the bank would inspect the property by the end of the week. Louise knew there was a law firm in her office building so upon leaving the bank they headed straight over and found a solicitor who was willing to act for them.

By this time their stomachs were seriously grumbling. Just at the end of the street 'Manly Ocean Foods' were known for serving up some of the best fish and chips in Sydney. The couple sat and indulged in a huge basket of crumbed John Dory fillets with chunky beer battered chips and a side of calamari rings.

A very late lunch now devoured they finally drove to Kevin's office and by 3:45pm the contract was signed. Everything seemed to be falling quickly into place. All searches and the pest inspection would be finalised within ten days so then it was just a matter of waiting for settlement date.

To celebrate early that evening, Ross and Louise enjoyed a chilled bottle of wine out on their balcony. No need to think about dinner tonight, both agreed they were still full from lunch. The pink-tinged sky reflecting the sunset in the west, was mirrored on the stillness of the ocean. An easy swell ran the length of the beach and in-between buildings the couple caught glimpses of the white surf breaking near the shore.

With almost eleven months remaining on the apartment lease, the Greens discussed their options and decided to proceed with the major renovation works. They were more than capable of doing a vast amount of it themselves; replacing the roof with aluminium sheeting, extending the deck and railings out the back, stripping existing paint and repainting, even removing most of the walls to open up the living area. Admittedly one of these walls was load-bearing so Ross deemed it would be necessary to get a builder in at that point to construct the supports.

"We've got this Lou," he assured her. "After working in the building industry with carpenters and plenty of other tradesmen, I've gleaned a lot of knowledge over the years. And I'm sure not afraid of a hard day's labour. We should get the wiring replaced, I wouldn't want to risk another fire and some of the plumbing should probably be checked out too."

"I'll drink to that," Louise chortled, raising her glass high above her head. "We'll get the final plans drawn up by a draftsman and submit them to council before we do any structural work but there's plenty to go on with in the interim."

Ross smiled and said, "That's for sure. A long list of things to do. And once we know the final dimensions, you can design the kitchen and hunt around for the materials you'd like to use. All those sorts of things we can do on the weekends."

Taking a final sip of wine from her glass, Louise added, "In that case, we'd better make the most of the weekends we have up until then. I'd love to see Taronga Zoo Ross, can we maybe do that on Sunday?"

"Yes, or course my sweet...but we can also monkey around now," he winked.

CHAPTER FOURTEEN

Seated at a cosy table for two in Dee Why's finest restaurant, Ross and Louise gently clinked their champagne flutes together. "Here's to our third wedding anniversary my love," Ross smiled at his wife.

Louise knew they shouldn't have been splurging on such a dinner but she wasn't going to begrudge her husband the opportunity to spoil her. Besides, as far as the Greens were concerned, it was worth every penny. Succulent garlic king prawns, oysters Kilpatrick and lobster mornay with stuffed rigatoni were the most divine dishes they'd ever consumed. Topped off with a crème brulée to die for, the culinary brilliance sent their tastebuds into sensory overload.

Within five minutes of the couple arriving back at their apartment, Louise rushed to answer the phone. *'Bit late for a call at this hour,'* she speculated.

"Lou, we have a beautiful baby girl!" Jillian announced with delight. "She's tiny, adorable and totally healthy. We couldn't be happier."

"Oh Jill, that's absolutely wonderful news. When was she born?"

"At 6:05am this morning. She weighs six pound, eleven ounces… and she already has black curly hair just like her Daddy. We named her Anthea Jane. I can't wait to send you a photo Lou."

"Oh, please do Jill, I can't wait to see her." Louise's heart was pumping with excitement.

"Sorry Lou, I have to go…feeding time. I'll call you next week and we can have a long chat."

Hanging up the receiver, Louise beamed a broad smile at Ross. "The baby arrived a week early and she's doing well. They've named her Anthea Jane."

"That's unusual," Ross commented. "I like it."

While Louise removed her make-up, she was elated and couldn't stop smiling at herself in the mirror. *'This evening was already exceptional...but now it's absolutely perfect!'*

• • • • •

Social life for the Greens continued to centre around Friday evenings at the Surf Club with Louise's work colleagues and attending the odd movie with Peter and Martha. They had little time for anything else.

Early in May, the Deans discovered that Martha was pregnant. They'd been hoping for a family over the course of the last few years and now, four months into her pregnancy, Martha was feeling fit and healthy.

"Peter and I are so thrilled," she told Louise. "I suffered a miscarriage early last year and as devastating as it was, we decided to keep trying. With the first baby, my scan at eight weeks revealed a very fragile heartbeat but this little one has the 'heart of a lion' our gynaecologist tells us."

Talking with Martha about the upcoming birth made Louise a little clucky. As did finding out that Jean and Don were also expecting their first child by the end of November. A few months after the Greens arrived in New Guinea, the Evans' eloped to Brampton Island in the Whitsundays. The couples regularly kept in touch and hoped to meet up again very soon.

Settlement date finally arrived for Ross and Louise's new house by mid-May and they couldn't wait to get started on it. Entering the front door, they studied what some may consider a daunting task ahead. Not for the Greens. They were enthusiastic and extremely positive about the project.

"Let's start by removing this tongue and groove panelling from the hallway," Louise suggested. "I can pull out the nails and sand them back to bare timber."

"Yep, sounds like a good plan," Ross agreed. "My first priority should be the roof. I can see where water has been slowly seeping into the living room ceiling, so rather than patch it, I think we should replace the whole roof."

Straight up the ladder with tape measure in hand, Ross surveyed the overall roof size then referred to their rough plans, adding what would be required to cover the deck.

The remainder of the day was spent meticulously calculating, double-checking and noting measurements for all proposed renovation areas in order to complete their sketches. The couple knew it was early days but they were having fun and could already visualise their finished home.

That evening while Ross drew up a scaled blueprint for the draftsman, he said, "With all of this work ahead of us, we really need a second vehicle, Lou. Just a cheap utility to carry ladders and all the heavy equipment."

"Sensible idea," Louise nodded, "and I might know where we can acquire one. Carl mentioned that his brother was selling an old Datsun ute and buying a new 4WD…but I don't know if he still has it. I'll ask him tomorrow."

By Saturday morning the Greens took possession of the yellow utility and because it had been advertised for months without any buyer interest, they managed to get the ute for a bargain basement price. Shortly thereafter Ross and Louise were loading the vehicle up with ladders, saw horses, sanders and numerous other tools they purchased from the hardware store.

After the renovation plans were drawn up and submitted to council, Ross and Louise were advised that final approval would likely take a further two weeks. The wait seemed interminable but meanwhile they began stripping much of the interior; ripping out the kitchen, removing wall panels in the hallway and all internal walls in the living area. They both loathed the wallpaper in the bedrooms so it had to go as well. A carpenter that Ross knew from work built the replacement supports and wherever possible they salvaged materials from the demolition for possible future use. All doors were substituted and dead locks applied to exterior entry points.

Out in the backyard, as no permit was required, the couple poured a concrete slab and erected a lockable aluminium shed in which to house their tools and building materials. After its completion that weekend, the Greens received council approval to commence work with no alterations necessary.

The Queen's Birthday long weekend allowed Ross and Louise

three full day days to work on the house. With the weather outlook being favourable, replacing the roof was a major priority. Peter offered to assist with the arduous task, so very early on Saturday morning they began removing sections of the old roof and replacing each one as they systematically progressed. Ross was relieved to see that the original trusses were in good condition. By lunch time on Monday, the entire job was finished; complete with guttering and downpipes.

Martha pulled up in the driveway with some freshly baked pies and sausage rolls for the famished labourers. Standing back to admire their work, Ross said, "The house looks fifty percent better already! It would have taken twice as long without your help Peter. Thank you so much my friend. We owe you."

Peter admitted to Ross, "It's certainly tough, physical work and I've gotta say...I ache all over. But what an accomplishment. It looks great." He chortled as he wrapped his arms around Martha. "Selling Insurance is a bloody breeze compared to this slog!"

• • • • •

Throughout the chilly winter months, Ross and Louise had the entire house re-wired with additional power points and switches installed. They scraped off wallpaper, freshly painted and re-painted white walls and ceilings whilst preserving the original intricate cornices and light surrounds of the old home. All windows were replaced and those at the front of the residence were enlarged to take in glimpses of the water view. New windows, frames and the addition of a large timber entrance door really modernised the street appeal of the home.

Louise gazed down the hallway and said to Ross, "It's lovely and wide now. I'd really like to make an art gallery of that wall eventually."

"You're the decorator, Lou. You do whatever you fancy. I certainly like the sound of it."

Plumbing fixtures were the next thing to be addressed. An ensuite and walk-in robe had to be added to the master bedroom, utilising space from the original fourth bedroom. The family bathroom needed to be totally refurbished and a new outdoor spa built into the extended deck. Keeping re-sale in mind during the renovation process, the Greens chose to maintain a neutral colour scheme throughout.

With so much expenditure to account for, Louise purchased a home computer in order to track their outgoings. One evening after discussing the building costs with her husband, she openly voiced her concerns.

"This is turning into a more costly project than we'd initially calculated but don't get me wrong…I know that if we hadn't done much of the work ourselves, that outlay would be far greater." She looked at him seriously and added, "Perhaps we should look at selling our land in Perth. Apparently, the property market over there is in a good place, thanks to the booming mining industry in the west."

Ross was aware that this scenario would eventually arise, so he was more than prepared to consider it. "Well, let's have a look on the internet and see what kind of prices they're asking," he remarked.

Honing into a Scarborough real estate website, the Greens were surprised to see that much had changed since they left for Lae a few years back. There were a number of homes for sale, mostly renovation properties, but only two vacant blocks of land available. Ross immediately decided to call Ken Wilson and find out a bit more.

"Hi mate, it's Ross. How are you going?"

"I'm great Ross. It's good to hear from you," Ken replied. "I'll get Janet to pick up the other phone so we can both talk to you."

"Hey Janet. Louise is just picking up the other phone in our bedroom now," Ross asserted. "So, Ken, we're just ringing to pick your brains a bit. We're considering selling the block of land. Our renovations are still a few months off completion yet but we're nearing the pointy end and that's when we're going to need more money. We don't want to increase our borrowing if we don't have to."

They discussed the situation at length and it turned out that the Wilsons were tossing up whether to sell or extend due to Janet being pregnant.

Ross hesitated for a moment. "Congratulations! That's terrific…"

"Oh my gosh! I'm so happy for you both," Louise quickly interrupted.

"We only had the pregnancy confirmed yesterday," admitted Janet.

Ken cleared his throat and said, "Back to your question Ross. Frankly, it's a seller's market at present, so I reckon it's a perfect time to offload it. That's my personal opinion but obviously the ball's in your court, mate. Let me know what you decide. I'll say hooray and let Janet and Louise chat."

"Yeah, thanks mate, greatly appreciated," Ross replied before hanging up the receiver.

"Are you still there Lou?" Janet queried.

"I sure am!" Louise smiled. "Wonderful news my friend."

"Yes, we're pretty stoked about it," Janet confessed. "Listen Lou, seeing we're already on the phone, I want to pass a business proposal by you. With your approval of course, I'd like to train up one of our graduate students. Her name's Katherine Bishop and she topped her class. Other than being a lovely young woman, she's extremely motivated and conscientious, engaged to an accountant over here. I'd still be available to oversee everything and ultimately, I'd like to buy the business, as you know…but right now we're so unsure with the baby and everything."

"That's totally understandable Janet. I'll certainly give it some serious thought. I know you're a good judge of character and if you think Katherine would be right for such a position, I could run with that provided you were able to preside over operations. Naturally I'd pay you a retainer for doing that. I don't want or need to sell the business at this point, so that sounds like a potential option. I'll get back to you in a day or two."

Both women hung up and Louise returned to the kitchen where her husband was making coffee. She sat down and explained, "The business provides us with additional income so I don't think it would be wise to sell it right now. Janet will probably work full-time for at least another few months so that gives us time to think it through. That being said…by then Katherine could choose a different direction and we could lose her altogether. There's a lot to think about there. Anyway, are we going to put the block on the market? It sounds feasible to me Ross."

He wholeheartedly agreed and resolved to phone the agent after work the following day. He wanted to discuss price range and enquire about the likelihood of it selling quickly.

Next afternoon, having spoken with the agent, Ross phoned Louise at work. "He knows the property and recalled the fire," he told her. "As far as sale price is concerned, the small loan we just took out would literally be covered if the asking price is realised. So…what do you think? Are you happy to list?"

"Yep, let's do it," Louise avidly encouraged.

By that evening the Perth property was up for sale and Louise phoned Janet to confirm that her suggestion to train a new manager was a very practical choice. They discussed remuneration for Katherine and a retainer for Janet. All that was left to do now was to ask Katherine if she wanted the position.

• • • • •

Gusty southerly winds swept through Sydney like a tornado and this August they were particularly severe. Numerous fallen trees and power lines caused property destruction throughout every shire. Fortunately, the Greens apartment and their house remained unscathed.

A tiler was currently laying white tiles in the living, kitchen, hallway and wet areas of the home. The carpet chosen for the bedrooms was a neutral cream colour with a small brown fleck through it. As soon as the tiler was finished, the carpet layer was due to commence.

In the warmth of their heated apartment, Louise set about designing her new kitchen. "I want lots of drawers and bench space," she informed Ross. "I'd also like to have an insinkerator and an appliance cupboard facing the benchtop, so I can just pull out the appliances as I want to use them. We need a decent-sized workable pantry, plenty of space for a large fridge/freezer, a range hood over four hotplates and a wall oven. I'm happy with stainless steel or white appliances."

Ross cracked open a beer and remarked, "As I said Lou, that's entirely your department. It all sounds good to me but you're the chef, so I trust your prudence."

Within a couple of nights, the kitchen design plan was complete and Louise delivered her drawings to a draftsman. He drew it all up to scale, making further suggestions along the way. Some Louise agreed with, others she didn't...but in the end, the Greens were extremely pleased with the technical drawings for their new kitchen.

Having already decided on the materials to be used, the couple took the draftsman's plans to two different cabinetmakers for quoting. Both companies returned similar quotes so the couple opted for the tradesmen who could commence work the earliest.

The following week, just as Sydney's gusty winds abated, Louise took her first business trip to the Gold Coast. The company had opened a new outlet at Nerang which required her training skills.

Met at Coolangatta Airport by the branch's new Manager, she was then escorted to a hotel at Broadbeach. It was in very close proximity to the new industrial area where the branch was located. Louise was astonished by the number of cranes along the skyline. She hardly recognised the place. It had really forged ahead in leaps and bounds within a few short years.

Recalling meeting her husband here and their happy days spent with Jean and Don immediately sprung to mind. She so wished to catch up with them but alas, this wasn't a holiday. When she last spoke with the Evans' they'd just purchased a new house in an estate on the outskirts of Brisbane and were busy fencing the pool they'd installed. Jean was now entering the final trimester of her pregnancy.

Before drifting off to sleep alone in her hotel room that night, Louise found herself reminiscing over the amazing, carefree year that she and Jean spent in Surfers Paradise. They were cherished, happy memories. Once again, a stirring maternal feeling engrossed her. "Maybe next year our turn will come," she said aloud.

Over the course of the following week, the crew with whom Louise worked were eager to learn which made her job extremely rewarding. She loved teaching and there was no doubt that she was very good at it.

CHAPTER FIFTEEN

Spring marks the birth of new life and for Peter and Martha, that analogy couldn't be more apt. Their daughter Skye entered the world late in September, her proud parents entirely besotted with their tiny bundle of joy.

Now only three months out from Christmas, the Greens wanted to take full advantage of the temperate weather and knuckle-down with the last of their renovations. They ordered a six-person spa from the local pool shop and this particular brand was manufactured in America, so shipping would take around five weeks. In the meantime, Ross constructed the brick hearth for the fireplace then started the massive task of sanding back paint on the exterior weatherboards. Fortunately, from the experience he gained working with Neville in Rabaul, Ross knew all the shortcuts.

Arriving home from work late one afternoon, the real estate agent from Perth phoned to say that he had a buyer for their block. A cash buyer no less, who apparently didn't even quibble over the advertised price. Contracts would be exchanged and the deal finalised within two weeks.

"Time to celebrate, Lou." Ross clapped his hands and rose from the dining table. "Want a gin and tonic?"

"I'd love one darling. Thanks," Feeling excited and relieved, Louise flopped onto the lounge. "The pressure's really off now. We can entirely finish the house…double garage, landscaping, furnishings, the lot."

In the kitchen Ross poured Louise's drink then proceeded to fix a rum on the rocks for himself. She hoped that he was only planning to have one, but sadly, that wasn't the case. Four stiff rums later and he was fast asleep in his chair.

Louise just left him, turned out the lights then went to bed. *'I hope he wakes up with a hangover in the morning'*, she admitted. *'And where did he hide that rum? It wasn't in the liquor cupboard. Obviously, there's a secret stash I don't know about.'*

• • • • •

By the end of December, the Green's house was really taking shape. They'd both booked annual leave between Christmas and New Year which allowed them nine solid days to complete some projects and begin new ones.

Meanwhile in Queensland, Jean and Don were celebrating the festive season with their one-month-old son, Gareth Ross Evans. His caesarean delivery wasn't exactly part of the couple's birth plan but after a few complications, it became a necessary procedure. Their baby boy was extremely healthy, weighing in at a whopping eight pound, nine ounces.

Ross finished the exterior painting in high-white to contrast with the black corrugated iron roof and the spa was installed on the deck. Whilst he stained the timber doors adjacent to the deck area, Louise ordered all of their major kitchen appliances including top-quality chrome tapware.

The kitchen was finally installed and fitted-out within the first week of February, the slab for the double garage had been poured and all of its construction materials delivered. Ross intended to slowly work on the concrete block structure once they moved in. With so many other small tasks yet to complete, the garage and the driveway certainly weren't a priority.

The lease on their apartment was due to expire in four weeks, so finishing all the major work on the house was perfectly timed. The Greens arranged final electrical, plumbing and building inspections then Peter insured the home and its contents before the couple took up residence.

With all inspections approved Ross and Louise couldn't wait to move in. They began packing up the apartment and had already decided to sell the majority of their second-hand furniture.

Each time they carted a load of belongings from the apartment to the house, it dawned on the couple that although they'd planned their home for re-sale, they may never want to leave the haven they were creating together. Only time would tell.

Louise organised connection of the telephone and emailed friends and associates to advise them of their new number, along with the house address. She also applied for a mail redirection at the post office.

On Saturday morning after the removalists collected the Green's unwanted second-hand furniture, Ross went for a surf while Louise thoroughly cleaned the empty apartment. When he returned the couple gathered up the remainder of their possessions and locked the door behind them for the last time.

Returning the keys to the estate agent's office, the Greens then went shopping for new furniture. With four major retailers to choose from, Ross and Louise had every intention of browsing through each one of them. The variety of lounge room, bedroom and living room furniture to choose from was enormous.

Like children at the zoo, the couple excitedly navigated their way through each section of every store. By close of business, they were ready to drop but managed to purchase almost every piece they wanted. The list was extensive and all items were currently in stock. Louise was taking the day off on Monday so the Green's scheduled all deliveries for that morning.

For the living room they chose a white leather lounge suite consisting of a two-seater and a three-seater with matching recliner chairs. The beautiful nine-piece dining setting comprised a table with a smoke-glassed top, supported by two white slate pillars. Upholstered leather on the eight dining chairs perfectly complemented the lounge and tied the whole living area together.

A cream two-pack bedhead with attached side tables was the perfect fit for their master bedroom. Together with a comfortably sprung queen-sized mattress and base their suite was simple, practical and modern.

They picked a superbly hand-crafted timber table with plenty of bench seating for the deck, along with two comfortable chairs to place at either end of the large space. For the bench cushions Louise chose a tropical design of ferns, palms and flowers in vibrant rainforest colours.

Heading home to spend the first night in their new house, the couple quickly stopped to grab a takeaway pizza. Despite being exhausted from all their decision making they couldn't wait to crack open a cold bottle of bubbly to celebrate the occasion. After all, they'd been looking forward to this night for almost a year now.

Sitting on their old stools at the kitchen bench, Ross proposed a toast to their new abode. Louise couldn't wipe the smile from her face as they hugged each other tightly. While peering out onto the deck Ross placed his hand on Louise's knee and said, "We should splurge on a big barbecue, Lou. Christen it before the weather gets cool again, I reckon. There's plenty of room to play with."

"Sure is, but in the morning, I need to tally up what we've spent today before we buy anything else. Our poor credit card must be just about maxed out!"

Growing weary within the hour, an early night was certainly called for. Louise was glad she'd already made up the twin beds they brought over from the apartment on Thursday afternoon. Too tired to bother showering tonight, the Greens crashed into bed.

Waking to the sun's rays beaming into the bedroom on Sunday morning, blatantly prompted Louise to consider what type of window coverings she wanted. Ross had already been outside for hours mulling over plans for the driveway and tossing up some ideas for the front yard.

Over a cup of coffee Ross and Louise did some quick calculations on their spending spree the day before. Surprisingly the balance on their card was far more than they'd initially estimated which allowed plenty of room to purchase Ross's much wanted barbecue. With nothing in the house for breakfast, the couple showered, jumped in the ute and drove back into town.

At a small café next to the Barbecue and Fireplace Centre, the Greens enjoyed a chicken and avocado toastie before entering the store. They were chuffed to discover all 'end of summer' stock was discounted by a minimum of twenty percent. Inundated by choice, Ross and Louise finally settled on a stainless steel, dome-topped Weber complete with a side burner, cupboards and a rotisserie underneath. The barbecue was too cumbersome to load into their utility so they arranged for delivery.

By the time Ross arrived home on Monday afternoon, all the new furniture was in place. The smell of fresh leather intermingled with a lamb roast, wafted down the hallway and met his nostrils as soon as he opened the front door.

Poking his head into each room while making his way to the kitchen, he declared to Louise, "Everything looks fabulous darling. You've certainly been a busy bee!"

"I certainly have," she smiled back at him. "I'm so happy with it all. How about you take a shower while I put these veggies in, then I'll meet you on the deck for a beer. I've set the table outside."

"Good plan," Ross replied looking himself up and down. "The chippies were lathing some exposed beams today, so I'm covered in bloody sawdust."

The evening was drawing in when Louise served up dinner. Roasts were always a favourite for the Greens and lamb with mint sauce, gravy and baked vegetables, undeniably topped the list. They quietly conversed in-between mouthfuls, bewitched by the pinky-orange glow of the evening sky through the trees of the national park.

"Isn't that a lovely sound, Ross?" Louise commented as twirping birds settled into their trees for the night.

"Yes, my sweet…and the bird-song is just an added bonus to a wonderful first dinner in our new home. Thanks Lou."

"Oh, dinner isn't over yet," Louise smiled as she gathered up the plates. "I made you a pavlova topped with mango, strawberries and passionfruit."

"Be still my pounding heart," Ross dramatically gestured. "If you keep spoiling me like this, I'll be forced to have my way with you."

Later that night, the couple spooned in their new bed then hands began to wander. Rolling over to face one another, their eyes filled with rapture before instinctively making love. This was an infrequent act for the Greens.

• • • • •

"A business woman, a great cook…and a seamstress. There's no end to your talents Lou," her husband remarked upon sighting the lounge cushions.

Louise had purchased a second-hand sewing machine and chose a bright, tropically-inspired calico fabric that she'd so admired in New Guinea homes and restaurants. Along with the white louvre shutters that were installed in the kitchen and bedrooms, their home now oozed sophistication.

Content with the interior decorating up to this point, Louise had more to achieve over the coming months but for now it was time to host a house-warming dinner party. Autumn was in full swing and again winter would soon be chomping at its heels. Wishing to utilise their outdoor deck space and barbecue for the occasion, a mid-April date, some two weeks away would be fitting.

After designing invitations on her computer, Louise distributed them to their Friday evening group of friends. Jean and Don would be in New Zealand visiting her family at that time and though Louise didn't anticipate Jillian and Claude would be able to come down from Queensland, she sent them an invitation regardless.

Two days later, much to Louise's surprise, Jillian phoned to say, "We'll be there. Claude's family have been wanting to see us for quite some time, so we can kill two birds with the one stone. We'll fly down on the Thursday afternoon…that gives us plenty of time to commute from the Sunshine Coast to Brisbane Airport that morning."

As Claude's parents lived on the south side of Sydney and owned three cars, Jillian planned for her in-laws to mind the baby on Friday night while they drove up to the Green's house-warming dinner. The women agreed that Jillian and her husband would stay overnight.

"On the Saturday around 2pm, Claude's mother wants to have a little party for Anthea's first birthday. Do you think you'd be able to come?" Jillian asked.

"Absolutely!" Louise answered excitedly. "We wouldn't miss that for the world Jill. Besides, Aunty Louise is really yearning for her first cuddle."

Jillian laughed and before they ended their call, she offered to arrive at the Green's house around 5pm to lend Louise a hand with preparations.

Meanwhile, the others were delighted to receive their invitations and everyone advised that they'd be attending. Peter and Martha were the only guests who'd ever seen the home before or during its renovation process.

Planning the menu, Louise sorted through her recipe books. As she'd be working that Friday, time was of the essence. A big antipasto platter before dinner was quick and easy to prepare. Main course: a marinated, butterflied leg of lamb on the barbecue accompanied by a selection of three salads and potatoes in their jackets with sour cream. Given the time restraints, a New York-style baked cheesecake could be made the night before and garnished with fresh, seasonal berries on the night.

The week of the party Louise spent a couple of evenings in preparation and on Friday afternoon, managed to slip away from work an hour early. Ross had already picked up the beer, wine and a small bunch of colourful gerberas on his way home.

Louise rushed to arrange the tablecloth, place settings, bright fabric serviettes and cutlery on the outside table then quickly polished the crystal glasses, arranged the flowers in a small bowl and placed the centrepiece on the table.

Standing back admiring her handiwork, Ross appeared on the deck. "Looks great, Lou. Drinks are done. I'll go and have a shower…unless you want one first?"

"No, I have to mop the kitchen floor. You go, but when you come out, please make sure it's dry before you walk on it."

At 5:10pm, Jillian and Claude arrived. The Greens went out to meet them and help with their overnight bag. Louise had only met Claude once before and their husbands were meeting for the first time. Introductions were hardly called for but as Ross and Claude shook hands, the excited women chortled and threw their arms around one another.

They all entered the house and Louise showed her guests to their bedroom. Jillian was enchanted with the décor. "It's not finished yet," Louise admitted. "I just need some artwork on the wall and eventually I'll sew some cushion covers for the throw pillows on the bed."

Proudly revealing the balance of the interior to their friends,

Ross and Claude then prattled whilst the women prepared salads. They were so happy to be in the kitchen together again. Within the hour their other four car-pooling guests arrived and introductions took place out on the deck.

"What a major difference," Peter exclaimed. "You two should quit your jobs and get into the renovating and decorating business. It's truly remarkable." Turning to Ross he asked, "No roof leaks in the storm last Tuesday mate?"

"No, of course not. We did a great job," he boasted.

The mood at the table was set early. Jillian, Martha and Carl's wife, Donna, talked about babies while Louise handed the platter around. The men appeared to be discussing construction and engineering. Joining the women, she felt her stirring desire for children arise once more and resolved to discuss the idea of starting a family with her husband.

All in all, the barbecue was a huge success and the simplicity of the menu made it easy for Louise to mingle and thoroughly enjoy her guests. Donna insisted on making coffee for everyone in order to give Louise a deserved rest and served it with delicious after-dinner mints she brought from home.

By 11pm guests were growing weary. After the Greens waved them off out the front, they returned to find Jillian clearing the table outside whilst Claude packed the dishwasher.

"Care for a nightcap?" Ross asked Claude.

"Thanks for the offer, Ross…but I'll pass. With the little one's party tomorrow, Daddy needs to be on his A-game," he laughed.

"Is there anything you need before bed, Jill?" Louise enquired.

"No thanks, Lou, we're good. See you in the morning."

Over a leisurely breakfast on the deck next morning, the two couples caught up on their respective news and Jillian sighed, "It's so nice to have a quiet, uninterrupted breakfast again. I have to say, this baby business is pretty exhausting Lou. We wouldn't change it for anything but once in a blue moon, it's great to have a night off."

Claude laughed, reached out and held his wife's hand. "Yeah, yeah…but you miss her already. I know I do…that's why we've hardly stopped talking about her."

The couple lovingly gazed at one another across the table and

Jillian bashfully remarked, "You're right. One night away from our baby girl is more than enough for me too. We'd best get a wriggle on."

Before Jillian and Claude left, the Greens agreed to meet them in Taren Point at their in-laws house a few hours later. Louise quickly tidied up the kitchen and the deck while Ross scrubbed the barbecue then they showered and headed off.

Just over the Captain Cook Bridge, in a prime waterfront location overlooking the Georges River, Claude's childhood home was nothing short of magnificent. A small pink and white striped marquee with purple and silver balloons sat poised in the centre of the double-storey mansion's sprawling manicured lawn.

With champagne in hand, adult guests enjoyed playing party games with the children in-between chatting and nibbling on hors d'oeuvres. Anthea was by far the youngest so she kept herself amused with some colourful satin ribbons and giggled as she watched the other children having fun.

Louise adored her and after gently swaying the baby on her hip for about ten minutes, she found it extremely difficult to let her go. To feel Anthea's tiny fingers on her face and gaze into her huge brown eyes, melted Louise's heart. She was absolutely beautiful.

Claude's mother had baked and flawlessly decorated a rainbow unicorn cake which was enjoyed by all. Everyone sang 'Happy Birthday' to little Anthea as she fell asleep in her grandfather's arms.

CHAPTER SIXTEEN

"With all our friends making babies, I'm feeling a bit clucky," Louise confessed. "How would you feel if I refrained from taking the pill and we started trying for a family of our own Ross?"

He promptly swung around with an unsettled look on his face. "No way! I'm never having kids! With the hereditary sight problems in my family, why would I bring a child into the world and run the risk of them being born with the same affliction."

Returning to face the television, he assertively shook his head and blurted, "I've been through hell because of this bloody eye and you know my sister's totally blind. What are you thinking? Forget it, Lou. It's never gonna happen!"

Louise was rendered speechless while she grappled to comprehend the words her husband spluttered. This revelation was monumental and the tone in which it was delivered seriously distressed her. Up until now, Louise had never even contemplated her life without children. She had no idea her husband felt this way and immediately wished they'd discussed it years ago.

Silence prevailed and Louise was compelled to leave the room. Choking back tears she walked out onto the deck and sat in total darkness to reflect on her emotions. Feelings of sadness, disappointment, confusion and utter emptiness deeply enveloped her senses.

Ross went straight to the liquor cupboard, poured himself a full tumbler glass of rum on the rocks and remained inside staring blankly at the TV set. He was angry that Louise even wanted to bring children into their lives. *'She knows I don't like kids much, surely? And even if sight issues weren't a problem, I don't want bloody rug rats! Stand your ground mate. It's your life too,'* he reassured himself.

Eventually, Louise came inside and poured herself a glass of water at the sink. As she began drinking it, Ross came over to replenish his rum. There was ample room between herself and the icebox but Ross harshly corked Louise's arm as he passed her.

With no forthcoming apology, she turned and looked at him alarmingly. Ice now in his glass, Ross spun around and viciously slammed his palm into Louise's sternum, sending her stumbling across the kitchen.

"Move over woman! Shit, not hard," he bellowed like a man possessed.

Louise was furious. "Don't you dare push me around and speak to me like that, Ross Green." Her bottom lip quivered as she attempted to regain her composure.

In retaliation he slurred, "Well…get out of me bloody way why don't ya!"

Making a B-line for the bedroom, Louise closed the door behind her and fully clothed, slipped into bed. A fierce battle between her head and heart ensued. Anger and disillusionment saw her question her own happiness and their entire marriage. But then again, maybe she was to blame. Raising the issue of having children clearly induced this evil rum session. If she'd kept her mouth shout, the incident would never have occurred.

As little respect as she had for her husband at this moment, Louise had to admit that she understood his genetic concerns. It was a valid issue. She lay wide awake, listening out for Ross's every move and ruminating over the possibility of adopting a child. Badly wanting to be a mother, that was certainly an option worth discussing. Maybe in another week or so she'd pluck up the courage to broach the subject again.

Finally hearing Ross stagger down the hallway, enter the guest bedroom and close the door, Louise changed into her night gown and went back to bed. Snuggling into her husband's pillow she silently wept.

Sunday morning, Ross was up early as usual. While Louise cooked breakfast she could hear him working on the garage. "Your eggs are ready," she called from the deck.

He slowly made his way up the stairs and sat down at the outside table. "Looks great Lou, I'm absolutely famished. Heard we could be in for some showers later this afternoon so I started at first light. Managed to finish that back wall so we can put the roof trusses up next weekend. Hope I didn't wake you? I tried to be as quiet as I could."

While her husband tucked into his poached eggs on toast, Louise replied, "No, I didn't even know you were out here." She lied to keep the peace. Truth was, Louise had been awake for hours.

Over breakfast Ross conveyed his landscaping ideas and asked for his wife's opinion on her preferred layout. His nonchalant demeanour was annoying her. It was as though nothing had transpired the night before.

"Thought I'd set out the driveway this afternoon. Have you got time to give me a hand?" he asked.

With eyes down, Louise just nodded her agreement whilst chewing on a piece of bacon. Her mind boggled. *'How could he not recall pushing me? We didn't share a bed last night. Surely that would indicate something went awry. And no mention of the baby subject either. He knew I was really upset about that.'* She was at a loss.

•••••

Louise found herself teetering on the edge over the course of the next few weeks. Constantly being wary of every word she uttered in Ross's presence. By the onset of winter her caution eased but their dynamics had certainly shifted. For Louise, life just felt hollow.

In front of their open fireplace the Greens cuddled up on the lounge one evening after dinner. They were listening to Ross's favourite Marvin Gaye record and with only one lamp providing muted light, the ambience in the room was romantic.

"Ross darling, I understand your reason for not wanting to have children of our own…but would you be willing to consider adoption?"

Flickering flames reflected in his aggravated eyes. "Louise… seriously, let it be. I don't want kids either way, so in short that's a definitive 'no'. I knew you'd bring this up again. If you want to piss off and have kids with someone else, then do it. We can sell this place, split the difference and go our separate ways."

He returned his attention to the fire while Louise hesitantly remarked, "I'm not looking to end our marriage Ross, I'm just saying that some couples don't want a family initially, but down the track many of them change their minds."

"Yes, some do," he smugly replied, "but I'm telling you for the last time, I'm not one of them. I've never wanted children and I never will. This conversation's over. Period!"

•••••

The following week Louise was still consumed with the stark reality of remaining childless and the fear of becoming yet another domestic violence statistic. She needed more stimulation in her life and the prospect of establishing and immersing herself in a business like the one in Perth, really appealed to her.

Arriving home from work late one afternoon, Louise pulled up in their roofless garage and discovered Ross in the backyard, erecting a barrier between the house and the existing fence of the national park. *'What on earth is he doing?'* she speculated.

Once out of the car, Louise could hear strange squeaking sounds behind the door that connected the garage to the laundry. Cautiously turning the door handle and peeking inside, two lively puppies came scuttling across the tiles towards her.

Louise immediately gasped and fell in love. Both pups had shaggy coats, one was black, the other brown with small white patches. Their big black eyes and floppy ears were adorable. As she placed her handbag on top of the washing machine, the puppies ran around her feet frantically wagging their tails.

She bent down to pat them and they leapt up on her legs, competing for attention. Whist one tried to jump even higher the other piddled from all the excitement, as puppies tend to do. Louise picked them up and laughed. The pups' bodies were small in comparison to their big feet. Two little heartbeats raced as she held them close to her chest.

Scanning the laundry Louise could see that they'd officially moved in. There were some toys on the floor, a bag of dried dog food on the shelf and a doggy bed big enough for both pups in one corner.

As she walked out into the backyard carrying the pups, Ross immediately downed tools and smiled as Louise walked towards him.

"How do you like our new family, Lou?" he asked with a grin from ear to ear.

"I love them. They're just so cute. What are they? Where did you get them? Do they have names yet?"

Ross patted the head of each pup and said, "I thought we could decide on their names together…but I really like 'Magic' for the black one."

"Magic," Louise repeated. "Then I think this one should be 'Jester'."

It was agreed and Ross went on to tell his wife that the Newfoundland breed originated in Canada. They're large dogs, known for their loyalty and sweet temperament. He ordered them from a breeder not long after they were born and now at eight weeks old, the brother and sister were finally old enough to go to their new home. Two pups would keep one another company while he and Louise were at work.

Magic and Jester were getting restless and struggled to be released from Louise's arms. She placed them on the grass and they tumbled around together, tripping over their own feet. While Ross proceeded with the barrier fence, Louise rolled in the grass with the two energetic fuzz balls. They snuffled in her hair and tried to chew on her ears and fingers. She was having a blast with them, much to Ross's amusement.

As the sun began to set Louise was feeling far more like a grub than a human being. "It's high time for a shower," she said, brushing the grass from her clothing.

"You can leave them out here, Lou. I'll keep an eye on them while I finish this off. Not much to go now."

It was almost 7pm by the time Louise dished up dinner. Meanwhile Ross had completed the fence, showered and the exhausted pups were fast asleep in the laundry.

"Are they going to stay inside Ross," she asked.

"I've been thinking about that. If we want to sell this place, probably not. There's plenty of yard so I thought I'd build a kennel for them at the back of the garage. We've got loads of concrete blocks left over and I could use some of the timber we stowed in the back shed. Until the kennel's built, hopefully next weekend, they can stay in the laundry. We might have a few sleepless nights for a little while. They're bound to fret for their mother until they get used to being on their own. I also thought we could set up that old bathtub somewhere outside to wash them."

"That's a great idea," Louise encouraged. "I really don't want that happening in the laundry tub...or heaven forbid, in our new shower!"

Whilst eating, the couple read through some information supplied by the breeder. It detailed exactly what, and how much to feed the dogs at each growth stage, how to care for their coats, vaccination information and general tips for their wellbeing. Ross told Louise that he would feed them morning and night.

"We'll have to keep our shoes away from them and close all the internal doors. They'll make short work of anything they fancy to chew on," Louise commented.

Noticing a pile of mail on the hall table, she retrieved it and scanned through the six envelopes. There was a letter from Rabaul. The Kiap (Local Government Officer) wrote, 'I am saddened to advise you that Joseph Soia has been killed as the result of a traffic accident. He fell from a PMV and was run over by a vehicle travelling behind. The boy died on impact'.

Louise was instantly in tears as she handed the letter to her husband. She had advised Joseph's headmaster of their change of address and in turn, he must have communicated with the Kiap.

"Poor Maria...poor Joe," Louise whimpered. "He was a beautiful boy with so much potential. What a horrible tragedy."

Ross comforted his wife by holding her tightly. He was also dismayed by the news and though he'd never openly admit it, Ross was very fond of Joseph Soia.

● ● ● ● ● ●

With their new family established, the Greens were the happiest they'd been in quite a while. Louise raised the feasibility of starting a new business. Ross agreed that given the success of her previous venture, there was likely even more need for her services here in Sydney.

Spending the evening formulating an advertisement for the local Narrabeen publication, Louise noted that students would be required to bring along their own computers. The course would be completed within a school term, allowing them enough time to gain a good grounding in basic computer and internet operations. If there were only a couple of people who showed interest, she'd be able to use the bedroom they'd set up as an office. Any more than that would require a rented space properly fitted out for teaching.

Within a week, much to Louise's delight, eight students were keen to enrol. She contacted each course applicant and advised them that classes would commence mid-September. Whilst speaking with one woman, she informed Louise that another two friends were also keen to participate.

On the Monday morning, granting Carl ample notice, Louise handed in her resignation. He was disappointed to be losing her, as they'd worked so well together.

"Would you be willing to continue teaching new staff every now and then?" Carl queried. "We could just employ you on a consultancy basis."

"For the time being that would be great…but honestly Carl, if the business grows as quickly as I hope it will, I may not have the time."

"Of course, that's understandable. We'll play it by ear, shall we? How does that sound?"

"Perfect," Louise smiled. "Thanks Carl…and please continue to include us in your Friday night get-togethers. We'll be there whenever we can make it."

"Indeed, I was hoping you'd say that," he grinned.

• • • • •

Finding a good-sized space within a modern office building in the heart of Narrabeen, Louise signed a lease by the end of July for twelve months. The Greens decided to use some of the profits from the Perth business to fund the purchase of second-hand furniture and equipment that was required. This included desks, chairs, white boards and basic stationery items.

In August Louise took a three-day business trip to Brisbane to train some more staff for Carl. On the third afternoon, with work complete, she'd arranged to stay with Don, Jean and the baby that night. Jean waited in the office carpark to collect Louise and her luggage while Gareth slept soundly in his car seat.

Quietly opening the passenger door Louise whispered, "It's so good to see you, Jean. You look fantastic."

"Oh, stop flattering me Mrs Green, you'll make me blush," she giggled. Alighting from the car, Jean walked around to Louise and widely opened her arms, "Give me a hug. I've missed you so much."

The two friends warmly embraced, packed Louise's luggage in the boot and prepared to leave. Louise looked over her shoulder and saw Gareth stirring. "He's so big now," she commented. "In the photo you sent me a few months ago, I'm sure he was only half the size."

"Yep. He's growing like a weed," Jean laughed as they drove out of the carpark. "I think he'll definitely be as tall as his father."

"So…how's parenthood?" smiled Louise.

"Well, apart from still being a bit sleep deprived, we're both loving it. Don can't wait to get home from work and play with him, which gives me a break while I prepare dinner."

The women continued to chat about the baby, Louise's new business and caught up on gossip regarding friends from long ago. Driving about 30km south east of the city, they arrived at the Evans' house in Redland Bay.

Don was waiting outside as they pulled up in the driveway. Greeting Louise with a hug and kiss, he then retrieved her luggage from the boot, placed it down and reached into the back seat to unbuckle his son. Gareth had only just woken. The baby let out a shrieking giggle when he saw his father's smiling face.

After showing Louise through the house and garden, the two women began to prepare dinner. All the while they could hear splashing and foolery emanating from the bathroom where Don was bathing Gareth. Louise couldn't help but laugh at their antics.

Pouring chilled wine for herself and her friend, Jean turned to Louise and asked, "So now that you two are happily ensconced in your Narrabeen home, when are you going to start making babies, Lou?"

"Probably never," she reservedly replied. "Ross is scared about the hereditary eye deformities than run in his family. He doesn't want to pass them on…and he blatantly refuses to consider adoption. So, Magic and Jester are our babies."

Jean sat her glass down on the countertop, stepped forward and hugged Louise. She could clearly see the disappointment in her friend's eyes. "I'm so sorry, Lou. You'd be a great Mum. You have so much compassion and empathy…not to mention patience and understanding."

"Thanks, Jean. It is what it is, and I've come to terms with the decision. Besides, I honestly love those dogs," Louise added wistfully.

With Gareth fed, Louise sat down and gave him his bottle while Jean finished cooking. He guzzled it down quickly at first but midway through, started dozing off. They all went into the nursery to put him down in his cot.

Dinner underway, the adults discussed their lives in general and Jean mentioned the possibility of taking Gareth to New Zealand at Christmas time.

"We're still yet to decide but the family have been hounding us about seeing Gareth. We've made our minds up about something else though," she said, smiling at her husband. "Don and I would be extremely happy if you'd agree to be Gareth's godmother. Please say you will?"

Louise's face lit up. "Oh, I'd love that. A true honour! Thank you both so much for considering me worthy of the role."

The couple laughed at Louise's obvious enthusiasm and sincerity. "We probably won't have a christening or anything official like that," Jean admitted, "but knowing that you accept the responsibility is so comforting to us. It means a lot."

Over coffee and a Baileys Irish Cream they toasted to the good health of Louise's godson as she perused Gareth's 'Baby's First Year' photo album. Meanwhile, the Evans' enjoyed flicking through some of the most recent photos of the Green's house and their adorable fur babies.

• • • • •

The traffic was bedlam when Louise exited the secure long-term carpark at Mascot Airport. She was beginning to feel more confident driving through the inner city but having to contend with thousands of commuters meant keeping her wits about her at all times.

That was easier said than done, given her concern for Ross's welfare over the past three days. He hadn't made any attempt to call her at the hotel or at the Evans' house. Each night Louise tried to call him but the phone just rang out. She knew something wasn't right.

Magic and Jester could hardly contain themselves when Louise drove into the garage. They were madly yelping a 'welcome home' from the backyard. She headed straight out to pat them and stayed for a short while. The yard was scattered with faeces and blowflies.

Returning to the house she unpacked her luggage, removed some lamb loin chops from the freezer and went back outside to clean up the dogs' mess. She'd just completed this onerous task when Ross pulled up in the ute.

Meeting in the kitchen he gave Louise a brief, perfunctory hug and said, "Good to have you home again. I'm filthy. Need a shower." He then swiftly left the room.

She could smell stale rum on him. Not only did he look tired and dishevelled, Louise noticed a large bruise on his cheekbone. While he showered, she tidied up the living room and put some dirty clothes in the washing machine in an attempt to alleviate the stench of perspiration throughout the house.

"How was your trip?" Ross asked as he returned to the kitchen.

"Busy and successful," Louise replied. "I finally met little Gareth. He's as cute as a button. Don and Jean send their love and they asked me to be the baby's godmother. I felt very honoured… and naturally I accepted."

"That's nice, Lou. What's for dinner?"

"I'm defrosting some lamb chops so we'll have them with peas, cabbage and mashed potatoes."

"Sounds good. I'm going out to play with the dogs," Ross told her as he made his way out onto the deck. "Bet they were happy to see you home."

"They were…but they stink. They've been rolling around in excrement," Louise pointed out, rather annoyed. "Where have you been each night after work? I tried to phone you numerous times."

"Oh, out and about," he replied. "Had drinks a couple of nights with the boys from work. Pub meal afterwards. Didn't get home 'til late so I haven't had time to do much, other than feed the dogs."

"I gathered that," Louise softy remarked as her husband descended the stairs to the backyard.

Half an hour later, Ross tethered the dogs at their kennel and came inside. Dinner was only a few minutes shy of being ready. Silently he poured a wine for Louise and a rum and Coke for himself, retreated to the lounge and watched the news.

"I picked up a couple of cash jobs while you were away," he announced during their meal. "I'll have to do them at night, after work. They're under lights, so that won't matter. One's near the city and the other closer to home. I'll probably work on them a couple of evenings each week."

"Okay, that's good love," Louise returned. "I was thinking that I might need to run some night classes too. I've just had so many replies for the course that I can't fit all the students in during the day. Some have asked if I'll be running evening classes so they can attend after work. I'm also toying with the idea of establishing a recruitment facility to provide employment for the graduates but I'll certainly go with the evening classes first."

"Sounds like a plan," was Ross's disinterested comment.

'What happened while I was away?' Louise mused. *'It feels like I've come home to a stranger.'* She couldn't put her finger on it… but Ross was definitely being aloof for some reason.

As her husband entered the kitchen he asked, "Want another wine?"

Louise politely declined his offer but Ross didn't hesitate to pour himself another rum. This time around it was neat.

CHAPTER SEVENTEEN

Louise worked diligently on her Basic Computer and Internet Operations course as term three seemingly materialised in the blink of an eye. Not only were her daytime classes full, capped at twelve students, she was compelled to hold evening classes just to accommodate the overflow of applicants.

This meant long hours each week but it was hardly a chore for Louise. Besides, it kept her mind off Ross and their deteriorating home life. Marking exams at the end of each term would be the only pressure she'd have to endure, as far as the business was concerned.

An enthusiastic and diverse cohort included a few mature women who were looking to return to the workforce; a mother and daughter keen to start university degrees, another lady wanting to draft and self-publish a novel and a pregnant woman wishing to write and illustrate children's books as a stay-at-home Mum. The balance of students were men from all walks of life.

Evening classes ran from 7pm to 10pm and were scheduled to cover two terms. On the majority of nights Louise returned home from the office, Ross didn't dawdle in before 11pm. As the weeks progressed, he didn't discuss work at all and Louise would clam up about her own.

On weekends, Ross worked Saturday mornings while Louise grocery shopped and attended to housework. In the afternoons the couple would either go to the beach or take Magic and Jester to the local dog park for a walk. Sunday, it was back to landscaping as there was still much to complete.

Ross had already done the hard yards during the preceding months. He'd strategically placed large boulder rocks to form a retaining wall for the higher parts of the yard and concreted mowing strips around the lower garden beds. This is where the Greens intended to plant low maintenance succulents.

Driving to the nursery, Ross surprisingly asked his wife, "Could you teach me how to use the computer, Lou? You know…just the basics. And how to get on the internet?"

"I had no idea you were interested, but yes, I can certainly do that," Louise replied.

"Seems like a part of life now," he said, shrugging his shoulders. "This Google thing looks interesting. A guy at work trades the Australian stock market and sometimes during the night he follows the overseas markets as well. His shares are booming. I spend half the night awake anyway, so I thought I'd have a look and possibly use some of the money from my cash jobs to start trading."

Louise was pleased to hear her husband express initiative towards future technology and their financial security. "Okay then. Next weekend I'll teach you all the fundamentals."

It's true that Ross's insomnia was still haunting him, despite the long hours he continued to work. He would wake during the night from dreams and often nightmares about their house going up in flames and find it impossible to return to sleep. The couple deduced that after their house fire in Perth, the incident was indelibly etched in Ross's psyche.

• • • • •

By mid-December the Green's landscaping was finally complete and their garden design integrated harmoniously with its picturesque national park backdrop. Beautiful plantings of colourful native grevilleas and flowering shrubs showered over variegated undergrowth. The gardens received little care during the week but on weekends, Louise looked forward to getting out into the yard early to avoid the summer heat.

The dogs were trained to stay away from the garden beds and for the most part, they obeyed their master's orders. Ross took care of the lawns which they'd envisaged to be thick and lush, but their two big fur babies couldn't resist digging in the soft, fertile soil.

With some time off over the Christmas/New Year period, the Greens completed the driveway edging and replaced the original rusty letterbox with a modern, stained timber structure. Ross spent the majority of his days surfing and most nights, after a short sleep, he'd quietly get up and spend hours in the office browsing the internet. Louise had also set up a personal email address and password for him. The stock market was gaining his interest and he started dabbling in share trading.

Two weeks into the New Year, during the very early hours of Wednesday morning, Ross was sifting through his share portfolio in the office when the phone rang. It was Louise's sister and she sounded very distressed. He immediately woke his wife and Louise stumbled into the lounge room to take the call.

"Mum had a stroke, Lou," Julie declared. "It's not looking good for her at all…so I think you should come over as quickly as you can. Dad isn't coping too well either. I think he'd be really grateful for your support right now."

"Oh Jules! Yes, of course. Please let him know I'll be on the earliest possible flight."

After much negotiating with the airline and scrambling to pack, Louise managed to book a 9am departure to Auckland that morning. Ross dropped her off outside the terminal at Mascot and promised to keep in touch with his very anxious wife.

During the flight, numerous consequences of her mother's condition played out in Louise's mind. Flashbacks of early childhood days spent with her flicked over and over like a slideshow. As the plane touched down, she couldn't believe they'd already been airborne for 3 hours.

Wading through Immigration and Customs seemed to take forever. Finally sighting Julie in the crowd, Louise read the trepidation on her sister's face. They tightly hugged for a few seconds before hurriedly making their way to the car.

As Julie negotiated the traffic, she looked at Louise and said, "I've really missed you, Sis. I'm so glad you're here, we all are. When I told Dad you were arriving his eyes lit up like I haven't seen them in years. A friend's minding the kids at her house, so we'll go straight to the hospital. They put Mum in Intensive Care and her face and the right side of her body are frozen. She can't speak or respond to questions and she doesn't seem to recognise anyone."

"How's Dad dealing with it?" Louise asked.

Julie shook her head and replied, "Well obviously he's pretty dejected. He asked John to be straight with him regarding Mum's condition…and John told him the truth. Highly unlikely that she'll recover to any form of normality or worse still, the outcome will be fatal.

After arriving at the hospital, Louise's eyes began to fill with tears as she followed Julie into her mother's room. William rose unsteadily from a chair at the head of her mother's bed where she was peacefully sleeping. As Louise walked towards her father, he opened his arms to greet her. He'd aged markedly within the last six years.

"I'm so pleased you're here my darling," he remarked, embracing his daughter in his shaky arms. "I don't think Mum has long to go but she isn't in any pain…so we can be thankful for that."

William dropped his head as he and Julie slowly left the room, allowing Louise some time alone with her mother.

"I don't know if you can hear me, Mum. It's Louise. I'm holding your hand."

Surprisingly Elizabeth looked relaxed and contented. A brief fluttering of her eyelids indicated that she recognised her daughter's voice.

"We'll look after Dad if you need to slip away," Louise assured her. "Thank you for giving me such a wonderful life Mum. Our happy days in the garden together and our long walks along the beach will be in my memory forever."

Louise then sat quietly for a few more moments, staring at her mother's hand resting in her own. While gently caressing her wrinkly fingers, Louise added, "I love you, Mum. I'll be back to see you in the morning."

With a tender kiss on her mother's soft cheek, she exited the room. In the corridor, William's daughters hugged him amidst an outpouring of tears and apprehension for the days that lay ahead.

No sooner had the family arrived at Julie's house when the head nurse phoned. "Your mother has just peacefully passed away, Julie," she sympathetically declared. "John was by her side and he's on his way home as we speak. I'm so sorry."

Looking directly at her father, their glazed eyes met. There was no need for words. Julie joined William and Louise on the couch, placing one arm around her father's shoulders. He heavily sighed and sunk his head into his hands. Completely dazed, the family sat in total silence.

• • • • •

Her heart ached as Louise peered out of the plane's window. The cloud-filtered sky beckoned her with its trance-like kaleidoscope patterns. Losing her mother four days ago was still a hard reality to grasp, as was the fact that her husband hadn't contacted her since leaving Sydney.

'You selfish bastard!' Louise cursed him. *'Where in the hell are you? Why haven't you answered the phone for five nights straight?'* The more she thought about it, the angrier she became.

Because Ross had no idea when his wife was returning from New Zealand, she had to arrange public transport from Mascot Airport. Catching a bus to Narrabeen, Louise then booked a taxi to take her the rest of the way home.

It was mid-afternoon when she walked up the path. Magic and Jester went berserk in the backyard upon hearing Louise's voice. She immediately unlocked the door, entered the house and looked around.

There were empty takeaway containers on the kitchen bench, covered in ants, the floors were a mess and their bedroom looked like a dumping ground. Going outside to greet the stinky dogs she found the yard in complete disarray; faeces everywhere, a portion of her garden completely dug up and plants wilting from lack of water.

Shaking her head, she then retrieved a spade and a plastic bag from the garden shed. After collecting the excrement, she fed the ravenous dogs, gave the gardens a thorough soaking and hit the shower.

Ross didn't come home until the following afternoon. Louise had not long returned from a walk with Magic and Jester when his ute turned into the driveway. He unlocked the front door and was surprised to see his wife standing in the kitchen.

He looked guilty as he approached Louise. She turned her cheek to avoid his mouth before he kissed her. "I didn't know you were home yet," he remarked, as the rum on his breath wafted to Louise's nostrils. "How's your mother?"

"Dead, but thank you for your concern," she replied facetiously.

"We need to talk," were the only words Ross returned.

Louise was fuming as she intently watched her husband pour himself a rum and coke. In that moment, she actually loathed him. He took his drink over to one of the recliners and made himself comfortable.

"Okay, talk," Louise said, bracing herself on the lounge.

"I want a divorce," he haphazardly declared. "There's someone else. You don't know her but we met a few months ago and we want to live together."

"Why do you need someone else?" she asked, totally flabbergasted.

"Because she doesn't want kids either, so it's not complicated. You can go and find another guy who'll father your damned children." His eyes quickly returned to his glass.

"And what if I won't give you a divorce? What then?" Louise snidely remarked.

"Doesn't matter," Ross snapped back. "We'll sell this place, split the difference, then Kylie and I will just live together."

Louise was far too irate to cry. Thinking on her feet she spluttered, "Come on then. I'll help you pack and you can leave now. Take the dogs with you."

Within seconds Ross rose from his chair, walked over to the lounge and violently back-handed his wife across the face. Louise swayed as she stood up and tried to flee the room but Ross snatched at her arm, forcefully pulling her back to him.

His face was red, his eyes wild. Louise was terrified and desperately attempted to release herself from his grasp. Meanwhile, Ross jolted her arm up behind her back and she yelped in agony. They both heard her forearm snap.

Giving her one final, assertive shove, Louise lost her balance and stumbled head-first onto the tiled floor. There she lay, completely unconscious while her husband roared out of the driveway.

In the dark of night, her mind wandered back to the past; her petite mother's dark curls and sparkling blue eyes, her kind, fair-haired father. As she opened her eyes, Louise's cold body ached all over, her head pounding like a hammer. *'Where am I? What time is it?'* she attempted to establish.

Pulling her arms to her body in an attempt to roll over, Louise screeched in pain. Suddenly all of her senses were alert and she recalled Ross's actions in crystal clear detail. *'Is he still here?'* She panicked at the thought, motivating her to slowly stand upright and turn on the light switch.

The front door was wide open and Ross's ute was nowhere to be seen.

With intense relief she made her way to the spare bedroom and lay on the bed, sobbing. She cried for her mother, her marriage and the severe pain shooting down her arm. Deciding to call an ambulance was her only option, as she rejected the thought of seeking help from friends. Louise was far too ashamed to do that.

When the paramedics arrived some ten minutes later, they looked at Louise then back at one another. A small nod passed between them. They'd seen it all before. Administering pain relief, Louise's arm was then placed in a sling and ointment applied to her swollen, blackening eye.

"It looks like you also have a broken cheekbone Mrs Green. Can you tell us what happened?" The senior paramedic placed his hand gently on Louise's shoulder as she hung her head, tears rolling down her cheeks. With no forthcoming answer, they vigilantly loaded their patient into the back of the ambulance and drove her to Neringah Hospital.

The attending doctor asked, "Do you want to tell me what caused these injuries?"

Louise slowly shook her head. He then went on to advise her about A.V.O. procedures with regards to domestic violence cases and offered her confidential counselling. "If you fear returning home, we have facilities where you can stay," he assured her.

During her x-rays, Louise remained completely silent. She could no longer see out of her left eye. The results confirmed that her left arm was fractured just below the elbow. It would require a plaster cast and her cheekbone needed surgery. This would be performed first thing in the morning and she'd be released later that afternoon. *'What about Jester and Magic? Did he take them? Would he feed them?'* she pondered.

All went well in the operating theatre and by 3pm Louise was allowed to go home if she felt it was safe to do so. No guarantees there…but either way she had to know if the dogs were alright.

Attempting to hide her face, Louise awkwardly climbed into a taxi and returned home to find Magic and Jester wild with excitement and extremely hungry. There was no sign of Ross or any indication that he'd been back.

Walking past a mirror she hardly recognised her own reflection. Her face looked like something the dogs had been chewing. After feeding them she locked all the doors and refusing to lie in their marital bed, opted to lay down in the spare room. Still fuzzy from the general anaesthetic, she dozed fitfully.

It was early evening when she woke to the clicking sound of the front door lock. Instantly alert and aching all over, she sat on the edge of the bed listening to every sound. Ross walked down the hallway and made his way out onto the deck to be greeted by an excited Magic and Jester.

Louise cautiously walked to the kitchen and began making a cup of coffee. Her husband took one look at her, grunted, and with a large suitcase he'd retrieved from the garage, swiftly entered their bedroom.

She could hear him packing and as he did so, heartfelt relief swamped Louise's body. *'How could I have been so stupid to marry such a monster?'* she ridiculed herself.

On his way out, Ross said, "I'll call you next week about putting the house up for sale."

"Take the dogs with you. I can't manage them," Louise returned.

"They have to stay here. You'll cope," he blurted, slamming the door behind him.

After throwing his suitcase on the passenger seat of the ute Ross gazed at it and thought, *'She's a real bitch. I certainly don't need her in my life. Kylie's bloody great in bed, doesn't want kids and knows how to have a good time. That's my kinda woman!'*

CHAPTER EIGHTEEN

With her course material now ready to commence Term 1, Louise's thoughts pivoted back to her private life fiasco and its monetary consequences. Fortunately, both businesses were in her own name, as was the income she received from them. Everything else was largely unknown except for one major fact. She no longer trusted her husband at all.

Magic and Jester patiently waited for Louise to feed them. It wasn't easy with one arm in plaster. "Just as well I'm right-handed," she remarked whilst slowly opening the can of dog food. They looked up at her and she smiled for the first time in days. "And the car's automatic, so that's a bonus."

Louise thought about the following day while the dogs woofed down their dinner. She had to be up early to apply her makeup. It was going to take time to fully conceal the bruising on her face. "You're on your own tomorrow you two, it's time for Mum to go back to work," she said as she stroked their soft coats.

On the Friday night at the end of that week, Ross phoned and got straight down to business. "We're moving to Melbourne so the house needs to go on the market now. I've organised the agent who sold us the place and made an appointment for Tuesday. You need to be there to sign the authority, so you'll have to meet me in town."

Absolutely fuming, Louise replied, "I won't allow you to dictate to me. You're the one who left. And aside from work, I'm not going anywhere looking like this. Your alcohol-induced tantrum made a mess of my face, so you can wait until it suits me." She drew in a deep breath and added, "Go to Melbourne or go to hell. It's of no consequence to me." She then hung up the receiver.

Having never spoken to anyone like that in her life before, Louise was shaking. Immediately she had four major priorities on her plate; transfer half the funds from their joint account to her own personal account, have deadlocks fitted to the doors, get a handle on her legal rights and organise a valuation on the property.

By the following Wednesday, Louise had attended to everything except sourcing a lawyer. In the phone book she found a solicitor in Narrabeen, Heather McCracken, who could see her on Saturday morning. Louise's battered appearance was of little concern as she knew the lawyer would have to be made aware of all the grizzly details anyway.

After applying thick makeup, Louise drove to her 10am appointment with Heather. She outlined Ross's violent behaviour, both past and present, and when it was strongly suggested that Louise take out a Domestic Violence Order against him, she decided not to do so, given the fact that he was moving to Melbourne.

Heather discussed divorce proceedings in detail and said, "Just let me know when you're ready to file and I'll take care of it for you." Louise thanked her and whilst paying the consultation fee, which was no small sum, clearly stated that her husband would be funding the divorce.

Driving back home, Louise felt somewhat relieved for having unloaded her problems but she really needed to chat with a friend. Someone she could trust, to bounce the whole mess off. By the time she pulled up in the garage, Louise had built up the courage to call Martha.

"Oh, I'd love to come over," Martha smiled. "We haven't seen you at the club for almost a month now. And Peter's home, so he can look after Skye if you want me to pop around this afternoon?"

It was agreed and at around 3pm Louise opened the door to her friend.

"Good heavens!" Martha exclaimed. "What did you do to your arm?"

Louise looked at her seriously and replied, "Let's go out to the deck, Martha. I have to talk to someone and guess what? I've chosen you."

"Oh, lucky me," she smiled. "Where's Ross?"

Dropping her gaze, Louise returned, "That's another part of the story. Come in and I'll make us a coffee."

While the kettle boiled, Louise unwrapped some shortbread biscuits and asked her friend for an update on family news. Peter had recently been promoted, apparently Skye was as cheeky as ever and Martha was still happy to be a home body for the time being.

Outside, as the dogs gnawed on two pig's ears in the yard, the women quietly sipped their coffee on the deck. "This isn't a pretty story, Martha," Louise began. "Thank you for taking the time to come over. At the moment I just really need a sounding board."

Martha listened intently while Louise relayed the whole story, including Ross's total lack of compassion for her mother's death. She also mentioned his prior bullying incidents and vicious outbursts whenever he'd imbibed too much rum.

Regularly shaking her head as the saga unfolded, Martha was aghast. "I'm so sorry Louise. I have to admit...I would never have guessed that Ross Green could be so violent. Where is he now?"

"No idea. He didn't leave a phone number so I can only presume he's living with his new woman in an apartment somewhere. I told him to take the dogs but he said there was nowhere to keep them. Then again, that could be a lie too. It certainly wouldn't surprise me. He only took a few clothes when he left, so no doubt he'll be back soon to get the rest of his things."

"I think there's something I should tell you Louise," Martha admitted. "About three months ago, Peter was at a Broker's Conference in Kings Cross and as he was leaving the venue's carpark to drive home, he told me that he saw Ross with a woman. Peter's work colleague told him that she was a hooker who'd been working the Cross for the last few years. She's quite young apparently. Peter assured me that Ross didn't see him that night."

"Ahhhh...so the plot thickens," Louise concluded. "Her name's Kylie, if that's the same woman. I'm so glad you told me, Martha. That makes my decisions even easier."

Happy to change the subject, the women then discussed Louise's burgeoning business. "I might have to lease larger premises and employ an assistant, maybe two, in time," Louise told her friend. "I'd eventually like to expand and develop a recruitment agency so I can place my students into qualified positions when they've completed the course. Currently though, I have other priorities. I'd really like to buy Ross out of this house and stay here…if I can afford to."

Martha was proud of Louise's vision and after a few hours of conversation she headed home to prepare dinner. Louise's shoulders felt lighter and with Peter's sighting of Ross presumably with Kylie, she was determined to seek out her own real estate agent to appraise the house.

Lying awake for many long hours that night, Louise brooded over the worst period of her life. Eventually she drifted off until the dogs started barking. Squinting her weary eyes at the bedside clock, she'd certainly slept in. It was already 8am.

Donning a dressing gown, she went outside to see what was causing the disturbance. Ross was standing at the kennel. He'd let the dogs off their lead and was making a huge fuss of them. Louise instantly wondered, *'Did he try to unlock the door or did he just go through the gate?'* She knew that his face would soon reveal the answer.

As Magic ran over to Louise, tail wagging, Ross looked up at her and said, "I've come to collect a few things. The rest of my clothes and some tools from the back shed."

While he retrieved his suitcase and two sturdy boxes from the back of the ute, Louise walked inside and unlocked the front door. In the kitchen she turned on the kettle and poured herself a bowl of cereal. Ross went about his business, loading the boxes and taking them one by one back to the ute.

With packing complete, he stuck his head through the front door and sharply remarked, "Haven't had time to get an estimate on this joint yet. Next week, I hope." He then left as quickly as he'd arrived.

The remainder of the day Louise spent walking the dogs, watering the garden and attending to some light cleaning duties. None of these tasks were easy with one hand but she managed as best she could. By that evening her facial swelling had subsided considerably and Louise was starting to look more like herself again.

• • • • •

After showing the estate agent original photos of the property, he was clearly impressed by the final renovations as Louise escorted him through the house and its surrounding yard. She withheld the fact that the appraisal was due to a marriage break-up, knowing that agents generally viewed the scenario as a 'desperate sale'. The final valuation would be available by the end of the week.

Late that evening as Louise lay in bed reading, the phone rang. It really startled her. The house was ever so quiet and she was utterly absorbed in a thrilling suspense novel. *'Really? What now?'* she grumbled whilst making her way to the lounge room. Picking up the receiver, all she could hear was whimpering. "Hello, who is this please?" she asked.

"It's me," her sister sniffled. "More bad news I'm afraid Lou." A few seconds of silence followed whilst Julie contained herself. "Dad passed away. His neighbour found him a few hours ago. He only knew that something was wrong because Dad's car was in the driveway and there weren't any lights on in the house, so he went over to check on him."

Without saying a word, Louise carefully sat down and began sobbing.

"I'm so sorry Lou. It looks like he suffered a massive heart attack. He was hopelessly miserable without Mum, so at least they're together again now." Julie tried to console her sister but there was no way of softening this heartbreaking blow.

Louise gently nodded her head and returned, "Yes, true...I'm just absolutely shocked that we've lost them both in such a short period of time. How are you, Jules? You've had so much to cope with over the last few weeks and I know that I've been no help to you from here."

"I'm okay Lou, honestly. John has been my rock and I don't know what I'd do without him."

"He's a true gem alright," Louise replied. In that moment her mind drifted and she couldn't help but secretly assess her own conceited husband. Snapping back to their conversation, she asked, "Do you know if Dad wanted a funeral?"

"As a matter of fact, we only talked about that after Mum died. He said he just wanted a family-only service and to have his ashes scattered in the ocean across from the house. We haven't even got around to doing Mum's yet, so I thought it would be lovely to send them out to sea together. What do you think Lou? I know it's really difficult with your classes and everything…but would you be able to come back again for the service?"

"Yes, I want so much to be there. Poor darling Dad. He was a wonderful father to us. We were lucky to be raised by incredible parents Jules. I've never taken that for granted."

"Neither have I," her sister confirmed. "John and I certainly have big shoes to fill when it comes to raising Lucy and Mark. I'm so sad about Dad but I also know in my heart that he's exactly where he wants to be."

The women then discussed contacting a funeral director and trying to make arrangements for a Saturday service. That way, if flights were available, Louise would be able to fly over on the Friday night and return Sunday afternoon.

As the busy week progressed, Julie and Louise constantly kept one another updated on their planning. The service was scheduled to commence at 11am on Saturday morning in the funeral parlour chapel and Louise's flights were booked accordingly.

With so much on her mind, Louise's emotional state was fragile to say the least. Her only hope was that Ross wouldn't make another appearance before she left…or find out that she was going away. Magic and Jester were booked into the nearby 'Comfy Kennels' from Friday morning and Louise would collect them early Monday morning before work.

On Thursday night the real estate agent phoned to advise Louise of the property valuation price. "It's quite a large block of land with glimpses of the ocean and of course it backs onto the national park," he began.

Impatiently she thought, *'Yes, I know all that. Just get to the point!'* Eventually he revealed the figure and it was within $10,000 of what she considered reasonable herself. Louise told the agent she'd give it some thought over the next month and contact him again if she decided to sell.

Opting to wrap up classes an hour early on Friday afternoon, Louise made her way to the airport and caught a 7pm Qantas flight direct to Auckland. With her arm still in plaster it was fortunate that she only had to contend with a carry-on bag.

The same sinking feeling that consumed her only a few weeks prior, quickly re-emerged with vengeance. Everything in the plane's cabin spun before her eyes as she battled to maintain complete consciousness.

• • • • •

"Where's Ross?" John asked with a quizzical look as he met his sister-in-law at the terminal gate. "And how did you break your arm?"

"Ross couldn't make it and if you don't mind John, I'll tell you about the arm tomorrow. I'm exhausted," Louise replied as she kissed him on the cheek.

"No problem at all. Are you okay? You look very pale," he said, casting a worried glance towards her.

Louise smiled and said, "I'm fine. This tough week is just catching up on me I think."

There was little traffic on the road and Louise found herself dozing on and off while John drove home. Julie and the children were already asleep so they quickly decided to follow suit.

So excited to see their Aunty Louise, Lucy and Mark were determined to wake the adults very early on Saturday morning. While John slipped down the street to grab everyone some McDonald's pancakes for breakfast, Louise thoroughly enjoyed the company of her niece and nephew. They were both adorable, affectionate children with a million and one questions to ask of their aunt.

With coffee brewing and the household fed, John took Lucy and Mark outside to play on their swing set. He knew the sisters needed some time alone to chat.

"Alright Lou, confession time," Julie started. "Where's Ross and what happened to your arm?"

Louise looked down at her cast and replied, "I fractured it above the elbow three weeks ago when I tripped over Jester in the yard. I even heard it snap." Instead of looking Julie in the eye, she then chose to peer at the children through the kitchen window. "Unfortunately, Ross is working on a cash job out of town and it has to be finished before the builders walk in on Tuesday."

"That's a real shame on both counts," Julie commented. "Listen…I found that copy of Dad's Will and Testament in his desk drawer. I'll show it to you tonight. As we suspected it's pretty old, but a solicitor friend of Johns has confirmed that it's valid. In part it reads: 'In the event both parents are deceased, assets will be sold and profits split evenly between both daughters, Julie and Louise.'"

They looked sadly at one another. "I still can't fathom that we've lost them both," Julie remarked. "It's almost surreal."

Remaining with their own thoughts for a while, the sisters sat at the table blank-faced until John and the children returned to break the silence. "Sorry girls, don't mean to rush you but Jules, do you have the kids' overnight bags packed?" John queried. "If not, I'll do that now, otherwise I'll take them straight over to the babysitter while you two get ready."

"Yes, they're in Mark's room, next to his dresser. Thanks love," she smiled.

Kissing and hugging the children before they left, Julie and Louise then showered and dressed before John returned. After he did so, a quick spruce-up saw the group heading to the funeral parlour. There would be five attending the service as William's brother and his wife would be joining them.

The chapel ceremony was short but poignant. Louise, Julie and John each spoke a few heartfelt final words to William and concluded with a very long hug. It was a fitting end to a magical era. One they'd never forget.

John had prearranged a peaceful lunch in a quaint little restaurant overlooking the Hauraki Gulf where they enjoyed a few drinks and a simple meal. He recalled many happy memories of living across the road from Julie and Louise when they were all children. Julie then suggested that they visit the family home in an attempt to figure out what to do with its contents.

Entering the old house where their parents no longer lived was an eerie experience for the sisters. Other than some cherished personal effects and pieces of furniture, it now felt as though the dwelling had lost its soul.

"It'll take a solid couple of weeks to clear out the entire house,"

Julie commented from the dining room.

Louise nodded as she looked around. "Yep. After all these years it's a huge job alright. I wish I could stay and help you Jules but I have to get back to the dogs and my students. Besides, I'm no use to you with one arm."

"Please don't worry about that Lou. I'm the one who isn't working, so I have the time to do it. But while you're here, select whatever you want to keep. We already have a house full of furniture. We can have the items shipped to Sydney for you. I know the furniture's old but some of it could be antique. John and I were thinking it would be wise to sell the rest, probably at auction as a house-lot. If you agree to that of course?"

"Absolutely. That sounds like a sensible way to approach it," Louise concurred.

Looking wistfully throughout each room, she picked a few of her most cherished pieces; the hat stand that had always stood just inside the front door; the old mantle clock that held particularly fond memories for her; two large crystal vases; a brass kettle on its stand with a burner underneath and the Canadian cedar glory box.

"If we could arrange to have a crate made for the glory box, the other items can be packed inside it," Louise suggested. "Are you sure you don't want any of these things for yourself Jules? she asked.

"Positive," her sister smiled. "And when I go through Mum and Dad's jewellery and other personal items, if I know there's anything else you'd like to keep, I'll put it in the box as well. The rest of it I'll store at home, along with their photo albums. I know we want to spread their ashes on a full moon high tide, so whenever you're ready to come back over and do that, you can go through the stuff at my place and see if there's anything else you want."

They returned to the Keane's home early that evening and John ducked out to get a couple of takeaway pizzas for dinner. Meanwhile the sisters discussed Louise's long-term business goals. Julie suddenly reached out and held Louise by both shoulders.

"I know you well, Lou," Julie smiled. "And I know you're grieving for Mum and Dad...but I also know there's something else bothering you. What is it? I thought your fractured arm story was believable enough but then I saw you doing your make-up this morning and I'm pretty sure you have the yellowing remains of a large bruise on your face. Don't forget Lou, I'm a nurse."

Unbidden tears welled up in Louise's eyes and before she knew it, they flowed down her cheeks like a waterfall. Julie hugged her sister closely then led her to the settee. John walked through the door, quickly assessed the scene and placed the pizzas in the oven. Just as he was preparing to make himself scarce Julie called him into the lounge room and said, "Come and sit with us John. We're a caring family, so you should also hear what Lou has to say."

Louise sighed heavily, wiped the tears from her face and out it came. The whole abysmal mess from start to finish. "I'm sorry that I lied to you earlier," she added. "I didn't want to say anything because I know you have enough to deal with right now…but there you have it. All the truthful rigmarole that I've been hiding."

The Keane's were naturally astounded by these revelations and didn't quite know how to react. "So, do you have a plan, Lou? Or is it all too soon?" John asked, immediately wishing he'd responded in a more empathetic way.

"A few…but they're really vague at the moment, John. I'd like to buy Ross out of his share of the house. And I know I can't keep the dogs, as much as I adore them. They need regular exercise and I just don't have the time for it."

Julie stepped in and said, "How about we have dinner before it spoils and we can continue this conversation while we eat." She then entered the kitchen, closely followed by John and Louise.

Opening a bottle of New Zealand shiraz, John was silently seething. *'We all need a drink to settle our nerves. Bloody hell… you're a real asshole Ross Green!'*

Whilst they nibbled away, Julie said, "When we wind up Dad's estate, you'll have the money to buy him out. The old place is on a prime piece of land and the north shore is much sought after. It would have to be worth around the two million mark I'd say. We'd just need to make it happen before Ross starts rattling your cage. Probate shouldn't take too long but then again, you know government departments. It's like the age-old question: How long's a piece of string? Anyway, I haven't looked further than the house at this early stage. Dad likely had shares and there'll certainly be cash in the bank but how much, I wouldn't know."

Louise looked pensively at her sister. "It feels like an awful thing to say…but this inheritance is quite timely for my situation, isn't it?"

"Yes," Julie nodded. "You could certainly look at it that way. There's no doubt Mum and Dad's legacy will make life a little bit easier for you. I wonder if you could apply for bridging finance in the event Ross starts applying pressure on you? I could arrange a letter through Dad's solicitor, outlining the value of assets. You could then give the lending authority a copy of the Will, proving that half of those assets will be forwarded to you. That should be enough for them to approve a short-term loan."

"That all sounds fine but for the time being, let's talk about more pleasant things," Louise suggested. "It's so quiet without the kids here, isn't it Jules?"

"Ah yes…peaceful!" was the wry response from her sister.

"Actually, I think the correct word is 'heavenly' my love," John laughed as he cleared their plates from the table.

Louise sipped her wine and said, "Although there's nine years between us, I think our early childhoods would have been pretty similar growing up. I clearly remember when you left to do nursing down in Hamilton. The dynamics of the household changed radically when your friends weren't coming around anymore. I remember going to swimming club at the Tepid Baths with my friend Irene when we were in primary school and after training, we'd go to that fish and chip shop at the bottom of Queen Street. For a shilling we'd buy our hot chips wrapped in newspaper and eat them on the ferry on our way home."

"Shirley and I used to do the same," Julie smiled. "Do you remember her? She used to live just behind us."

"I do," Louise nodded several times. And do you remember Miff? She lived in the city but she'd come and stay with her grandma. We still send one another a Christmas card every year. She's in Rotorua now. Oh, we used to love it when the north easterly winds whipped up. We'd sit on the edge of the promenade wall with our legs dangling over the edge while the waves crashed against it. The water would spurt into the air and drench us."

"Yes, I recall that you were very fond of her," returned Julie. "I think my favourite memories would have to be at the beach, in summer with the full moon tides. Mum and Dad would come down and enjoy the sunshine while we swam or built sandcastles. In the school holidays when the city dwellers flocked to their beach houses, there were always heaps of kids to play with. At night on low tide, we'd play touch footy on the beach until it was too dark to see."

Louise, John and Julie continued to enjoy their waltz down memory lane for almost two hours before calling it a night.

The following morning John collected the children shortly after breakfast then headed to the hospital for a few hours. Louise hugged Lucy and Mark as she said, "I don't have to be at the airport until mid-afternoon, so…we're going to the beach. How does that sound?"

"Yippee!" The two balls of energy replied in unison. They couldn't wait to get straight back out the door.

A nostalgic stroll along the beach at Milford, their old stamping ground as children themselves, was a perfect start to the day for Julie and Louise. Lucy and Mark ran ahead, amusing themselves and when they reached the promenade, jumped off the wall onto the sand just as the sisters had done as youngsters. Many changes had taken place over the years. Old renovated beach shacks were now palatial abodes and three large townhouses had been built beside their old family home.

Julie smiled, reached out and held her sister's hand. "Even though most of the houses have changed Lou, the lifestyle remains the same. I think Mum and Dad would be proud to see us walking in their footsteps like this."

"I know they would," Louise replied as she hugged her sister tightly.

When they arrived back at the Keane's house, on the doorstep they discovered an arrangement of flowers and a small blue giftbox with a silver ribbon. While Julie placed the flowers in a vase, Louise opened the box and retrieved a silver dragonfly strategically placed on top of a folded piece of parchment paper. It read:

The Dragonfly

In the bottom of an old pond lived a grub family. Every now and again, a member of the family would crawl up a lily stem and make it to the top of the water. They would never return and the rest of the family couldn't understand why.

One day they vowed that the next family member who was called to make the upward climb, would return and tell the others what happened.

With an urgent impulse to seek the surface, one of the brothers rested on top of a lily pad and gloriously transformed into a dragonfly with beautiful wings. Whilst flying back and forth over the pond, he thought about the promise he and his family had made. Suddenly he realised that even if his family could see him, they wouldn't recognise such a radiant creature as one of their own.

The fact that we can't see our loved ones after their transformation (death) is no proof that they cease to exist.

Love, Shannon.

CHAPTER NINETEEN

Ross phoned Louise on the Friday night after class. "You can't put this valuation off any longer Louise. We have to get the house up for a quick sale so I can move on," he bluntly demanded.

Little did Ross know that his wife had already arranged bridging finance with their bank manager earlier in the week after receiving a faxed copy of her father's Will. Along with an assessor's valuation on her parent's home, the bank pre-approved a loan which was valid for six months from the date of contract. Signing the paperwork was all that was required.

"It's all, 'I', 'I', 'I' with you, isn't it Ross? Now it's my turn to have a say," Louise replied. You take the cash that's left in the joint account. I've already withdrawn my half as you're probably well aware. If you want a divorce, I won't contest it…but you're footing the bill. And you have to take the dogs, there's no way I can properly care for them with the hours I work."

Ross was growing more impatient by the second. "I'm talking about the bloody house Louise, not all this other bullshit!"

"Hear me out Ross, I'm not done yet. I already have a valuation from a reputable agent and there's no need for a second one." She then told him the assessed price.

"Well, you could have told me that you'd already organised it!" he blurted.

Louise chuckled. "And how would I do that Ross? I don't even have your phone number."

"Yeah, right. Well, that figure sounds reasonable enough. Let's get it on the market and add another $10,000 to the asking price to cover the agent's commission."

"That won't be necessary because if you agree to everything I've asked, in return, I intend to buy out your share of the house,"

Louise declared. "I'll keep the furniture and pay half the legal fees."

Ross was speechless as his mind quickly did the math. "Where in the hell did you get that sort of money?"

"Let's just say…that's none of your business," Louise retorted. "This is a cash offer Ross, so let me know within three days if you're prepared to accept it or not. If you do, make sure you come and get all your personal stuff by the end of next week and bugger off."

Hanging up the receiver, Louise suddenly felt empowered by her own tenacity.

On Sunday, without any preliminaries Ross rang Louise and accepted her offer. "We need a solicitor to arrange the Change of Ownership papers. You have the title deed in the safe so will you sort that out?' he asked.

"I will. Call me again tomorrow night and I'll confirm an appointment day, time and the address of my lawyer's office in Narrabeen," Louise instructed.

Before their meeting with Heather McCracken, Louise drove to the bank in Manly, signed the paperwork for the bridging finance and arranged a bank cheque for Ross. He had informed her that he'd drop by the house afterwards to collect the last of his personal items together with the dogs and their associated gear.

In the solicitor's office, whilst Heather's legal secretary drew up the revised Title Deed papers for the Greens to sign, Ross and Louise avoided eye contact at all times.

Breaking the silence, Heather smiled and said, "It's great to see you out of that plaster cast Louise. And it looks like your face healed really well."

"Yes, it is a relief. Thank you," Louise answered, extremely surprised that she raised the issue.

Ross squirmed uncomfortably in his chair as he gaped at Heather, embarrassed by the fact that she may well know the cause of his wife's injuries.

Holding his gaze, Heather cunningly remarked, "You look surprised Mr Green. Didn't you know that the police sent Louise to me for a domestic violence consultation after she was released from hospital? You're very lucky that your wife chose not to press charges."

Sinking even further into his chair, Ross looked away from her and began fidgeting with his shirt buttons. Heather winked at Louise and she smiled. After retrieving the bank cheque from her handbag, Louise placed it on Heather's desk.

"There's my payment for our agreed amount on the house Ross," Louise said, looking at him. "I may as well give it to you now, so Heather can witness the transaction."

He stood up and grabbed the cheque just as Heather's secretary returned with the final paperwork. After signatures were acquired, Ross practically bolted out of the office.

Ross was already waiting out the front when Louise arrived home. She unlocked the garage and garden shed then he gathered up the dogs and their belongings, plus the balance of his tools. Unlocking the front door, Louise made her way to the kitchen and offloaded her handbag and a large envelope containing the new Title Deed paperwork.

Magic and Jester were eagerly awaiting a pat as Louise made her way out onto the deck. She said a tearful goodbye as she cuddled the dogs for the last time then quickly made her way back inside before Ross loaded them into the back of the ute. After hastily gathering up his personal paperwork from the office, the rest of his shoes and a large bag of winter clothing, Ross exited the front door, leaving it wide open…and left without a word.

Louise rested her saddened body up against the door frame and watched her family drive away. She would miss the dogs dearly. Taking in a long, slow sigh, she then closed and locked the door as she gazed down the hallway. "So…this is how a marriage ends," she said aloud, dabbing her tears.

Deciding to indulge in a quiet coffee to pick herself up before returning to work, Louise knew that through all the disappointment, she also felt relieved that it was finally done and dusted. She could honestly admit that she no longer loved Ross Green.

• • • • •

Louise and Julie's family home sold at auction within six weeks of her leaving New Zealand. There was a large crowd in attendance and five fiercely competitive bidders drove the price way beyond what the sisters had anticipated. They knew that investing wisely would set them up for life, all thanks to the arduous work and forethought of their wonderful parents.

Shortly thereafter, Louise paid out the bridging loan. She had a successful business from which she could diversify and she was debt free. Her future was now entirely within her own control.

When the shipping crate arrived, there were obvious signs that Customs had taken it apart to assess its contents. As she excitedly began to demolish the protective timber with a claw hammer, her only hope was that they'd repacked it carefully.

Relieved that the glory box remained undamaged, Louise opened it up and was thrilled to find surprise pieces that Julie had added. Some jewellery that she recalled her mother wearing, a tiny etched-silver thimble that she used when embroidering and two pieces of framed artwork. One was a large sepia photograph of 'Takushinama', who was a friend of her grandmother. She was the last of the pure Canadian Indian women in British Columbia and Louise had been told numerous stories about her. The picture proudly hung in the hallway of their family home. The other piece adorned Louise's bedroom wall when she was a child. A black ink sketch of dandelions, depicting the soft petals blowing off in the wind to become fairies. The caption on the bottom in Yugoslavian translates to 'Promises of Spring' in English.

As she studied the sketch, Louise knew she had to inform all her friends of their separation. Obviously, the Deans were aware, but in regards to the others, it was a secret that she no longer wished to keep. Time to remove the dead weight and enjoy her friendships once again.

She met up with Carl, Donna, Peter and Martha for drinks after work and they were all so happy to see her. As soon as Martha saw Louise enter the club's foyer, she walked over and hugged her. "Carl and Donna already know about the break-up," she said. "They were hounding us for information weeks ago and we couldn't lie to them. I'm sorry if you wanted to tell them yourself Lou."

"No, not all," Louise returned. "In fact, I'm glad you did Martha. Saves me having to do it. Now I can just fill in any blanks and enjoy a drink with friends. That's what I want more than anything."

The group had a few questions that Louise couldn't avoid answering but for the most part, she felt comfortable doing so. They were sympathetic to all that she'd endured, including the loss of her parents...and relieved to hear that Ross had moved interstate. By the time they left the club, everyone was back to their usual banter and sharing a few laughs.

Phoning the Wilsons that evening, Louise and Janet first discussed business as they did on a regular basis. Janet was aware of the passing of her friend's parents but Louise had kept the balance of her private life to herself. When she revealed what had transpired in her marriage over the past few months, Janet wasn't surprised that the Greens had separated. On more than one occasion she'd witnessed Ross's deplorable attitude towards his wife, particularly after drinking. The shocking part for Janet was to hear of the horrible injuries that he'd inflicted on her friend.

"Do you have any plans for the end of term break? Janet queried. "It's only three weeks away now."

"Not yet. This whole mess with Ross and working thirteen-hour days has been chaotic to say the least. I haven't had a chance to scratch myself."

"You need a proper break from it all, Louise. And that means getting away," Janet suggested. "Why don't you come over and spend Easter and some of the holidays with us? Ken just finished the extension and the granny flat's perfect for you."

"I'd love to do that Janet. Thank you so much for the offer. I'll have a look at some flight schedules over the course of the next week and ring you back. Give Ken and baby Craig a hug from me."

Janet was really pleased. "I certainly will. We can't believe he's four months old already, so he should be close to sitting up by the time you get here."

After the call, Louise was as happy as a frog on a tap and her holiday couldn't come soon enough. There were numerous other things she wanted to do in Perth while she was there: finally meet Katherine their manager, see what had been done with the block of land they sold, swim in the Indian Ocean and try to meet up with some other old friends.

By the end of the week Louise had booked flights to Western Australia. She'd also phoned Jean and Jillian, informing them of her marriage breakdown. Collectively the calls were well over two hours long and though they were exhausting for Louise, she was very grateful for her friends' support. Both women praised her for having the gumption to pick herself up and move forward within such a short period of time.

• • • • •

Peter dropped Louise at the airport at 6am and said, "Have a great trip. I've got your return flight details so I'll pick you up when you get back. If anything changes along the way, just let us know."

"Thanks so much, Peter. I really appreciate it. Have a lovely Easter," Louise smiled.

"Just as well you said that," he returned, quickly opening the glovebox. "I almost forgot." Handing Louise an Easter egg wrapped in gold foil with a red bow he added, "From Martha. She said it's just in case the Easter Bunny can't find you in Perth."

Louise laughed. "That's so sweet. Please thank her for me."

Upon boarding the plane, she was extremely surprised to discover that her seat had been upgraded to business class. This was an unusual privilege for any airline to offer. About an hour after take-off from Mascot, the pilot emerged from the cockpit and sat beside Louise on a vacant seat. He immediately introduced himself.

"Hi Louise, my name's Murray Corbet. I'm a friend of Peter and Martha Dean. I had dinner with them during the week and they mentioned a friend who was booked on this flight. As I was scheduled to fly, I offered to look after you," he grinned.

Louise smiled back at him. She was instantly charmed by this handsome gentleman. "Hence the upgrade I'm assuming? Thank you very much Murray. I think I was born for this sort of luxury but having never had the honour, I'm just learning. It's a lovely start to my holiday."

He laughed and they chatted for a short while. Murray then asked, "When are you returning to Sydney? Depending on seating availability of course, I'll try to arrange a little more luxury for you."

More than happy to pass on her flight information, Louise provided it to him, along with the Wilson's contact phone number. His beaming smile revealed a set of perfect white teeth as he said, "I'd best get back to work. Enjoy your trip. Nice meeting you Louise."

With seat reclined, feet up and a glass of champagne on the table beside her, Louise then took up her book. After reading a few pages, she realised that she hadn't absorbed a single word of the story. Her thoughts were still with Murray. *'I wonder if I'll ever see him again?'* Reaching for an eye mask she then settled in for some much-needed sleep.

As the plane touched down, Janet was already at the arrival gate to meet her. Craig was nestled comfortably in his mother's arms. After they collected Louise's luggage from the carousel and made their way towards the exit, she felt a hand gently rest on her shoulder. Looking up she was very surprised to see Murray.

"Enjoy your holiday," he said quietly, whilst striding past with his co-pilot.

"Wow Louise, how do you know that hunk of manhood?" Janet asked, scanning Murray up and down.

Louise laughed and said, "I'll fill you in later but for now I'd love to have a nurse of Craig while he's awake. Is that okay?

"Of course," Janet smiled as she began offloading the infant. "My arms could really do with a rest. How about I wheel the suitcase to the car and you carry the baby?"

Louise's eyes lit up as she cradled him. "Oh, he's just beautiful Janet. His little features are picture prefect…he has your mouth and eyes…and Ken's button nose. Turning her attention back to her friend, Louise added, "And look at you. My goodness your figure's amazing. If I didn't know otherwise, I'd say there's no way you gave birth to a baby less than five months ago."

Janet timidly shrugged her shoulders. "That's lovely of you to say. I feel good too."

Reaching the car, Louise handed Craig back to his mother and asked, "How did he go with his first bottle the other night?"

"Like a duck to water," Janet smiled. "And to be perfectly honest, I'm glad the breastfeeding's over. It just wasn't working for me."

Making their way to the Wilson's house, Janet looked in the rear vision mirror and said, "Craig's out for the count. I'll feed him and put him down when we get home and that should give us a good hour for a peaceful lunch."

The renovations Ken and Janet undertook on their cottage certainly paid off. They'd added two bedrooms, one with an ensuite, and extended the outside area with half of it undercover. The kitchen had increased in size and ducted air-conditioning was installed throughout the house. Attached to one side of the exterior, a spacious granny with a two-way door allowed easy access to the home.

While the women conversed over a roast beef salad that Janet had prepared earlier, Louise pointed out the differences between the Perth and Sydney operations along with her plans to diversify later in the new year.

Janet's mind was ticking over at a rate of knots when she remarked, "I wonder if evening classes and an employment agency would work well here? Ken plays competition squash on Monday nights but he's here every other evening. I'd have to discuss it with him of course, but I'd love to teach evening classes. And if Craig or Ken happened to be sick and I couldn't be there, I'm sure Katherine would be prepared to stand in for me. We'll mention it when we see her. I know it's only an idea at this stage but we'd need to know she's onboard."

Before Louise had arrived in Perth, she and Janet arranged to meet with Katherine at the office for a few hours that afternoon to discuss business. When Craig woke, Janet strapped him into the baby capsule and they headed into town.

Katherine's professionalism and cheerful nature pleased Louise. There was an instant connection between them. Over coffee, Katherine brought her owner up-to-date and revealed the final results of her first term students. When Louise mentioned the possibility of running evening classes, Katherine informed her that she'd already received many enquiries.

"It would be great to provide students that opportunity," she smiled. "I'm more than happy to step up and fill the breach if Janet can't make it."

"Excellent," Janet nodded. "Obviously I need to talk to Ken about it but I'm pretty sure he'll be happy for me to return to teaching a few hours each week. Perhaps we can look to commencing these classes in Term 3."

"I already have a list of names and contact numbers for those who enquired, so we can start there," Katherine suggested. "Sorry Janet, I feel bad for not mentioning these requests earlier."

Janet placed her hand on Katherine's forearm and replied, "Oh please, don't apologise. I couldn't have dealt with it in my sleep deprived state anyway. Now that Craig's on the bottle, it changes everything. He's sleeping right through the night and Ken can feed him if need be, so I'm happy to get out of the house for some mental stimulation."

Katherine looked at Louise and said, "Before we wrap things up, I was wondering if you could use some help in Sydney? Janet told me how many hours you're working each week and that must be really tough on your own. I have a graduate student from last year's course, Beth Phillips, and she's been working in a job-share position but would much prefer full time work. Her husband's currently a tutor at the university here and he accepted a transfer to the ACU in North Sydney. They leave in a month. Beth's a lovely woman. Always smartly dressed, friendly, well-spoken and she's highly intelligent."

"An assistant is exactly what I need," Louise sighed. "I've been thinking about that for a while and it would be great to employ a graduate of our own. Thanks Katherine, sounds like she'd be a perfect fit for the job. In the meantime, can you email me through her details and if you happen to be in touch, please let her know that I'll be phoning when I get back."

It was then decided that the group would discuss the employment agency agenda at another time. After all, they were on holidays and Louise had promised Katherine a very brief meeting.

After dinner at the Wilsons, concerned, Ken asked Louise if she felt lonely.

"No, not really. I don't have much time to think about it during the week," Louise admitted. "Obviously I'm really missing the dogs but the only time I feel a bit secluded is on weekends when it's 'family time'. I don't want to encroach on friends who have young families…and that's most of them. So, I'm thinking about taking up golf again. And I still love walking on the beach, tending to my garden, watching movies and reading. I bought an old sewing machine too. Wouldn't mind doing an interior decorating course."

"We're glad you decided to come west for the holiday Louise," Ken smiled. "We're having a few of the old gang over on Monday, along with some of our new friends. I'm looking forward to introducing you."

"That sounds like fun, Ken. Any friend of yours is a friend of mine. Unless of course his name's Ross Green!" she laughed.

The next morning while Janet caught up on some washing, Louise borrowed her car and drove into town to do shopping. She'd yet to buy a gift for the baby and this was the ideal opportunity to do so. There was so much to choose from in the baby supply store but in the end, Louise settled on a Jolly Jumper. It could be hung from a door architrave or any other sturdy structure to allow an infant to safely swing and bounce around. The second gift was a large, stuffed Panda bear for Craig to cuddle and play with. Louise just couldn't resist its lovable blue eyes and podgy tummy.

Returning home just before lunch with three cheese and bacon pies from the local bakery, Louise took them into the kitchen. While Janet prepared plates and a few glasses of ginger beer, Louise slipped back out to the car and smuggled her gift shopping into the granny flat wardrobe.

"There was a call for you while you were out, Louise," Janet told her. "He didn't leave a name or a message, I just told him that you'd be back around lunchtime and he said he'll try again later."

"It's probably Peter, Martha's husband. He's keeping an eye on the house for me while I'm away. I hope everything's alright."

Janet sat the plates down on the table and said, "No, it was a local call. I didn't hear any long-distance beeps."

They'd only taken a few bites out of their pies when the phone rang again. This time Ken answered the call. "Yes, I'll just put her on," he said. Cuffing the mouthpiece, he looked at Louise and said, "It's for you. I think it's that guy again."

"Hello," Louise answered, half swallowing a piece of pastry.

"Hi Louise, it's Murray Corbet. We met on your flight to Perth. I hope you don't mind me phoning you?"

Eyes wide she answered, "No, not at all. I was wondering who phoned earlier. Funnily enough, Peter and Martha are the only other people I gave this number to."

"Well," Murray declared, "to keep a long story short, I've flown my maximum hours so I'm grounded and have to take a stopover. I'm here in Perth until mid-afternoon tomorrow and I was hoping you might have dinner with me tonight?"

Louise could hear the smile in his voice. "That would be lovely Murray…but I'd need to speak with my hostess first. Can I call you back?" she asked.

"Please do," Murray returned. He then provided her with the phone number of the hotel along with the extension number for his room.

As Louise hung up the receiver, Janet continued to nod excessively. She knew it had to be the pilot from the beaming grin on her friend's face. "Whatever it is, don't ask, just go," Janet insisted. "It's time for some excitement in your life girl! Take my car. You know your way around this city."

After calling Murray back, they arranged to meet out the front of his hotel at 7pm. "There's a nice restaurant nearby which the flight crew regularly frequent," he told her. "If you're happy to drive we can dine there…otherwise there's a little place just a few blocks away. Well within walking distance."

"I don't mind driving Murray," Louise informed him. "Happy to. See you then."

Janet was glued to her friend's eyes for the entire length of the call. When Louise hung up the phone, Janet pumped her fist in the air and said, "I'm so excited for you. What are you going to wear?"

Louise smirked. "That's an easy decision. I only brought one dressy outfit with me!"

Late that afternoon, having played with the baby for a few hours, Louise then wrapped Craig's gifts and placed them back in the wardrobe. Whilst showering and preparing for the evening, she questioned her decision to accept Murray's offer. *'Is it too soon? Am I ready to start seeing another man?'* By the time her makeup was done, she took a close, final look at herself in the mirror and said, *'Stop overthinking it…it's just dinner with a very handsome pilot. What single woman in her right mind would say no to that?'*

Dressing in black crepe wide-legged pants with a black and white blouse, she then added a pair of small diamond earrings and mandatory black stiletto heels. Murray was fairly tall so she felt comfortable adding a little more height. Last minute, Louise considered phoning Martha for information about him but concluded, *'If he found out, he might resent the fact that I pried. Just play it by ear, Louise.'*

Janet and Ken wished her all the best as they waved her off in the driveway. Approaching the city, she began to feel nervous. *'Just be yourself,'* she recited over in her head. Knowing exactly where the Hilton was located, Louise pulled over about thirty metres from the entrance and gently tooted the horn when she saw Murray standing on the curb. Her heart began to flutter as he walked towards her.

Opening the passenger door he said, "Good evening. You look lovely Louise. Allow me to direct you to our destination."

"By all means," she replied as he sat in the passenger seat. The restaurant was only a five-minute drive from the hotel and after Louise parked, Murray opened the driver's door for her. Something Ross had never done.

Crossing the street, he positioned himself towards the oncoming traffic and gently held Louise's elbow. Another very polite gesture that didn't go unnoticed. Louise was growing more nervous by the minute and hoped they'd be having a drink at the bar before dinner. She needed something to take the edge off.

Upon entering the establishment Murray asked, "What would you like to drink, Louise?"

"I'd love a gin and tonic, heavy on the tonic…in a tall glass please Murray."

"Ah, yes of course, you're driving. I would have preferred to pick you up but alas I don't have a car."

"It's no problem at all, honestly," she smiled. "I'm staying with friends in Scarborough and Janet was more than happy to lend me her vehicle. I lived in Perth about four years ago so I know my way around fairly well."

After being served their drinks, Murray took a sip of his scotch and dry. "I'm afraid I don't know Perth very well at all. We just fly in, sometimes have a short break, then fly off to the next destination. I really only know the CBD."

They continued chatting about Louise's time in the west and Murray was surprised to hear that she'd lived in New Guinea for some time. "A few of my colleagues have put in a lot of flying hours up there," he commented. "I've heard the Territory is quite challenging and I'm told there are some formidable landing strips."

Conversation flowed easily and time flew by. When Louise finished her beverage, she went to the lady's room while Murray asked the waiter to be seated at their table. He ordered two glasses of white wine and when she returned, they browsed the dinner menu.

"The barramundi with creamy lemon pepper sauce is divine," Murray suggested, having chosen the dish numerous times before.

"Yes, I'm happy with that," Louise smiled. "And for entrée I wouldn't mind the crumbed prawn cutlets."

"Great choice. I think I'll have the same," he nodded.

While Louise scanned Murray's striking facial features, she deduced that he was close to her own age. Picking up conversation from where they left off at the bar, she discovered that he was single and lived in nearby Dee Why. He liked to play golf and enjoyed a game of squash whenever time allowed.

"Getting back to golf is something I was planning to do after the holidays," Louise admitted. She then went on to briefly describe the business. "I'm hoping to employ a woman to takeover two of my day classes and perhaps a few of the evening classes as well. My plan is to expand and add a recruitment agency to both operations. I've been putting in some very long hours up to this point but now I'm ready to share the burden and delegate."

"That's great. Balancing work and play can be quite tricky but I think it's crucial to one's overall happiness," Murray remarked. "Perhaps we can play golf together, Louise?"

"Could be fun…though I need some practice. I'd also like to establish a handicap in order to play competition golf. Haven't had time to play squash since leaving Rabaul but that's something I thoroughly enjoy as well."

Murray said, "I try to play squash once a week wherever I end up. After sitting in the cockpit for hours on end it's important to stay active during stopovers. Some of the crew play as well. A number of the hotels have their own squash courts and a gym, so that's handy."

Louise's nervousness had greatly diminished by the time they finished the main course so she plucked up the courage to inform Murray that she was married but recently separated. He didn't appear to be the least bit perturbed by her admission.

Mutually deciding to skip coffee at this hour, Louise gazed at Murray while he paid the bill. Given his easy manner, flawless olive complexion, perfectly cut short, thick dark hair and startling, expressive blue eyes, she could only assume that he often dated.

When they walked back to the car, Murray opened the driver's door for Louise and thanked her for the evening. On the short drive back to the Hilton he said, "I really enjoyed your company, Louise and I'm delighted that you could make it tonight. I'd like to do it again in Sydney if you're willing. Perhaps Martha and Peter could join us."

"Thank you, Murray. I've enjoyed the evening too. And yes, it would be a pleasure to catch up at home."

Pulling up outside the hotel he imparted his final words. "Have a great holiday with your friends and I haven't forgotten your return flight. I'm not scheduled for that day but a friend of mine will be, so I'll touch base with him." He then gently squeezed Louise's hand and with a smile added, "Happy Easter," as he got out and closed the door.

Glancing in the rear vision mirror as she left the curb, Louise could clearly see Murray watching her drive away. "Wow...what a catch!" she said aloud whilst navigating the inner-city streets. "He'd be a calm port in a storm, that's for sure." Recalling their conversation during the course of the evening she found it uncanny that they shared exactly the same sporting interests. *'I certainly hope he calls me again,'* she thought wishfully.

The lights were still on in the Wilson's house when Louise pulled into the driveway. Ken and Craig were asleep but as Janet opened the front door, she looked at her friend expectantly. Louise walked in, all smiles.

"I see you had a good time," Janet remarked. "Where did you go? Is he as nice as he looks? What did you talk about? Will you be seeing him again?"

Louise hugged her and said, "That's a lot of questions. Let's just say he's a true gentleman in every sense of the word. He suggested having dinner again in Sydney with Peter and Martha." Covering her mouth to conceal a yawn she added, "I'll tell you everything else in the morning."

•••••

It was a real treat for Louise to be in the kitchen preparing Easter Sunday breakfast with Janet. She hadn't cooked for anyone but herself in quite a while. They chatted about Louise's dinner date with Murray and Janet was pleased to see her friend in such high spirits.

Craig contentedly amused himself in his rocker with two shiny rattle toys while the adults devoured their scrambled eggs, chipolata sausages and English muffins. After clearing the plates from the table Ken left the kitchen and returned with two small gift-wrapped boxes. He placed one on the table in front of his wife and the other in front of Louise.

"Happy Easter ladies. From Craig and me," he declared.

"Oh love, that's so sweet," Janet smiled as she stood to kiss him on the cheek. Both women opened their gifts at the same time. Inside the boxes were an assortment of Roses soft-centred chocolates, Guylian seashells and two bars of white Belgian chocolate.

"That's incredibly thoughtful Ken," Louise beamed at him. "Thank you so much. Oh, I almost forgot…I'll be back in a jiffy." She walked into the granny flat, retrieved Craig's presents from the bottom shelf of the wardrobe and reappeared with her arms full. Looking at Janet she said, "I should have sent you something when he was born but with Mum and Dad and all the Ross debacle, I just couldn't find the time."

"There was no need to do that Louise. Honestly, your beautiful card was more than enough for us," Janet assured her. Ken nodded in total agreement.

"I wanted to buy him a gift, so I did," Louise replied adamantly. "Now I'm going to pack the dishwasher while you two help your son unwrap them. It'll take all day if we wait for Craig to do it," she laughed.

The baby showed enormous interest in the colourful wrapping paper, particularly because of the noise it made. His tiny fingers pulled at it while Ken attempted to remove the sticky tape. Janet watched on with sheer joy written all over her face. Craig's eyes widened when his father slowly placed the Panda bear on his son's stomach. He clutched the toy, pulled it up under his chin and snuggled it. Within seconds he was sucking on the bear's nose.

Janet unwrapped the Jolly Jumper and immediately looked at Louise. "Thank you so much. Ken and I were looking at these a few weeks ago but with all the other stuff we had to get for the baby, our budget was pretty tight. What a fabulous gift. Not only will it keep him amused but he'll also learn to get those leg muscles working." She then walked over to Louise, hugged her and turned the kettle on.

Meanwhile, Ken clipped the Jolly Jumper onto the door architrave in the living room and slowly placed Craig into the harness. For a short while his little legs didn't move. He just dangled from the contraption like a broken puppet. After a minute or so, he tucked his chubby legs under his body and began to push up off the floor. Ken, Janet and Louise cheered in unison. "Good boy," they smiled, encouraging him.

A short time later he was bouncing up and down spasmodically, dribbling and giggling. Louise burst out with laughter. "I'm enjoying this as much as he is," she admitted. Janet was already lying on the floor beside her son in hysterics while Ken photographed the shenanigans on his camera.

For the remainder of the day, they were all happy to stay at home and enjoy one another's company. There was only some grocery shopping to be done for tomorrow's barbecue lunch, which Janet and Louise attended to late that afternoon.

An early start in the kitchen the following morning saw the two women preparing for an Easter feast. Janet had always loved to entertain and she was a fabulous cook. They shelled 3kg of West

Australian king prawns and marinated them in garlic, white wine and orange juice. In the meantime, Ken took Craig for a walk in his stroller and brought home some pancakes for breakfast to ease the girl's workload.

They then made a rye and sunflower seed cob loaf and baked it in the oven along with some roasted capsicum, onion and slivered almonds for the mango salad. With eleven adults to cater for, Louise and Janet agreed that combined with a large portion of rump steak, there was plenty for everyone.

Guests began arriving around noon and there were hugs and kisses all round. Louise already knew six of them and she noticed straight away that two of the men were scanning the yard for Ross. It quickly became apparent that the Wilson's hadn't informed them of the Green's separation. In fact, they'd kept Louise's visit a complete surprise.

When the chatter subsided a little, Louise took it upon herself to enlighten her friends. "I'd just like to say a few words before we settle in for a lovely afternoon," she announced to the group. "It's wonderful to see you all again and to Bronwen and Laird… it's lovely meeting you for the first time. I can see that some of you are wondering why Ross isn't here but you're just too polite to ask. Truth is, we separated a few months ago and he's no longer part of my life. It's time for me to move on. Now I'm certainly not in the business of slandering him because we're all friends here and I hope that will continue. So, if you want to ask me any questions when we chat, feel free. I'll do my best to answer them. Happy Easter everyone."

Ken poured wine and cracked open beers while Louise wandered around the deck with a plate of nibblies. Craig became the star attraction when he finally woke from his nap. All agreed that he was such a contented baby. Even though he was teething and drooling everywhere, the infant hardly ever grizzled.

Tongues loosened from the wine and most of the women showed concern for Louise. They'd not seen the Greens since they left for New Guinea but there was no doubt that Louise had lost a considerable amount of weight.

"It was very hot in the Territory," she explained. We spent

almost a year renovating an old house together in Sydney and since then I've opened a new business, lost both my parents and separated from Ross, so it has gradually just fallen off. I'm a bit underweight but that's only temporary," she smiled.

When asked to elaborate on her parents, she briefly explained their deaths then the group immediately moved on to questioning why she and her husband had separated. "It's pretty simple really," Louise replied. "Ross didn't want children and I did." She made no mention of domestic violence whatsoever. "He doesn't have many friends in Sydney and the last thing I want to do is jeopardise his friendships over here. So, I hope he keeps in touch with you all." She knew full well that the odds of Ross maintaining contact with any of them was about a hundred to one.

By 6pm Craig was well and truly ready for a bath and bed. Janet slipped away to tend to her son while Louise stacked dishes in the dishwasher and washed up anything that wouldn't fit. The only leftovers were two crusts of the cob loaf. Within the hour guests were saying their goodbyes and dispersing.

Ken, Janet and Louise were far too full from lunch to require dinner, so they opted for a nightcap instead. Baileys Irish Crème liqueur on the rocks was a perfect end to a wonderful afternoon.

"You handled that well, Louise," Ken remarked. "We expected there'd be questions but we also knew you'd handle them in your own way. It wasn't our place to divulge the details you discussed with us in confidence. Very nicely done."

"Thanks Ken, thank you both. I appreciate you more than words can say."

It was back to work for Ken on Tuesday morning and over the course of the next four days, Janet, Louise and the baby enjoyed their time together. Craig was no trouble at all. He'd have a bottle anywhere and just dozed off whenever he was tired, even in the noisiest of places.

They spent time at the beach and drove past the Green's old block of land where a partially constructed double-storey, modern, sandstone brick home now stood. In Fremantle one morning as they began strolling around the city, Louise said, "I'd like to make a gallery-type display in my wide hallway at home and I was hoping to find a couple of artworks while I'm here in the west."

"There's a terrific new gallery on the corner of the next block," Janet returned. "They stock a range of spectacular artwork from professional photographers all over the State. Let's have a sticky beak and see if anything tickles your fancy."

Upon entering the gallery, Louise was particularly struck by a scene depicting a bright red cliff face, rippling white sand and emerald blue water typical of the Dampier Peninsula. The foreground showed clumps of tussock among boulders and behind that, the contrasting colours of the beachscape. Whitewater within the shore break almost appeared to be moving.

Suspended from the ceiling at the back of the room, hung another large photograph of the same dimensions. It was a Cable Beach scene in Broome. Rippling wind-blown dunes in the foreground, cream cliff faces and a darkening sky at the end of the day was just as Louise had remembered it. The tips of the dunes were highlighted by the setting sun. The two contrasting photos were perfect for her hallway space. Falling in love with them both, Louise arranged for the gallery owner to pack and ship the pieces to Narrabeen.

Leaving the metropolitan area by mid-afternoon, Louise took in her surroundings. Not much had changed in recent times, except for the addition of numerous al fresco establishments which added a great vibe to the old historical precinct. Some new housing developments had also popped up, mostly along the coastline, thanks to the West Australia mining boom. Perth was certainly a city on the move.

That evening after a lovely lamb roast, Louise cleared her throat and gazed at Janet. "You're going to the Crown Towers for dinner tomorrow night with your amazing husband," she announced. "All expenses paid. I'm staying here to babysit Craig while you two enjoy a well-earned night off. And I've organised a limousine, so you don't have to drive. I want to show my gratitude not only for a wonderful holiday but also everything you contribute towards the business. I owe you a lot."

Unbeknown to Janet, for the past few days Louise and Ken had been secretly making these arrangements for the final night of her stay. At first Ken adamantly declined Louise's overly kind offer but she persisted until he was forced to yield.

Janet shrieked with delight as she gazed at Louise. "Really? Are you kidding? Her attention then swiftly turned to Ken. "I can't believe you didn't tell me about this!"

Louise reached across the table and placed her hand on Janet's forearm. "He swore to secrecy because I begged him to. I really wanted it to be a surprise and he promised not to blab. Besides, it was hard enough twisting his arm to agree to it, let alone pass it by you as well," she laughed.

"Yes...well I can see why," Janet responded. "It's the Crown Plaza! I can only imagine how expensive that is. We would have been happy to go to any restaurant."

"I know," Louise smiled.

"And it's so up-market. What would I wear? Ken has a nice suit but I don't own anything you'd consider to be formal."

Louise looked at Ken and added, "We knew you'd say that." He gently nodded and relaxed back into his chair. "So tomorrow you and I are going shopping to buy you a new outfit."

"I don't quite know what to say Louise," Janet replied, shaking her head. "The words 'thank you' hardly cut the mustard. I'm so excited."

"Terrific," she smiled. "Then let's get an early night because you'll need your beauty sleep Mrs Wilson."

Browsing through 'La Plage', Janet's favourite fashion boutique in the city, she selected three black evening dresses to try on. All of them were stunning but she was mindful of the fact that she'd like to be able to wear it again on special occasions, so nothing too formal. That eliminated two of them immediately. More than happy with her choice of a simple chiffon over silk slip dress, Louise then found some strappy black heels that completed the look perfectly. After much hunting through the storeroom at the back of the shop, the sales assistant returned and said, "It's your lucky day. I did find a size 7 and it's the last pair."

Louise paid for the items then they had a light lunch at 'The Stanley' before taking Craig home for a nap.

Later that afternoon, Louise discretely handed Ken her credit card and said, "I've already paid for the limo so you need only pay at the restaurant after dinner. And please don't scrimp on your orders.

Have entrée, main, dessert, wine…whatever you like." She knew that the menu wouldn't display any prices, therefore her friends would be guided by their choices, not the cost. And that's exactly the way Louise wanted it.

At 6pm on the dot, a black stretch limousine drew up at the front gate. Janet felt like a queen as her husband escorted her to the vehicle. Louise was holding Craig on her hip while she waved them off at the door.

Knowing that the baby would only be awake for another hour at best, Louise wanted to enjoy every moment with him. After placing Craig in the Jolly Jumper she asked, "What would you like to do little man? We could play a game of Monopoly or perhaps Scrabble?" she joked as he bounced up and down. "Yes, you're right. I'll probably get the seven-letter word way before you. I tell you what…if you're happy here for a while, you can watch me make a toasted ham and cheese sandwich."

Before entering the kitchen, Louise turned on the record player. Craig's favourite album, which she had heard numerous times during her stay, was Patsy Biscoe's Children's Songs. While she prepared her toastie, Louise found herself singing along to the music, much to the baby's amusement.

Within fifteen minutes, she could see that Craig was beginning to tire so she turned off the record, placed him in his bouncer and prepared his bottle for bed. She'd often watched Janet make up his formula and knew exactly what mixture and temperature it needed to be.

Feeding him on the lounge, she then gently placed Craig against her chest and patted his back. A few small burps escaped his tummy and he rested his tiny head on her shoulder. By the time she walked into the nursery to change his nappy, he was fast asleep. That made the process much easier. Placing the baby in his cot and tucking him in, Louise then kissed his soft cheek and thought, *'You'll make a great Mum one day Louise.'*

'Cleopatra', the movie Louise was watching on television, had just finished when she heard the jingling of keys in the front door. Ken and Janet emerged absolutely beaming.

"Oh, you're still up," Janet smiled as she removed her heels.

"Yes, of course. I wanted to keep an eye on your beautiful boy until you got home," Louise smiled. "I haven't heard a peep out of him and he's been down since about 6:30pm. So…how was it?"

"Janet looked at her husband and replied, "Absolutely incredible! Luxury at its very best. The food, the service, the atmosphere… what a night."

Ken placed his arm around Janet's waist and said, "That's for sure. I know we'll be talking about it for a very long time. Thank you so much for this experience, Louise."

"I'm so glad you enjoyed it," she returned. "Now I'll leave you two alone and toddle off to bed. In the morning I can't wait to hear all about it." She hugged them both and gave them each a peck on the cheek before retiring to the granny flat.

Even though they didn't need to leave for the airport until 10am the following morning, Louise was fully packed within half an hour of rising. She then entered the kitchen to join Ken and Janet for coffee. Craig was lying on his tummy on the playmat, arms outstretched, desperately trying to pull his knees up underneath him.

"Good morning beautiful," Janet said as she smiled at her friend. "It won't be long now. Once he starts crawling, we'll have to put locks on everything."

Placing a fresh mug of coffee in front of Louise, Janet sighed and said, "Oh the coffee last night was divine. Apparently, the beans come from the Atherton Tablelands in far north Queensland. It was strong and sweet. Almost had a hazelnut flavour to it, didn't it Ken?"

Without allowing her husband time to answer she continued. "And we had these beautiful hand-made chocolates sculpted like a rose in their own tiny gold patty cases. I have to show you the carnation corsage too. All the ladies got one before they were ushered to their tables. Ours was right next to the window and it overlooked the dazzling lights of the city." Janet stopped for a short breath then added, "We had sea scallops for entrée, lightly grilled in butter with the roe still on. They just melted in our mouths and then we had Esperance lobsters. How good were they Ken?"

Again, poor Ken couldn't get a word in edgeways before his wife carried on.

"We shared a bottle of Margaret River Sauvignon Blanc then we slow-danced on the most magnificent dance floor I've ever seen," Janet grinned. "We had the whole view of the city literally at our feet."

Louise could hear the elation in Janet's voice and she was choking up with emotion as her friend spoke.

"My turn," Ken interrupted. "And we had a glass of Moet champagne in the limo on the way there…in crystal flutes and everything."

Amidst Janet's enthusiastic account of the previous evening, none of the adults realised that Craig had managed to worm his way to the kitchen. It was only when Ken felt something brush past his foot that he looked down.

"And where exactly do you think you're going Mr?" he chuckled with his hands on his hips.

The baby looked up at him and let out an ear-piercing shriek. Janet and Louise couldn't contain their laughter. Tears welling, she said to Louise, "What you did for us was incredibly considerate. And I don't just mean dinner. I'm talking about the dress, the shoes, looking after Craig…everything! It was just a magical night that we'll remember forever. Now before I start crying, Ken's making breakfast so I'm going for a shower." She then hugged her friend, kissed her husband and headed to the bathroom.

With breakfast over, Ken cleaned up the kitchen while Louise read Craig a story from one of his little picture books. The two women then left for the airport. Being Saturday, Ken offered to stay at home with Craig.

Upon check-in at the terminal, when Louise handed the hostess her ticket she smiled and announced, "Here's your boarding pass Mrs Green. It appears you'll be travelling business class today. Enjoy your flight."

As Louise made her way to the departure gate she grinned and thought to herself, *'It's not what you know, but who you know. Good on you, Murray!'*

CHAPTER TWENTY

Good to be home and feeling well rested, Louise placed a frozen pizza in the oven, threw on a load of washing and sat down to sort through the mail. Amongst a myriad of marketing flyers, a vibrant yellow envelope immediately caught her eye. It contained a card from Jillian, the front of which was a hand-painted watercolour depicting a manta ray that she'd photographed whilst snorkelling on Lady Elliott Island some years ago.

With dinner done, she was just about to call Jill when the phone rang. "Hi Lou, Peter tells me you had a lovely time in Perth," Martha commented.

"Oh yes, I did, thank you," Louise smiled. "The city's booming. Changed quite a bit. I caught up with some old friends and met the manager over there. We're going to expand our operations to align with the business here. The Wilsons were fabulous hosts and baby Craig is just a delight. I enjoyed every moment of it."

Martha deliberately cleared her throat and added, "I heard on the grapevine that you had a dinner date with a mystery man."

Louise could hear the smile in her friend's voice. "That's true… and I have you and Peter to thank for that," she replied. "Murray introduced himself on the flight over. He kindly upgraded my seats, both ways. I certainly enjoyed having dinner with him. It was all very unexpected."

"Apparently he was quite taken with you," Martha remarked. "Just so you know…Murray's a super guy. Peter sold him a life insurance policy years ago and they've been friends ever since." Suddenly Louise could hear caterwauling on the end of the line. "Sorry to cut you short Lou but I have to go. Skye's running a temperature and obviously its woken her up. Poor little thing, she's been miserable for a few days now. We'll catch up really soon. Bye."

Momentarily, Louise called Jillian and thanked her for the card. They swapped news and after almost an hour of conversation she asked, "Could I please commission you to paint the Dicky Beach wreck for me Jill? I'm making a gallery on one side of my hallway and you know I've always wanted to own one of your beautiful paintings."

"Of course, I'd love to do that for you!" Jillian remarked. "My obligations list is pretty lengthy at present but if you're prepared to wait a few months, I'd be honoured to do a painting for my bestie."

By 10:30pm Louise could no longer conceal her spontaneous yawning. She moseyed off to bed and while thoughts of Murray entertained her mind, the sound of drizzling rain on the corrugated roof above eventually sent her into a deep sleep.

The following morning brought a brisk change in air temperature as the showers continued. Autumn was nearing its end and the winter months were slowly nipping at its heels. Louise donned her dressing gown, made herself a cup of coffee and started scrolling her email inbox. As requested, Katherine had sent through Beth Phillips' contact details.

'This is your last week off, so use your time wisely,' Louise said to herself as she began to prepare a 'to do' list for the week ahead. *'Call Beth today, that's first priority!'*. From there she noted researching her employment agency concept and working on a financial and feasibility assessment for its implementation; booking her car in for a service; paying the electricity and phone bills; organising another delivery of mulch for the gardens…and that was just for starters.

Beth was extremely happy to hear from Louise. After much discussion, the women concluded that Beth would take over two of the day classes, plus three night classes each week. This would free Louise up to establish the employment agency aspect of the business. They agreed that her employment would commence in week 4 of Term 2.

Tuesday was yet another miserable day. After hauling her golf clubs from a cupboard in the garage, she cleaned the cobweb-covered bag and removed the contents of its pockets. Nothing but a few old score cards from Rabaul and some old balls and tees. The clubs themselves had been cleaned before they were shipped to

Australia but the grips had badly perished.

Mid-morning she drove to Cromer Golf Club which was located adjacent to the Narrabeen Lagoon, applied for membership and dropped her clubs into the Pro Shop for grip replacements. "Thanks to the weather, it's pretty slow here today," the manager remarked. "I'll have them ready by this afternoon if you want to come back and get them today."

As Louise was already out and about it allowed her time to drop into the office and collect a few things, do some much-needed grocery shopping and refuel her car. "Suits me to a tee," she replied, smiling at her intentional pun.

The manager quickly acknowledged her wit and they exchanged some friendly conversation before she exited the shop. Standing in the undercover area out the front of the Golf Club, waiting for a torrential downpour to pass, a man came running in from the carpark. He was drenched by the time he stopped and looked up at Louise.

"Oh my gosh…what are the chances? This is a lovely coincidence I must say," Murray puffed as he wiped the excess water from his face. "I intended to call you tonight."

Louise's heart skipped a beat. She was equally surprised. "I had no idea you were in Sydney," she smiled. "You poor thing, you're soaking wet. What are you doing here?"

Murray continued to shake the water from his jacket whilst saying, "I'm meeting a few friends for brunch in the bistro. This is our local club. I flew in from Darwin this morning and now I've got four days off. And you? Surely, you're not playing golf on a day like this?"

"No, no, just came down to sign-up for membership and have some grips replaced on my clubs."

"That's great news," he smiled. "Sadly, I doubt we'll be able to get a game in over the next few days, especially given the dismal forecast. But at least we're all set for next time. Would you like to join us for brunch while you're here?"

Given her extremely casual appearance and complete lack of make-up, Louise was amazed that he'd even suggest such a thing. "Very kind of you to ask Murray, though I'll have to decline. I'm heading to the office then I have to grocery shop. My fridge at home is practically empty."

"Sorry. I shouldn't have put you on the spot like that. I'm just excited to see you again," he smiled. "Did you enjoy the rest of your holiday?"

"I did, thank you. Had a great time…and my upgraded seat on the way home finished it all off very nicely."

Murray laughed. "Any time. Where are you tripping off to next?"

"Gosh…nowhere in the very near future," Louise admitted. "I want to expand the businesses before I take another break."

"Busy girl by the sound of things," Murray replied. "Hope you aren't too busy for dinner. I'd like to ask the Deans to join us…if you're prepared to risk another date with me. I was thinking perhaps Friday night? I know it'll depend on whether Martha's mother can look after Skye but if not, we can go on our own if you're brave enough."

"I'd really enjoy that, either way Murray. Thanks. And yes, I can be brave when necessary," Louise laughed. "Best get going and leave you to brunch. Just give me a call after you've spoken to the Deans and we'll go from there."

"Certainly will," he shouted as Louise made a dash for her car. Thankfully the passing deluge had abated somewhat.

While negotiating the grocery aisles, Louise's mind was hardly on food shopping. Her chance meeting with Murray and their prospective dinner plans absorbed her thoughts. She grabbed only the basic necessities and suddenly realised that she'd failed to drop by the office on the way. *'For Heaven's sake…don't forget fuel Louise,'* she reprimanded herself. *'The office can wait until tomorrow but the last thing you need is to be stranded on the side of the road in the pouring rain because you ran out of petrol!'*

Arriving home with her repaired golf clubs and shopping in tow, Louise noticed a large box under the front porch as she pulled into the driveway. A bright red and white 'Fragile' sticker immediately caught her attention. "They're here already!" she excitedly declared.

Hurriedly packing food into the fridge and freezer she then unlocked the front door and carried the box into the dining room. Fortunately, it was completely dry. There was no sign of any water damage. Like a child on Christmas morning, she removed the cardboard and styrofoam packaging to reveal the artwork she'd purchased in Fremantle. Standing back to admire them, she was absolutely delighted with her choices.

Within a few hours she'd unpacked the balance of her groceries, vacuumed and mopped the floors and spent much time deliberating where in her gallery the photographs should hang. Making her way to the garage to source a stash of picture hooks, she hastily returned to the house when the phone rang.

"Hi Louise, it's Murray. I just spoke to the Deans and Friday night works for them. I hope you like Thai cuisine? Martha said she thought you did, so I reserved a table at a little family-owned place I frequent in Manly."

"Sounds wonderful," she smiled. "I haven't had Thai in quite a while but I certainly enjoy it."

"Great," Murray responded with a slight sigh of relief. "I'm picking you up this time. What's your address?" He noted it down and added, "I'll be there at 7pm. Until then, enjoy the rest of your week and don't work too hard, will you?"

"I'll try my best Murray," Louise replied, picturing his handsome face smiling at her on the other end of the line.

● ● ● ● ●

"Sorry I'm early. Wasn't exactly sure where you lived, so I kept some extra time up my sleeve," Murray explained as Louise opened the front door.

"No need to apologise," she smiled. "Come on through. I'm almost ready."

He followed her to the living room, stopping at intervals in the hallway to admire the artwork. "Beautiful photography. North Western Australia I'm guessing?"

"Indeed. I purchased them in Fremantle last week and they arrived a few days ago. Over time I want to make a full gallery of this wall. I think the width of the hallway lends itself to that."

Murray nodded and returned, "I completely agree." As he entered the living room he added, "Gosh, Louise, the décor's wonderful.

Who was the interior decorator?"

Louise gently lifted her shoulders and proudly replied, "I did it myself. I really enjoy it."

"Well, it's a credit to you," he commented as his eyes closely perused the space and its surrounds. "Great taste, I must say."

"Thanks Murray. I'm happy with it. I'll just be a minute," Louise gestured, making her way towards the bedroom. After quickly applying her favourite Estee Lauder perfume, she grabbed her handbag and returned to him. "Ready when you are."

As they made their way towards the front door, Murray broadly smiled at the recently hung Dampier scenes then escorted Louise to his car. Only a ten-minute drive down Pittwater Road saw the couple arriving at the restaurant.

Upon entering the establishment, the host greeted Murray like a long-lost friend then directed them to a table where Martha and Peter were already seated.

"I've already taken the liberty of ordering wine," Peter told Murray as they shook hands. Meanwhile the women shared a warm hug and Martha commented that Louise looked particularly elegant.

The waiter took their orders and conversation flowed. Murray and Peter chatted between themselves while Louise told Martha about her holiday in Perth and the business expansion they were instigating.

Louise was keen to learn more about Murray so naturally her ears pricked up when he spoke about work and the interesting destinations he'd encountered. Mention of a small business enterprise that he and a fellow pilot were discussing also came to the fore. "In-between flight schedules, there's often a lot of down time," he went on to explain. "We're looking to buy and renovate a house for rental or sale...and we'd like to build a real estate portfolio from doing the same thing repeatedly."

"That's interesting," Louise remarked, sipping her sauvignon blanc. "Obviously you know that Peter and Martha renovated their old home. My ex-partner and I did that too. That's the house I'm living in now. I bought out Ross's share last year."

Their stir-fried noodles, green curries and coconut infused Mai-style pork meatballs were delivered to the table and conversation continued to centre around the potential that renovation investments provided. With time passing quickly, Martha kissed her husband on the cheek and said, "We should be getting home to relieve Mum of her babysitting duties." All agreed and by 9:30pm the couples left the restaurant and parted ways.

Whilst driving home, Louise deliberated over inviting Murray to stay for coffee. She certainly wanted to, but thought it may be improper at this very early stage in their friendship. By the time they pulled up in front of the house, she'd convinced herself otherwise.

"Would you like to come in for coffee, Murray?"

"Yes, I'd like that very much. Thanks, Louise," he smiled as he turned off the ignition.

Inside, Murray sat on a stool at the kitchen bench while Louise set about making coffee and dishing up some of her Rocky Road specialty.

"I noticed Martha calls you Lou. Which do you prefer?" he questioned cautiously.

"I don't mind either way. I'll answer to both," she grinned.

He observed her closely, admiring Louise's friendly charm and wit. They were both qualities that he found very attractive in a woman. Though she wasn't stunningly beautiful by any means, she was very easy on the eye. And Louise was different to most of Murray's past dates, none of which had lasted long term. Travelling had always made relationships difficult and he simply couldn't be bothered with anything 'problematic'. "Please tell me about yourself, Lou," he started. "What paths have your life taken up to this point?"

Speaking in her quieter tones, Louise delivered a short precis. She didn't divulge the reason for her marriage breakdown or speak ill of Ross in any way. Murray listened intently whilst they enjoyed coffee and conversation that spanned an hour or so.

"Well…it's getting late, so I'd best be off," Murray smiled as he took their mugs to the kitchen sink. "I have two trips to Adelaide and Darwin starting tomorrow afternoon but I'll be back in Sydney next Friday, so if you like, I'll call you when I fly in."

When Murray turned, Louise was right behind him. He gently placed his arms around her, urging her body forward. They locked eyes before he kissed her softly on the lips. They kissed again and their bodies immediately moulded together. Louise could feel his arousal as much as her own. Butterflies began to scatter throughout her chest.

Slowly drawing apart, Murray looked at her with a wry grin and sighed, "Okay…now I really, really should go."

Walking hand in hand to the front door, he thanked her for coffee and said, "We'll have a game of golf when I get back, promise," before making his way to the car.

• • • • •

Term 2 steamed ahead with Louise's workload increasing exponentially. Her desperately needed assistant, Beth Phillips, was finally due to commence training on Monday. Up to this point, Louise and Murray hadn't spent a great deal of time together over the course of the past five weeks but hopefully that was all about to change.

They did however manage to enjoy a few outings for dinner and the occasional game of golf. Murray had been introduced to Carl and Donna via their Friday afternoon drinks at the Surf Club and all of the friendship group agreed that he was a perfect match for Louise. His feelings for her were genuinely sincere and it was evident that the couple's relationship was starting to get serious.

Teeing off from the third hole during an early game of golf on Saturday morning, Murray asked Louise, "How do you feel about a harbour lunch cruise tomorrow? You said you'd love to see the city and its surrounds from the water, so I thought what better way to do it?"

"I'd love that Murray," she smiled. "And the weather's perfect. Might as well take full advantage before winter really kicks in."

"Fabulous. Then it's a date," he grinned, kissing her gently on the lips. "The boat departs Circular Quay at 11:30am, so I'll pick you up at say 10am? That should allow us plenty of time to find parking and purchase our tickets."

Sunday morning traffic wove its way into the city without too much fuss and Murray decided to utilise a nearby parking station that he often used for work purposes. As the couple wandered down to the Opera House, Louise was astonished by its enormous presence.

Strolling along the waterfront they encountered a barrage of overseas tourists from a passenger liner tied up at the terminal. Most of them were taking photographs of Sydney's iconic harbour sites. Nearing 'The Rocks' area, the couple noticed a major yacht race underway. Large motor cruisers and smaller watercraft buzzed around dodging one another while the legendary harbour ferries carried out their busy routine schedules.

With tickets purchased Murray and Louise boarded the boat and settled into seats that provided a great vantage point for the excursion. Once all passengers were aboard, the cruise commenced with complete commentary explaining visual landmarks and their associated history. Luxurious homes belonging to famous identities were also pointed out as the well-appointed launch motored in and out of the many arms of the city's waterway.

Murray ordered a bottle of Leeuwin Wineries sauvignon blanc from West Australia, which Louise highly recommended. An hour or so into the cruise, waitstaff distributed menus and the couple chose an irresistible seafood platter for two. Sydney rock oysters, muscles, crab, swordfish, Moreton Bay bugs and fresh tiger prawns were presented in due course, along with finger bowls and large cloth serviettes. It was an ocean feast to behold…and every bit as scrumptious as it looked.

Returning to Circular Quay around 4:30pm, the couple disembarked and as Murray and Louise made their way down the jetty he said, "I've arranged a pass for us at Qantas Headquarters. It's on the top floor of that tall blue building." He pointed out the structure and added, "There's a cafe and bar up there. I thought we could grab a coffee and watch the lights come on around the city. It's a magnificent sight."

"Well…you're just full of surprises Murray Corbet," Louise smiled up at him. "How could I possibly resist?"

Hand in hand they strolled the foreshore and after making their way up Hunter Street to Chifley Square, entered the modern building and took the elevator to the twelfth floor. Choosing a lounge next to the sweeping curtain wall of greenish-tinged glass, a waitress promptly appeared to take their order for coffee and lamingtons.

Outside the pink autumn sunset shimmered on the harbour and its surrounding structures while lights in the city began to sporadically glow. One cruise ship was lit up in all its spectacular glory as it slowly motored east towards 'The Heads'.

Chatting for well over an hour as darkness engulfed the last of the daylight, Louise remarked, "This is simply stunning Murray. Thank you for such a memorable day."

He smiled and returned, "It was my absolute pleasure, Lou. Great company with an amazing woman and a fabulous day out… what else could a man ask for?"

"Well, I suppose we should get going," she blushed. "I have an early start tomorrow. Beth's meeting me at the office an hour before class commences."

Driving back to Narrabeen, the couple discussed Louise's plans for her new assistant. The induction process would consist of a week's teacher training alongside her mentor, followed by a debrief after the students had departed each day. This would allow Louise ample time to answer any questions that Beth may have and allow her to properly prepare for the next day. The procedure would continue until her assistant felt comfortable and confident enough to teach alone.

Pulling up in the driveway, Murray placed his hand on Louise's thigh and beamed a smile at her. "I hope all goes well tomorrow. I'll call you when I get back from Cairns on Wednesday." He then leant over and passionately kissed her.

Within moments, Louise could feel the heat in her loins. "You're a tender, gentle man…and a gentleman, Murray. I'm so grateful that our paths crossed."

He sensed her arousal. Looking seriously deep into her eyes, he cradled her face in his hands and admitted, "My feelings for you are so strong…I don't know how much longer I can contain myself." Again, he laid the sweetest kisses on her lips.

"I can't believe I'm saying this right now…but would you like to come inside for a while?" she nervously asked.

"Would I ever?" he returned promptly. Within seconds he

hastened to the passenger side of the vehicle and opened Louise's door.

As she stepped out of the car and retrieved the house keys from her handbag, Murray held out his hand and she passed them to him. Unlocking the front door and allowing her past, he then closed and locked it behind them.

Louise immediately excused herself and went to the bathroom while he sat patiently at the kitchen counter. She emerged a few minutes later and walking up behind him, placed her arms around his waist. "I have to admit, I'm very nervous Murray. I've never slept with anyone but Ross, so I hope you'll forgive my inexperience."

Turning his head towards her, Murray rose from the chair, turned his body and pulled Louise tightly into his chest. "I have a few butterflies myself," he confessed. "Been a while for me too… but that's okay, we'll take it slowly. This isn't just a tryst, Lou. I've never felt this way about anyone before. I guess that's why I'm a bit quivery."

Murray's admission was the final encouragement Louise needed. Releasing herself from his arms she clenched his hand in her own and wordlessly led him down the hallway to the bedroom. Their kisses were sweet to begin with, but urgency lay festering just beneath the surface. As he gently held her from him, their eyes met, aflame with simmering passion. His hands crept down the sides of her body, brushing her breasts, causing Louise to catch her breath.

Kicking off their shoes, she found herself again enfolded in his arms as he slipped her dress straps from each shoulder. She then unclipped her bra and removed it, revealing her soft, supple breasts. Reaching out she began to undo the buttons on Murray's shirt. He took her already-hard right nipple into this mouth and with a moan gently fondled the other nipple between his thumb and forefinger. Louise then pulled his shirt out of his trousers as he eased her dress down over her hips.

"You're so beautiful," his husky voice remarked. Overwhelmed with desire, leading her towards the bed, he pulled back the bed cover and eased her body down onto the crisp white sheets. Taking off his trousers, socks and underwear, he then removed Louise's silk lace nickers.

She watched his every move with deep anticipation before he lowered himself onto the bed beside her. Their passionate kisses intensified as Murray took his lips to her breasts, one hand sliding down her stomach to the thick, dark mound below. Creeping his fingers even further, he discovered her wet desire.

Almost at bursting point, Louise whispered, "Please take me now, Murray. I can't wait any longer."

Lifting his head, he gazed at her whilst manoeuvring himself into a kneeling position between her thighs. For a brief moment he scanned her body in wonderment then Louise raised her hips to meet him. As he entered her, they both gasped with sheer pleasure. Murray was almost powerless to refrain from ejaculating but he was determined for them to climax together. Fortunately, the wait was short-lived.

Louise moaned as her body trembled and pulsed through the orgasm. She'd never experienced such tingling euphoria in her life. It was pure rapture.

Finally, Murray moved his body to lay beside her. While their breathing slowed, he raised himself on one elbow and searched Louise's smiling face. After tenderly running his fingers through her hair, he kissed her on the lips and said, "Well...you were certainly worth every moment of the wait."

She softly placed her hand on his face and replied, "I'm glad. I thought this time with you would never come...and it was truly incredible!"

CHAPTER TWENTY-ONE

Concealing her private affairs had almost become second nature for Louise. A defence mechanism of sorts which allowed her to cope in an abusive marriage, without the added scrutiny of external factors. But with Murray Corbet now in her life, she was happier than she'd ever been before. It was time to shed her old skin and celebrate their relationship.

"Hi Jules, it's Lou. Is this a good time to chat?" she asked, twirling the telephone cord around her index finger.

"Sure is," Julie smiled. "The kids are in bed. Mark is absolutely exhausted. He had his first Athletics Carnival today and managed to win the 100-metre sprint for his age group. It was the funniest thing Lou…when the sports master presented him with the first-place gold ribbon, he just cried. He couldn't believe he'd won."

"Aww…that's so cute. Please tell him I said congratulations and give him a big kiss from me. And how have you been?"

"Well, truth be told, I'm on a bit of a health kick at the moment," Julie admitted. "With the shifts I've been allocated for the past month, I'm not eating anywhere near as well as I should…and I've put on half a kilo. So, I've just started jogging whenever I can and trying to take a couple of yoga classes each week. I'm even having a green tea right now, as we speak."

"Good for you Sis. Just don't overdo it. I know what you're like…once you commit yourself to something, there's no stopping you."

"Oh, that's rich, coming from one of the most motivated women I know," Julie laughed. "So, what's going on in your world? Have you met any scrumptious eligible bachelors yet?"

Louise swallowed and replied, "In fact…yes, I have. That's why I'm calling you. I should have told you a while ago."

There was a moment's silence before Julie blurted, "Okay, spill it. Who is he? What does he do for a living? How did you meet? When? How old is he? Is it serious?"

"Enough with the Spanish Inquisition," Louise jested. "His name's Murray Corbet and he's a Qantas pilot."

"Wow!" Julie returned, sipping her tea. "I think I need a wine for this…but I'll refrain. So? Keep going."

Twenty minutes later Julie had been comprehensively briefed on the new man in her sister's life, including the fact that they were sleeping together. "I'm so happy for you Louise, seriously," she smiled whilst placing her hand on her chest. "You deserve nothing but the best and Murray sounds like a true keeper."

"He is an incredible guy but you know what they say…once bitten, twice shy. I'm just trying to remain objective and not get too carried away in the romance of it all. I know he seems perfect but everyone has their imperfections. I just haven't found any yet."

"And maybe you never will," Julie suggested. "It's true, he probably isn't perfect…but nonetheless, he sounds pretty close. Hey…speaking of 'Mr Right'…John has to fly to Sydney for a 3-day medical conference at the end of next month. It's a symposium for nuclear medicine trials and I think it's at the Western Sydney University. Do you know where that is? He found a locum to stand in for the time he's away, so our Medical Director gave him the green light to attend.

"Excellent. Yes, I know exactly where it is. It's in Martin Place, practically the centre of the city. He's more than welcome to stay with me if he needs to arrange accommodation. I'd love to spend some time with him."

"That's very generous of you Sis. We're not sure about all the details yet…but as soon as we receive the schedule next week, I'll be able to give you a bit more info.

• • • • •

Slowly and sensuously Murray seduced Louise into a sublime frenzy. She and Ross had never participated in oral sex, so this was an entirely new experience for her. The exhilaration of the newfound ecstasy left her breathless.

Murray lifted his head from her, wriggled his body up the bed and sunk his head into the pillow beside Louise. She was absolutely sated. "I know this is a very personal question," he started "…but I was wondering if you've had oral sex before?"

"No, I haven't Murray…and I've never felt so alive. Thank you for introducing me to such a beautiful, almost out-of-body experience. It was unbelievable."

He softly kissed her and said, "I really want us to be relaxed and enjoy one another. You're the light in my life Lou…and I promise to try and please you any way I can."

Louise's eyelids grew heavy and though she fought to maintain her focus on Murray, she was asleep within seconds. He pulled up the bed cover and gently tucked it around her neck and shoulders, ensuring that she'd remain warm during the cold night. After laying his lips gently on her cheek, he smiled, placed his arm across her stomach and closed his weary eyes.

Both sitting back against their pillows the following morning after enjoying a hot, freshly brewed coffee, Louise smiled at Murray and said, "We'd better hit the shower. Gordon's coming over in about an hour, isn't he?"

"Yeah, he said around 10am. That gives us plenty of time…so… can I propose to have you for Sunday breakfast?" Murray snickered, lifted the bed sheet and kissed her belly button."

"By all means Mr Corbet," Louise replied in a sexy voice as she made her way to the ensuite. "Meet me in the shower in five minutes."

Only a few weeks ago, Murray and his pilot business partner Gordon Perry purchased their first old 60's residence just out of Narrabeen. It had remained empty for a few months and the men managed to obtain the house for a very fair price. The ocean views were great and they knew that if they added another floor, they'd be even more spectacular. A thirty-day pending contract was conditional upon the usual inspections which included the ability of the current foundations to withstand a second storey.

Murray had already asked Louise if she'd consider decorating the place when it was finished. She agreed that while Beth was working out to be a perfect fit for her business, it was certainly a possibility…depending of course on the timing of things, as starting up the recruitment agency was still a major priority.

Gordon had heard about the amazing work Louise did on her own renovation and asked Murray if he could possibly see the house. Naturally Louise was only too happy to oblige and suggested that he come over to view some photos from the renovation process. Besides, being Murray's new business partner, Louise was very eager to meet him.

Whilst preparing a plate of Danish pastries purchased from the local bakery, Louise heard a knock on the front door. It was Gordon, arriving bang on time.

As Murray greeted him, Gordon looked his friend up and down and said, "It's a bit nippy for a t-shirt and shorts Muzz? I feel like I'm catching a cold just looking at you."

"It's only a few days shy of Spring mate," he returned. "Besides, this place is well insulated. Come on through and meet Louise."

Upon entering the kitchen Murray announced, "Lou, this is Gordon Perry. Gordon…meet my girlfriend, Louise."

Gordon wasn't quite as tall as Murray, but he looked to be rather fit. His piercing blue eyes were unmissable. Short auburn hair framed his clean-shaven round face and as he reached out to shake Louise's hand, she liked him immediately. "Charmed," he smiled. "I've heard a lot about you…all good, of course."

As he gazed at the dining and lounge room, very much liking what he saw, Louise said, "Please, feel free to look around. Excuse the state of the master bedroom, I've not had time to make the bed this morning."

He looked at the pastries and saw that Louise was making coffee. Upon turning he said to Murray, "Well I can see Louise is busy…so why didn't you make the bed Muzz? Any good boyfriend would do that for his lady."

"In my defence," Murray started, "I did offer…but apparently it's linen washing day."

"Ah, yes. Any excuse will do." Gordon then quickly turned and jokingly winked at Louise before making his way into the lounge room. The décor was practical but it also had great appeal. He liked the bright colour touches and after surveying each space, the serene ambiance of the entire home impressed him.

Meanwhile, Louise retrieved the renovation photo album from her office and placed it on the kitchen bench. Whilst Murray flipped through the 'before' and 'after' snaps, Gordon returned to join him.

"Do you take milk and sugar in your coffee, Gordon?" Louise asked.

Smiling, he answered, "A dash of milk and no sugar, thank you."

Once Louise was seated with the men, Gordon began his enquiries regarding the project that she and her husband had undertaken. "Murray tells me that you might possibly be interested in lending us a hand with the interior decorating side of our business. I know you're not a 'qualified' designer but…judging from what I see here, you hardly need to be. This place is fabulous and I'm so pleased that you live up to the accolades Muzz showers on you. I'm also well aware that you have your own computer business, so do you think you could find the time to work with us? And given your experience, we'd love your input on some of the renovation aspects as well."

Louise sipped her coffee and replied, "Actually Gordon, I'd love to sink my teeth into another refurb. Currently I'm taking on more staff and expanding the business, which I anticipate will take another six months or so…but I have a few people in mind who'd be capable of managing the new enterprise. By the time you're at the fit-out stage of your project, I may well be in a position to assist."

Gordon smiled and said, "That would be terrific. Do you mind if I pinch an apple and cinnamon scroll?"

"Please do, mate," Murray replied. "In fact, take as many as you like. There's no way Louise and I can eat them all on our own."

"If I can help in any other way, just let me know," Louise offered. "I was more than happy with the tradies we employed…so I can pass on their names if that would be useful. I still have all material and paint colour samples on file too. They might provide you with a bit of inspiration."

The two men grinned at each other and 'high-fived' before Gordon turned to Louise and said, "That would be invaluable, thank you Louise. "And we're both very excited about the prospect of working with you. I think we'll make a great team."

After showing Gordon around the deck area and the back garden, he expressed his gratitude for Louise's hospitality as they walked him out to his vehicle. "Oh…Muzz…just when I thought I'd heard them all, someone told me a new pilot joke yesterday. What's the difference between a jet engine and a co-pilot? He didn't wait for a response from his friend before adding, "The jet engine stops whining when the plane shuts down."

They all laughed and Murray said, "That's not too bad, even for you Gordy!"

Waving him off the couple then went inside and Louise said, "Gosh Murray. What am I committing to here? I'm certainly going to need a pretty good manager to handle the employment agency."

"You're right…but I don't want you take on too much, Lou. You said that you were trying to reduce your workload to enjoy some leisure time but it feels like we're just getting busier. I know that working with you would feel like leisure time to me anyway…but that's because I only sit in a cockpit for twenty-five hours a week."

Louise looked at him knowingly and said, "Well, if I can get this recruitment thing off the ground, I can hand it over to a manager and just oversee the business dealings. Then I'd be in a position to concentrate on home décor, and that's what I love. In fact, it was only last week that I had a brainwave. Martha told me she was looking for some serious mental stimulation now that Skye's a bit older and it crossed my mind that if she was interested, we could possibly set up the marketing side of the agency from her home office. That might suit her down to the ground so I'll give it some serious consideration. If I think it's viable, I'll approach her. I have to admit, I used to be apprehensive about employing friends but it worked out so well for me in W.A."

Murray placed his arms around Louise's waist and replied, "Sounds like a sensible idea to me, my lovely…but let's not talk shop anymore today. I'll help you clean up and we'll do that load of washing because the golf course is beckoning us."

• • • • •

Wednesdays for Louise were set aside to work on solid planning for her employment agency. While Beth taught the daytime class, Louise relished being in the peace and quiet of her own home office. But this privilege still had its distractions and for Louise, thoughts of Murray and their evolving relationship became the main culprit. They'd been together for six glorious months now.

Staring out the window into her well-established garden, she smiled upon noticing tiny flower buds appearing all over the Jasmine vine. Even the native Gardenia trees were showing hints of the delicate lemon-scented blooms to come.

'I think I'm in love,' she uttered aloud, then quickly cupped her hand across her mouth. On hearing those words, suddenly the magnitude of their meaning warmed her heart. The voice in her head replied, *'What do you mean 'think'? You know damn well you love him. Just admit it!'*

At that very moment she heard the postman's motorbike pull up at her letterbox. Getting little work accomplished anyway, she decided to go outside and collect it. A few general letters and a parcel delivery collection notice from the post office. *'That looks interesting,'* she thought. *'I need to grab some milk and cream, so I might run down and pick it up now.'*

When the postmaster took the slip from Louise, he retreated to the back storeroom and returned with a long, cylindrical tube.

"Oooh…I think I know what this is," Louise excitedly smiled at him. "Thank you, sir…and please excuse me, but I have to run."

Once at home she scoured through her desk drawers and finally found a pair of scissors. Upon opening one end of the tube, she carefully retrieved the canvas and unrolled it on the dining room table. The Dicky Beach wreck painting was everything she had hoped for…and so much more. The waves looked so real that she could imagine Jill and herself body surfing in them. She was absolutely thrilled with it.

That evening she phoned her friend to sincerely thank her and request an invoice, as it had been excluded from the package. Jill advised that after many years of friendship, the painting was a gift. "Let's call it a labour of love," she concluded. "Whenever I get a chance to go down and visit my brother, you can shout me a wine."

Speaking of brothers…it was now only a week before Louise's

brother-in-law was due to set down in Sydney. John had planned to spend the Wednesday and Thursday night at an associate's apartment in Haymarket and on the Friday night he agreed to join Louise and Murray for a barbecue at her house and stay for the evening. She would then take him to the airport for departure first thing Saturday morning.

• • • • •

"You cook a pretty mean steak Murray," John smiled. "Just a shame that the beef's not quite as good as our New Zealand yearlings…but I guess I'm just a biased Kiwi."

"Yes, that you certainly are, John," Louise retorted. "And no offence intended Murray, but I think I'd have to agree with him."

In jest Murray replied, "Okay you two…I know when I'm outnumbered. But just remember you're talking about the animal, not the chef who cooked it."

"Touché my good fellow," John announced, raising his wine glass.

They all chortled at his comment and Louise was very much enjoying the banter between the two men. She held a great deal of respect for John and his fabulous sense of humour, so she suspected they'd hit it off.

John turned his attention back to Murray and said, "Flying those big kangaroos is a huge responsibility. I take my hat off to you mate."

"Thanks John, yes, there's a lot at stake but I hear you're a doctor, so our obligations are really one and the same…to preserve human lives. The only difference for me I suppose is that I also have an expensive aircraft to account for."

"True, very true," John returned, "but there's never a day I have to contemplate the possibility of losing hundreds of patients at once. And the aircraft themselves…just how expensive are we talking? It's something I've always been curious to know."

Murray sipped his wine and said, "Around 24 million, give or take."

John's eyes bulged as he blurted, "Holy mackerel! I think that could build an entire hospital.”

"I'm just waiting for a call-up to do a training course which will hopefully keep me in town for a few weeks. Qantas is due for a new fleet of aircraft and about twenty of us have been told that we'll be flying them, so we have to be briefed on all the upgrades and run a few test flights. It means a promotion and unfortunately that could lead to a transfer. Because my beautiful lady's here, obviously I'm not too happy about that prospect," Murray remarked, placing one arm around Louise and squeezing her tightly.

"And where's that transfer likely to be, Murray?" John curiously enquired.

"Probably Brisbane. They figure the single pilots are the easiest to relocate and they're currently looking at four of us to be based elsewhere. We'll also be flying offshore and that's something I haven't done for quite a while."

Although Murray had mentioned a transfer before, Louise had never really given it a second thought...until now. Hearing him discuss it with John suddenly triggered alarm bells and placed the scenario front and centre in her mind. It was indeed a real and distinct possibility.

Around 7:30pm after they'd discussed John's work at the hospital, Louise's business expansion venture and numerous political issues, Murray announced that he was leaving. "Got a 5:25am flight to Perth in the morning, so I'd best be off. It was a pleasure to meet you John and I hope we can catch up again soon. You never know, I could be flying to N.Z. by the end of the year and if so, I'll be sure to get in touch."

"Please do," John smiled, standing and shaking Murray's hand. "You're welcome any time. Please look after our girl...she means the world to us."

"She means the world to me too, so I certainly will," he replied, kissing Louise on the forehead.

After seeing Murray off at the door, Louise noticed that John had already begun cleaning up. "How about you do the dishwasher and I'll clean up the barbecue? Sound like a plan?" he queried.

"That would be terrific, thanks John, I really appreciate it. There's a scourer and some other cleaning equipment in the cupboard underneath and I've got a hot plate spray here under the sink if you need it. I'm just going to the bathroom. Won't be long."

John was hunting through the kitchen cupboard when the phone rang. Knowing that Louise was unavailable, he took the liberty of answering it on her behalf. "Good evening, Louise Greens' residence," he answered.

"Who are you?" the male voice blurted back at him.

"John Keane. I'm her brother-in-law. Is that you, Ross?"

"Yes. Is she there? Please put her on the phone."

Reluctantly, John didn't say another word and fought to bite his tongue. Placing the receiver on the hall table he slowly walked to Louise's bedroom door and called out, "Louise, sorry to bother you, but Ross is on the phone."

"Really?" she questioned as her heart rate increased. "What the hell does he want?"

"I didn't ask," John admitted. "What do you want me to tell him?"

"Nothing, thanks John. It could be important so I'd better grin and bear it. I'll be out in a moment."

John retreated to the lounge room and when Louise emerged, he whispered, "take some big breaths Lou."

Hesitating before taking up the receiver, she followed his advice then said, "Yes Ross."

"I was wanting to talk to you Lou, but it seems you have company."

"I have family here. What do you want to talk to me about?"

"I'm in Sydney for the weekend. Going back to Melbourne on Monday. I just wanted to see you. You know...see how you're going," he prompted.

"Ross, like I said, I have family here," Louise reiterated. "Besides, I don't want to see you, nor do I want to talk to you... unless of course, you finally want a divorce. I'm all for it...but again, I'm not footing the bill."

"Are you alright Lou?" he questioned with a skerrick of sincerity in his voice.

"What would you care?" she burst out. "Yes, I'm perfectly fine. Very busy, very happy and no one knocks me around anymore. I'm hanging up now. Don't call me again. If you have anything else to say, do it through my solicitor. You know where her office is."

Shaken, she placed the receiver back on its handset and dubiously looked at John.

"What did he want?" John could feel anger rising in the pit of his stomach.

"Just a chat apparently," Louise sighed. "He's in Sydney for the weekend, returning to Melbourne Monday…and that can't come soon enough from where I'm standing. The hide of him. Can you believe it?"

"Maybe the girlfriend's dumped him. Who knows?" John deduced. "Either way, he's nothing but trouble with a capital 'T'. You need to watch your back for a while, Lou. Does Murray know you've suffered violence at the hands of your husband?"

"No, he doesn't," she admitted. "And I have no intention of telling him unless I have to."

"Well now, I strongly suggest you do…because this isn't a secret you should keep from him."

CHAPTER TWENTY-TWO

Over the past couple of weeks Louise had found time to formulate a proposal to put forth to prospective businesses that she felt would benefit from her service. She was open to their suggested requirements and very much looking forward to any further recommendations.

Sitting at her office desk she began delving into The Yellow Pages directory. After sourcing applicable firms, Louise introduced herself by phone and enquired about correspondence with the appropriate personnel. Noting their names and email addresses in order to send out her proposals, she constructed a long list.

All the establishments she contacted that day expressed interest and asked for written information. She advised that they would receive the relevant details before the end of the week. Initially hoping for perhaps 40% of them to be receptive to the service, it appeared as though that percentage would in fact be much higher.

Between classes she continued along this track for another two days then stayed back late at the office preparing hard copy proposals for those who'd requested them, and emailing the balance. After 4pm on Friday, she sat down with Beth to debrief.

"My confidence is growing with every class I take," Beth smiled. Her response was upbeat and cheerful. "I thought that adding the evening classes might be a bit tiring but I'm actually feeling stimulated."

"That's fantastic," Louise responded, "and you're doing a great job. Listen Beth…I'm giving considerable thought to hiring someone to take over 'my' other classes. If you happen to know of anyone, we could train them up or perhaps see if any of our own students would be suitable for the position? I thought that if we could find another teacher, it would free us both up for a day off here and there…or if either of us got sick or wanted to take a holiday, we'd have a substitute teacher. Anyway, I've kept you long enough. Just have a think about it. Enjoy your weekend. Any plans?"

"We're off to the Hunter Valley for our wine tasting feast," Beth replied.

"Oh yes, that's right," Louise recalled. "Where are you staying?"

"At the Pokolbin Vineyard. It's supposed to be lovely and we can sample as much as we like without having to worry about driving anywhere."

Louise nodded and said, "I like the sound of that. Well…have a wonderful time. Did you get your sofa delivered yesterday?"

"Sure did. It's a perfect fit for the townhouse and honestly, anything's better than our clunky old bug-infested lounge suite! You could certainly do with some relaxation Louise. You've had such a huge week. Is Murray home?"

"No, he's away this weekend but he'll be back on Tuesday. Gives me time to tie up a few things and I really need to get into the garden and do some fertilising. I missed the start of Spring so the least I can do is prepare them for the hot summer ahead."

• • • • •

Within a month, after attending numerous meetings involving their owners or department managers, Louise had received a great response to the service on offer. By the end of this period, she'd contracted more than forty committed clients including some current and former students. Now the business officially had another notch under its belt.

Janet called from Perth and advised her boss, "The employment agency framework is in place over here and it's up and running… but obviously still a work in progress. We're continuing to pursue more clients as students graduate. The night classes are set to commence next semester, so it's all systems go. Busy, busy, busy! Naturally we envisage that all students seeking work will be placed into positions."

"That's great news, Janet. Thank you for bringing me up to speed," Louise acknowledged. "Between yourself and Katherine, you've both worked so hard to bring this to fruition and I sincerely appreciate everything you do. Before the end of the year, I intend to reassess your salaries and rest assured, you'll both be receiving a handsome Christmas bonus."

Knowing that she desperately wanted to enrol for the interior decorating course at night school, Louise decided it was time to approach Martha. Would she possibly be interested in working from home to arrange graduate student interviews and employment opportunities, as well as attempting to secure new clients? Louise knew that her friend was the perfect candidate for the job, so there was certainly no harm in asking.

She pre-arranged a visit to Martha's house on Saturday afternoon while Skye was having her nap. Over coffee, Louise told Martha exactly what she proposed. In the beginning it would require a half-day in the office, maybe more, until such times as the agency was firmly established.

Much to Louise's delight, Martha was absolutely thrilled at the prospect and could hardly wait to tell her husband. Peter knew full-well that 'baby talk' was hardly the mental stimulation that Martha craved. This would be the perfect solution for her.

"Not only is it wonderful for me," Martha admitted to Louise, "it's great for Skye as well. I can arrange childcare for when I'm at the office and this gives her the interaction that she really needs with other children her own age. I'm over the moon with your offer Lou, when can I start?"

Her enthusiasm pleased Louise no end and she replied, "Any time you like. The more clients we have, the better. We'll start with some of our own students who are graduating at the end of the term because they've already enlisted in the service. Perhaps after that, we can expand to clients who require trades people...which would mean enlisting trade companies. Honestly Martha...who knows where this could go? Today's Wednesday, so I'm happy if you even want to come in on Monday for a few hours? We could go through the finer details and I can show you what I've achieved to date. That way you can take over from me whenever you feel comfortable to do so."

Louise then went on to inform Martha of her intention to do some home decorating for Murray and Gordon's house, as well as commence a course in interior design.

"There's no doubt about you, Lou. You don't sit still for long. Murray's such a good guy and you two really deserve each other. And a huge 'thank you' for offering me this opportunity. It means the world."

Hugging Martha she replied, "You're most welcome my dear friend…and I couldn't agree more, Murray's a thoroughly decent gentleman."

That weekend while Murray was working, Louise visited a few Art Union homes and display villages, noting decor ideas that appealed to her. She also completed an enrolment application for the interior design course of her choice, due to commence in Term 1. Being mid-October already, Louise knew this would be ample time for Martha to settle in. The evening class would be held at the local high school and Louise was excited about applying herself to something completely different.

Curled up in bed with a book on Sunday evening, she was contemplating an early night when the phone rang beside her.

"How are you darling?" Murray asked. "I hope I didn't wake you. I'm still in Cairns and we have about twenty minutes before our last flight to Townsville…so I really wanted to hear your voice. I miss you."

Smiling, Louise answered, "Me too. I'm looking really forward to you coming home Murray. I got your message on Thursday. Great to see you'll be commencing your course later next week."

"Yes, I think we're supposed to kick off on Thursday or Friday, not sure which yet. Once we start, I've been told we'll be grounded for about six weeks of simulator work and loads of study. I'll be glad when that's over. These courses are pretty intense but the end result will be well worth the effort. During that time Gordon will have to cope with the renovation on his own I suppose…but he's more than capable, so I don't have any problem with that. How has your week been?"

Louise was pleased to inform him that Martha was now onboard and everything seemed to be fitting together nicely. "Beth's training up a former graduate student, Grace, to be an assistant teacher…so that will really free up my time to work with you and Gordon."

"That's terrific," Murray returned. "Sounds like you've had a very full week indeed. Mine's been pretty much the usual…sick of sleeping in hotel rooms and eating out. On Wednesday we flew two return flights from Sydney to Melbourne…then Cairns and back to Townsville overnight. Down to Brisbane this morning then Sydney and back up here to Cairns. Sydney to Perth tomorrow, stay overnight and back Tuesday morning via Melbourne."

"I'm amazed that you even know what city you're in half the time," Louise confessed. "It must be very confusing on such a tight schedule."

"It can be," Murray admitted, "but honestly Lou, you get used to it."

"Listen, before you go…I was wondering if you've made any plans for Wednesday yet?" Louise questioned him. "I'd love to see the house you're buying. Is there access to get inside before settlement?"

"Probably not…but I can certainly show you around the outside and we can attempt to peer through its filthy windows. I'd love for you to see it, Lou. More than happy to take you over whenever you want to go. I'll call you again on Tuesday night when I'm back in Sydney and we'll take it from there. Goodnight my darling. Sweet dreams…I'll be thinking of you as I shoot across the night sky.

• • • • •

Wednesday morning at 9am Murray phoned Louise before leaving his unit. "I should have thought to mention this on the phone last night but I was tired and it completely slipped my mind. Do you have any other plans for today? After I show you the house, I'd love for us to take a walk on the beach and maybe grab some fish and chips for lunch. The weather forecast is superb. What do you say… can I twist your arm?"

"No need," Louise replied. "I'm absolutely up for that. We haven't strolled the foreshore together in quite a while and I could certainly do with some fresh, salty sea air in my lungs. There's nothing pressing that I have to attend to until later in the afternoon, so why not?"

"I apologise for the short notice Lou…but that's exactly what I was hoping you'd say," Murray smiled. "Do you want me to pick you up a little bit later now?

"10am is still fine with me Murray, I'm basically ready to go. Just need to hang out a load of washing and do a bit of ironing I've been putting off."

Murray arrived at Louise's house right on time and after knocking on the front door, the couple couldn't wait to throw their arms around one another. He picked Louise up off her feet and slowly turned complete circle as they shared a passionate kiss. "I wish I could hold you every day," he smiled.

Whispering in his ear Louise replied, "In my dreams, you do."

Locking the front door, Murray then escorted Louise to the passenger side of the car and opened the door for her. Once seated himself, he looked in the rear vision mirror and said, "Who owns the black sedan parked across the road?"

"I'm not sure," Louise returned. "Harry must have visitors staying with him."

Seven minutes after pulling out of the driveway, Murray and Louise drew up in front of a half-brick, half-timber low set dwelling. It was situated at the end of a quiet cul-de-sac facing east and west. What had once been a garden was now overgrown with vines and weeds.

"The roof tiles can come off," Murray remarked as he looked up at the apex, "and after sleeping at your place, I definitely want to keep hearing the sound of raindrops on a metal roof of some sort. Gordon received the engineer's assessment report on Tuesday and it confirmed that the slab and cavity brick walls will withstand another floor."

Louise smiled and said, "That's great news," whilst taking his hand and resting it gently in her own.

"We're taking some rough plans to a draftsman next week," Murray continued. "We're hoping to put the living area and kitchen upstairs and build a large deck on the north and eastern side to capture the view and the northern sunshine. If we can weather-proof it, there's plenty of room for a children's play area underneath. Bedrooms and laundry will be downstairs. As you can see, there's no undercover parking…so on the southern side we'll build a double garage. On top of that we'll have the master bedroom, ensuite and walk-in robe which connects to the upstairs living area. I think it'll end up being quite a large home. There's an old path near the boundary fence, so do you want to hop out and have a look around?"

"Absolutely," Louise returned. "Try keeping me here."

Vision to the interior through any of the windows was virtually impossible but at least Louise could get a feel for the house. She was particularly impressed by the block's size and generous backyard.

"We're thinking timber-framed windows and bi-fold doors onto the deck," Murray commented as they perused the rear of the dwelling. "Obviously we'd like to talk to you about that…and a few other things before we firm up the plans. Gordon was also talking about replacing the downstairs timber exterior with cavity brick, like the rest of it."

Louise nodded and replied, "I totally agree. The brickwork will bring the whole house up-to-date and give it a punchy street appeal too."

Placing his arm around Louise's waist, Murray continued sharing his thoughts on the renovation. "We'll rip out some of the interior walls that aren't weight bearing to make a couple of the downstairs bedrooms a bit larger and we can add a second bathroom as well. Perhaps a couple of feature walls, the rest plasterboard, renew all the wiring and add extra power points. So…what do you think of the place?"

"There's obviously a lot of work to be done Murray," Louise admitted, "but it will be incredible when it's finished. Great location, close to the school and everything that Narrabeen has to offer. You both stand to make a very nice profit if you're wise with your spending."

"True…and that's where your renovation advice and expertise will be invaluable to us Lou. Now how about we hit the beach? Make the most of this glorious morning?"

Strolling the foreshore hand in hand from the Narrabeen Beach barbecue area, south to Collaroy Surf Club and back, the couple discussed Murray's upcoming course. Louise was very curious to know exactly what it entailed. The aviation industry had always fascinated her and she was keen to learn about every aspect of it.

After an hour of withstanding the sun's vibrant rays, the couple welcomed the air-conditioned interior of the surf club. Here they quenched their thirst with a chilled lemon squash and enjoyed some freshly battered snapper with shoestring fries.

"Before I drop you home, would you like to stop by my unit and have a look at these rough house plans before we take them to the draftsman? We'd really appreciate it if you could cast your eye over them first, Lou," Murray queried.

"Yes, happy to. Beth's calling me at 3:30pm, so I don't need to be home before then."

Inside Murray's ultra-modern apartment, the dining room table was covered in renovation sketches of every description. "Please excuse the mess," he remarked. "I was having a quick look through everything and making some minor adjustments when I got home yesterday afternoon. I won't have time to work on them after tomorrow and Gordon's keen for my take on it."

"No problem at all," Louise returned. "Where there's mess… there's progress." Still standing, she began to sift through the drawings one by one.

Murray leaned over the table beside her and pointed out a few key features that could perhaps impact building costs. Within two minutes of discussion, he turned to Louise and said, "I have to make love to you, Lou. Right here. Right now. I can't keep my hands off you a second longer."

Turning to kiss her, Louise met his lips with insatiable desire. In a whirlwind the couple's clothing was strewn across the floor and they found their naked bodies entwined on the lounge. An intense, almost primitive love-making session was over almost as quickly as it had begun. Both Murray and Louise were totally satisfied. Rolling over onto their sides to snuggle together, Louise exhaled and whispered, "Wow! That was explosive."

"Yes, I know," Murray admitted. "Sorry about that Lou. I just couldn't resist."

"Don't apologise. I absolutely loved every second of it. Gee whiz…I didn't even know I had that animal instinct in me! Thank you, my darling. You've opened my eyes to a whole new world."

After spooning on the lounge for quite some time, the couple finally rose and dressed themselves. Murray made coffee for them both while Louise returned to perusing the plans at the dining table. After much deliberation three of the drawings were revised. Louise was pleased that she could help and Murray sincerely appreciated her input and opinions.

Pulling up at Louise's house, they noticed the black sedan was gone. "Okay then, I'll see you in a few days for drinks on the deck. Looking very forward to it," Murray smiled. "I'll grab the pizzas on my way over. Extra mushrooms and easy on the capsicum, right?"

"You've got it," she smiled back at him. "Some garlic bread would be great too."

• • • • •

"If I didn't know better, I'd think you were an accomplished barman, not an experienced pilot," Louise remarked in the kitchen as she kissed Murray on the cheek.

"Ah...but I'm both," he replied. "When I was training for my pilot's license, I worked part-time in a Kings Cross bar to pay the bills."

"Is that so?" Louise remarked, accepting the tumbler of gin and tonic that he'd prepared for her.

Outside on the deck, the sun had just sunk beyond the horizon. Silhouetted gum trees starkly contrasted against their pastel-coloured backdrop. "What a beautiful view," Murray commented. "It's so serene. Here's to us, lovely lady," he added as they clinked their glasses together.

"I'll drink to that," Louise smiled. After taking a sip of the chilled alcoholic beverage she said, "A barman, hey? I'd love to hear the whole 'Murray Corbet story'...but at least some of the chapters would be great for now. You know quite a bit about me but I've come to realise that I know very little about your life. Thus far I'm aware that your brother Ryan is two years younger than yourself, lives in Melbourne with his wife, Paula. He's a pharmacist and she's a nurse...and they've been married for just over a year. But what about your parents? That's if you don't mind me asking of course?"

"Well, Dad died when Ryan and I were in our early twenties. I'm thirty-two, so that would be a good ten years ago now…and sadly Mum passed only two years after him. I wouldn't say that we were a wealthy family but certainly far more privileged than most. With only four of us, naturally we were a tight-knit group. We loved our parents dearly and their love for us was reciprocal. We couldn't have asked for a better childhood. It was always full of fun and an abundance of laughter."

Louise smiled and said, "That explains a lot about your cheerful personality and zest for life. What about things like…when's your birthday, past relationships?"

After gently swirling the ice cubes in his glass and sipping the gin, Murray replied, "January 6, five days before yours."

Very pleasantly surprised, Louise raised her eyebrows and asked, "How do you know my birth date?"

"Ah…that's secret information," he jested. "No…truth be told… when you put your driver's license on the kitchen counter the other day, I quickly had a sticky beak when you weren't looking. As far as girlfriends go…I've never lived with a woman. I did date a girl for about a year when I first joined Qantas and the few relationships I've had since were more platonic than anything you'd consider serious. What else? I have a small mortgage left on my apartment, which I'm determined to pay out by the end of February…um… what else would you like to know, Lou? I'm an open book for you, my lovely."

Clearly Murray felt comfortable engaging in their conversation so she decided to continue. "I know navy blue's your favourite colour but when it comes to entertainment and other enjoyments, what tickles your fancy?"

"You would certainly be at the top of my list," he admitted, rubbing his chin as he closely observed a blushing Louise. "I don't think anyone could tickle my fancy quite like you do. Ah…movies? Love a feel-good movie for sure. No blood and thunder. Music…I particularly like traditional Jazz, you know, the old crooners. I'm also quite taken with that Michael Buble CD you're playing now. Don't like much of the modern, noisy stuff. I never mind a dance and obviously travel's a huge enjoyment. I'd much prefer long, hot summers and shorter winters. I'm looking forward to getting overseas and seeing more of the world. I've been to New Zealand and Fiji and after Mum and Dad passed, Ryan and I took a trip to Bali. I'd really like to see Canada and Alaska in particular. New Orleans for the Jazz music. Switzerland, Spain, Portugal, France, South America, Vietnam, China...my list goes on. There are too many countries to mention. I have no real desire to see the U.K. although Southern England and Ireland could make my bucket list. Where would you like to go, Lou?"

She gently swayed her head from side to side and returned, "There's plenty of this vast country I'd still like to see...the Kimberleys, Longreach, Uluru, Darwin. I lived in Canada for a while so I saw quite a lot of it, as well as the States. New York is a city I'd love to visit again. I think New Year's Eve in the 'Big Apple' would be so much fun. Ah...the Caribbean, Hawaii, some of those lovely tropical places. I still have a Pen Pal in Sweden and when she talks about the Baltic and the Fjords, they sound fascinating. Maybe the moon? I don't really know. It's all just a dream at this stage."

Inside, while Murray was preparing their third drink, he called out, "Please come and slow dance with me, you gorgeous creature."

The second last track of the CD was just about to start when Louise locked the door behind her and entered the living room. She placed her arms around Murray's neck whilst he tenderly held her waist. Staring into each other's eyes as they swayed around the room, neither of them even noticed that the last song had finished playing. They were thoroughly absorbed in each other.

A Tawny Frogmouth's hooting call from the tree outside the kitchen window eventually broke their trance. Hand in hand, Louise led Murray down the hallway and into her bedroom. The couple made passionate love several times before midnight.

Early morning, they were rudely awoken by a group of boisterous Kookaburras heralding the new day. Murray sighed as he raised himself on one elbow to gaze into the face of the woman he'd fallen deeply in love with. He yearned to be with Louise constantly, to take care of her, cherish and protect her.

Looking back at the face of her handsome lover, Louise realised she had never been in love before. She now knew that her feelings for

Ross weren't true love at all. With Murray there were no inhibitions whatsoever. She felt free to completely be herself and their sexual chemistry was off the charts.

Murray sensed tears welling in his eyes as he traced the contours of her delicate face. "Louise, I've fallen in love for the first time in my life," he confessed. "You mean everything to me and I've never been happier than the day you entered my life." He studied her eyes carefully while his own glistened with emotion...desperately awaiting her response.

Reaching up Louise gently brushed a tear from his cheek. She could feel her bottom lip starting to quiver as she fought to smile. Her heart was thumping. "It dawned on me about a month ago that I've never been in love before either. What I had with Ross came from habit, not from love. To hear you say that you love me...makes my heart sing." Immediately she began to cry. "I'm madly in love with you Murray...and it's such a relief to have the courage to say it. Now I'm begging you...kiss me before I burst!"

CHAPTER TWENTY-THREE

Before she knew it, darkness had fallen on a rather unusual Saturday. Louise felt as though she'd accomplished very little other than a few mundane, weekly chores. Unseasonal gusty south-westerlies hampered her numerous attempts to plant some hybrid hibiscus in the front garden. Frustrated by the wind's strength and the sweltering heat it carried, she finally gave in and retreated to the still, coolness of her home.

'*I need a bath…and a glass of wine wouldn't go astray,*' Louise said to herself whilst retrieving the wok from the kitchen pantry. Preparing some Asian greens to accompany the chicken strips, she added garlic and ginger to the mix before tossing it in a drizzle of fish sauce. Within minutes her stir-fry dinner was ready.

Pouring herself a Riesling, she then locked the back doors, snapped on the television and scrolled through the stations to find Sydney's weather forecast for the rest of the weekend. Her efforts were futile. Instead, she settled for the final ten minutes of a British sitcom while she ate her meal then decided to call her sister.

"Oh, wonderful. I was just thinking about you," Julie said as she answered the phone. "What's going on in your life since we spoke a few weeks ago?"

Louise brought Julie up to speed on her latest business enterprise and added, "Carl asked if I'd go to Cairns early in February for another training gig. Murray suggested spending a few extra days when I'm finished to do some snorkelling on the Great Barrier Reef."

"Sounds wonderful. I was just going to ask you about Murray. How is he? I take it all is well…because I can hear you grinning on the phone."

"You're as bad as Mum, Jules. You have this uncanny knack

of knowing what I'm about to say before I even know myself." Louise paused while her sister laughed. "Anyway…I'm very happy to inform you that Murray and I are in love. We only confessed our feelings to one another about a week ago."

"I knew it!" Julie announced proudly. "That's wonderful news. John likes him a lot and he's a good judge of character, so I like what I've heard of him. We think you two are a great match. Now I have to ask Lou…have you heard from Ross again?"

Louise sighed and said, "No. Thank goodness. I think he got the message loud and clear when John was staying."

"Excellent, but we still worry about you being alone. Perhaps Murray could move in…now that you two are officially love birds."

"Hold the fort, Jules! It's early days. We're not there yet." At that moment Louise could hear another call coming through. "I think Murray might be trying to ring me…I'd better go. Give my love to John and the kids and keep a big chunk for yourself."

As soon as Julie hung up the receiver Louise said, "Hello?"

"It's Martha, Lou. Just wondering if you're spending the weekend with Murray?"

"He sat his final course exam this morning then all the team took off on a test flight to Perth late this afternoon. They're staying overnight. I think they're due back at about 8pm tomorrow night but he's had a huge week…so we agreed to catch up on Monday night instead. Why do you ask?"

"I was wondering what you're doing tomorrow? How about you come over and have lunch," Martha suggested. "Nothing fancy. Just you and me. Peter's made plans."

"I'd love to. I want to get up early and plant these hibiscus shrubs. Dug the holes today…but that wind made it virtually impossible to stay outside."

Martha nodded and said, "I know. It's unrelenting. My petunias look like they've been hammered in a storm. They're saying it won't ease until Tuesday."

"In that case, I'd better hold off," Louise concluded. "What time are you thinking? I'd love to see Skye."

"A play date with Aunty Lou…she'll adore that," Martha admitted. "Let's say around 11am. That will give you about an hour before I put her down."

"Perfect. Do you want me to bring anything Martha?"

"No thanks Lou, not at this stage…but if I think of anything, I'll let you know," she replied. "See you when you get here."

After hanging up the phone, Louise packed the dishwasher then poured herself a bath. The fragrant aroma from the coconut salts and frangipani bubble bath quickly permeated the bathroom. With her head now comfortably rested and eyes closed, she gently swayed her fingers through the tepid water. Relaxing completely, tender thoughts of Murray filled her mind.

The wind was still up and she could faintly hear the latch rattling on the side gate. As each gust whistled beneath the bathroom's tinted awning window, its intensity increased. While retrieving the sponge from the soap holder, she thought she could also hear movement in the hallway. Immediately sinking lower into the water, she kept her eyes firmly fixed on the doorway.

"Hello, Lou. Why did you change the locks?" Ross asked as he stood perfectly calm in the centre of the door frame. The smile on his face didn't match his scruffy, unkempt appearance.

Louise froze in fright. Managing to stifle a scream, she was determined not to let on that he had struck terror in her. "How did you get in Ross? What are you doing here? What do you want?" she queried in the most composed manner she could muster.

"That's a lot of questions," he returned with a sinister grin. "I jimmied the back door of the garage. I had to…because you changed the locks.

"Why didn't you just knock, instead of breaking in?" she questioned.

Ross attempted to slick back his matted hair as he said, "I want to talk to you…because I want to come back and live in Sydney. Here. With you."

Silently panicking, Louise's brain scrambled in an attempt to come up with an escape strategy.

First, she had to get out of the bathroom. That way she stood a chance of making a dash for the front or back door if necessary. "Can I at least get out of the bath? I'll get dressed and we'll talk about it," she suggested.

"Sure. Whatever…but I'm not letting you out of my sight. I just don't know if I can trust you, Lou. You're married to me…but I saw you kissing another bloke and I know he stays overnight a lot. Does he live here now, in our house?"

Louise gulped as Ross threw a towel in her direction. She avoided his questioning and covered herself before stepping out of the bath. "I need some clean clothes so I'll be back in a minute."

"No, you won't," he returned, deliberately blocking her exit to the hallway. "I'm coming with you. Let's go." Grabbing Louise's arm, he directed her through to the bedroom.

Once inside, she requested some privacy to get dressed but Ross blatantly refused. "I've seen it all before. I'm your husband remember?"

Now fully clothed, Louise stood beside the window, crossed her arms and glared at him. "Why do you want to come back? Where's the girlfriend?"

Ross rubbed his hand across his mouth. "She's in Melbourne. It's over with her. I made a huge mistake."

"There's just no place in my life for you, Ross. I can't live with the violence. And this is no longer 'your' house, remember?"

"Having another guy here sleeping with you doesn't go down well at all with me." He nervously began rubbing his chin as he looked around the room.

In that moment, Louise knew she had to choose her words wisely. "I'm sorry Ross but I've moved on and built a new life. You no longer have the right to tell me what I can and can't do?"

Fire flared in his eyes as he bolted towards the window, lunged at Louise and pinned her arms hard against the wall. She was cornered with nowhere to run. He snarled at her and whispered, "Is that so? Well…if I can't 'tell' you what to do anymore, I'll just have to 'show' you. Won't I?"

Grabbing her by the hair, Louise begged for him to stop before he dragged her forward and punched her in the face with all his strength. Instantly she flung back against the wall and tried to remain on her feet. Involuntarily tears sprung to her eyes through distorted vision.

"You ungrateful bitch!" Ross yelled into her face, spraying

saliva as he again grabbed a handful of hair. Louise couldn't escape the stale stench of rum and hygienic neglect on his breath. She was repulsed. "You belong to me! Do you understand?" he ranted. "I'll kill you before I see you with another man again!"

Shaking in intense pain, Louise tried to push him away. Ross back-handed her across the mouth with full force. Immediately she felt her jaw dislodge while attempting to knee him in the groin. His rough hands gripped around her neck and he drew her face close to his. Vial breaths increased in strength, as did his fury.

Louise felt her head swim before she took her final breath of air. Knees collapsed beneath her as she slid to the floor, Ross's hands still tight around his wife's throat. Before totally losing consciousness, she knew this was the end. Ross was actually killing her.

Staring at Louise's limp body lying prone on the floor, Ross's rage intensified. He kicked her several times in the ribs with his heavy boots before lifting her shoulders and slamming her head against the skirting board. Blood oozed from Louise's nose, mouth and head like a trickling stream.

With one final vicious kick to her thigh, he then trod on her stomach with his full body weight before leaving the room. Slowly making his way back to the door he'd jimmied open, he slammed his fist into the wall, jumped in his car and spun the tires on the bitumen while he roared away.

Ross had no intention of killing her…but Louise had goaded him to the point of losing control. His heart almost thumped out of his chest by the time he reached the intersection. *'Will they suspect it was me who killed her?'* he theorised. *'The airline ticket proves I flew from Melbourne to Sydney. Fuck Louise! I loved you and it was a mistake to leave…but you were screwing some arsehole in our own bloody house!'*

Finally pulling up in a carpark overlooking the ocean, Ross retrieved a large bottle of Bundaberg rum from the passenger seat and proceeded to down it like a bottle of water. The black dog was back, filling his head with despair. More rum. *'I killed my wife,'* he cried aloud several times in a row. Holding his head in his hands, tears flowed as he sobbed like never before.

• • • • •

By noon on Saturday, Martha Dean was becoming increasingly concerned about her friend. She'd attempted to phone Louise numerous times during the course of the morning, all to no avail.

Peter returned from the local nursery at 12:45pm and his wife met him in the garage as soon as she heard the car pull up. Opening the driver's door, he could see that Martha looked worried. "Is everything alright honey?" he quickly asked.

"I'm worried about Louise, Peter. She should've been here almost two hours ago. You know that's very out of character for her. And no phone call to say she's been held up either."

"Yep. That is strange," he frowned. "I thought you two would have finished lunch by now. I'll just unload this fertiliser out of the boot then I'll drive over and see what's going on. In the meantime, could you call Tommy and let him know that I'll have to pass on snooker this afternoon?"

"Yes, of course," Martha replied as she kissed him and made her way back to the house.

Ten minutes later, Peter parked in the driveway of Louise's house and knocked on the front door. No reply. As suspected, it was locked. Swiftly scanning the perimeter of the house, he discovered that the fence gate was ajar. After walking around to the back deck, he peered through the glass sliding doors into the living room. There was no sign of activity so he made his way behind the garage to find the back door fully open. Louise's car was there and he immediately noticed damage to the lock barrel. Peter surmised a forced entry and suddenly his heart rate increased four-fold.

Rushing into the house, he called Louise's name whilst popping his head into each room down the hall. Eventually he spotted her face-up on the floor of her bedroom…pink pyjamas mottled with blood, a heavily beaten-up head and face, one leg twisted out of its joint…and not a skerrick of movement. He was absolutely horrified.

To comprehend the physical torture inflicted on his friend's body was a real battle for Peter but somehow, he managed to push his emotions aside and bent to feel for Louise's pulse. It was barely detectable, though she was alive. Dashing to the phone he dialled triple zero, announced Louise's address and urgently requested an ambulance and the police.

The six-minute wait felt like an eternity. Peter ran back to Louise, knelt beside her and gently held her fingers. Tears pooled in his eyes as he said, "It's going to be okay Lou. Help is on its way now. Please hang in there, I'm begging you." Suddenly he felt nauseous and sprinted to the toilet, throwing up the contents of his breakfast.

Wiping the vomit from his mouth, he could finally hear distant sirens. Slowly rising to his feet, Peter entered the hallway and unlocked the front door before picking up the phone to call his wife.

"I found her darling," he sighed heavily then went on to describe the gruesome discovery. "Police and ambulance are almost here... so I'll call you again when I can."

Martha was shocked to the core, so much so that she couldn't even respond. She simply hung up the phone and wept uncontrollably.

The ambulance was first to arrive, closely followed by the police. While three paramedics attended to Louise, the two police officers entered the hallway. One questioned Peter thoroughly whilst the other entered the bedroom to inspect the crime scene.

"What's the name of the victim?" The senior constable asked, retrieving a small note pad from his top pocket.

"Louise Green," Peter quietly answered. "I don't know if she has a middle name."

"And your relationship to her? Do you know her well?"

Peter could faintly hear a medical apparatus being used by the paramedics when he said, "Yes, my wife Martha and I are her good friends. In fact, Martha works for Louise. She has a computer training business here in Narrabeen." He studied the constable's face and added, "She was supposed to be at our place for lunch at 11am but when she didn't show up by 1pm, or answer any of Martha's calls this morning, we started to get concerned. Louise lives alone so I drove over to check on her."

The constable looked at Peter sternly. "So why didn't your wife drive over herself?"

"Well, I'd been out for a few hours and..."

"You weren't at home this morning?" The constable interrupted. "Could you please tell me your whereabouts?"

Peter rubbed his chin and replied, "I left home at around 10:30am and went down to buy the paper and pick up some nappies at the supermarket…then I went to Foleys Nursery for a while. When I pulled up in the garage at about 12:45pm Martha came out and told me that Louise still hadn't arrived. Our baby daughter was asleep so my wife went back inside and I drove straight over here."

"Do you think anything has been stolen?"

Looking around, Peter gently shook his head and returned, "Honestly…I couldn't be sure about that."

"Mr Dean, do you know anyone who'd have cause to batter this woman in such a way?" the constable urged whilst continuing to take notes.

"No. Absolutely not. Louise is a wonderful person. We've known her very well for a couple of years now. I know she's been separated from her husband for probably eight months but they're not divorced. He moved to Melbourne with some woman. Louise has a terrific new guy in her life and she's really happy. His name's Murray Corbet. Been a very good friend of mine for many years."

The constable requested Murray's contact details, along with his home address. Peter willingly obliged and informed him that his friend was a Qantas pilot currently undertaking his final weekend of exams and test flights for the new Boeing fleet.

At that moment the younger officer briefly entered the hallway and announced, "Forensics are dispatched. Five minutes out Sarge," before returning to the bedroom.

"They'll need to fully examine the property and dust for prints Mr Dean," the constable explained, "so I need to know exactly what you've touched since you arrived."

Scanning the hallway, Peter folded his arms and retraced his steps. "When Louise didn't answer the front door, I tried the handle to see if it was locked…and it was. Then I went around the back and the side door to the garage was already wide open, so I didn't touch that when I came inside. Obviously, I felt Louise's neck for a pulse… and I unlocked the front door for the ambulance guys." Fidgeting, immersed in thought, he added, "Oh…and two more things. I threw up in the toilet and I also used the phone to call emergency services then my wife."

With Louise on a stretcher, the paramedics exited the bedroom and after carefully loading her into the ambulance, one medic swiftly returned to the constable and reported, "We'll be under siren to Manly. She's in a pretty bad way," before leaving as quickly as he'd appeared.

Restoring complete focus on Peter, the constable continued with his questioning. "Do you happen to know who her next of kin would be?"

"She has a sister in Auckland who's a nurse…and she's married to a doctor. Their names are Julie and John Keane but I wouldn't have a clue about their contact details."

"Alright. We'll try to get in touch with them. Meanwhile, would you mind coming down to the Manly Police Station to make a formal statement, Mr Dean? We may have some more questions and we'll need you to read and sign that declaration. You're welcome to drive your own car down, or you can come with me."

"I'll drive…but can I please call my wife before I leave? I need to know that she's okay."

"Yes, of course. Officer James will remain here with the forensics team," he explained, just as the young policeman appeared in the hallway again. He was carrying Louise's computer and answering machine. "Oh…and will you sign for these items please? I need to take them now."

Peter signed the form, handed the pen back to the constable then phoned Martha immediately. She answered within seconds and said, "Oh, Peter. I feel useless sitting here. There must be something I can do? How is she?"

"I know my love but we have to sit tight for now," he sighed. "The ambulance has just left. They've taken her to Manly Hospital. She's unconscious which the medics say is probably a good thing… because she's lost a hell of a lot of blood and her injuries are extensive. I'm leaving for the police station now to give an official report. Can you think of anyone who'd do this to her Martha?"

"No…but then again…remember Ross bashed her up before he left for Melbourne with the prostitute. Lou had to be hospitalised after that episode, so I'm sure their administration would have a record of it. Does anything look out of place inside Peter?"

"Everything's tidy, just how Lou likes it…but there was a wet towel on the carpet in her bedroom and the bath's still full of water. Whoever did this obviously broke-in through the back door of the garage because the lock had been jimmied open. I have to go. I'll be as quick as I can. See you when I get home."

Arriving at Manly Police Station, Peter's head was in a spin. As he relayed to the sergeant what Martha had told him about Ross Green's previous violence towards Louise, he again felt ill. Holding his hands on his stomach he added, "She said that the hospital might have records of Lou's previous physical abuse." Staring vacantly into the sergeant's eyes Peter informed him that he used to do a bit of surfing with Ross. "I never saw any signs of violence in him but as I said, we'd only known them for a couple of years. Martha and I first met the Greens when they arrived back in Australia after spending two years in New Guinea. Before that, they lived in Perth…and I'm pretty sure that's where they got married. I know Ross was born in Sydney and he's a bricklayer by trade. Louise was born in New Zealand."

During their brief moments of silence, the rapid sound of typing on a keyboard by a female clerk seated in the corner of the room, somehow began to ease Peter's nerves.

The sergeant then asked, "Do you have any photographs of this Ross fellow, Mr Dean?"

"Possibly. I'd have to ask my wife about that," he concluded.

Once the official statement was typed up, the clerk handed it to Peter while the sergeant instructed him to read it aloud. After signing and dating the document, they thanked him for his time and valuable assistance in the case. The sergeant then shook Peter's hand and said, "If you happen to find a photo of Mr Green, please drop it down to the station as soon as you can. We'll be in touch if we need any further information."

Driving home, many thoughts crossed Peter's mind but first and foremost was how he could contact Murray. He knew that his mate wasn't home, so there was no point in trying to call him. Then the penny dropped. He quickly did a U-turn, headed for Dee Why and arriving at Murray's unit, left a hand written note under his door that read: *'Call me urgently please mate. Pete. D.'*

CHAPTER TWENTY-FOUR

Shocked to the core, Murray rested his head against the window and stared out at the turbulent ocean. Ferocious winds lashed and gyrated the waves like a colossal washing machine while squalls of fury swept through him.

Having just spoken with Peter on the phone, Murray attempted to absorb all the gruesome details of Louise's attack and her subsequent injuries. *'Broken ribs, a collapsed lung, fractured femur, broken nose, head trauma, internal bleeding…what deranged bastard's even capable of this?'* he questioned himself.

Slowly backing up to the lounge suite he sat down and hung his head in his hands. Peter's final words played over in his mind like a nightmare…"In my opinion, he intended to kill her…and very likely thought he'd succeeded!" Wiping tears from his cheekbones, Murray grabbed his wallet and car keys then left the apartment.

Hurtling into the first available car space at Manly hospital, he locked his vehicle and broke into a run towards the entrance doors. An elderly receptionist answered his immediate questions, asked a few of her own then provided directions to the Intensive Care Unit.

"I have to advise you Mr Corbet, as the patient's in ICU and you're not a relative, they won't permit any form of visitation."

"We'll see about that," he assured her. "Thanks for your time."

As he wound his way through the labyrinth of corridors to the eastern wing, Murray reached the nurse's station and requested to see Louise Green.

One nurse quickly rose from her chair and unashamedly gawked at him. A handsome pilot in uniform was certainly a rare sight in the ICU ward. After closely observing the identification tag pinned to his jacket pocket, she smiled and asked, "Are you a relative…Mr Corbet?"

"No, I'm not," he admitted. "Louise doesn't have any relatives in Australia. But I'm her fiancé, so I certainly hope that counts for something?" He didn't feel the least bit guilty about stretching the truth if it enabled him access.

"Oh, I see," the nurse replied whilst jotting down a note at her desk. "In that case, you can have a few short minutes with her. Take the second corridor on your right and you'll find a police officer seated outside the door of her room."

The duty policeman stood as Murray approached him. "Ah...Mr Corbet," he announced, "we've been trying to get in touch with you since yesterday afternoon."

"I was interstate, W.A. Only touched down about an hour ago. A friend told me what happened. Can I please see her now?" Murray pleaded.

"That all depends on your willingness to cooperate with our investigation, Mr Corbet. You're Louise Green's boyfriend. Is that right?"

"Fiancé," Murray impatiently corrected him.

"Really? Interesting. Our report doesn't contain this information." The officer paused and eyeballed him carefully. "Do you have any witnesses who can verify the fact that you were interstate last night?"

Murray gaped at him and blurted, "Are you serious?" He swiftly scanned the passageway. Suddenly conscious of prying ears from numerous medical staff, he lowered his voice and added, "Do you consider me a suspect?"

"It's just protocol Mr Corbet," the officer returned. "No one's pointing any fingers but I cannot grant you access to the victim on hearsay alone. I'll need the contact details of a primary witness."

"Very well," Murray conceded. Retrieving his wallet, he flipped it open and handed over a business card for Patrick O'Hare, Qantas' Chief Training Officer. "We've all been under O'Hare's command, a group of fifteen pilots, since 8am yesterday morning."

"Okay. Take a seat," the officer instructed whilst walking a short distance down the corridor.

Murray silently stewed as he observed the policeman speaking on his two-way radio. After a couple of brief calls, the officer returned and declared, "You have five minutes Mr Corbet. In you go. I'll need to ask you a few more questions before you leave."

Upon entering the crowded room, Murray gazed at unfamiliar faces before a nurse advanced towards him. "I'm looking for Louise Green," he sighed.

She pointed to the back left corner and answered, "Bed 3. I'll be with you shortly," before rushing off to consult with a team of doctors.

Sighting Louise, Murray hardly recognised the woman he loved. After staring at her for a few moments he drew up a chair and gently took her hand. A network of monitoring equipment and intravenous tubes enveloped her frail body like a spider's web. He studied her partially bandaged head and severely bruised, swollen face. Seven stitches to her temple, a clearly broken nose, blackened eyelids and a bloodied gauze across her bottom lip.

When Murray examined the bruising around Louise's neck, he felt sick to the stomach. Clearly the perpetrator had attempted to strangle her. As tears sprung to his eyes, the nurse slowly approached and said, "It's a miracle that she survived such a heinous attack. The doctors say she'll pull through…but it will take time. For now, she's in an induced coma. Due to the extent of her internal injuries, Louise lost a lot of blood…so they're administering a transfusion. We've carried out all the major radiography scans and done countless x-rays. Her broken ribs will heel and we've placed her leg in a plaster cast. It was fractured in several places. These injuries should mend fairly well over the course of about six weeks but she will require some ongoing physio after that."

"Does she need any surgery?" Murray asked with his eyes still firmly fixed on Louise.

"Yes, she does," the nurse confirmed. "Her right lung has a severe laceration that won't heal of its own accord, so they'll need to operate on that within a few days. Whist she's in theatre under anaesthetic, the surgeon will also straighten her broken nose. The only other possible concern is some major bruising around her lower stomach. It would appear as though something heavy may have fallen on her...or perhaps she was forcefully kicked during the attack. It's certainly an area we'll investigate further when we bring her out of the coma."

Murray looked up at the nurse and asked, "How long will she be in a coma?"

"I'm afraid I can't answer that question," she empathetically responded. "We're carefully monitoring her around the clock and for now Louise is stable.

Rubbing his weary eyes, Murray said, "I've only just finished work so I'll quickly go home and shower then come back. Is that alright?"

"You look exhausted to be honest…and she won't respond to you. I'd suggest you try and get some sleep and come back tomorrow morning. That would be preferable."

"Thanks. You're probably right," Murray agreed. "Doubt I'll get much sleep but I suppose anything's better than nothing."

The nurse smiled back at him before making her way to the patient in Bed 2. Meanwhile Murray kissed Louise's hand and muttered, "I'm so sorry Lou. And I promised John that I'd look after you…hardly! You must have been so frightened. I can't even begin to imagine."

Momentarily, a matron appeared to advise Murray that his visiting time was over. He stood and placed a gentle kiss on Louise's swollen left cheek. "I love you, Lou. Fight like hell my darling. We have our whole lives ahead of us. I'll see you in the morning."

Exiting the room Murray was transparently distraught when confronted by the policeman. "I know this is a seriously tough time for you both, Mr Corbet…" the officer started, "but I have to ask… do you know of anyone who could be responsible for this assault on your fiancé?"

"No. Neither of us associate with lowlife mongrels…let alone a monster like this," Murray snarled. "I'm sorry. I'm buggered and I just need to go home."

Agreeing to leave any further questioning until morning, the officer thanked Murray for his cooperation and watched the heavy-hearted pilot slowly shuffle off down the corridor.

Arriving home within fifteen minutes, Murray noticed the light flashing on his answering machine. There was one message from detective Ian Tulloch earlier that afternoon and another from Louise's sister only an hour ago. The distress in Julie's whimpering voice was almost unbearable. She left her contact number so Murray immediately picked up the receiver to call her back.

In Auckland, Julie snatched up the phone on the first ring. "Julie Keane."

"It's Murray, Julie. I've just seen her at the hospital."

"How is she? I'm going crazy over here. I feel totally helpless," she cried.

Murray sat down at the kitchen bench and explained everything he knew about the attack and Louise's condition.

Julie couldn't quite believe what she was hearing. "When the police called to tell us what happened, they didn't go into any details about the severity of her injuries…and they're much worse than we suspected. I asked them for your phone number. Thank you so much for calling me back. We're trying to organise flights to Sydney now and John's madly sourcing a locum to fill in. He wants to assess Lou himself and know exactly what treatment she's receiving…and I have to be with her too. We've already arranged for the kids to stay at a friend's place. Do you have a key to the house?"

"Yes, she gave me one a couple of weeks ago but as it's a crime scene, I don't know if you'll be able to stay there. I'll phone the police and ask them as soon as I hang up. If you can't, please stay here in my apartment. My mate's away for three months so there's a spare room with an ensuite. When you've booked the flight, let me know. Do you want me to pick you up from the airport?"

"No thanks Murray. We'll grab a cab," Julie replied. "And thank you for offering us a room, we may have to take you up on that."

He cleared his throat and added, "Peter seems to think that whoever did this to Lou intended to kill her…and after seeing the bruising around her neck tonight, I'd have to agree. It just doesn't make sense that a break and enter would lead to someone wanting to strangle a woman to death. Who could possibly want her dead?"

Julie remained silent for a short while then replied, "There's only one person I can think of…and that's her husband. I wouldn't put it past him. He's a mean piece of work. Lives in Victoria but I know he was in Sydney a few weeks back. Ross phoned Lou at the house that night John stayed over. Apparently, Ross told her that he was there for three days and wanted to see her. Lou refused. Who knows…

maybe the scumbag's been in the city ever since? You knew about the call, didn't you?"

Without hesitation Murray returned, "Yes. Yes, I did. I have to make a few other calls so I'd better go Julie. I'll call you back about staying at the house as soon as I can."

Upon hanging up the phone, Murray felt guilty lying through his teeth. There was little point in worrying Julie unnecessarily. But could her theory be a reality? Knowing very little about Ross Green, Murray was shocked to hear Julie speak of him in such derogatory terms. And why wouldn't Louise have mentioned Ross's call?

Within seconds he phoned Manly Police Station and asked to speak to the detective handling Louise's case. Personnel informed him that the case was now being reviewed as an alleged attempted murder and therefore escalated to the Central Intelligence Bureau. After connecting him with the CIB, detective Ian Tulloch took the call.

"Detective, my name's Murray Corbet. I'm Louise Green's fiancé. I've just been speaking with her sister in Auckland and the Keane's are arranging to fly to Sydney. They're wanting to stay at Louise's house. Is that possible?"

"Well…forensics have finished in there but the house is still a mess Mr Corbet. We've cordoned off the back door and battened it to secure the place but I can't see any cause for entry denial."

"Thank you, detective," Murray replied.

"I tell you what…I'll send a cleaning team out there first thing in the morning. They'll get rid of all the chalk and finger print dust around the place and remove the blood from the carpet. Then I'll organise a few undercover cops to keep the house under surveillance while your family are here. How does that sound?"

"Like a very generous offer detective. Thanks again. I certainly want them to feel safe in the house while Louise's attacker is still out there."

"Terrific. Consider it done," he smiled. "We're still interviewing neighbours who may have seen or heard something on Saturday evening and following up a few leads. We're also trying to get in touch with her husband. I understand they're separated but not divorced. Is that correct?"

Murray confirmed. "Yes, that's right. Ross Green lives in Melbourne somewhere and has done so for about ten months now. Strangely enough, Julie just confirmed that he was in Sydney for a few days only weeks ago. He phoned Louise the night her brother-in-law was staying over. From what I've been told, Ross wanted to see his wife but she refused his request."

"Extremely useful information. We'll certainly chase that up and keep you well informed as the investigation progresses. I'll be releasing a statement to the media tonight in the hope that the public may step forth with any information for us. And please remember Mr Corbet…this is officially an attempted murder investigation, so all information must remain confidential and shared only between the parties who are directly involved. Good evening to you."

Murray showered and after watching some of his despair wash down the drain, he dressed and climbed under the covers in his darkened bedroom. Tension and worry crept through his veins but eventually he drifted into a restless slumber. Accustomed to surviving on power naps, he was reasonably alert when the phone rang.

"Sorry if I woke you Murray…it's John. We're booked on QF348 arriving Sydney at midday. We'll go straight to the hospital from the airport."

"Okay," Murray replied. "Forensics are finished at the house so you can stay there. I'll be at the hospital all day tomorrow, so I'll give you the keys when I see you. Have a safe flight."

"You're a good man. See you soon pal," John yawned.

●●●●●

"We're gradually trying to bring her out of the coma," a nurse informed Murray as he gently ran his fingers through the ends of Louise's hair. The love of his life looked so serene until her eyelids began fluttering erratically.

"I think she's trying to open her eyes," he remarked, smiling up at the nurse.

"Yes, she is…and hopefully that will happen within the hour."

As the nurse jotted down her observations on Louise's chart,

Murray left the room and called the Deans from a public phone in the corridor. There was a new duty policeman on guard this morning and his attitude towards Murray was extremely friendly.

Peter answered the phone and promptly said, "Hi Mate. How are you? How's Louise?"

"I'm at the hospital this morning and they let me sit with her for a few minutes last night. Sorry I didn't call you when I got home but I had to speak to Lou's sister and one of the detectives overseeing the case." Murray quietly brought his friend up-to-date with Louise's condition, the police investigation and told him that John and Julie were on their way. "Is Martha there? Could I have a quick word?" he added.

Martha was right beside her husband, listening to every word of their conversation. "Hi Murray," she said. "We can't believe this has happened. I think Peter's still in shock. I've taken the liberty of phoning Beth Phillips, Lou's assistant…and briefly told her what occurred. Between the two of us, we'll handle the business for however long it takes."

"The police want to keep this investigation under wraps as much as possible so can you ask Beth to do the same, please Martha?" Murray asked.

"Of course. We'll just say that she's away on an urgent assignment if anyone asks, that way no-one will attempt to contact her. When she's out of the coma, will you tell her we're taking care of everything? And do you think it's alright to let Carl and Donna know? Obviously, I'll tell them to keep it to themselves."

"Yes, by all means, they're good friends," Murray concluded. "I'll tell Lou you're thinking of her. Thanks Martha. John and Julie will be staying at her place and I'll let you know when she's scheduled for surgery. Could be tomorrow."

Returning to Louise's bedside, Murray found a new nurse scanning through her chart. She looked up at Murray and beamed a radiant smile. "I'm Judy Baldwin. I take it you're Louise's fiancé?"

"That's right. Murray Corbet. Nice to meet you, Judy."

"The gynaecologist was here very early this morning," she informed him. "He has scheduled Louise for surgery tomorrow morning. I'm so sorry." With that Judy turned and left the room while Murray sat holding Louise's hand. *'What does she mean she's sorry?'* Murray wondered. *'I don't even know what this operation involves. I'll have to ask John.'*

Suddenly he felt Louise's fingers twitch. She was aware of a human's touch and the comforting feeling sent memories of pleasant teenage years spinning around in her head.

"Good morning," a voice greeted Murray from behind. It was the same nurse from the evening before. "The team are preparing to insert a breathing tube in Louise's throat and that procedure will take about twenty minutes. Would you like to go and grab a coffee or something?"

"Yes, a coffee would be great…and I have to make a call, so I'll do that now," Murray smiled up at her.

Entering the small café area in the east wing, he grabbed a copy of the Sydney Morning Herald and began flicking through the pages whilst a barista whipped up a cappuccino. Page 3 carried the headline:

'NARRABEEN WOMAN BASHED AND LEFT FOR DEAD
A Narrabeen business woman is fighting for life in hospital having been found by a friend, severely bashed in her home. Police are investigating a number of leads.'

Murray's complexion paled and his chest tightened after reading the article. Quickly folding up the paper and collecting his coffee, he paid the barista and headed to a table near the phone.

A call to Qantas HQ soon had Murray speaking with his boss, chief pilot Warren McMahon. After informing him of the attack and Louise's condition, Warren agreed that a short leave of absence was certainly warranted.

"You have a great deal of accrued sick leave Murray, so I'd suggest you tap into that and we'll reassess the situation as it unfolds. I've just received your exam results and as expected, you passed with flying colours…so I'm honestly not concerned about you missing this first week of Phase 2 assessment. You'll catch it up. Call me again on Friday and we'll take it from there."

"Thanks Warren. Could I please ask a favour while I have you.

Louise's sister and her husband are on their way over from NZ and as I don't have access to a computer here, could you please tell me if QF348's ETA is still twelve hundred hours?"

"Ah…hold on. I'll have a look in the system. I think they're grounded in Auckland."

While Murray patiently waited on the line, he could hear Warren speaking to a colleague. "Sorry my friend. Just had confirmation the flight was cancelled due to a severe weather front crossing the north island. The storm cell's a doozy and it just keeps building, so we've had to can all flights in and out this morning. If conditions improve, we'll possibly reschedule this afternoon, but more than likely we'll have to hold off until tomorrow. Hard to tell at this stage."

Murray thanked him for the update and after finishing his cappuccino, re-entered the ICU corridor. He immediately noticed the policeman on his two-way radio. The officer began walking towards him and signalled for Murray to exit the corridor the same way he came in. Both men stood closely facing each other at the back of the waiting area.

In a quiet tone the officer said, "I just received information from detective Ian Tulloch and the bureau have asked me to pass it on to you. Ross Green hired a black sedan through Budget at Mascot Airport on two occasions in the past few weeks. The latest rental agreement was signed last Thursday afternoon, at which time the car was released. It should have been returned to the airport by 6pm last night but up until now…there has been no sign of him, or the vehicle. We have the rego number and highway patrol have been issued with an alert for its sighting."

"The bastard!" Murray burst out. Now he felt certain that Ross had done this.

Instantly, an image of the black sedan with heavily tinted windows sprung into his mind. The vehicle had been parked across the road from Louise's house on several occasions over the course of the past few weeks.

"Thank you, officer," he politely replied before storming back through the corridor with the policeman hot on his heels.

From the door of the ICU room, Murray abruptly halted when he saw a curtain encircling Louise's bed. His heart pounded frantically.

Within a few seconds, Louise's nurse emerged from behind the screen and approached him.

"Good news, Mr Corbet...your fiancé's out of the coma and we're just giving her a bed-bath now. Won't be long. The breathing tube has been inserted in her throat, so she's unable to speak but her airways are nice and clear."

"Oh, thank you. That is a relief," Murray smiled as the nurse retrieved a chair for him.

Whilst observing the bustling activity in the room he felt like he was caught in the midst of his own emotional crossfire...elated that Louise had regained consciousness...and furious that Ross was capable of such a savage attack on his wife. Suddenly the nurse reappeared and said, "You can see her now."

Louise slowly turned her head in Murray's direction. One eye remained closed but the other lit up on sighting him. As he moved to her bedside, he kissed her gently and lovingly scanned her battered face. She returned a watery smile as he reached for her hand.

"I'm unspeakably sorry Lou," he whispered. "I should have been there to protect you. It's a miracle you're alive...and for that I'm so very grateful. I love you with every essence of my being. John and your sister will be here tomorrow and we're all going to take excellent care of you. There's also a police officer guarding the corridor outside, so you're safe here. No further harm can come to you, my love."

Attempting to smile, Louise reached out her arm then placed her hand on Murray's cheek as a sign of her appreciation and love for him.

"I know you're unable to speak my darling...but I need to ask you a serious question. Can you blink once for 'no' and twice for 'yes'?"

Louise immediately returned two blinks.

Staring at her anxiously, Murray urged, "Who did this Lou? Was it Ross?"

She dropped her gaze for a few seconds before clenching the bedsheet with both hands. Quickly returning her focus to Murray, the unquestionable sadness on her face said it all as she blinked at him twice.

CHAPTER TWENTY-FIVE

"Sorry to disturb you, Mr Corbet," Louise's nurse smiled at him. "The officer in the corridor would like a quick word."

"Yes, of course," he replied. Rising from his chair he kissed Louise on her forehead and said, "I'll be back in a jiffy darling."

Outside the room Murray was relieved to see the Keanes standing beside the duty officer with their luggage in tow. After exchanging a solid handshake with John, Murray opened his arms and embraced Julie as though they'd met numerous times before. She returned his warm welcome and sighed, "It's so lovely to meet you, Murray."

"Sorry to hear your flight was cancelled yesterday," he remarked. "That must have thrown a real spanner in the works?"

Gazing at her husband, Julie nodded then rolled her eyes and said, "Even this morning's flight was delayed for another two hours. We finally took off at 8:40am."

John added, "Jules handled the situation like a real trooper. She just overdosed on caffeine and paced up and down the airport several hundred times until she wore holes in the carpet! How's Lou, Murray?"

"Doing well, all things considered. They're taking her for surgery in about fifteen minutes. She's in Bed 3. I'll wait out here… to give you some privacy."

Just as the Keanes were about to enter the room, Murray said, "Before you go in, I asked Lou yesterday when they brought her out of the coma if Ross was responsible for the attack. She confirmed it was him."

"I bloody knew it!" Julie scorned behind clenched teeth, her raging eyes firmly fixed on Murray.

John remained completely silent for a few moments before placing his arm around her shoulders. "You have to try and stay calm for Lou's sake, Jules," her husband advised. "Take a big, deep breath and let it go for now."

"Easier said than done...but I'll do my best." Reaching for John's hand she filled her lungs and gradually exhaled. "I'm ready."

"Excellent," he responded. "I want to see the patient chart before they take her to theatre."

Bedside, Julie looked in horror at her sister before gently kissing her swollen cheek. Louise opened one eye and smiled weakly. The tears began to well as she squeezed John's hand.

"It's great to see you Lou," he admitted.

Whilst John removed her patient chart from the end of the bed and began painstakingly perusing the reports, Julie explained to Louise, "He arranged a locum for a week and then he'll return to Auckland. John's sister is going to take care of the kids while I take care of you."

As Julie continued talking, she was mindful to avoid anything relating to the assault. Her only objective was to raise Louise's spirits. She spoke about the children and the new station wagon that they'd recently purchased.

Meanwhile, John completed the grim assessment of his sister-in-law's medical reports and Julie noticed him having a quiet chat with the matron. After a few minutes he returned to Louise's bedside. Now aware of the hysterectomy that was about to be performed, John struggled with his emotions. She would never be able to have children. The matron confirmed with him that Louise understood and consented to the procedure but he wondered if Murray knew exactly what it entailed. Either way, John was fully aware that a complete hysterectomy was imperative. Louise's crushed reproductive organs were the major source of her internal bleeding.

"Are we all set?" the anaesthetist quietly enquired as he approached Louise.

She nodded affirmatively before looking at her brother-in-law with hopeless despair. John leant over and whispered, "Chin up. I know this one's really tough but we are all here for you girl. You're in good hands. I'll go and get Murray."

Filled with assorted emotions, he then left the room while Julie confirmed her love for her sister. When Murray appeared at Louise's bedside, Julie rose from her chair and smiled at him. "We'll meet you out in the corridor."

"You look very tired my darling," Murray told Louise as he kissed the back of her hand. "You'll be asleep soon. Sweet dreams. I love you Lou…we're going to get through this together. I'll be here when they bring you back from the recovery room."

The three then wordlessly meandered their way out of the hospital. According to John's estimates, Louise's surgery would take approximately four hours, so there was little point in hanging around.

"I could strangle that animal myself," Murray confessed to the Keanes as they drove to Louise's house. "I phoned detective Tulloch yesterday afternoon and told him that Ross did this. They need to catch the bastard and nail him to the wall!"

In the back seat, Julie was reading the newspaper article when she concurred with Murray's assertive statement. "Mum and Dad never liked him…said he was a hard man to read and always kept his cards close to his chest. John was never too fond of him either. I just thought he was a bit shy but when we found out that he'd physically abused Lou, my opinion of him changed completely."

John jumped into the conversation from the passenger seat. "We didn't even know they'd split until Lou came back for William's funeral. She was recovering from a broken cheekbone and a fractured wrist after Ross attacked her in the kitchen during a drunken rampage. Apparently, he'd been having an affair with a young hooker from The Cross for a while, so after this incident, which wasn't the first, he took off to Melbourne to live with her. Did you know about that?"

Murray kept his eyes focused on the road and slowly shook his head.

"Did she tell you that he phoned the night I was here, wanting to see her?"

Again, Murray looked straight ahead and replied, "I only knew that Ross called her because Julie told me he did. I know very little about their marriage…and I certainly wasn't aware of any physical abuse."

"But you said you knew about the call when I spoke to you on the phone the other night?" Julie probed.

"I lied," Murray admitted. "I was a bit shocked that Lou hadn't told me…and I didn't want to worry you any further. Sorry Julie. I did it to protect you, and myself I suppose."

"And now I can see why. Honestly, you needn't apologise Murray. We feel terrible just springing all of this on you. I just assumed…"

John swiftly interrupted his wife. "I'm really sorry that you weren't aware of their history either, mate. After Ross's phone call that night, I practically begged Lou to tell you about his previous rum-induced assaults on her…and the fact that he was in Sydney. I knew that up to that point she hadn't disclosed her marital issues with you, so for her own safety I told her it was time to do so. I feel partly responsible because I should have just told you myself. Maybe I could have prevented it. Who knows?"

"There's no stopping a man on a hell-bent mission John," Murray returned, briefly gazing at him. "He'd have got to her one way or another, whether I knew about it or not…so please don't beat yourself up. If Lou even suspected that she was in some sort of danger, I know she would have told me. The only blame in this entire atrocity lands on Ross Green."

Pulling into Louise's driveway, Murray noticed a white Ford Falcon parked a few doors down. In the driver and passenger seats, two casually clothed men appeared to be studying a large street map. Having seen photos of Louise's husband in the past, Murray knew that neither man was Ross Green. His alert senses remained focused while they unloaded the Keane's luggage from the boot and unlocked the front door.

John and Julie placed their suitcases in the spare room and sauntered into the kitchen. Meanwhile, as Murray looked around the hairs on his arms stood on end, quickly followed by a shivering chill. He was relieved to see that the cleaners had done a good job. From the gruesome scene Peter described, Murray could only imagine the mess they faced. Other than a large, cracked dent in the plaster beside the window, the room was fully intact.

Finally joining the Keanes in the kitchen, Murray said, "I need to make a few calls, so I'll do that now if you don't mind?"

"By all means Murray, do whatever you need to do. I'll see what I can find to make us some lunch," Julie replied.

Getting through to detective Tulloch took a while but eventually he answered the phone. "Ah, Mr Corbet...I just tried to get hold of you at the hospital and I was about to call you at home. How's Louise?"

"She's undergoing surgery now but she's making progress, thank you. The Keanes and I have just arrived at the house and I can see two men in a white Ford parked down the street. Are they police officers?"

"Certainly are," the detective replied. "Constables Lewis and Cunningham will remain on surveillance duty until further notice. Please don't approach the vehicle, otherwise our cover will be blown. I also assigned an officer and a sniffer dog to the back fence perimeter of the national park, so you can rest assured that you're all very safe at the property. If a possum so much as strays into the yard, we'll know about it. Until Green's caught, I'd strongly recommend you stay at the house as well for a few days at least. We don't have the additional resources at this time for surveillance on your apartment...but we need to take every possible precaution."

"Yes, of course. I understand. That's a wise recommendation." Murray agreed.

Detective Tulloch continued. "We've had our tech experts screen the computer from your fiancé's office and it would seem that her husband had a penchant for hard-core pornography. All of this lewd material was viewed from an offshore website in the very early hours of the morning for about five months straight. I'll ensure that it's wiped from the hard-drive before returning it."

Murray rubbed his chin and said, "Good idea. That's not something I'd want her to see."

"Now back to Green's whereabouts and the reason for my call," Tulloch asserted. "He was scheduled to fly back to Victoria yesterday but didn't make the flight. We have an 'all points' out for the sedan between Sydney and Melbourne, in the event he's driving back. Obtained his address. He's renting a room in a boarding house and works for a local bricklayer. Didn't turn up for work this morning and hasn't been back to the boarding house either. No witness leads from the public as yet but one of the neighbours across the road confirmed that he also saw the black sedan parked at the curb several times. He just assumed that Louise had visitors."

Murray asked, "Have you been able to establish exactly when she was assaulted?"

"From coagulation of the blood, paramedics estimate that it occurred somewhere between the hours of 8:30pm and 11:30pm."

At that moment the intercom on Tulloch's desk buzzed. "Please stay on the line Mr Corbet," he advised Murray before placing their call on hold.

Within a minute the detective returned and said, "We've just had a breakthrough. One of the highway patrol guys found the car at the cliff end of Eastern Avenue, Dover Heights. I'm leaving now. Be in touch when I have more info."

"That's …". Murray hardly got a word out before Tulloch was gone. Hanging up the receiver he swiftly turned to the Keanes and declared, "They just found the car. It's in Dover Heights, near Bondi…on the other side of the city."

Julie instantly placed her hands over her mouth as John sighed, "Finally…some good news."

Murray seriously looked at John and explained, "He was supposed to fly back to Melbourne yesterday but he wasn't on the plane. And now they've found the car, we know he didn't drive back either. That means he's still here somewhere."

"Excellent! Time to flush the bugger out," John smirked.

"I just have to make another brief call," Murray informed the Keanes as he dialled Gordon's number. As far as he knew, his friend wasn't rostered to fly today.

"Hi, Gordy. Glad you're home mate. I need to have a quick chat. While I was away on the weekend Louise's ex broke into the house and bashed her up pretty badly. She's in Manly Hospital undergoing a big operation now."

"Oh, God Muz!" Gordon returned. "That's horrendous news mate. Is there anything I can do?"

"Actually, Gordy, there is. Obviously, I've got a lot on my plate right now so I need to ask for a few favours. Louise's sister and her husband are here from Auckland and we're all staying at Louise's house for a while. I'll be spending quite a bit of time at the hospital so would you be able to arrange for her back door to be replaced? Her ex jimmied open the lock and destroyed it. I'll pay the bill but I don't have time to arrange and co-ordinate the installation. You have the phone number, so just give us a call before you come over. If I'm not here, you can liaise with John and Julie. And one more please mate…no rush on this one…could you call Dan and ask him to price me up a security system for Lou's house. The one he installed in my apartment's great, so I'm thinking a larger version with cameras at the front, back and down the northern side fence. Thanks Gordy. Really grateful for your help mate."

"No problem at all Muz. Leave it with me. I'll get one of the builders pulled off the job and we'll get it done. How's the course going?"

"Passed my first exam but with this major setback, I haven't had a chance to start the next training instalment. The boss granted me a week of sick leave and then I'll hit the books again my friend."

Gordon smiled and said, "Stay strong Muz and give my love to Louise. We'll talk again soon."

Julie had set about making sandwiches for a late lunch, though her appetite was negligible. Murray produced a beer for each of them and they remained at the kitchen bench to eat.

"John," Murray started. "A nurse told me yesterday that a gynaecologist scheduled the op that Lou's having now. Do you know exactly what it involves?"

Looking down at his beer, John began twisting the bottle around in circles on the bench. It was a direct question that he wasn't sure he should answer. Glancing left at Julie then right at Murray, he drew in a deep breath. "The scans revealed that as a result of the injuries to Lou's abdomen, her reproductive organs were irreparably damaged. The rupturing caused the majority of her blood loss so she's undergoing a complete hysterectomy. I'm afraid she won't ever bear children." He quickly placed his hand on Murray's shoulder.

"I'm sorry I had to tell you this, Murray. It probably should have come from Louise herself but at least now you're prepared and you can support her."

Rapidly blinking to curb his tears, Murray looked at John and said, "The hospital staff think I'm her fiancé. I intended to propose in Cairns when we were scheduled to be up there at the end of next month. Now…I think I'd like to do that sooner. We haven't discussed marriage or kids yet…but I'm sure we could adopt, couldn't we?"

"Sure, you can," John returned in a positive, cheerful tone.

Tears also began to flow from Julie as she looked into her husband's sad face. The hysterectomy came as a total shock. Rising from her seat she placed her arms around Murray's shoulders and hugged him tightly.

Resting their heads gently against one another, Murray declared, "I'm just so sad for Lou because I know she wanted a family. As for me, I just want her…and for her to be happy. I love your sister more than I can say and I'll always be there for her. If we don't have children, we can enjoy yours. I'm happy to go with whatever she wants."

John smiled to himself as he observed their compassionate interaction. Murray was a decent man with a sincere depth that Ross Green never possessed. He was certain that Louise and Murray would have a wonderful life together.

•••••

Unlike the previous afternoon, their hospital visit found the patient a little brighter this morning. Louise's surgery had all gone to plan but being heavily dosed on morphine meant that she was barely responsive.

Finally out of ICU, it was a relief for Murray to see her in a general ward for the first time. The tube had been removed from her throat and although Louise's face was still very bruised, the contusions were beginning to yellow. Swelling in her left eye had partially subsided, allowing her eyelid to open slightly.

Still a little groggy, she blanketed her family with a sweet, sleepy smile. "I can talk now," she said huskily. "It really hurts though. In fact, everything's sore."

"You're a brave girl, Lou," Julie smiled as she kissed her sister. "It's so wonderful to hear your voice again. The nursing staff will monitor your pain levels and administer relief whenever you need it.

Try not to talk too much today and by tomorrow, you'll be chatting our ears off!"

"Ha, ha," Louise jested.

"John and I are just going to the café for a cuppa, so we'll leave you two love birds alone."

"What I'd give for a coffee," Louise started. "The nurse said maybe tonight. And they're going to help me have a proper shower." Her eyes lit up at the very thought.

As the Keanes left her bedside, Murray pulled his chair closer and manoeuvred his head to carefully kiss Louise on the lips. The large laceration on the left side of her mouth was healing incredibly well and her nose was completely covered in red tape from the rhinoplasty surgery the day before. John was happy to know that both surgeries could be carried out at the same time.

"Should I call you 'Rudolph' with that shiny red nose?" Murray asked, stroking her matted hair.

"Absolutely. It's an honour," she smiled.

The couple conversed happily for about fifteen minutes then Louise's mood completely changed. As drowsy as she was, taking Murray's hand she said, "I need to tell you about the operation I had yesterday."

"No, you don't my darling," he swiftly responded. "Julie and I already know about it. John told us yesterday."

Looking directly into his eyes, Louise was amazed by his calm demeanour. "Because I can't have children, I just want you to know that if you were considering a future with me…you may want to re-think that now. I love you so much, but I certainly understand if you want to walk away."

Leaning close to her ear Murray whispered, "Never! Loving you is all that matters to me and I'll be in your life for as long as you'll have me. Hopefully, that will be to the end of our days."

With glazed eyes Louise asked, "But what if I remain a reindeer forever?"

"Then I'll turn into one myself. 'Dasher'. Yep, I'd like that. I already know how to fly so it wouldn't be too much of a transition, surely?"

"And this is why I love you Mr Corbet," she smiled affectionately as the Keanes re-entered the ward.

John again perused Louise's patient chart while Murray and Julie spoke to her.

"I don't know if Murray told you, but he's staying at your house with us for a few days. You know, to help us settle in and find our bearings," Julie explained.

"Yes, he did," her sister replied. "Please use my car while you're here. You'll need to do some grocery shopping, that's for sure."

"We will," Murray returned. "Might do that now on our way home. And late this afternoon I'll drop into the Dean's house. Peter and Martha are desperate to see you. Do you think you might be up for visitors by tomorrow afternoon, Lou?"

"Yes, I'd love that. After a shower tonight, at least I'll feel semi-presentable," she replied. "And I'll be able to talk properly, so Martha and I can discuss the business."

While Murray and John gazed at each other, slowly shaking their heads, Julie blurted, "Incredible! You can't stop thinking about work even at a time like this."

Louise simply smiled at her sister and said, "Jules...stop being such a worry wart."

● ● ● ● ●

Julie was preparing dinner in the kitchen when the phone rang. Murray quickly answered it, hoping the call was from detective Tulloch and not the hospital.

"Ian here, Mr Corbet. I think we may finally have our man."

Murray immediately signalled for John and Julie to rush to the phone. With their three heads huddled together, Murray held the receiver slightly away from his ear whilst the detective continued.

"Investigation squad found two smashed liquor bottles beside the vehicle in the carpark yesterday. The sedan was unlocked and on the passenger seat there was a note that read, 'I didn't mean to kill her. See you all in hell'. After scouring the area for a few hours, we found no sign of him. An abseiling specialist was called to descend to the bottom of the cliff and comb the rocks because the sea was far too rough to access the area by boat. We didn't turn up anything until a call came through from a fisherman at Bondi just before dawn this morning. He reported spotting a body wedged between a crevice on the high tide mark at North Bondi headland. Throat cut, deep lacerations all over him. I would have called you earlier but it took quite a while to cordon off the scene and retrieve the body. They'll have to do an autopsy of course but first we need a relative to officially identify him at the morgue. Will Louise's brother-in-law do that?"

"Yes, no problem at all," Murray replied. "When do you need him there? And where is the morgue exactly?"

"I'll meet you both out the front at say 7am in the morning. It's on Parramatta Road in Glebe…at the Coroner's Court. About a half-hour's drive from Manly. Make sure he brings identification for the medical examiner. Just keep in mind that we've only ever seen two photos of Green. The one your mate brought down to the station and the one on his driver's license, which we found in his wallet in the car. I can't be certain that it's him because his face is pretty smashed up, presumably from leaping off the cliff…and a body that's waterlogged, particularly in salt water, swells like a balloon after a few days. At this stage, we can only assume it's Green."

Murray remained silent for a moment. Meanwhile, Julie covered her mouth and dashed to the bathroom. "Thanks, detective Tulloch," he responded. "John and I will see you in the morning."

Hanging up the receiver, silence prevailed as Murray and John dwelt on their own thoughts and emotions. Eventually John huffed, "That'd be right…took the coward's way out. Couldn't face the consequences of his actions when he thought he'd killed her…and almost did!"

Whilst John made his way to the bathroom to check on Julie, Murray felt irate and relieved all at once. Angry because he knew that when Ross was found, he intended to confront him…and solaced by the reality that he was no longer alive.

By lunchtime the following day, Murray and the Keanes arrived at the hospital to find Louise in good spirits. The family had already debated over their decision to tell her the truth about Ross. Would they simply say that he was in police custody…or reveal the fact that he was dead? In the end, they concluded that honesty was the best approach. Besides, they'd much prefer she hear it from the family before being informed by police.

"They found Ross, my love," Murray said solemnly. "He killed himself."

Louise looked away and said nothing at all.

"I know this is a big shock Lou," Julie added, "but the police are wanting to know if there will be a funeral."

Without turning her head to face her sister, Louise shrugged and replied, "I don't know…and I honestly don't care. It isn't my problem. I hope he rots in hell as far as I'm concerned. His sister can take care of all that. Her phone number's in the little blue book beside the filing cabinet in my office at home. Just give it to the police and they can handle it from there. It's not up to us to have to deal with his sister."

Immediately sensing Louise's irritation, Murray leant over and kissed her gently. "You're absolutely right darling. That's none of our concern. Your recovery and knowing that you're safe with me for the rest of your days is all that matters now. We all love you so much." Quickly changing the subject, he then asked, "How was your shower last night? Have the nurses given you any indication as to how long you'll be in here?"

Louise smiled at him and said, "Aside from the pain, especially in my ribs, it was heavenly. Great to feel human again. And I ate my first meal last night. Not exactly restaurant quality but it was very satisfying nonetheless. They're thinking I'll be here for another six days at least." Finally turning to face Julie she added, "Having Jules at home should get me out of here a bit faster. They just want me to completely rest my stomach muscles before they release me, take a few more x-rays of this nose to see how it's healing, then poor Jules will have to put up with a broken-ribbed, punctured-lunged, leg-plastered nuisance under her feet. If I were you Jules, I'd be hoping they keep me in here as long as possible."

They all laughed and Julie replied, "Not on your life girl. I'd have you home tomorrow if I could."

CHAPTER TWENTY-SIX

For Murray, the month following Louise's assault was nothing short of hectic. Endless study, gruelling training schedules at Mascot Airport and staggered exams left little time to spend with her. Though they spoke regularly on the phone during the week, he only saw Louise and Julie at home for a few hours each Saturday.

Thankfully, Julie remained in Australia for a total of five weeks. She was a godsend to her sister during this time, not only by way of caring for Louise's every need but also keeping up with the housework and maintaining the yard. Obviously, she missed her husband and children dearly, so as soon as her sister could manage on her own, Julie returned to New Zealand.

Within the first few days of being discharged from hospital, Louise phoned detective Tulloch and thanked him for his tireless assistance in the case. "Just doing my job Louise," he humbly returned. She then called her closest friends to inform them of the attack and advise that Ross had taken his own life. All were horrified upon hearing of the incident and Louise's subsequent injuries, though few were astonished that Ross was responsible.

Publicity-wise, there had been very little…which was somewhat of a relief. Only one small snippet in the newspaper stating that she was recovering in hospital and that the body of the perpetrator, Ross Green, had been discovered washed up on rocks by a local fisherman. The autopsy concluded death by suicide.

From black and blue to lighter shades of the same, the bruising on Louise's face and body diminished as the weeks progressed. Sutures were removed and the scars remaining on her face would fade in time. Providing she didn't exert herself too much, breathing became easier as her ribs and lungs healed. Chronic headaches that she'd been suffering for well over a month also began to subside.

If it wasn't for the large cast on Louise's leg, she'd no longer be house-bound. One morning after waking she said to her sister, "I feel like a prisoner in my own home, Jules."

"I understand your frustration Lou but need I remind you…I'm a nurse, not your warden. You're free to leave at any time, but you'll put your back out within two minutes of lugging that plaster around."

Louise knew that Julie was right, as always, so she attempted to busy herself as best she could. Beth and Martha were doing a fabulous job maintaining the day-to-day running of the business in Louise's absence and she did as much as she possibly could to assist them from her home office. The Deans and the Hoffmans occasionally dropped by to offer their friend invaluable support and these visits were welcomed with open arms.

● ● ● ● ●

"Well…aren't you a sight for sore eyes," Murray remarked as Louise opened the door for him. She looked truly radiant in pale pink slacks and a predominantly pink blouse. The hues kindled a faint glow in her complexion. Medium-healed white shoes and pearl earrings completed the ensemble perfectly. She almost took his breath away.

Smiling back at him Louise said, "The x-rays confirmed that my ribs are completely healed now, so…can I finally have a big, firm hug? Please?"

"With great pleasure my lovely lady," Murray replied.

The couple stood solidly embraced for almost a minute, relishing the scent and touch of one another. Not a word was spoken as they slipped into a blissful world of their own.

Finally, the whir of a distant siren snapped them back to reality. Louise locked the front door and entered the security code into the keypad before heading to the car.

Reaching the intersection, Murray gently placed his hand on Louise's thigh and asked, "How's the leg feeling after a week out of the cast, Lou?"

She looked down and said, "Surprisingly good. The physio sessions are tough but other than that, it really only aches when I'm doing the exercises at home. I can feel it getting stronger every day." Nervously she gazed at Murray and enquired, "Now, where exactly are you taking me?"

"Seafood is the cuisine for this evening, my love. I've booked us the finest table at Hugh's in Manly. Have you been there before?"

"Ah, no, I haven't…but I'm certainly aware of their five-star reputation," Louise admitted. "To be completely honest Murray, I'd be happy to dine anywhere tonight that isn't my own kitchen. It's wonderful to be out of the house again. That being said, now I'm super excited…and probably a little underdressed."

"Oh balone," Murray responded. "You look gorgeous Lou."

Parking near the foreshore, Murray took Louise's hand and slowly walked her over to the restaurant. She still had a slight limp in her step but appeared to be managing with little pain.

Upon entering the establishment, the couple were ushered to a romantic corner table for two, overlooking the water. A crisp white linen tablecloth and serviettes, accompanied by a small posy of red roses and babies breath arranged in a crystal vase, sat in one corner of the setting. Candlelight polished off the private position, made so by two potted Cascade palms separating the table from view of other patrons. Outside, the glimmering lights of Manly reflected on the ocean's edge.

"What a perfect location this is," Louise commented as Murray pulled out the chair for her.

Within seconds a waiter arrived with a beaming smile and a bottle of Moet Chandon. He poured it into their crystal flutes and quickly disappeared.

Murray raised his glass and declared, "To us, my beautiful girl… and to your remarkable recovery."

"To us, dear Murray," Louise concurred. "I'm so happy to be alive. And here's to you for being by my side every step of the way. Oh, and one more…congratulations on achieving the second highest score in your course. A well-earned result for all your hard work."

The waiter promptly returned with menus and the couple ordered their customary seafood platter for two. Whilst the meal was being prepared, he briefly returned to top up their glasses then discreetly floated off again.

Murray rose from his chair and took Louise's hand as he bent down before her on one knee. Gazing into her lovely eyes he asked, "Lou, would you please marry me?"

This was an easy question for Louise to answer but as tears welled in her eyes, she just couldn't find words. Nodding enthusiastically, her eyes didn't leave Murray's face as he reached into his pocket and retrieved a small velvet box. Extracting the solitaire diamond ring he'd selected that afternoon, Murray placed it on the third finger of her left hand. Louise had never felt true happiness like this in her life before. She could barely see the ring for flooding tears.

Quickly dabbing them away to prevent her mascara from running, Louise took Murray's face in both hands and passionately kissed him on the lips. "Of course, I will. I couldn't be happier. This is such a surprise."

Murray resumed his seat, leaning forward to gently wipe away another tear as it ran down Louise's cheek. Now holding hands across the table, he was wholeheartedly relieved that his proposal had been accepted. He really hadn't considered anything beyond that. Should she have refused him, Murray knew that he'd be utterly devastated.

"Thank you, my darling," he beamed. "I feel like the luckiest fellow on earth right now. I was going to ask you in Cairns but with everything that has happened, I just couldn't wait that long. I was so worried that you might reject me."

"Never, my love…but as I can't give you babies, I did consider walking away from our relationship so that you wouldn't feel obligated to continue on with it. Selfishly, I wasn't strong enough to do that."

"You're anything but selfish, Lou. If we decide to have children in our lives, I'm open to adoption. There's no hurry. I just want you to be happy. We've discussed travelling and we're in a great position to do that…given the perks that my job offers. The world is our oyster, Lou."

Meanwhile, the waiter had been diligently keeping an eye on his patrons and was thrilled to witness the proposal. Bringing the platter to the table, he congratulated the happy couple before refilling their glasses and hurrying off for a brief chat with the owner. Upon his return from the cellar, the waiter then presented Louise with a boxed bottle, sporting a wide red ribbon. Shaking Murray's hand, he announced, "An engagement gift, compliments of the house."

At 9pm after a fine meal and dessert, Murray could see that Louise was growing weary. They moseyed home and sat on the lounge for a while with lights dimmed and background music playing softly. Despite Louise's excitement as they discussed their future together, she was clearly exhausted.

"Would it be alright if I just cuddled beside you tonight?" Murray quietly asked. "No hanky-panky. I promise."

"That would be very comforting, my handsome fiancé," Louise smiled. "It's a long time since we've had a bit of privacy."

In bed, Murray studied Louise's tired face. "Do you like the ring I chose, Lou? If not, it can be swapped for a different one."

"It's perfect darling," she yawned. "Exactly what I would have chosen myself. Thank you. I love you."

Snuggled into Louise's back, Murray held his fiancé gently until contented sleep took over.

The next morning, Murray and Louise were very excited to phone their respective families and friends, announcing the engagement. Everyone was delighted with the news. Murray promised to fly Louise to Melbourne to meet his brother Ryan and wife, Paula. They were unaware that Murray even had a special someone in his life, so this news came as quite a revelation.

• • • • •

With her physiotherapy appointments now wrapped up, Carl phoned Louise to confirm that she was still keen and well enough to do some training in Cairns. The new branch's grand opening had been delayed by three weeks due to a builder's industrial dispute. As far as timing was concerned, it was the perfect opportunity for Louise to travel interstate once again.

Like every other branch, the Far North Queensland team were an absolute pleasure to tutor. Always willing to go above and beyond that which was asked of them and their thirst for advancement was insatiable.

By the end of the training week, Murray arrived at Louise's hotel where they spent the night before flying south east to Hayman Island for a week of rest and recreation. The Island Resort had recently undergone extensive renovations following a tropical cyclone that ripped through the Whitsunday islands over a year prior. The result of the refurbishment was luxury at its finest.

For the first two days the weather was overcast but improved each day thereafter. The couple were enjoying getting to know one another more, both intimately and intellectually.

Day three saw them on a charter to the outer reef where they snorkelled and free-dived amongst the beautiful corals and vividly coloured fish and clams. Some fellow tourists were of a similar age and their varying walks of life made for interesting conversations. A sumptuous lunch was served onboard followed by another snorkelling session.

Back at the resort that evening, they joined two other young couples for dinner. George and Noelle Smyth hailed from Thredbo in the Snowy Mountains, and Bill and Robyn Johnson lived at Mt. Tamborine in the hinterland behind Queensland's Gold Coast. Murray was very familiar with both locations. Louise on the other hand could only relate to the coastal strip of the Gold Coast. She'd never seen the area known as 'The Green Behind the Gold'.

A game of golf was certainly on the agenda as Murray and Louise hadn't played together for many months. A new course had just been built on Lindeman Island so they decided to join a group the following day. The fast-cat launch left the jetty within an hour of the couple feasting on their mouth-watering buffet breakfast.

Motoring to Lindeman on the open top deck, guests were treated to an unexpected sight. It was whale migration season and the first pods from the Southern Ocean were arriving in the warm waters off the Queensland coast to give birth to their calves. Witnessing their tail-slapping and breaching in the passage delighted everyone onboard.

The golf course was exceptional. Views from the fairways to the nearby islands nestled in the brilliant aqua waters were breathtaking. The game itself wasn't too flash. Murray and Louise were clearly out of form...but it didn't bother them in the slightest. They were just happy to be together, relaxed and relishing the fresh sea air.

A half-day champagne lunch extravaganza on Whitehaven Beach concluded their day-tripping activities. The pure white silica sand reflected like snow in the midday sun. Louise had never seen anything quite like it before. She was mesmerised by the landscape, wishing the day would never end. That evening they ordered room service and watched a comedy movie that left them in stitches of laughter. Playful shenanigans quickly spilled over into their memorable love-making session.

Sadly, as work beckoned, their Whitsunday adventure came to an end. The couple had only scratched the surface of this incredible island playground and all it had to offer but both agreed…they'd certainly return again one day.

During the flight back to Sydney, comfortably settled in first-class, Murray smiled at Louise and said, "The new aircraft have just been commissioned…so I suppose it's time to find out whether I'll be relocated. We're all having a meeting with the 'Powers that Be' on Thursday afternoon."

Given that Louise was consumed with her burgeoning business and he and Gordon were well underway with their renovations, Murray sincerely hoped that he could remain in Sydney. As did Louise.

Relieved to be completely healed of all her injuries, Louise was looking forward to sinking her teeth back into the business. There were still numerous loose ends that had been left dangling during her recovery time so she was determined to tie them all off, one by one.

Arriving home at 9:30pm from her first decorating class, Louise fumbled for the light switch and rushed inside to answer the phone.

"I was hoping you'd be home by now beautiful," Murray said as she answered. "How was it?"

"Hi darling," Louise replied. "Just pulled up. It was terrific. Our teacher's a lovely woman and I can see that I'll learn a lot from her. I'm almost too scared to ask…but what's the verdict on the relocation issue?"

Murray cleared his throat and returned, "I'm staying in Sydney. Hip hip hooray!"

"Oh, what a relief," Louise sighed before whooping for joy.

"Four pilots are moving to Brisbane and that's what got me off the hook. Two of them have families up there and the other two have partners in the city. Wish I'd known these guys were applying in the first place, it would have saved me all this angst. Anyway Lou… now we can get on with our lives. I was thinking…what sort of wedding do you want my love? Let's make it soon."

"I agree. There's no reason to hold off," Louise smiled. "I'd just like something small and intimate Murray. No idea about location. I'll leave that up to you because I've been down this track before."

"What about Auckland?" Murray queried in a bubbly manner. "Ryan and Paula could fly over and I'd like Gordy to be there. It'd be really nice if Peter and Martha could attend too. After all, they're responsible for bringing the two of us together. I wonder if Jean and Don would be able to come? I'm sure they'd like for Jean's family to see little Garth."

By this stage, Louise was almost laughing. She'd never heard Murray so excited. "It's a bit late in the evening to make these decisions now my darling. When next we both have a day off, we can sit down and start making some sort of list. How does that sound?"

"Perfect," he replied, "and I have to be up at the crack of dawn, so I'd best get some sleep. Love you, Lou. Sweet dreams. I'll call you tomorrow night."

Later in the week, after making plans for Saturday, Gordon joined Murray and Louise for a game of golf. The day was perfectly still, idyllic conditions. Louise was impressed to discover that she and Murray had improved greatly since their round on Lindeman Island. Gordon was also a very reasonable player so the competition was immensely enjoyed by all.

At Louise's afterwards, they discussed the various stages of Murray and Gordon's house renovation and Gordon asked, "Do you two have any plans for tomorrow? I thought I'd check out the annual Home Show and I was wondering if you'd like to join me?"

"Well, we hadn't planned anything, so I'm keen if Lou is," Murray replied, smiling at his fiancé.

"Love to," she smiled back at him. "I have a bit of homework to do for my course but I can fit that in tomorrow night."

The following morning, Gordon met the couple at the showground's northern entrance, as prearranged. A quick cappuccino and a few donuts later, they all began winding their way through the myriad of stallholders, company displays and sponsor's tents. There were so many interesting concepts and modern innovations to absorb.

Nearing the end of their complete loop around the showground, Louise came across a small cubicle displaying unusual works by a Brisbane artist. One painting in particular caught her eye. It was titled, 'Storm Surge': a limited-edition acrylic on canvas in varying ocean blues with white highlights. At the top of the painting a wave crested aqua made her feel so alive and she immediately envisaged it under a spotlight to further enhance the luring crest. The work was stretched over a timber formwork, making it appear frameless.

"This should be in my gallery at home," she commented to the artist as he sat painting. "I grew up close to the beach and I've always had a deep connection with the ocean."

"Me too," he smiled up at her. "I think it's in my blood. My grandfather was a sailor and Dad was a naval officer, so I suppose it stands to reason."

Murray overheard their conversation whilst perusing some brochures with Gordon. When Louise said to the artist, "I just have to have this painting," Murray looked up to inspect the subject of his fiancé's enthusiasm.

'*Wow, she's right. It's magnificent,*' he admitted. Taking the credit card from his wallet, he walked over and handed it to the artist. Looking at Louise affectionately, Murray declared, "I also love it, Lou. Consider this my wedding gift."

Louise reached up and kissed him, completely oblivious of interested glances from onlookers. "Thank you, my love, that's so very generous. We can both admire it for many, many years to come."

"Just as well I didn't pick you guys up this morning," Gordon joined in. "We're going to need every square inch of the station wagon to get this masterpiece home!"

Quietly smiling to herself, Louise watched the artist carefully wrap the painting in heavy, corrugated cardboard. She could scarcely wait to get home and hang it.

CHAPTER TWENTY-SEVEN

It was rare for Louise and Murray to spend a Wednesday together, so naturally they took full advantage of the privilege from sun-up till sun down. Packing a large picnic blanket, a few throw pillows and an esky, they headed off to Avalon Beach.

Under the shade of an enormous Norfolk Island pine, the couple set out their belongings whilst admiring the pristine ocean before them. High tide had just peaked on this glorious autumn morning.

"I made us a fruit salad with the works," Louise declared whilst cuddling Murray from behind. "Would you like some?"

"Absolutely," he replied, pulling her arms even more firmly around him. "I don't know what 'the works' entail…but I'll try anything once."

Removing a large Tupperware container, two bowls and two dessert spoons from the esky, Louise began dishing up the colourful array of diced fruits. "Here you go. Not quite the one we had on Hayman…but it's pretty close. Thought I'd take advantage of the last of these seasonal sweeteners."

Murray's tastebuds danced with every mouthful. "Oh, that's good Lou. Really good. It's like eating a tropical rainbow." Poking around in his bowl amongst all the pineapple, watermelon, mango, strawberries, oranges, apples and kiwi fruit, he held up his spoon and asked, "What's this pink one?"

"Guava," Louise chuckled.

"Beautifully tangy. And this orange stuff?" he questioned. "Tastes like a banana and a mango at the same time."

Still smiling, Louise returned, "That's papaya, commonly known as pawpaw. I ate a lot of them when we lived in New Guinea. It's my favourite of all the tropical fruits." For a brief moment her thoughts turned to Ross as she looked across the ocean.

Murray placed his hand on her shoulder, detecting a hint of sadness. "What did you think about the Auckland idea for our wedding Lou? A co-pilot I used to work with got married on Waiheke Island and he said it was magical. Have you heard of it?"

"I know it extremely well. It's a lovely place. In fact, the island's part of my heritage. The logistics of a big wedding could be difficult to manage over there, but a small affair would be a breeze."

"Your heritage?" Murray queried. "How so?"

"Well…it's a an interesting but rather long story, my love. Not sure if you'd want to hear it right now."

"Now's the perfect time," he suggested. "We've got all day."

"Alright. You asked for it," Louise smiled cheekily.

Placing their bowls and spoons in the esky, the couple then laid back on the picnic blanket with a pillow each to rest their heads. Holding hands, perfectly relaxed, they gazed up into the pine tree's dense foliage. "Okay, I'm ready," Murray smiled.

Louise began to explain, "An Englishman named Joseph Hodgson sailed from England to Sydney in 1839 aboard one of his father's ships. He was the third son of a wealthy Lancashire family who owned barques, which were very large sailing vessels. His two older brothers were both captains aboard these barques and they traded goods in Sydney and New Zealand. Joseph had trained in veterinary surgery but before taking up his profession, his father granted him permission to holiday in Sydney during one of the brother's trips. Whilst their ship was being loaded, Joseph sailed off to New Zealand in another of his father's ships. I think it was the *Duke of Marlborough*. Calling in at Port Nicholson, Wellington, a passenger named Mary Prouse embarked for the Bay of Islands. She'd been employed as a maid for Reverend Henry Williams' wife, who, at the time was in Wellington."

After swiping a nuisance fly away from her nose, Louise continued. "This part is merely conjecture but it would appear that Joseph, having become interested in Mary on their voyage north, stayed in the Bay of Islands and became a regular visitor in the Williams' home. It's known that Joseph worked as a farm manager in Pakaraka before moving to Auckland after marrying Mary at the Waimate North Mission Station in November 1840. Because he didn't return to England as planned, Joseph was cut off from his family's fortunes. His brothers are recorded as being regular traders to New Zealand ports. Joseph and Mary lived in the Bay of Islands at Russell until 1845. At that time, all settlers had to take refuge aboard the warship *H.M.S. Hazard* due to the attacks on the Maori people of Heke's tribe. The settlers were then taken to Auckland and disembarked on March 22nd. It was here that Joseph Hodgson established the first butcher shop on the corner of Queen and Shortland Streets. I don't think he ever practiced as a vet. There's certainly no record of it. After three years, in 1848, the family moved to Rocky Bay, Waiheke Island. They were some of the first settlers and Joseph established a dairy farm which he operated for many years. He also started a company made up of ship owners and wood and coal merchants. Joseph and Mary had nine children and the Hodgson family became very prominent in yachting. Am I boring you yet?" She turned her head and smiled at Murray.

"Not at all," he admitted. "I'm fascinated. Please carry on."

"I just need to go to the ladies' room first. Be back in a minute."

As Murray watched Louise walk to the nearby amenities block, he thought to himself, *'We should definitely get married on Waiheke Island. I've heard it has a picturesque vineyard as well.'*

Within a few minutes Louise returned to lay on the rug. This time she snuggled into her fiancé, placing her head on his shoulder. "That feels better," she sighed. "Now where was I?"

"They were a well-known yachting family," Murray prompted her.

"Ah, yes. So, Joseph was sailing home to Rocky Bay from Auckland one day in about 1850 when he heard that two twelve-year-old boys had jumped ship in the Rangitoto Channel. That's in the Hauraki Gulf. Presumably they swam to Rangitoto Island, so Joseph went looking for the deserters himself. He could only find one of the boys, whom he took back to his farm at Rocky Bay. Realising that the authorities would be searching for the lad, Joseph hid him in a hollow tree on the farm for five days while a government boat searched the area. It's unknown what became of the second boy. Joseph's eldest daughter, Jane, was given the task of taking meals to the deserter in his hiding place. Being well educated, Joseph managed to communicate with the boy, even though he didn't speak English. His name was Inez Perez and later, he changed his name to Ennis Parris, being the nearest translation in English. Ennis worked for Joseph Hodgson for several years and when not required to work the farm, sat in on lessons with the nine Hodgson children, taught by their mother. Jane, who was born on Waiheke Island, married Ennis Parris in July, 1861 in Freeman's Bay, Auckland. She was twenty years old and Ennis was twenty-one. They farmed in the Rocky Bay area for a short time then in 1865 purchased Pikau Bay, later known as Cowes Bay. Here they hand-built a homestead constructed from materials logged and milled on the property. Ennis and Jane had eleven children before she died in 1883. Joseph remained on Waiheke until his death, resulting from an accident in Auckland. The 125 acres of land that Joseph and Mary owned on the island were left to their sons, as was the company."

Murray was almost dumbfounded. "That's a great story Lou… but how in the heck do you remember all those names, dates and statistics? Sounds like you should have been an historian?"

"I researched and wrote it all out years ago while Dad and his siblings were still alive. Sadly, I lost it all in the house fire but I think Julie still has a copy. I must ask her. I did send one to my cousins with all the births, deaths and marriage dates of our ancestors…but obviously that would need updating by now."

"Do you know much about the lives of the Hodgson children?" Murray asked inquisitively.

"Certainly do," Louise proudly confessed.

Smiling, Murray said, "I thought you might. Feel like a coffee while we continue to delve deep into the past?"

"I'd love one," Louise replied, "but I'd also like to stay here a bit longer. It's such a glorious morning."

Murray stood up and stretched his back whilst announcing, "You can have both, my sweet. I packed a thermos this morning before I picked you up. I've got instant coffee, sugar, some long-life milk and a couple of mugs, so we're sorted."

Louise quickly sat up, quite astonished. "There's no doubt about you Murray. You're one in a million."

Heading towards his car he shouted back at her, "Only a million?

I was hoping for ten million at least Lou!"

She laughed to herself whilst watching him retrieve a small picnic basket from the boot. Returning, Murray set about making their beverages.

"Almost forgot a teaspoon," he smiled. "Only remembered it when I grabbed the biscuits. We've got some Arnott's shortbread creams and a packet of Kingstons. Wasn't sure which you'd prefer."

"You've gone to so much effort my darling, thank you," Louise acknowledged. Deliberately batting her eyelids and leaning in to kiss him, she added, "You're going to be a wonderful husband."

A grin from ear-to-ear dominated Murray's face before he returned her kiss. "I'll certainly try my darnedest lovely lady. So… did Ennis, can't remember his surname, remarry after Jane died?"

"Yes, he did. About five years later, Ennis Parris married a hard-working Swedish woman named Bertha Eversen. She was born in 1852 and basically raised his children. At some stage, two young local men sailed their girlfriends over to Cowes in their Cutter, which is smaller type of vessel. Bertha made them all welcome and the men promised that if the Parris' could build additional rooms, they'd be able to acquire boarders. So, Ennis felled more trees and built five rooms which Bertha furnished with simple beds and heavyweight cotton-covered boxes. The rooms were soon filled with visitors brought ashore by boats. With the help of the Maoris and Ennis's sons, he continued building with their own timber to construct a larger homestead, more guest rooms and a Post Office. Around 1890 it opened for business and became the first establishment of its type on Waiheke Island. Ennis and his team had built the structures well and they stood for seventy years, until fire destroyed them. It was a very popular resort with yachtsmen and launch parties from Auckland, so it quickly turned into a boating haven. Some of the largest racing yachts of the time sailed there. The regatta was moved from Arran Bay to Cowes Bay and in the early 1900's became an annual event. They raced a course from Arran Bay to south of Ponui…then north behind Ruthes Island, now known as Rotoroa, to Rabbit Island, now known as Pakatoa, and back. Sometimes it was vice versa. Steamer excursions would also run to Cowes on New Year's Day. They'd be stacked up at the end of the wharf while visitors promenaded along the beach."

After sipping her coffee, Louise continued. "My Great Uncles, who were Ennis's sons, became mariners. Adolphus captained Northern Steam Ship vessels and the government oyster vessel *Te Waipounamu*. Edward owned and skippered the speedy trading cutter *Janet*, who won the Auckland Anniversary Regatta six years in a row. Bertha became the Postmistress and as Ennis was aging, they sold the place in 1906 when my father was three years old. Ennis would have been a comparatively rich man at that stage but within a few years, Bertha died and he remarried a woman named Mary Shepherd. She was reportedly his nurse and it's believed that she cared for him through an illness but only stayed with Ennis for two weeks after they married. Mary then absconded to Australia with his wealth. Ennis's whereabouts was unknown until he became the publican of the Golcondal Hotel in Coromandel from 1912 to 1914. There are few records of him after that...but we do know that he was dependent on his sons William and Edward, for his keep during the last four to five years of his life. One of his daughters, Mary Johnson, lived in Thames and provided her father with a home until he died of senility in December, 1924, aged 78. Son William, married Alice Reeve, who were my grandparents...and they bore eleven children. So, there you have it. That's the abridged version but I think it's pretty accurate. Perhaps I should get that copy from Julie...I could bring it all up to the present. I know we have nineteen cousins."

"Wow, that really is an incredible background. I definitely think you should Lou, while your cousins are still around," Murray concurred. "I wouldn't mind looking into my own family history one day. It's fascinating stuff."

Louise laid down on her side and jested, "I already suspect you're a direct descendant of Prince Charming my love, so there's really no need!"

•••••

There was a full contingent on Friday evening at the Manly Surf Club. Martha and Donna were anxious to catch up with Louise and her pending matrimony news. A wonderful evening was enjoyed by all, as they celebrated the couple's engagement and discussed their plans for the future.

After returning to Louise's, Murray was keen to tackle their wedding arrangements. He poured two glasses of Riesling and proposed, "Let's make a list for our big day, Lou. How do we start?"

"With the bridal party I suppose," she replied, sipping her wine. "We chose not to have any groomsmen or bridesmaids because the whole thing was a secret. Guests just thought they were joining us for lunch." Louise then went on to briefly outline the small beach wedding. "Do you want any attendants? Your brother perhaps?"

Shrugging his shoulders, Murray said, "I really don't know, Lou. It doesn't bother me one way or the other. I suppose it depends whether you want to have bridesmaids?"

"For me, honestly…because it's in New Zealand, that makes the whole 'attendants' business a bit complicated. It kind of defeats the purpose of keeping things simple."

"True. No attendants," Murray agreed. "What about guests?"

Taking pen to paper, the couple spoke about the Deans, the Hoffmans, Jean and Don, and Ryan and Paula. Louise would also love it if Jillian and Claude and Janet and Ken Wilson could attend. Naturally, John and Julie would already be there.

"Do you think Gordon would want to bring a partner?" Louise enquired.

"I suppose we should allow for one. There is a lady he's seeing but no-one permanent."

"Well, that makes sixteen," Louise deduced, "not including ourselves. We'd need to arrange overnight accommodation for everyone on the island. Oh…plus the children of course. As we speak there are nine in total."

Murray smiled and remarked, "That's terrific, Lou. It shouldn't be difficult finding rooms for a group of that size."

"No, but then we'd possibly have to arrange transfers to the island, depending on their flight dates and times. That could be a bit tricky." Taking another sip of wine, she thought for a moment whilst admiring the shimmering diamond in her engagement ring. "You know what Murray? I think we should call Julie in the morning and have a chat with her. She's the 'girl in the know' over there and it might be best to leave all the wedding arrangements to her. That way we can just focus on our ourselves and our guests."

"I like your way of thinking, Lou," he admitted. "That would certainly take a big load off."

Louise slowly reached over, kissed her fiancé on the lips and said, "My Uncle actually installed the electricity on Waiheke when I was a child. I used to go down to Palm Beach and stay with my cousin, Laura, during the school holidays. It really is the perfect place for us to get married. I'm so glad you suggested it, my love."

Next morning, after a much welcome sleep-in and a light breakfast, Julie answered her sister's call.

"Hey Jules, we've got a project for you…if you're up for it," Louise prompted.

"Sounds rather ominous. Do tell?"

"Murray and I were hoping you might be interested in arranging our small, simple wedding at the Waiheke Island Winery in about two months from now? You whinged so much about not being involved in my last wedding…I thought you might like to do it all this time? If everyone on our list turns up, there'll possibly be eighteen adults and nine children. There's overnight accommodation to book for everyone and we'll need a celebrant too."

"Hell, yes! I'd love to do that," Julie blurted excitedly. "Tell me about your colour scheme, floral preferences, seating arrangements, reception menu…you know, all that sort of stuff."

Quietly laughing at Julie's enthusiastic response, Murray placed his arms around Louise as she replied, "We haven't got anywhere near that far yet, Jules. We just wanted to know if you could do this because it wouldn't be easy to arrange from here. And you've done so much for us already in the past couple of months, I really didn't know if you'd have the time to do it."

"Are you kidding me? I'll make time, don't you worry," Julie returned. "I'll look into a venue tomorrow and you can let me know the balance after that. Gosh, Lou…I'm ecstatic that you're coming home to be married! John and the kids will be thrilled too. Can't remember if I told you that we took them over to Waiheke last Summer for a weekend. I wanted them to see where their ancestors lived. There's nothing left of the old Guest House at Cowes but the school house is now a private residence. Looks like numerous extensions have been carried out through the years however the original chimney stack still remains and the Pohutakawa trees on the foreshore are enormous. I could imagine Dad and his siblings climbing them. While we were there, I even remembered Dad telling me that they used to ride to school on their horses from Rocky Bay, over the hill to Te Whau."

"Sounds like a pretty nostalgic experience Jules," Louise smiled. "I'd love to show Murray around those haunts while we're there. He was captivated by the story of our heritage."

"How about instead of going over the day before the wedding, we go two days before? That gives us plenty of time to have a good look around."

"Brilliant idea," Louise responded. "Please book that extra night along with the remainder of the accommodation."

Julie paused for a moment and added, "The other thing we need to do is spread Mum and Dad's ashes. Do you think that would be a nice time to do it, Lou?"

"Definitely. If we could aim for the weekend before the wedding that would be fantastic. Obviously, this would mean coinciding both events around the full moon but hopefully that's possible."

"Can't see why not," Julie told her sister. "Should we just have family present at Mum and Dad's final farewell? I thought it would be respectful to invite some of their friends."

"Of course, I'll leave that with you, Jules. Thank you for everything. You're going to be a busy girl. If you didn't have a lot on your plate before, you certainly have now."

Murray called into the receiver, "Yes, thank you so much Julie. We really appreciate it. Take care. Say 'hi' to John for me."

"Will do Murray," she replied. "Lou, I'll call you back as soon as I have some info. Get cracking on the rest of those wedding arrangements, okay? You know how quickly time flies. See ya, Sis."

• • • • •

Six days later, Julie phoned with a confirmed wedding date in

August. The venue was set and besides their immediate family's accommodation needs, tentative bookings had also been made for guests. A local celebrant on Waiheke would be performing the ceremony. Louise and Murray now had everything they required to start organising official invitations.

By the end of the following week, Murray and Louise flew down to Melbourne to stay with Ryan and Paula. Hiring a sedan at Tullamarine Airport, the couple then drove south-east for approximately an hour and a half before arriving in the picturesque Dandenong Ranges.

Welcomed at the door for the first time, Louise instantly felt accepted. Ryan was a similar build to his brother with a fairer complexion but the same thick head of hair. In stark contrast, his wife Paula was rather tiny with straight, blonde hair framing her striking blue eyes.

Ryan smiled at Murray and said, "I see she's worth hiding away brother," before they firmly shook hands. "Come on through Louise. Glad we could finally meet you. Paula will show you around while I get us some drinks to celebrate."

Their house was small, cozy and very much in keeping with the hilly terrain that surrounded it. An unusual timber pole home, made so by the fact that some of the long pillars came up through the floor of the structure. Others were on the outside of the dwelling. The poles and beams held up the roof, so there were no load-bearing walls. It was nestled perfectly in harmony with the landscape and being elevated, it boasted distant ocean views. Paula explained that they had plans to add another floor below the existing level.

Furnishings throughout the home were quite rustic and whilst Paula showed Louise each room, she mentioned that her favourite hobby was restoring old furniture.

"Some of these antique pieces have been completely transformed from the neglected state we found them in," Paula explained.

Louise was enchanted by the concept of the entire structure and asked, "Would you mind if I took a few photographs? It would be fabulous to build something like this one day. Maybe a weekender somewhere. I've never been inside a pole home before."

Pleased by her future sister-in-law's reaction, Paula replied,

"Yes, of course you can. Feel free. It was fun watching it all come together, Louise. The site has an eighteen-degree slope so it would have been virtually impossible to build conventionally…besides, Ryan and I were keen to capture that view if we could."

"I really love it, Paula. It's just amazing."

Earlier in the week, Louise had received their printed wedding invitations from a local supplier near her office. She required so few of them that they were ready within a day or so. Having brought Ryan and Paula's invitation with them, after lunch, Murray handed his brother the envelope.

Excitement resulted and quickly plans to fly to Auckland in August became the topic for discussion. "We're well overdue for holidays," Ryan smiled. "We'll certainly be there. Paula and I could hire a motor home after the wedding and explore the country." Gazing lovingly at his wife, he asked, "Do you reckon you could get three weeks off, honey?"

"I can certainly try. But what about you? Do you think you could source a locum at this short notice?"

Ryan nodded and replied, "I believe so. There are a fair few retired pharmacists up here in the hills…and they need to reach the minimum quota of weeks per year in order to retain their licenses. I'll put out some feelers as soon as I can."

"So, where are you two going for your honeymoon?" Paula asked.

"Oh, we haven't got that far," Louise smiled in return.

"Yes, we have," Murray proudly admitted, "but that's a surprise for my beautiful bride."

Louise's eyebrows shot up as he leaned over and kissed her on the cheek. Reaching for her hand he added, "It isn't entirely organised yet, lovely lady…but you'll find out all in good time. Just leave everything to your future husband."

Grinning, Ryan patted his brother on the back twice before announcing, "Who knew? Murray Corbet…a hopeless romantic! Should we break out the violins, Muz?"

CHAPTER TWENTY-EIGHT

With only three months to their wedding, Louise and Murray began to conscientiously knuckle down in their respective jobs and finalise planning for the ceremony. Nationally piloting Qantas's new Boeing aircraft invigorated Murray's passion for flying and busy schedules saw him interstate and overseas on a regular basis. This allowed Louise ample time to prepare staff in readiness for her three-week absence and with Ross's Death Certificate now in her possession, she could blissfully contemplate her new life as Mrs Louise Corbet.

The weekend prior to their nuptials, an exhilarated Murray and Louise touched down in Auckland very late on Saturday afternoon. Greeting them at the airport was the equally excited Keane family. Mark and Lucy threw their arms around Louise with all the love they could muster.

"Aunty Lou, we're going to the Grill Room for dinner," Mark blurted.

Quickly examining Murray, Lucy smiled up at him and said, "Hello Murray. I'm Lucy…and that's my brother, Mark. Do you like the Grill Room too?"

"I'm sure I will," he smiled back at her.

The adults warmly embraced before collecting the couple's luggage from the carousel and departing the airport. Arriving right on time for Julie's 6pm reservation at the restaurant, they thoroughly enjoyed their meals then headed to the Keanes' at around 8:30pm. All growing weary, the entire household was asleep within the hour.

Sunday morning the weather was superb. A light offshore breeze with perfectly predicted tides. Venturing down to their old stomping ground with family in tow, Julie cradled her parents' ashes whilst Louise carried a small basket of red rose petals. Surrounded by long-standing friends and acquaintances, all stood on the shore quietly gazing out over the magnificent Pacific Ocean that lay before them.

As Louise tossed the delicate petals high into the air, a zephyr carried them out beyond the break. Closely followed by the ashes, Julie and Louise smiled and hugged one another tightly as they watched a gentle tide propel them out to sea.

Meanwhile, a musician friend of the family sang 'Never Walk Alone'. It was such a fitting song choice. Other guests joined in and through teary eyes, everyone watched the rose petals disappear out of sight. Given the happy childhood memories created on this beach, Julie and Louise knew their parents would be proud of them for making this their final resting place.

John produced some cold drinks and nibblies for everyone in attendance. The group mingled, catching up on one another's lives and reminiscing over the past. A nostalgic but ultimately happy occasion to farewell such a loved and respected couple. For the rest of the day, Louise and Murray enjoyed the company of the family as they walked the foreshore, built sandcastles with the children and played a highly competitive game of beach cricket.

From Monday to Wednesday, while the Keane children were at school and their parents worked, Murray and Louise explored the city and some of its surrounding areas. A gentle hike of the Mercer Bay Circuit at Piha was a particular highlight, as were the Auckland Botanical Gardens.

By Thursday afternoon, as planned, Ryan and Paula joined Murray, Louise and the Keane family for the 'Baroona' ferry transfer to Waiheke Island. Their first night's accommodation was extremely restful for all. On Friday morning they piled into a hire van and armed with a comprehensive map, began their exploration of Julie and Louise's historical family sites.

Leaving a main road, John parked the vehicle then they all navigated their way down a bush track to the beach where the sister's grandparents had built their original home. There was no sign of the structure but it was obvious from the lay of the land where the homestead would have been situated. Louise retrieved a small piece of driftwood and a polished stone from the sand to take home with her.

While they stood on the track above the site, three curious

women taking their morning walk, stopped for a chat with the group. Seldom did they see tourists in this area.

"We're on a discovery tour," Julie explained. "This is where our grandparents and father lived as a child. He used to ride a horse to school from here."

One of the women smiled at her and said, "Well then…this will come as a pleasant surprise. I own the old school house. It's my home."

"Oh, my goodness. That's incredible!" Louise remarked. She then introduced herself and the remainder of the group. "I traced the history of our family some years ago. It would be wonderful to see the school site."

The woman continued to smile and added, "Be my guest. We'll be another hour or so…but you're welcome to have a look at it whenever you like."

Noting the directions, Julie offered her thanks before the group returned to their van. The white timber dwelling with its central chimney was relatively easy to find. Surrounding it, a beautiful terraced garden containing huge trees sloped down to the beach. Just as Louise imagined her father climbing them, Lucy and Mark proved that this enjoyable pastime was still alive and well…some four generations later.

As Murray watched on, he said, "Imagine how many children have climbed the limbs of these monstrous trees."

Looking up into them, Julie returned, "Many scores, I'd say. They're well over a hundred years old. In summer these Pohutakawas, which line many beaches in New Zealand, are literally smothered in deep-red flowers. They're a magnificent sight."

Stopping at Onetangi for lunch, they then drove across the island to Cowes Bay. From the top of the hill the view out to Pakatoa Island was stunning. In more recent history, this was a place where alcoholics were sent to dry out. Cowes had since been transformed into an exclusive, privately owned resort. It was closed for the winter months, so sadly the group weren't able to walk in the footsteps of their ancestors.

Nonetheless, all agreed that they'd had a wonderful, memorable time together. That night, as pre-arranged, Murray stayed in Ryan and Paula's room to allow Louise plenty of time to prepare herself for the big day.

On Saturday morning the remaining wedding guests arrived. At the ferry wharf, they were met by the Winery Transit bus and taken to their accommodation. Julie had planned a midday wedding in consideration of the number of children in attendance. As for Louise, she knew very little about any of the arrangements her sister had made. Being well aware of Louise's penchant for surprises, Julie was determined to keep it all under wraps.

Though the early morning dawned showery, by 11am the heavens cleared and a blue, cloudless sky prevailed. Louise would be attending to her own hair and makeup, so there was no need to leave the comfort and warmth of her bed before breakfast arrived at the door.

After a leisurely bath, dressed in her white robe, Louise slowly began applying makeup and styling her hair. Within an hour there was a gentle knock at the door.

"Lou, it's me. Are you decent?" Julie asked.

Unlocking the door, Louise declared, "Jules, you look so beautiful. Come in." Admiring her sister's pale pink lace-over-satin dress, Louise's attention then focused on the stunning floral arrangement she was holding. "And that bouquet is incredible. I absolutely love it." A blend of cream roses, baby's breath and sprigs of silver fern were arranged in a small bunch, forming a trail of around six inches.

"I know, right?" Julie smiled. "And here's a coronet. I thought you might like it…but honestly, if you'd prefer…"

Louise promptly interrupted her sister. "I'm definitely wearing that. It'll sit perfectly amongst my curls, don't you think?"

"Yes, I do," Julie smiled. "Those tiny cream roses with the sprinkling of white baby's breath will look gorgeous in your dark hair."

"How long have you been up Jules? You're as bright as a button," Louise commented, making her way back to the bathroom to finish her makeup.

"Since about six, I think. John took the kids down to explore the beach, so I thought I'd get ready early, in peace. He assured me they'll all be showered and dressed by 11:30am, so…I've come to assist the bride. If you don't need any help, that's fine…but I'm staying here to annoy you either way."

Louise laughed as she exited the bathroom and turned her back to her sister. "Are my curls soft enough Jules?"

"That depends, Lou," she replied, gently lifting Louise's hair at the ends. "Are you going to spray them?"

"I don't think so. I'd prefer a more natural look."

"In that case, they're a bit tight now…but they'll drop anyway. They look great. You've done a beautiful job of your makeup too. If I didn't know any better, I'd say it was done by a pro. Gorgeous foundation, the perfect coverage…and those brownish-gold eye shadows really make your eyes shimmer."

Louise gently turned her head from side to side in the mirror above the desk and said, "Thanks, Jules. Would you like to make yourself a coffee while I get dressed? I just had one with breakfast."

"Absolutely. I'll have a sticky beak at these magazines too. If you need anything, just let me know."

The sisters continued conversing while Louise was in the small bedroom, slipping into her cream silk wedding outfit. She wore a camisole for warmth underneath the two-piece creation which consisted of a pair of wide culotte-style full length pants and a top with long, fitted sleeves. The neck of the top fell in a soft cowl, revealing a hint of cleavage. A few self-covered buttons fastened the back and a row of smaller ones embellished the wrists. High-heeled shoes of an identical cream colour completed the sophisticated outfit.

After clipping on the small pearl earrings that she borrowed from her sister, Louise strategically placed the delicate coronet on her head. Emerging from the bedroom holding their mother's necklace, she asked, "Would you please help me with Mum's pearls?"

Julie's heart instantly melted. She fanned her face whilst enchantingly gazing at her sister. "Of course I will, Lou. You look so incredibly happy and absolutely stunning. Just give me a second to pull back these tears, otherwise I'll have mascara everywhere."

With yet another knock at the door, John quietly uttered, "Sorry to disturb you girls. There's no need to open up. Just a gentle reminder that it's 11:30am. Will you be coming back to the room first, Jules?"

"Yes, darling," she replied. "I won't be long." Returning to face Louise, Julie took both her sister's hands and said, "Okay, I'm off. We'll see you on the lawn out the front of the reception room just after twelve. Don't forget your bouquet and never forget that I love you with all my heart. You're the best sister any girl could ever hope for…and I know that Murray loves you as much as I do. Well… almost," she smiled.

Waiheke Winery was an acclaimed wedding venue with fabulous sea views overlooking the beach and Pakatoa Island. By midday a small congregation of Murray and Louise's family and friends were seated in rows either side of the red carpet that would lead the bride towards her groom. All invitees were in attendance. A colourful, native floral arch at the end of the carpet indicated where the vows would take place.

As guests quietly chatted amongst themselves, a nervous but dashingly handsome Murray Corbet stood facing the arch. He was attired in a dark grey tailored suit with a cream satin tie and a buttonhole that perfectly matched Louise's bouquet arrangement.

Lucy, carrying a small basket of cream rose petals, left the seat beside her parents and made her way to the back of the congregation. As Louise approached her niece, Lucy produced a huge smile and nodded her head. Within seconds, the Lou Rawls song, 'Wind Beneath My Wings' began to play. Julie felt it was an apt alternative to the traditional wedding march, given that the groom was a pilot. This subtle touch of humour wasn't lost on Murray, Louise or their guests.

Walking several metres ahead of her aunty, Lucy scattered petals whilst making her way down the carpet. Louise slowly followed. Murray turned and immediately tears welled when he saw her. Upon noticing the emotion in his eyes, she too became overwhelmed with deep happiness.

Immediately reaching for her hand as she stepped under the arch, Murray kissed Louise on the cheek. Gordon, who was seated in the front row, said, "You're not supposed to do that yet, mate." His comment caused a ripple of laughter.

Having written their own vows, filled with commitment, love and smatterings of humour, the marriage celebrant only said a few short words before allowing the couple to deliver their pledges to one another.

With the ceremony over, guests mingled with the newlyweds in this relaxed, romantic setting. Meanwhile, the children kept themselves amused by gathering up all the rose petals and tossing them over their unsuspecting parents. The photographer took a number of formal photos before discreetly taking some candid shots of the guests and the children at play.

Inside the reception venue, lunch was ready to be served. Tables were arranged in a 'T' shape enabling easy conversation and intimacy for the adults. Julie chose a traditional, New Zealand themed menu consisting of Seafood Chowder with crusty fresh bread for entree, green lip muscles, kina, Bluff oysters, crayfish and a variety of colourful salads for the main course. The children were delighted with their own table in the centre of the function room…and the chicken nuggets and sausages were a real hit. Mark proudly oversaw the menu for the little ones, which included kiddy wine whilst the adults indulged in some of the finest wines that the vineyard produced.

A masterpiece in every sense of the word, all agreed that the wedding cake was almost too impressive to eat; a small tower of mini pavlova meringues bound together by cream with toffee drizzled down from the top. Tiny edible flowers were strategically placed throughout the toffee to add a touch a colour. Not a traditional cake by any means…but certainly spectacular. Naturally a light-hearted argument ensued between Aussie and Kiwi guests, as to who invented the pavlova.

Some brief speeches were delivered. John spoke on behalf of the bride, Ryan for the groom, and the newlyweds also said a few words of their own. Both gratefully thanked Julie for all her hard work in delivering a wedding that was far above and beyond their expectations. After the formalities concluded, the older children took the younger ones outside to play. Meanwhile, the adults danced, mingled, and bubbles flowed until the magnificent red sunset reflected on the waters of the Hauraki Gulf.

• • • • •

On the flight over to San Francisco, Murray told Louise that they'd be travelling to numerous destinations during their honeymoon but still refused to disclose exactly where and when. She was extremely excited about the mystery surrounding their adventure. At home, Murray had only advised that she pack for both warm and cold climates, but that's as much as she knew.

After registering at the Mark Hopkins Hotel, the couple ventured upstairs for dinner. Murray had reserved a table at the 'Top of the Mark' restaurant with views over the amazing city, the harbour, and its famous Golden Gate Bridge. Louise had briefly visited 'San Fran' before, but she'd never seen it from this perspective.

The following day, after taking the cable car to Fishermen's Wharf, the couple sat in the sunshine and ordered Clam Chowder for lunch. The dish was everything it was reputed to be. During the afternoon they took a boat tour to Alcatraz and concluded that it was indeed an isolated, miserable place to be incarcerated.

By 8am the next morning, the jovial couple boarded a six-hour flight to Juneau, Alaska. Here they walked over the Mendenhall Glacier then took the Mount Roberts Tramway to the top of the peak. Looking down, they could see five large cruise liners docked at the wharf, spewing out tourists by the hundreds. The view was absolutely spectacular and surrounding them, some of the higher mountains still retained brilliant-white snow. At the tiny souvenir shop, Louise purchased two small round timber boxes, each with a dragonfly etched into the lid. One for herself and one for Julie. In Alaska it was customary to place written, heartfelt wishes inside the box.

Returning to the base of the mountain, Murray and Louise strolled through the small town of Juneau and entered a pub with sawdust thick on the floor. It was a busy, noisy establishment but as they ordered a counter meal for dinner, the couple realised that all the commotion added to the hotel's vibrant atmosphere. That evening they stayed at the historic Alaskan Hotel where every room boasted an open fireplace.

Walking through town again at daybreak, the newlyweds made

their way to the wharf and boarded a small ship which would take them into the rugged Alaskan Wilderness. The vessel only carried a hundred passengers so given its size, this allowed guests the opportunity to visit small ports that the larger ships couldn't access.

At Bartlett Sound, a National Park area, passengers were taken ashore by tender to watch a documentary at the small cinema. The film featured some of Alaska's unique sites and customs before introducing visitors to its famous Iditarod Sled Dog Race and their booming salmon industry. The ship's tour guide, who was extremely knowledgeable in the field of arctic flora and fauna, then took the group on a short bush hike. During the walk, all were fortunate to witness a mother bear and her three cubs playing in the forest. With cameras in hand, the group managed to get a few shots whilst giving the mammals a wide berth.

In the many inlets, they experienced the spectacle of carving glaciers and countless animal and bird species. Soaring Golden and Bald Eagles, schools of cheeky sea otters, mountain goats, moose, bears with their cubs, dolphins, Orca and Humpback whales…even the birth of a seal pup on a small iceberg. Joining some like-minded fellow passengers, Murray and Louise kayaked around the shore of Sitka Harbour before landing on the beach to inspect several totem poles and watch a carver working on another.

Louise particularly enjoyed the enchanting fishing village of Elfin Cove. Its twelve residents, thirteen in the summer, lived on tiny houseboats all perfectly lined up along the jetty. Given the size of the population, she was fascinated when they found a tiny well-stocked bar…about the size of her ensuite at home.

Leaving the chilly climate behind, the couple then flew south with Alaskan Airlines to Honolulu, Hawaii. Murray had reserved a garden view room at the Royal Hawaiian Hotel, a lovely old pink building that oozed tropical charm. An area out the front on Waikiki Beach was roped-off from the public to allow hotel guests to relax and partake in a bit of longboard surfing.

On the second evening of their stay, they attended one of the island's finest Luau gatherings to absorb the heart of Hawaiian culture and some authentic Polynesian cuisine. The enchanting atmosphere was one of celebration and togetherness…and the food, unforgettable! As the couple joined the performers for some traditional dancing, Murray placed a beautifully fragrant frangipani and hibiscus lei around his wife's neck and said, "I don't want this night to end Lou, but we have to be up just before dawn, so we should be heading back soon. I've booked a taxi to the foot of Diamond Head and I thought we'd walk up and watch the sunrise from the top. Afterwards, if we have any energy left, we might walk back to the beach via the suburbs…check out some markets along the way."

"Did you say 'markets'?" Louise beamed at him. "Well, I suppose I'll allow you to drag me away for that."

Up early, they taxied to the parking lot at the base of the famous landmark and climbed the path to a look-out point at the summit. Hundreds of people had the same idea, mostly Japanese groups with their tour guides. In one section of the track, they crouched down for some time to navigate a narrow tunnel. From the peak of this broad, saucer-shaped crater, the sunrise glistened on the crystal clear North Pacific Ocean surrounding O'ahu.

Slowly strolling back to the hotel in the glow of the morning, the couple observed how the locals lived and even stopped to chat with a few inquisitive residents. After sampling and purchasing some pieces of their home-grown fruit and eating it along the way, they arrived at the Waikiki Family Markets. Here they perused the intricate work of some island artisans and Louise picked out two vibrantly floral sarongs, known as 'pareos', to take home. On stepping back into the hotel, they quickly donned their swimmers and hit the ocean for a well-deserved dip.

The island of Maui, only a half-hour flight from Honolulu is where the newlyweds spent the next three days. Their room at the resort within the exquisitely manicured Wailea Golf Course was superb. Playing nine holes of golf was first on the agenda then they ventured into the quaint town of Lahaina, formerly a whaling station with some interesting little shops.

For Louise, the long-extinct volcano 'Haleakala' brought back memories of Rabaul. In one of the stores, she purchased a pair of scrimshaw earrings. They were made of whale bone with ancient sailing ships on them. She explained to Murray, "Scrimshaw was originally an ancient maritime art. Sailors would carve nautical images into whale bone or whale's teeth. When I lived in Perth, I bought a beautiful scrimshaw whale tooth. It's in my china cabinet at home. From what I remember, it was quite expensive…but you know me, coming from a seafaring family, I just had to have it. I'll show you when we get home."

"Ah, yes. Speaking of home Lou…only two more days in paradise and it's back to Sydney we go," Murray sighed as he cuddled her from behind.

CHAPTER TWENTY-NINE

Moving into Louise's house was an obvious living arrangement for the newlyweds. She'd devoted a great deal of time and effort to her Narrabeen property and for Louise, it was her sanctuary. Murray was more than happy to rent out his furnished apartment and leave the busy suburban street that he'd called home for the past three years.

Two weeks after returning from their honeymoon, Murray had officially moved in. His unit was then professionally cleaned and a local agent found a tenant within four days of listing it. Meanwhile, Louise was fully engaged in her business whilst Murray's international flight schedules expanded to include Port Moresby, Nadi, Hong Kong, Kuala Lumper, Bali, Bangkok, Hanoi and Saigon.

These longish hauls required numerous overnight stays but this afforded him extended time at home in Sydney with his wife. The latter also allowed for Murray and Gordon's renovation to proceed more quickly. Stage one was complete; second floor built, including the large veranda, associated plumbing and wiring, and the aluminium roof of course.

As the old house was fast becoming a new home, Louise set about designing the kitchen and had sourced all samples in readiness for the decision-making process. Keeping to the neutral theme of white, black and timber was a wise choice. Tapware, doors, and associated hardware were now onsite. Lighting fixtures would be next. With her Interior Decorating course drawing to an end, Louise felt that she'd learned a great deal from it.

Within a matter of a month, the entire house renovation was complete. Gordon invited three local real estate agents to inspect the property, in order to gauge a ball-park figure on its value. They knew exactly what they needed to cover costs…thanks to Louise's thorough account-keeping methods. Naturally, Murray and Gordon hoped to make a good profit.

One of the agents, Carol Kerr, was the woman who originally sold them the property. "I've been watching the progress as I drive past each day," she remarked. "What a transformation! Congratulations. And you've made the most of these ocean views. It was a brilliant idea to establish the living area upstairs and take full advantage of the outlook. I don't think you'll have any trouble selling it at all. Could be a home for a family with teenagers, or an older couple who really enjoy entertaining." She then suggested that they consider auctioning the property.

The other two agents more or less agreed, one proposing an auction, the other recommending it be marketed as an 'exclusive' property…due to the fact that it was unusual in its layout, boasted exceptional water views and was situated in a coveted area of Sydney.

Gordon, Murray and Louise had been keeping an eye on the local market and auctions appeared to be quite a popular selling choice. After attending a few themselves, all agreed to utilise this method of sale. In consultation with Carol Kerr, the vendors settled on a reserve price. It may have been a little high for the current market but that could be negotiated down if necessary. Carol suggested a five-week marketing campaign with open house inspections each weekend. They discussed the option of 'dressing' the home with furniture and window treatments but decided against it. The group consensus was to allow potential vendors to imagine the spaces with their own choice of furnishings. So, with everything sorted, the property was now in the agent's hands.

Auction day saw Gordon and the Corbets excited but nervous at the same time. It was an overcast morning with little wind. Five registered bidders and a crowd of about forty onlookers were in attendance. The auctioneer wasted no time introducing himself and describing the property before calling for the first bid, which was well below the reserve. A cautious second buyer's offer was then made, quickly followed by a third party. Already they were about to meet the reserve price.

An Asian gentleman standing at the back of the crowd raised his arm and made a bid on behalf of his client. This was succeeded by yet a higher bid, so he increased it again. The figure was now $10,000 above its reserve. The agent made another offer and the field appeared to be narrowing between two bidders. When the agent began to close the bidding, the Asian man again stepped up his bid. The competitor then surrendered and the auctioneer declared the bidding closed, congratulating the new buyer on his purchase.

Gordon and Murray cleared $85,000 after expenses, which included Louise's designer fee. They could hardly believe their good fortune. And they'd so enjoyed the whole process that it didn't seem like work at all. Over a celebratory dinner, the men decided it was well worth doing again and within a fortnight they'd purchased a run-down duplex on a large block, zoned to accommodate four apartments.

• • • • •

Arriving home from the office early one afternoon, Louise retrieved her mail from the letterbox and amongst a heap of junk mail, was surprised to find an envelope from Michael East, a former solicitor. The Greens had contracted his conveyancing services when they sold the block of land in Perth and at the same time, Michael drew up their respective Wills.

Upon entering the house, she opened the envelope and began to read the Letter of Testament. Astonished to discover that Ross had neglected to change his Will after they separated, Louise was equally baffled to grasp the fact that she hadn't either. It completely slipped her mind. Reprimanding herself and taking a mental note to attend to it promptly, she continued to absorb the letter's contents.

It stated that Louise was now the executor of Ross's estate, which meant everything was legally left to her. The solicitors had also listed his assets; one motor vehicle, his bank account balance and all shares and investments. An itemised portfolio of shares and his Term Deposit account revealed that almost all the money Louise had paid him for his half of the house had been invested. There was no debt whatsoever and Ross's net worth was staggering.

Gobsmacked, she immediately phoned the solicitor at his Manly office. "This is incredible, Mr East. I can't believe it! Are you aware of the circumstances surrounding Ross's death?" she enquired.

"Partly, Mrs Green," he replied.

Quickly interrupting him, Louise said, "I've since remarried Mr East. My name is now Louise Corbet."

Clearing his throat, the solicitor returned, "Pardon me, Louise. I do apologise."

"That's alright. Murray and I have only recently married, so I'm still getting used to it myself."

"Well, in that case I offer you both my congratulations," he responded. "Now back to your question. The Coroner's verdict states 'death by his own hand' and I was informed that the two of you had separated...but that's as much as I know."

"And I have two other questions if I may," Louise started. "Given that Ross committed suicide, I thought his Will would be null and void? And now that I'm no longer his wife, doesn't that change everything?"

He smiled and answered, "No. On both counts. His last Will and Testament is valid and legally binding. 'Death by his own hand' has no bearing on the balance of his assets or acquisitions. The fact that you've since remarried is also irrelevant. Your surname may well have changed but you are still the same entity. He certainly left you a fairly substantial estate, Mrs Corbet."

"Yes, evidently he did. I must say, I view this entire scenario as 'poetic justice' in a way. Ross Green almost destroyed my life before taking his own. I don't know what I'll do about the shares...I don't really know much about the stock market," Louise admitted.

"One of two possible outcomes there. Either transfer them into your name or simply sell them off. I'd strongly advise you consult a financial advisor before making that decision."

"You're right Mr East," Louise concurred. "That's very sound guidance. Thank you. Now I have one final question and I'll make it quick, as I've taken up a lot of your valuable time already. My husband and I need to revise our Wills...so should I organise that with one of your colleagues?"

"Unless there's a conflict of interest, I can do them both Mrs

Corbet. Would you like to book an appointment now?"

Louise smiled and replied, "I'll just have to check Murray's availability first, then we can arrange a date and time. Thanks again Mr East, I'll be in touch again very soon."

Hanging up the phone she silently stood in the hallway, gazing out into the backyard. *'Good heavens...I'm officially wealthy,'* she acknowledged. *'Ross would be furious to know that not only did I survive, I remarried...and Murray and I received all of his assets. He'd be turning over in his grave!'* Smiling at the very thought of it, she yelled out, "That's karma for you, Ross Green...and it tastes so sweet!"

Meanwhile, Murray was scheduled to touch-down at Mascot after a flight from Bali. Louise knew that he'd be home within the hour so she excitedly made a dash to the bottle shop then quickly showered and slipped into a floral cotton dress. After dimming the lounge room lights she selected some jazz music and slowly began dancing throughout the space.

Unlocking the garage's internal door, Murray did a double take when he saw Louise. "Hello my darling. You're looking very radiant this evening. Are we expecting guests?"

"No, my love," she smiled as they kissed. "How was the flight back?"

"Departure was fifteen minutes late but we had a nice tailwind all the way, so arrival was pretty much on time. I'll just put these bags down Lou and jump in for a quick shower. Is that okay?"

"By all means, please do Captain Corbet. Take your time."

He disappeared into their bedroom and Louise prepared some blue cheese and crackers on a small platter. When she heard him getting dressed in the ensuite, she removed the chilled champagne glasses and bottle of Moet Chandon from the fridge.

"Is there anything I've forgotten Lou? Clearly, we're celebrating something," Murray remarked as he entered the kitchen and placed his arms around her.

"Very observant of you my darling. Yes, it would appear we are," she smiled. "And no, you haven't forgotten anything...except to tell me that you love me. Why don't you pour us both a bubbly."

Murray inquisitively replied, "Mmmm, this is very mysterious...

but just to set the record straight, I told you that I loved you this morning when I phoned from Denpasar."

"I know. Just keeping you on your toes," she jested.

As Murray popped the cork and poured the champagne, he said, "Okay Lou, out with it. You can't leave a man hanging in suspense like this."

Taking their glasses to the lounge, with smiling eyes Louise began to tell her husband what had transpired. She concluded her revelation with the total amount that she bequeathed.

Murray threw his head back and roared with laughter. "However inadvertent this may have been on Ross's part, you deserve every single penny of it, my darling. Consider it compensation for all the hell he put you through."

Louise grinned, replying, "I agree. It's pretty hilarious. Anyway, I thought you and Gordon could use the utility for the business and as for the shares, we'll have to decide what we want to do there."

"We?" Murray surprisingly returned. "You're more than capable of making your own decisions Lou. This is your legacy, not mine."

"As far as I'm concerned my darling, we'll both thrive from these assets. They're not mine alone, so I want you to be involved in every financial decision we make. Remember that we agreed to share everything. This just means that now we need to upsize to a bigger bucket."

"Fair enough," Murray conceded, "but I think we'd better make it a barrel!"

• • • • •

Louise was managing to take more time away from the business which allowed her to focus on herself whenever Murray was away. She joined a women's golf competition at her local club where the ladies played one day a week. By adding her name to the draw, Louise was meeting different people which also enabled her to forge new friendships.

Fellow golfers were from various walks of life, some retired, others who were employed as shift workers and a few school teachers who only played during the term holidays. Quite a number of the women had migrated to Australia from all parts of the globe. Louise was enjoying their company and her game was improving considerably.

One of the women, Penny Morgan, was the ladies club captain. She'd retired from the police force and taken up painting and piano as hobbies, enjoying regular classes in both. Within a very short time, Louise and Penny became good friends.

Most days Penny walked her German Sheppard, Shannon, and often called into Louise's for a coffee while the dog romped around the backyard. She would fetch and retrieve a very sloppy ball for as long as someone was willing to throw it…and she loved to chase dragonflies. Louise was happy to see the animal enjoying the wide, open space, just as Magic and Jester had done before her.

Louise showed her friend a photograph of the beloved dogs she once owned as a sigh escaped her lips. "It's so sad when I think about it. I really have no idea what happened to them both after Ross left."

Penny asked to borrow the photo briefly and when she returned a little over a week later, proudly presented Louise with an acrylic portrait of Magic and Jester to hang in her gallery. Naturally, Louise was overwhelmed with emotion. It was a perfect representation of the pair and her friend had even managed to capture each canine's unique personality.

In-between her leisure and work days, Louise concentrated on plans for the outfitting and interior decorating of Murray and Gordon's four townhouses. Builders were well underway and on track to have the complex at lock-up stage by mid-January. Contractors had already been assigned to complete the interior work soon thereafter, though the cabinetmakers were already busy working on kitchen and bathroom fixtures. Each townhouse was designed to have unique, individual textures and different colour pallets.

A few weeks before Christmas, the Corbets received a call from Bill and Robyn Johnson. They'd met the Mount Tamborine couple on Hayman Island and spoken on the phone a few times since. Robyn wanted to know if Louise and Murray had made any plans for the Christmas/New Year period and if not, suggested that the couple return to Queensland and stay with them for a while.

"To be honest Robyn, we hadn't even thought about Christmas," Louise admitted, "but we'd really love to. It just depends on Murray's roster really. I'll call you back in a few days and let you know."

Discussing the option over a cold beer, Murray was as keen as mustard. "With the statutory days plus a week's holiday, we could probably pan it out to ten days up there Lou. You'll be on holidays and the tradies won't be working over the break. The building industry just grinds to a halt over Christmas. We'll be lucky to see them back by the second week in January."

Louise smiled at him and asked, "Do you think they'll give you a week off? It's pretty short notice, plus you just took three weeks off for the wedding and the honeymoon."

"I certainly hope so," he replied. "I had eight weeks of accrued annual leave at the beginning of the year and I've only taken four of them. Flying internationally changes everything too. It's much easier to switch in and out with other pilots compared to domestic routes. I'll have a chat with Warren tomorrow."

Murray's leave was fast-tracked and approved by Wednesday. The following week saw the couple boarding a flight to Coolangatta only a few days before Christmas.

Late in the afternoon they were met at the airport by the Johnsons and driven towards Mount Tamborine via the scenic route. Driving up Wongawallan Drive to a lookout facing east to the ocean, and west to the mountain, Bill parked the car. He then extracted a chilled bottle of wine and four glasses from the boot whilst Robyn produced a selection of cheese and crackers which she placed on a rug.

"What a lovely touch. Thank you both," Louise remarked with enthusiasm. "The perfect start to our time together."

Toasting to their mutual good health and happiness, the couples sipped their local wine as the sun settled over the back of the mountain. It sent a reddish golden glow across the sky that briefly reflected on the high-rise buildings along the coastline from Surfers Paradise to Broadbeach and beyond. Darkness fell rapidly as they packed up and continued their journey to Bill and Robyn's unit.

Overlooking a lovely parkland to the east, their spacious unit was centrally located to the small township of Mount Tamborine. It caught the morning sun and without Daylight Savings in the State, by 4:30am a lovely variety of birds welcomed the new day.

Romano, a long-term friend of the Johnsons, phoned to invite them all for Christmas Eve drinks at his home on top of the hill at Wongawallan. He lived on the eastern side of the elevation and had been renovating the home for many years. The twilight view from his veranda was absolutely spectacular. It took in the entire Gold Coast skyline from Jacobs Well to Tweed Heads and inland to the mountains. Apparently, it was equally as breathtaking during the day as it was at night.

"Oh, this is like a fairyland," enthused Louise as they sat observing the lights switching on across the entire coastal stretch. Romano's house was perched high on the hill surrounded by rainforest on all sides, providing not only the spectacle before them, but privacy as well. He could never be built out and it was only a ten-minute drive to the highway and thirty minutes from the beach.

Their consummate host was of Italian descent and had prepared the group a platter of pickles and olives that he'd marinated and preserved himself. He also bottled his own delicious beer and had an apparatus for distilling alcoholic spirits under the house, which he co-owned with friends. He proudly smiled whilst announcing, "I can offer you beer, whiskey, gin, brandy, bourbon or a variety of fine liqueurs." All agreed that they were more than happy with a 'Romano beer'.

"Do you know if there's any land for sale around here?" Murray enquired as Romano returned with their beverages then settled into his chair.

"Yes, there are a number of blocks. All around ten acres and like this one, they're steep and largely unusable but they do offer a measure of privacy and an abundance of native wildlife. The developer established house pads on some of the blocks years ago… but there's no garbage collection up here and no street lighting either. We're on tank water and residents are serviced by the rural fire brigade who occasionally come up and burn off for training exercises. Our rates are low because we don't have the council facilities of urban areas. There's talk about further development past the end of this road too. The land's owned by a farmer in the valley just west of here and he has plans for some housing blocks."

"I'd be interested in seeing what's available, Romano," Murray replied, completely surprising his wife.

"I can show you a couple if you like. There's one on the western side, two lots down from here and another one on the eastern side with a small cabin on it."

Murray sipped his beer and replied, "That would be terrific. If you're free anytime between Christmas and New Year we'd love to check them out. Thank you."

Driving back to Mount Tamborine later that evening, Louise raised the subject of looking at land in Wongawallan with her husband. "So, you really like it up there, do you my love?"

"Yeah, I certainly do. The views are spectacular and from the moment I stepped foot on Romano's veranda, I envisaged a pole home like Ryan and Paula's. This type of construction can be built on a precarious site with very little disturbance to the land. If it was located on the western side of that steep hill, the poles would provide enough height to take in the easterly and westerly views. Perhaps it's just a pipe dream but I'd love to take on such a challenge Lou. Wouldn't you?"

"Sounds wonderful to me. I'd be into that for sure."

Waking to a splendid but very humid Christmas morning, the couples devoured a large plate of Danish pastries and freshly-squeezed orange juice before organising their picnic lunch. Whilst the women attended to food and drinks, Bill and Murray made themselves useful in the garage. They gathered up picnic items, filled a small esky with ice and began packing the car.

Outside, the Johnson's street was already a hive of activity. Parents watched on as children excitedly played with their gifts from Santa Claus. Some were riding shiny new pushbikes and skateboards, others were playing ball games in the middle of the road. Joyful laughter and the occasional shriek of delight echoed throughout the entire neighbourhood.

Just as Bill was rearranging the boot, a young boy holding a large tin of assorted shortbread appeared beside him. "Merry Christmas Mr Johnson," the child beamed. "This is from Mummy and Daddy and Sarah and me."

"Oh, thank you Riley. Merry Christmas to you too, dear boy," Bill smiled, patting him on the shoulder. "This is my friend Murray. He's from Sydney. We're heading up to the falls now, but I know that Robyn has a present for you all as well. She'll bring it over when we get back this afternoon. What's that in your pocket?"

Riley quickly whipped out the action figure and held it high above his head. "It's G.I. Joe. He's the most bravest soldier in the whole widest world! He can move his arms and legs and everyfing." Giving Bill and Murray a quick demonstration he then added, "I got it from Santa but Mummy says he can't come to Kindy 'cause he might get lost."

Bill smiled. "Mummy's right Riley, he's far too special to be at Kindy. I tell you what…when our friends go home next week, I'll come over and we can build a battleground for him in your sandpit. How does that sound?"

"Awesome, Mr Johnson. He'd love that! Maybe you could ask Mrs Johnson if you can have a G.I. Joe too? We could fight each uva."

"Good thinking. I'll see what I can do. Please thank Mummy and Daddy for the biscuits."

Running back into his yard next door, Riley shouted, "I will, Mr Johnson. Merry Christmas."

"What a cute little fellow," Murray commented as Louise and Robyn appeared in the garage.

"We thought you two had disappeared," Robyn smiled, noticing the shortbread tin in her husband's hand. "I see you have morning tea sorted. Let's pack that esky and we're ready to go."

Within a ten-minute drive from the Johnson's unit, the couples entered the Joalah National Park. Pulling up at the entrance to a short walking trail they unpacked the car and made their way through to Curtis Falls. The lush rainforest setting was both picturesque and cooling. A large swimming hole at the base of the falls was surrounded by towering basalt rock faces.

Their day was spent paddling in the refreshing, crystal clear waters of Cedar Creek, relaxing on their chairs beneath massive ghost gums and enjoying a delicious Christmas lunch. Besides their silverside, coleslaw and Turkish rolls, Robyn also dished up some of her home-made Christmas pudding with brandy custard. A few glasses of white wine topped off the afternoon perfectly.

A pre-booked dinner that evening in the hinterland's finest restaurant, saw the establishment filled with around sixty cheerful patrons. It was festively decorated with meticulous attention to detail, including hundreds of tiny string lights adorning the ceiling. All agreed that it was a Christmas wonderland to behold.

"What a beautiful place," Murray remarked, "and the outside deck just spilling over into the rainforest like that is really incredible. Everything around Mount Tamborine is so aesthetically perfect."

Robyn nodded and replied, "We knew you'd enjoy this spot. Bill and I have been here a few times and we always encourage others to try it. They don't do much advertising but then again, they don't need to. They have a great reputation up here on the mountain."

Soft classical music and Christmas carols played in the background whilst a buzz of convivial chatter continued between the Johnsons and the Corbets. Having heard earlier in the day all the details regarding Murray and Louise's wedding and honeymoon, Robyn enquired about the expansion of Louise's businesses whilst the men discussed Murray and Gordon's soon-to-be completed townhouses.

Leisurely sipping their varied cocktails, the conversation quickly became a group affair when Louise announced that she was wanting to become an Australian citizen. "I've been mulling it over for a while now," she admitted. "Some of the women in our golf competition gained their certificates last year. I wouldn't have to renounce my New Zealand citizenship, it would just mean having dual rights. I'm married to an Australian, I've lived here for a number of years now and I own two businesses that pay Australian taxes. The timing's right, so it seems to make perfect sense."

Murray smiled and took her hand. "As my wife, you already have the privileges afforded to any Australian, Lou…but if that's what you want, I think it's a great idea.

Bill and Robyn concurred. "It's a great excuse for a party too!" Bill added.

Louise laughed. "You're right. I'm happy to have a party any day Bill. I just want to be Australian in my own right. I love this country, its people and their fabulous sense of humour. They really know how to 'take the mickey' and have a good laugh at themselves."

Waiters arrived at their table with Christmas dinner in hand, impeccably presented. Glazed duck with chestnut stuffing, figs and watercress. This was later followed by red velvet trifle with fresh berries for dessert.

"Tomorrow, I definitely have to walk off all the calories I've eaten today," Robyn announced, patting the corners of her mouth with a serviette. "Oh, and I promised Doreen that I'd help her plant those seedlings in the morning."

Bill placed his arm around Robyn's shoulder and whilst looking at Murray said, "Remember to take Robyn's car whenever you want it. No doubt there's much of the coast you'd like to see while you're here and honestly, most of the time it just sits in the garage doing nothing."

"That's very kind. Thank you both," Murray replied.

By 9pm the couples left the restaurant and headed back to the Johnson's unit. A small nightcap was in order to complete their Christmas day celebration before flopping into bed.

For the next three days, Murray and Louise visited Sea World, spent a day swimming at Broadbeach and lapped-up a shopping spree in the heart of Surfer's Paradise. The balance of the Corbet's time was spent in the company of their gracious hosts and meeting some of Bill and Robyn's closest friends.

On Friday morning, Romano kindly took Murray and Louise to inspect the two blocks of land for sale in the Wongawallan area. The first was on the eastern side of the road and though it provided a similar view to Romano's site, the topography was much flatter... hence the rather hefty price tag. The second block was located on the western side and its steep terrain particularly lent itself to a pole home construction. The couple loved it immediately.

"Absolutely beautiful, Murray. So tranquil...and listen to those birds," Louise remarked.

As they moved further down the block, a family of bush turkeys could be seen scratching in the undergrowth. Looking back up towards the road, Romano suggested, "The house pad up there would be a perfect place to install the water tanks...and you'd capture the coastal view if you built up at road height. Then you could split another level further down."

Nodding in agreeance Murray replied, "Yes, I can envisage it Romano. That would be perfect for this site." Turning to Louise he asked, "So, my darling wife…your thoughts?"

Louise slowly turned full circle and beamed, "I can already picture it too. I don't think we should let this opportunity pass, so…I think we should buy it."

"Just like that?" Murray quizzed her.

"Yep. Just like that," she returned. Smiling at Romano she added, "You only live once, isn't that right Romano?"

He threw up his hands and shouted, "Vivi la tua vita al meglio! That's right…so live your life to the fullest."

Only half an hour after arriving at the block, they returned to Romano's house and Murray called the real estate agent whose sign was displayed on the allotment. Some two hours later a contract was drawn up and a cheque written out for the deposit. Settlement would be reached in twenty-eight days.

"You just bought a block of land? Here? Today?" Bill questioned when Murray and Louise arrived back at the unit. He heard what Murray said, but couldn't quite believe it.

"Yes, we did Bill," Murray smiled at him. "Bit the bullet and dived right in."

"Wow! I'm shocked…and absolutely delighted for you both."

Meanwhile, having overheard the conversation from the kitchen, Robyn burst into the living room and congratulated the couple. "So…which one is it?"

"The one on the western side. We love the aspect and it's the perfect site for a pole home," Louise smiled, embracing her friend.

Over dinner that evening Bill informed the couple that Brian Clarke, who lived at the end of their street, was a pole home builder. "Prestige Pole Homes is the name of his business. He's a lovely young guy. We've spoken numerous times and Robyn and I have seen a few of his projects under construction. Perhaps you could have a chat with him when he gets home from work tomorrow afternoon…you can't miss his dark green work ute, the business name is plastered right down the side of it in gold lettering."

"Well, that's very convenient, isn't it?" Murray smiled. "Sure, we'd love to talk to him, Bill. Thanks."

Brian's utility passed the Johnson's unit at around 4:30pm the following afternoon and parked in the culdesac. As the Corbets commenced their walk to the end of the street, Louise informed her husband, "Robyn said it's house number 82."

Murray rang the chime and a petite Thai woman soon opened the door. She was cradling a tiny infant in her arms. Murray introduced himself then quickly apologised for the intrusion before asking if he could speak with Brian.

"I hope we didn't wake the baby?" Louise quickly remarked.

"Oh, no…I'm just about to give him a bath," she replied, right as Brian appeared at the door.

After Murray explained that he and Louise were staying with the Johnsons and had just purchased a block of land, he asked if it would be possible to inspect any of the homes that Brian had built in the area.

"Ah, yes, by all means…provided the owners are home. There are two at Helensvale, not far from one another, so I'll make a couple of calls then phone you back tonight."

As arranged the evening prior, Brian met the Corbets and the Johnsons at his first specified address. The home was built on a very steep slope. Entry to the front door was via a rough huen timber ramp that joined the street's footpath. As they all removed their shoes, the proud home owners opened the door to welcome the group.

Brian smiled and hugged them before introducing everyone. "Ted and Mary are such a wonderful couple," he told Murray and Louise. "They're always receptive to me showing potential clients through their beautiful home…and I sincerely appreciate it."

"Always a pleasure Brian," Mary replied. "Please, everyone, come in and take a look around. We'll just be out in the front garden if you need us."

Most of the rooms throughout had polished timber floors, except for the living room and all three bedrooms. They were covered in thick, woven carpet. All but two of the poles were on the outside of the dwelling and the living, kitchen and dining areas were open plan. Huge beams ran in two directions, supporting both the exterior and interior poles. A pot belly fireplace stood in one corner of the living room.

Brian pointed out the major advantages of building a pole home as opposed to conventional structures whilst the group made their way through each space. "You can see that if you didn't want any interior walls at all, that's entirely possible because the poles and beams take all the weight of the roof...and together they stabilise the entire building."

"Incredible," Bill declared as he stared up at the ceiling. "I had no idea that a pole home could literally be a small arena."

Thanking the owners for their hospitality, the group then moved on to the second house where they found the occupiers equally accommodating. It was located on similar terrain amongst gigantic ghost gums and dense bushland. This dwelling contained more internal poles as it was a larger, four-bedroom home. Cork tile floor coverings appeared in the kitchen and wet areas whilst the balance of the house was carpeted. Again, it was extremely open plan and the living room flowed onto a large timber deck on the northern side. Two split levels separated the space; one dividing the living area from the bedrooms and the other stepping down onto the deck. Each level was connected by two steps. The design concept was brilliant. Descending to each level gave the impression that one was actually stepping down the hill....and vice versa.

"As you can see," Brian started, "this kind of construction is extremely flexible. Council require plans to conform to regulations in the usual way, but the interior of a pole home can be configured pretty much any way the owner desires. There really are no rules."

Murray said thoughtfully, "Yes, this method of building completely lends itself to one's own creativity. It's very innovative. I love it."

The group then returned to the street after extending their gratitude to the home owners. Brian handed Murray his business card and a couple of brochures. "I like to see owners develop their initial concepts then we collaborate on the house plans to ensure you get the end result you're looking for. I have to head off to Nerang now, so enjoy your holiday and have a safe flight back to Sydney. If you need anything further, just let me know. Pleasure meeting you."

After Murray agreed to stay in touch, they parted ways. Louise suggested that on the drive back to the Johnsons, they divert up to the block to take some photographs for reference purposes. Standing on the street, overlooking the land and admiring its views, Murray and Louise were super excited about the prospect of their pole home. Bill and Robyn were equally as thrilled for their friends.

New Year's Eve saw the Johnsons and the Corbets join numerous other party guests at Romano's Wongawallan house. From the front veranda they witnessed two spectacular fireworks displays. As New South Wales was an hour ahead of Queensland, due to Daylight Savings, the first flashes of colour at 11pm could be seen down on the State's border. An hour later the world lit up from Tweed Heads in the south, right through to Sanctuary Cove in the north.

Around lunchtime the following day, having all slept in after a late evening, the Corbets packed their suitcases and by 1:30pm Bill and Robyn were returning the couple to Coolangatta airport. Hugging their gracious hosts and bidding them farewell, Murray and Louise then boarded their flight to Sydney. Unbeknown to the Johnsons, Louise had left a token of their gratitude on the dresser in the spare room...an envelope containing $200 cash, along with a fine dining restaurant voucher to 'Corby's on Broadbeach'.

Fastening her seatbelt in preparation for take-off, Louise smiled, kissed her husband on the cheek, then held his hand and said, "Well, I was hoping to do a bit of shopping while were here, and we did... but if you'd told me before we left home that we were going to buy a block of land while we were away, I'd have called you 'crazy'!"

CHAPTER THIRTY

Meeting Murray and Louise onsite, Gordon brought the couple up to speed with the townhouses' completion schedule. "Carpenters have been here all week, so now the architraves and skirting boards are finished and internal doors hung. The kitchens are due to be fitted early next week and there's a painting contractor around here somewhere…he's firming up the quote and said he'd like to start as soon as the tilers are done."

"That's great Gordo," Murray returned. "It's full steam ahead by the look of things. I'll touch base with that landscaper in Wollongong again when we get home and tell him that we're all set to go. I envisage in about three weeks from now, we can probably put them on the market."

While Louise was discussing colour palettes and sifting through numerous swatches with the painter, Gordon asked Murray, "Do you think we should sell all four of them… or possibly keep one as a rental?"

Murray contemplated the proposition for a few moments. "Well, they found great tenants for my unit and there have been no complaints either way. So, I suppose, depending on what we make out of selling the other three, you're right…it might be prudent to hang onto one."

Both agreed that going to auction worked extremely well for them the first time around, therefore they'd opt for the same strategy again, with the same agent.

Over the next fortnight all four interiors were finished and the landscapers had added their final touches to the easy-care gardens. Carol Kerr inspected the townhouses to offer her valued opinion in regards to a realistic asking price. She was so impressed by each unit's layout, design and colour and texture choices, that she recommended Louise advertise her skills by way of signage placed inside each unit.

"I'm almost positive you'll get more work," Carol asserted. "There are so many new buildings going up in this area and quite a few renovations. Do you have any business cards that you could leave on the kitchen countertops for open inspections?"

"No, sadly I don't...not for this business anyway," Louise admitted. "I could organise some easily enough. That's clever thinking, Carol. Thank you. I'll do that."

Between the vendors and their agent, open inspection dates and the all-important auction date was decided upon. Louise thoroughly enjoyed designing her A4-sized corflute signs and business cards which were produced by the local printer she'd used numerous times in the past. On collection, the owner said, "I didn't realise you were diversifying into interior decorating Louise. I pinched a couple of your cards before we packaged them. Hope you don't mind? My sister and her husband have just started building at Dee Why and she mentioned wanting someone to style the new house for them." Naturally Louise was chuffed and kindly thanked Harry for his recommendation.

Within ten days, two of the townhouses sold prior to auction. Gordon and Murray received the asking price for each of them and a week later, at auction, the third was purchased after a lengthy bidding war. Altogether, their sale profits more than covered the cost of the fourth townhouse, so they decided to hold onto it for the time being.

Placing it in the hands of Sara Cuttance, the agent who already held the rental contract on Murray's unit, was an obvious choice. Though Sara was young and relatively inexperienced in the rental market, Murray felt that she'd proven herself extremely worthy of the task. Her 'can do' attitude and exuberant motivation was almost infectious.

Gordon and the Corbets deliberated over whether to furnish the townhouse prior to listing it for rent, but within days Sara received an eager enquiry from a young couple who solidified their decision. On inspection, they loved the place but needed furniture and were wanting to move in within a week.

"I've interviewed them both," Sara informed Murray over the phone, "and they're absolutely lovely. They've only recently married, so neither of them have previous rental references but they do work locally. I called their respective employers and a few of their friends. All sang their praises; a trustworthy, hard-working couple who dedicate a lot of their spare time to numerous charities throughout the North Shore."

"Sounds like a perfect match," Murray smiled. "It doesn't give Lou very long to source the furniture and I'm away all week…but I'm sure she'll manage. Gordy's home for the next three day, so he can lend her a hand."

"Terrific. In that case, you officially have yourself some tenants. They'll need a fridge and a washing machine. Other than that, just do the bedrooms, a television and a small dining table for the lounge room…oh, and a small setting for the veranda. I've added \$35 to the weekly rent payment to cover the furnishings. Is that fine by you?"

Murray was already nodding when he replied, "Yep. All good, thanks Sara. Lou will call you when everything's in place." Hanging up the receiver he quickly turned to his wife.

"Exactly how long do I have?" she asked anxiously.

In a feeble attempt to butter her up, he answered, "Only a week… my hard-working, adorable, generous, supportive…"

Louise interrupted him. "Flattery goes a long way, Mr Corbet… but I'm not sure it'll take you that far." She then smiled and placed her arms around his waist.

"Wait…there's more," Murray hinted as he kissed her. "If you let me whisk you off to the bedroom, I'll show you my full appreciation."

Squirming to release herself from his grasp, she smiled up at him. "Oh, I don't doubt that for one moment…but now's not the time. Good heavens. One week! I'd better get a wriggle on.

• • • • •

With occupiers now in the rented townhouse, Louise was looking forward to taking a breather but enquiries for her interior decorating services began flooding in. Numerous consultations were scheduled over the next few months and within a week she'd landed her very first contract.

Before delving into some décor and styling ideas one afternoon, Louise received a call from the Fotomat reminding her that prints which had been developed over a month ago, were still awaiting collection. She apologised for the oversight and immediately drove to the Narrabeen Shopping Centre to pick up and pay for the photos.

Scanning through them in the driver's seat, a beaming smile suddenly appeared on her face when she came across one particular shot; a coastal view from Romano's deck in Wongawallan depicting an artistic cloud formation over the high-rise buildings dotted along the ocean's fringe. In the top right-hand corner, she'd also managed to capture the branch of a Casuarina tree which perfectly set the scene.

Only a few blocks away, Louise pulled up outside the picture framing shop and with photo in hand, entered the premises. She asked the sales assistant if the photo could possibly be enlarged, applied to canvas and mounted on a wrap-around frame.

"I'll just check that for you," the young woman replied before slipping out the back to consult with her superior.

The assistant and her boss soon returned to the front counter. "Ah, Louise," he smiled. "I knew I recognised that voice. It's a great photo. The Gold Coast, I take it?"

"Yes, it is," she returned. "I'm hoping I haven't left my run too late, but I was hoping to have it ready for my husband's birthday next Friday…and I'm more than happy to pay accordingly. Is there any chance of that?"

"For you Louise, I'll make it happen," he nodded. "Enlarged as much as I can without losing focus?"

"I think so. I'll leave that to your expert judgement."

Whilst writing up the job ticket he said, "Consider it done. I'll call you as soon as it's ready."

Knowing that she had little spare time between now and next Friday, on the way home Louise purchased a sizable amount of silver wrapping paper, some wide blue ribbon then conscientiously selected a birthday card.

Murray also had a busy week ahead of him. Currently in Hong

Kong for the past three days, he was now scheduled to spend the next five in Kuala Lumpur before returning to Sydney on Friday morning.

Delighted with Louise's styling concepts, by Wednesday her client gave the green light for Louise to begin sourcing everything required to decorate the new unit, including a three-piece sofa, dining table, chairs and window coverings. After scouring through furniture, fabric and homeware stores for a full day, Louise chose and purchased all the décor pieces on her list. Each item superbly hit the brief; earthy tones and textures with a hint of emerald green and an emphasis on rusty-browns. The deliveries would be made directly to the client's unit within a fortnight, at which time Louise was scheduled to arrange their layout.

Extremely dense, low-lying mist that covered most of Malaysia, delayed Murray's departure flight for well over four hours. Louise was relieved to learn that her husband would still make it home, as she was preparing a special meal for his thirty-third birthday. 'Amat pis' a la New Guinea for entrée, a pidgin English term for raw, white fish marinated in coconut milk and lemon juice; pork fillet, broad beans and cherry tomatoes for main course; pavlova topped with whipped cream and Grand Marnier marinated strawberries for dessert.

When she received a call from Murray to advise that he'd landed and would be home around 5pm, Louise applied some makeup and got changed into a red, low-cut blouse teamed with black jersey pants and stiletto heels. She thought her black triangular earrings with a ruby-red centre, completed her outfit perfectly.

Having already set the dining table with her parents' beautiful silverware and crystal champagne flutes, she ventured into the garden to cut a variety of brightly coloured flowers for the centrepiece. Returning to the back deck, Louise was surprised to look up and see Murray casually leaning against the sliding door with arms folded.

"I'm just admiring the scenery," he smiled. "You look absolutely gorgeous, Lou."

Still holding the flowers in one hand and her secateurs in the other, she placed her arms around Murray's neck and passionately kissed him. "Thank you…and Happy Birthday my gorgeous husband. You've had a long week, so I thought we'd celebrate at home. A nice dinner, some champagne…"

"Mmmm…I've missed you, my sweet. That sounds wonderful. I hope I can have you for dessert?"

"If you play your cards right," she smiled. "Do you want to take a shower while I prepare the entrée?"

Murray kissed the back of her hand, turned on his heels and made his way down the hall. "I hope you haven't gone to too much trouble Lou?"

"Never," she smiled whilst arranging the flowers in the bowl.

Within ten minutes Murray re-emerged wearing his favourite chinos and a casual shirt he'd purchased on the Gold Coast. Looking fresh and handsome he presented himself to his wife. "What can I help you with darling?"

"Well…this is ready in about five minutes, so you could pop the champagne and pour us a glass."

With entrée served, Murray savoured the new taste sensation of 'Amat pis' while the couple enjoyed their chilled beverages and caught up on one another's news for the week. The pork still had fifteen minutes remaining in the oven, so Louise collected Murray's gift from the office and placed it on the chair beside him.

Reading the card, Murray said, "They're beautiful words. Thank you, my love," then slowly started unwrapping the gift. He looked up at Louise before removing the tissue paper completely. "Oh wow! Wongawallan. Who took the photo?"

"I did," Louise smiled, "while you were on the phone to the real estate agent."

"It's beautiful, Lou. Can't wait to hang it in the gallery first thing in the morning. Weren't the clouds amazing that day? And I love the tree branch in the foreground."

"That's a Casuarina tree. Sometimes they're called 'she oaks', but I don't know why."

Placing his arm around her, the couple then headed to the kitchen to dish up main course. While Murray carved the roast pork fillet, Louise placed the beans to one side on the plates and arranged the piping hot tomatoes at intervals around the edge. With the pork now in place, its succulent juices were drizzled over the entire meal.

Another glass of champagne consumed with dinner, Murray and Louise began discussing plans for the pole home. "I know we agreed to take our time and not bite off more than we can chew," Murray started, "but I had to kill some time during the layover in Malaysia, so I started sketching out a few ideas. I was thinking possibly two levels. The top floor would have views both ways and the second level could take in Mount Tamborine through the trees. If both levels were self-contained, we could earn income from two rentals. Or, we could just rent out the lower level and keep the top free for whenever we choose to utilise it. What are your thoughts on that idea Lou?"

"I think it's very sensible being able to have leverage like that. We were considering the two levels, so it just means a more expensive build with an additional kitchen, bathroom and laundry…but that's neither here nor there in the overall scheme of things."

Murray reached out and held Louise's hand. "The townhouses just pulled a decent profit and that might go close to covering the cost of the Queensland build. Besides, if we did decide to build two levels, we wouldn't have to build them both at the same time."

"True," Louise returned, "but you'll need that equity if you start another project. I'd be happy to put some of the profits from the businesses into the pole home…and the rental income from your unit more than covers the rates and upkeep around here, so you could possibly look at putting the balance into it as well. And remember there's all the money we have invested."

"I wouldn't want to dip into that, Lou. Those funds are yours… not for any of my possibly hair-brained schemes."

"I appreciate your concern darling, but it's there if we need it. Why would we borrow when we don't have to?" Louise then stood up and took their plates and cutlery to the dishwasher.

"Okay, okay, I'm hearing you," Murray conceded, closely following her with their empty champagne flutes.

"Are you ready for dessert?" Louise asked.

Murray smiled and pulled her towards him. Running his hands down the length of her arms he replied, "Am I ever! I think you'd better kiss me before I burst."

"I meant pavlova, birthday boy," she smiled back at him.

"Oh Lou, will it keep for tomorrow? I have plans for birthday dessert tonight...and it involves you, me, and some body chocolate I bought in Hong Kong. What do you say?"

Louise starred deeply into his eyes. "You know I can never resist chocolate, let alone the thought of licking it off every square inch of my husband's fabulous body."

With that, Murray quickly grabbed Louise's hand and whisked her off to the bedroom for some slow, very playful lovemaking. The kitchen was still a mess but when they surfaced from the bedroom at around 11pm to further indulge in Louise's delicious pavlova, neither of them could care less.

•••••

On Friday evening of May 25th, crazy celebrations were in full swing at the Corbet's house. Louise had officially been 'naturalised', along with seventy others at a Citizenship Ceremony held in the Manly Council Chambers earlier that afternoon.

Around thirty friends and work colleagues joined Murray and Louise to party in true Aussie-themed style. All were asked to dress in their worst 'okka' attire and only one couple bucked the trend. John and Julie Keane's presence, along with the outfits they were wearing, completely surprised and delighted Louise no end. They appeared in reed skirts, Julie in a halterneck top with a maori print, and both were wearing headbands with mokos painted on their chins.

"So...now you're officially an Australian Kiwi. Congratulations Sis," Julie smiled as she embraced Louise.

Placing her hands over her mouth, Louise held back tears while she mumbled, "Oh you guys, I can't believe you came all this way!" Murray swiftly appeared behind her. "Did you know the Keanes were coming? she asked him.

"Maybe," he returned with a grin, kissing her on the cheek. He then shook John's hand and warmly hugged Julie. "You two look fantastic, I must say. Let me grab you some drinks and we'll introduce you to everyone."

Peter and Martha kindly set up the food on a large trestle table on the deck, consisting of Vegemite sandwiches, meat pies in paper bags, little boys with tomato sauce, fairy bread and lamingtons. The beer keg was a real hit with the men, as were the sparkling lemonade sodas for the children.

"Okay everyone," Murray shouted. "Could I have your attention please. Before we really crack on with this party, I'd just like you all to join us around the side of the house because we have a surprise for Louise." As he made his way down the steps into the yard, his intrigued wife and their party guests followed.

Unbeknown to Louise, a large flagpole had been erected between the fence and the house, about midway down the yard from the street. On sighting it she beamed with elation. Murray took her hand and said, "Being a proud Kiwi…and now a very proud Aussie Lou, we thought you'd like to proclaim your dual citizenship for all to see. Would you do us the honour of raising the flags to mark this special occasion?"

"What a bewdy…you little rippers!" Louise announced as she scanned the crowd. "I'd absolutely love to." Heaving three flags high into the air, everyone loudly clapped as each flag was raised. The Silver Fern, the Boxing Kangaroo, and the Aboriginal flag now took pride of place in the Corbet's yard. Tears flooded Louise's eyes as she watched them catch the breeze.

Raucous shenanigans followed, including singing and dancing to some of Australia's best country artists. John Williamson and Slim Dusty were high on the playlist with songs like 'Give me a Home Among the Gum Trees', 'I've Always Been a Drover', 'True Blue', 'Old Man Emu' and the crowd favourite; 'Pub with no Beer'.

Meanwhile, the hosts and their guests also enjoyed playing some good old fashioned Aussie games in the backyard. Cricket was first up and each batter had to wear the customary floppy hat with swinging corks, a navy-blue singlet and stubbie shorts. The great thong toss became highly competitive amongst the children, with all players receiving a small bag of Fantales for their efforts. Egg and spoon races also kept the kids occupied whilst the adults participated in some extremely entertaining three-legged races.

It was nearly midnight by the time guests departed. All tuckered out from a fabulous evening, the group still managed to bellow out one final cheer as they headed to their vehicles. 'Aussie Aussie Aussie, Oi Oi Oi'.

CHAPTER THIRTY-ONE

When to broach the subject of starting a family with his wife, was somewhat of a conundrum for Murray. He'd questioned himself about asking her numerous times. Even though the couple had been happily married for just under a year, he was still unsure if she was ready for the discussion.

Over dinner one evening, he finally struck up the courage to raise the issue. Thrilled by his wife's enthusiastic response, they delved deep into the prospect of adoption. Did they want an infant or an older child? A boy or a girl? After weighing up the alternatives, Murray and Louise agreed that given the choice, they'd prefer a baby boy.

An initial enquiry was made by phone. The Child Services representative who spoke with Louise thoroughly explained the steps involved in the process and advised the Corbets to fill out and lodge a formal application for adoption. Once received, the application would be screened and moved onto the interview stage. This required a representative from the department to personally interview the prospective parents and inspect their home.

"We attempt to establish a suitable time for all parties, Mrs Corbet," he pronounced. "You'll be required to answer a myriad of questions in relation to your respective backgrounds. The purpose is to try, wherever possible, to match the baby's history with your own. In other words, we attempt to complement the heredity and interests of the adoptive parents, with those of the birth parents. As you can appreciate, the welfare of the child is our number one priority... so this process takes quite some time to get it absolutely right. All going well, you could be looking at up to eighteen months."

The Corbets were disappointed with the lengthy procedure but agreed that it would allow ample time for preparation. While the endless bureaucracy was underway, Murray and Louise collaborated on their plans for the pole home. It was decided that they'd build the top level first, though technical drafts for both floors would be submitted for approval simultaneously.

"There are too many trees to be bothered keeping a pool clean, so I'm happy to set a spa into the deck on the upper level…but I do think we should install fireplaces on both floors," Louise suggested. "Apparently it can get pretty cold up there in the mountains during winter."

Murray tapped his finger on one specific area of the drawing and said, "I love this concept…you're a design genius, Lou. It'll be the drawcard of the entire top level and I'm pretty confident Brian will react the same way."

A sunken area, recessed into the floor on the mezzanine level was a funky brainwave Louise had after seeing a similar idea in a magazine. A mattress would fit snugly into the recess with large, oversized cushions scattered on top to casually watch television, curl up in front of the fire or simply enjoy the view.

They discussed the exterior building materials and as painting would be a nightmare, opted for Brian's recommendation; pre-stained woodgrain sheeting. Murray had also queried him about building the ramp from the street to the front door. Brian advised that any additional external requirements could be built on the trot, once the house was at lock-up stage.

"When I spoke to Brian yesterday," Murray started, "he reckons the ramp will be structurally sound enough to support the weight of a large 4WD."

Louise carefully perused the plans and asked, "What about access to the undercover area downstairs?"

"He said we could build a retaining wall and take a driveway down there."

"Excellent," Louise returned, smiling at her husband. "If we were to rent it out, the tenants would require easy access to their front door. That's about all I can think of for the moment…we've pretty much covered everything. Are you still going to meet up with Brian next week when you're in Brisbane?"

"Sure am, my sweet. I'll hand over these plans so we can get them finalised and ask him to provide us with a quote."

Louise reached out for Murray's hand and said, "Must say, I'm pretty excited now we're at this stage…and I'm really happy with our vision. Brian will probably need to tweak a few things but overall, the design's extremely practical for the climate up there."

"I sense the wheels spinning, Lou. What else is going on in that pretty head of yours?"

She looked at him seriously and replied, "Just thinking about the baby and all the adoption stuff. I understand that nothing's a given…and I don't want to get my hopes up too much yet…but if all goes well…"

Murray quickly interrupted her. "All will go well, Lou. I truly believe that. We're going to be terrific parents and there's no reason for them to deny us a child. I know it isn't easy but we just have to be patient. Now, what were you going to say?"

Smiling up at him she replied, "That I've given some thought to the nursery. When I was looking over these plans a few nights ago, it occurred to me that we could build another room above the garage, probably about the same size, and make it my office. That way we could convert the existing office into a nursery. I still want to have two guest rooms for when family visit with their children, so there's the spare room here…and we could put a queen-sized fold-up bed in the upstairs office for any additional visitors. Does that sound like a crazy idea?"

"Are you kidding me Lou? Far from it!" He kissed her hand and asked, "Do you know if the slab can handle another level? That would be my only reservation."

"Good question, my darling. Don't know if Ross would have thought that far ahead. He only intended to live here for a year before selling up and doing another reno."

Murray rose from his chair to put the kettle on. "Tell you what… I'll call Gordy and get the number for that guy who checked the foundations on our place before we built the second storey. He'll inspect it and we'll have an answer back the same day.

• • • • •

A letter arrived from Child Services advising the Corbets that they'd successfully passed their assessment interview and were therefore deemed suitable to adopt. Now the balance of formalities could proceed after they attended a three-hour 'Preparation for Adoption' seminar to be held in the department's headquarters at Five Dock. Murray and Louise were over the moon to know that within a year at the extreme outside, they would become proud parents.

It was resolved that the garage slab could support an upper level, so visiting their draftsman, he drew up the simple extension which would be accessed via the laundry. Four weeks later the approved plan was released from council then the couple asked Murray and Gordon's builder to quote the job. Mate's rates were applied for the straightforward construction and within another eight weeks, the Corbet's extension was complete.

With her new office relocated, Louise couldn't wait to start decorating the nursery. She slowly began fitting it out with all the requirements for their new baby boy. There was ample room for a single bed, a cot and a change table. Selecting linen, towels and toys was a shopping experience that delighted her no end.

Meanwhile, Gordon and Murray decided it was time to build another block of four units. They dropped into Carol Kerr's office to see if she had any vacant land listings available.

"I believe I have something you'll both be very interested in," she informed them. "We officially have the contract but it hasn't even hit the market yet. It's the old run-down place only two doors up from the townhouses you built."

"You're kidding?" Gordon excitedly replied. "That's a bloody great block. Isn't it Muz?"

"Oh yeah…plenty of room for what we want."

The group then discussed the purchase price, which was a pittance compared to the townhouses block. Carol then agreed to give the men a week to arrange their finances.

"I've taken into account the fact that we no longer need to advertise and market the property, so that's a nice saving too," she smiled.

"What would we do without you Carol?" Gordon asked.

"Make far less profit, I'm guessing," she jested.

At home that evening, the men decided to pool their investments and as Murray still refused to borrow any of Louise's assets, only a small bank loan would be required to complete the sale. Given the solid remunerative portfolio they were establishing, Gordon and Murray considered the option of renting out all four units once they were built.

Louise had finalised another two interior design contracts during the extension process and she was immensely enjoying her newfound career. Though it absorbed much of her time, the I.T. business always remained a priority. She continued to frequent the office and teach whenever required, apply herself to overseeing operations on a weekly basis, and remain hands-on.

Martha had diligently pursued new clients over the past twelve months from both trade and retail sectors which bolstered the business into a fully-fledged recruitment agency. They listed potential employees from all facets of industry, as did the Perth enterprise…and with equal success.

Rewarding her staff's loyalty and diligent work ethic, Louise was committed to providing them with six monthly reviews and bonus incentives. The Narrabeen staff, whom she periodically took out for lunch, also benefited from regular meetings to ensure that any concerns were discussed and resolved. Janet followed exactly the same protocol in Western Australia.

At around 9:30pm, one Tuesday night, Murray was wearily pottering around the house in his pyjamas when the doorbell rang. Quickly ducking into the bedroom, he donned a shirt and shorts, calling out as he did so. "I won't be a minute."

Unlocking the deadbolt, he opened the front door and was surprised to find a young woman, carrying a small boy on her hip, standing before him. She appeared to be rather untidy and the child was wearing oversized, threadbare clothing.

Looking up at Murray she asked, "Is this the home of Louise Green?"

"Ah, yes," he hesitantly replied.

"Can I speak with her please?"

"She's teaching tonight, so I'm afraid she isn't here," Murray returned. The child reached out to him as if wanting to be cuddled.

"May I ask who you are?"

"I'm her husband's niece, Dale Burns…and this is Joshua. I heard my uncle died so his lawyer has probably been looking for me. Uncle Ross would have left me money in his Will."

Murray was speechless at first then thinking on his feet enquired, "Can you show me some form of identification?"

"I've got my pension card."

"But that could belong to anyone," he remarked. "Do you have a Driver's License?"

"Nah, I don't drive," she replied bluntly, readjusting the infant on her hip. "Anyway, who are you?"

"Murray Corbet. I'm married to your uncle's widow now. Her name's Louise Corbet."

The woman's body language suggested that she was growing impatient. "Look, I just need to know when she'll be home. I have to speak to her. Tonight."

"I'm sorry but I think you're wasting your time," Murray retorted in a commanding tone. "Your uncle's estate has settled and there was no mention of anyone other than Louise in his Will."

Anger flared in her eyes. "That can't be right. I need you to give me the name of Uncle Ross's lawyer."

"No, I won't…it's late and I think you should leave," he responded whilst stepping back inside.

The woman quickly attempted to place her foot in the door as Murray closed it, but to no avail.

She yelled at him from outside. "I'll be back…Mr whatever your name was."

After locking the deadbolt Murray entered the bedroom and covertly observed her from the window. Slowly making her way down the street, he wondered, *'How on earth did she get here? Walk? Catch a bus? That poor child shouldn't be awake at this hour.'*

Whilst changing back into his pyjamas, he concluded that he wouldn't tell Louise when she arrived home. It could wait until the morning.

Giving his wife a warm hug at the kitchen bench while he made coffee with breakfast, Murray mentioned the strange incident that occurred the night before.

"That's bizarre," Louise admitted. "In all the time we were together, Ross didn't have any contact with his family. I only know that his sister's legally blind and he told me that she had two daughters."

"She said she'd be back," Murray added.

Louise rubbed her eyes and said, "Oh gosh…I hope she isn't here to cause trouble. That's the last thing we need."

• • • • •

That weekend with Murray in Port Moresby, and whilst the summer weather was relatively mild, Louise wanted to spend time in the garden. Her husband meticulously maintained the lawns but with the tremendous rainfall they'd received this season, some thorough pruning was also required. Upon closer inspection of the flowerbeds, an abundance of pesky insects were devouring Louise's blooms like a three-course meal. Immediate action would hopefully deter them enough to save the new buds from suffering the same fate.

Driving down to the local plant nursery, she purchased an environmentally friendly insecticide and some new gardening gloves. Happily humming as she drove home, Louise was looking forward to getting her hands dirty. With the Corbet's busy lives, it was refreshing to have the opportunity to spend a day in the yard.

Pulling into the driveway she remotely opened the garage door and whilst glancing over at the front of the house, noticed a woman seated on the step with an empty stroller beside her…and an infant crawling around on the lawn. *'Oh dear. Here we go,'* she thought to herself. *'Has to be Ross's niece.'*

Closing the garage door behind her, she then ventured out the front. The woman rose to her feet and approached Louise. "Hello. My name's Dale Burns and this is my son, Joshua."

"How can I help you, Dale?" Louise asked as she observed the young child. He looked to be less than twelve months old; a cute, handsome little man who sat back on his bottom and stared up at her with huge brown eyes and a broad, happy grin.

She replied, "I spoke to your new husband the other night. He wasn't very helpful. I brought something to verify who I am. It's an expired passport I never got to use."

Digging into her tatty handbag she then withdrew the document and handed it to Louise. The photograph comparison was quite different to the person standing before her. Dale's hair was short and jet-black in the photo, but now it was a yellow-blonde straggly mop. Her sad, dull eyes had matured, revealing a great deal of stress for one so young. According to the passport, she was almost twenty-one years old.

"Uncle Ross was my mother's brother. Mum thinks, and I believe her, that his Will would have included us both. I know you've been living here for a couple of years now and this is a nice house...so obviously he had plenty of money. I want to see a copy of the Will."

Louise was slightly taken aback by her frankness. "The passport identifies you, Dale...but it doesn't prove that Ross was your uncle. I'm sorry, but as my husband already told you, there's no mention of anyone but myself in his Will."

"I don't believe you," she blurted. "I want the name of his lawyer?"

Louise could see that the woman was determined in her quest for the truth. After agreeing to provide her with Michael East's name, address and phone number, she wrote them on a piece of paper and handing it to Dale said, "It'll cost you money to find out exactly what I've just told you."

"Thanks, but that's my problem," she remarked, quickly placing her son in the stroller.

Louise watched on as mother and child made their way to the bus shelter at the end of the street. *'Wow! I certainly hope that's the end of that,'* she declared to herself.

Thinking about Dale and Joshua as she worked in the garden, Louise found herself feeling sorry for them...especially the little boy. She deduced that Dale must be a single mother, as she wasn't wearing any rings and it was obvious that she was struggling financially. *'I wonder if I should give her some money?'* Louise pondered. *'I could phone Michael, ask him to get me her address then send her a cheque. I'm just not sure if that could open a whole can of worms. I don't know. I'll talk to Murray about it when he gets back.'*

When her husband did arrive home on the Monday, Louise raised the subject of Dale's visit and her inclination to help the young woman. "We're just so comfortably well off…and she's obviously in desperate need of assistance. The money from Ross's estate was totally unexpected and there's a lot of it to go around."

Murray nodded, adding his own thoughts. "I understand where you're coming from Lou and I agree that she looks as though she could use a hand-up or a hand-out. The decision has to be yours but in the first instance, I think you'd be wise to find out a bit more about her…and her circumstances. If she's a tenant somewhere, it might be better to pay her rent for a while as opposed to giving her a dollop of cash. She may just squander it, instead of spending the funds on necessities for herself and the child."

"As always, you're absolutely right my love. I think I'll phone the solicitor to see what he can find out."

Late the following afternoon, Louise received a call from Michael East just as she was about to contact him. "I'm advising that a Ms Burns came to see me this morning," he started.

Louise cut him short. "Sorry Mr East, I should have phoned earlier. After the conversation I had with her, it was fairly clear that she'd be in touch with you."

"No problem at all," he assured Louise. "She requested to see a copy of her uncle's Will and after asking numerous questions and making a few calls to attempt to confirm her relationship with Ross Green, I obliged. Let's just say Ms Burns was extremely upset to discover you were the sole beneficiary."

Louise shook her head and replied, "I already told her that, but she obviously thought I was lying. My husband and I have discussed the possibility of helping her out a bit, as far as money goes…but obviously we need proof that she's Ross's niece. Did any of your phone calls confirm that?"

"Not by any legal means at this stage. I only spoke to her mother and her landlord. There's no question regarding her identity, her name is Dale Burns. Vouching for her relationship to Ross Green is another matter entirely. That would require the services of a private detective. For what it's worth, I'm convinced that she is Green's niece, but that's purely a gut feeling. Would you like me to put you in touch with the detective who handles most of the cases for our firm's clientele?"

Louise thought for a moment before replying, "Thank you for everything Mr East. I don't think we'll get anyone else involved at this early stage but if you could please provide me with her address, I'll personally go and talk to her."

CHAPTER THIRTY-TWO

Dale's address was located in a back street of St. Mary's, Western Sydney. The area was littered with run-down flats and rusty vehicles nestled amongst overgrown, neglected front yards. A vast majority of its residents lived in semi-darkness, as their shattered windows were boarded-up with timber battens or fibro sheeting. Overturned rubbish bins covered in graffiti, which bestrewed the footpath from one end of the street to the other, was a sight Louise had rarely seen.

'What a dreadful place to live,' she reasoned, pulling up outside the tiny terrace house. After carefully examining her surroundings, she locked the car and navigated her way up the cracked concrete path to the front entrance. She could hear a baby crying inside. After four rounds of knocking, Dale peered through the keyhole before finally opening the door.

Wearing a faded dressing gown, despite the afternoon hour, she looked surprisingly at Louise and asked, "What are you doing here?"

"I'm sorry to just drop in on you like this…but I wanted to see you," Louise explained. "Perhaps get to know one another a little bit. After all, by marriage, you are my niece."

Dale brushed her finger across her nose and said, "Do you want to come inside?"

"If I may, yes, thank you," Louise replied.

Stepping into the sparsely furnished, poorly-lit room, she watched Dale lift her son up from his play mat. Two wooden chairs either side of a small formica table, made up the only pieces of furniture in the entire space. It was clean and tidy, though the heavily-cracked linoleum floor would be difficult to wash. A clutter-free, tiny kitchen was situated at the western end with one door leading to a bathroom and the other to a small bedroom containing a single bed and a cot.

"How did you find out where I live?" Dale enquired, after offering Louise a seat at the table.

"The solicitor phoned me after you left his office, so I asked for your address."

Almost offensively, Dale blurted, "What do you want from me?"

"I don't want anything from you…except for possibly a friendship," Louise admitted. "After you left my house, I gave the matter some serious thought and decided that I'd like to get to know you. If you don't mind me asking, where's your mother?"

"In a nursing home. Been there for a while now. She's blind."

Louise could sense the sadness in Dale's voice. "Does Joshua's father live with you?"

Jiggling the baby up and down on her knee, she looked towards the front door and said, "Nope. He took off before Josh was born. No idea where he is."

Attempting to uplift the conversation, Louise remarked, "You keep this place really clean and tidy, Dale. It's a credit to you, especially with a little one to look after. Do you work at all?"

"I'd like to, but there's no one to leave Josh with…and I can't afford a babysitter. I used to work on the check-out at Coles during the day and stack shelves at night. Mum went into the nursing home when Dad died and she thought Uncle Ross would have taken care of us in his Will. She couldn't afford to pay for his funeral and since then, she hasn't spoken about him. Why do you want to know all of this stuff anyway?"

"I'll get to that in a moment," Louise assured her, "but first, I have two final questions. Did you finish Grade 10 at school?"

For the first time, Dale smiled as she answered. "I finished Grade 12, with pretty good marks too. I also did a typing and bookkeeping course."

Impressed by her response, Louise said, "This is my final question." Pausing for a brief moment to smile at the young mother and her baby, she then asked, "Will you let me help you, Dale?"

"I don't want charity from anyone," she responded, shaking her head. Joshua began to giggle and mimic his mother's movements.

"It wouldn't be charity, Dale. We're related…or at least we were. I'm not sure of the technicalities since Ross is no longer with us. Either way, I can see that you're in need and I'm in a position to help you. And I want to. I think you'll agree that this is hardly a good area to raise a child and I know that your Uncle Ross would have felt the same way. If I was to help with rent and childcare, would you be receptive to the idea of living in Narrabeen, near us?"

"Why would you want to do that, Louise?" Dale asked quizzically.

"I'm not really sure. I just feel it in my heart and I want to give you the opportunity to get ahead. Would you be prepared to accept my offer?"

"Should I call you Aunty Louise?" Dale asked shyly.

"Just 'Louise' is fine. How far in advance is your rent paid?"

"Up until Sunday."

"Okay. My husband's back on Thursday night, so we'll bring our two cars over on Saturday morning to collect you both and all of your belongings. Do you own the furniture?"

Grim-faced, Dale looked around her. "Other than the pram, we literally only have the clothes on our backs and a bit of linen. I do own Joshua's cot and it dismantles. Where will you take us?"

"Well…," Louise started, "if I can't find you suitable accommodation within the next three days, you'll stay at our place until I do. Are you happy to do that?"

Shyly, Dale smiled and nodded in agreement. Her back straightened as though a weight had been lifted from her shoulders. Joshua began squirming in his mother's arms, wanting to be put down, so she allowed him to crawl over to Louise.

After using her leg for leverage in an attempt to pull himself up, Louise bent down, picked him up and placed his tiny body on her knee. "I think we're going to be good friends, little man," she smiled at him. Joshua's big, brown eyes gazed into her own as he giggled and dribbled, revealing four tiny teeth. Placing him gently back down on the floor she said, "I really should get going now Dale. Thank you for taking the time to chat with me."

Both women stood up from the table and Louise widely opened her arms to her niece. Without hesitation, Dale walked straight into them, her warm tears of relief and gratitude seeping through Louise's blouse as she held her tightly.

"You're the first person to offer me help since I had the baby,"

Dale declared, pushing herself back from Louise's shoulder. "I've been so lonely. No idea where to turn. Thank you for giving us this chance. I promise you…you won't regret it."

"I'm sure I won't, Dale. We still have a lot of talking to do, but that can wait for another day. We'll see you on Saturday morning. Just put everything you want to take in a pile. I'll buy you a new bed and linen." Reaching into her handbag to retrieve her purse, Louise added, "Here's my business card. You can call me at home if you want to ask any other questions. Failing that, we'll be here at around 9am." Producing a $50 note, she handed it to Dale and said, "Now I want you to treat yourself."

"Thank you so much, Louise. I'm going to buy some cloth nappies and I'd love to get a haircut." She then picked up her son and walked Louise to the front door. "I can't believe this is actually happening."

After hugging Dale and planting a light kiss on Joshua's cheek, Louise returned to her car and drove for a few blocks before pulling over at the curb. Her emotions were overwhelming and she could no longer contain them. Leaning back against the headrest, she happily smiled through her tears, knowing that she could make this work.

On the way home she discovered a large Baby Bunting store in St. Ives and called in to purchase a high chair and more importantly, a car seat. Murray would have time to fit it before collecting their extended family on Saturday. Louise considered the fact that these practical investments could perhaps be reused when their own son arrived.

Making an appointment the following day with Sara, the real estate agent, Louise advised her that she was looking for a small, ground floor apartment or a small home with a fenced yard. Preferably two bedrooms and convenient to most facilities, as the occupier would be reliant on public transport.

That afternoon they inspected two properties; the unit was currently vacant, and the other small house would be available for tenancy in a fortnight. Interior repainting and carpet replacement was currently being carried out by the landlord. The latter option was within walking distance of Narrabeen's main street. It consisted of two large bedrooms plus another compact room. The enclosed yard, completely private from the street, would keep Joshua safe. Electricity costs were included in the rental, as was a small fee for lawn mowing.

Advising Sara that the tenants would be her niece and baby son, Louise opted for the house and explained, "Dale and Joshua will stay with us until their rental lease commences. I'll be responsible for the rent and the bond."

Louise was excited about the prospect of Dale and the baby living with them for around ten days. It would allow time to get to know one another. Her only concern was for Murray, as she'd not yet had the opportunity to discuss this arrangement with him.

• • • • •

Thursday evening, whilst seated at the dining table for a roast pork dinner with seasoned pumpkin, sweet potato and stewed apples, Louise told her husband what had transpired in his absence.

Murray sat fascinated by the animation and excitement exuding from his wife.

"I feel so good about this," she concluded, smiling and warmly clasping his hands in her own. Suddenly her face fell. "I'm sorry my darling, a thought only just occurred to me. You don't have a problem with Dale being Ross's niece? Do you? I'd never want to cause any sort of resentment between us..."

Murray promptly cut her short. "Look Lou, I admit to thinking she was an angry little waif when I met her, but now knowing her story, I can see why. Honestly, you have me feeling good about it too, my love. I'm sure everything will work out just fine...and the fact that she's related to Ross means absolutely nothing to me."

Hugging him, Louise looked up into his face and said, "Thank you," as tears of happiness and tenderness threatened.

• • • • •

In convoy, the Corbets drove to St. Mary's and whilst unpacking boxes from the car, Murray remarked, "What a feral dump! Gosh, you've done the right thing here, Lou."

Dale flung the front door wide open, accompanied by a beaming smile. Joshua came crawling behind her in hot pursuit. "I was scared you wouldn't come for us," she shouted.

"Your hair looks great," Louise commented, hugging her. It had been cut short and re-coloured to remove the bleached yellow-blonde. Quickly placing her arm around her husband, she declared, "You remember Murray?"

"Yes. Hello, Murray," Dale responded, smiling up at him. "I'm sorry I was so rude to you when we first met."

"That's all history, Dale. Now you have a whole new future ahead of you." He patted her on the shoulder before bending down to pick up her son. "Hi, Joshua. I'm Murray," he smiled at the baby. "I think you and I are going to be great pals." Holding his little body high in the air provoked a high-pitched, shrieking giggle, to which they all laughed.

Once mother and son's belongings were packed into Murray's vehicle, Louise opened the back door of her car. Dale exclaimed, "Oh wow! You even have a car seat for Josh. This'll be exciting. He's never been in a car before, let alone sat in his own seat."

After placing Joshua securely inside the vehicle with his little toy bear 'Barney', Murray kissed Louise on the cheek and said, "Okay girls, drive safely and I'll see you at home."

Following closely behind, Louise brought Dale up to speed on what would occur over the next ten days. "I found you a little cottage within walking distance of our place and everything you'll need in Narrabeen. It even has a third, small room…so I was thinking if your Mum's well enough to leave the nursing home, we could pick her up and bring her over to visit you once in a while. If you want her to, of course. The smaller room could be a temporary place for Joshua's cot while she's there. The agent will let us know when they've finished painting and carpeting. Meanwhile, you'll be staying with us, so you and I can haunt the second-hand shops while you choose your furniture."

"That all sounds amazing Louise, really…but it just feels like way too much. Are you sure you want to spend all this money on us?"

"Yes, I'm sure Dale, so don't you worry about that. It's my

pleasure. If you're comfortable leaving Joshua with Murray for a while this afternoon, I thought you and I could go to the Lifeline shop. It'll be fun…and you can buy a new wardrobe of clothes for yourself and bub."

"Are you serious? I'd love that. It feels like all my Christmases have come at once. Thanks so much Louise." Tickling the bottom of her son's feet, Dale began to softly sing the 'Incy Wincy Spider' song, which was apparently Joshua's favourite.

He clapped his tiny hands several times and when the final words of the song were delivered, he mumbled, "mo, mo, mo."

"Okay…but only one more time," his mother replied, holding up her index finger. "Do you mind, Louise?"

"Not at all. You have a lovely voice…and please…no need to whisper this time." As she listened to the lyrics for a second round, Louise had an epiphany. There was almost a direct correlation between the song and the adversities that Dale had endured in her life up to this point. The thought of a bright future now ahead of her, warmed Louise's heart no end.

Pulling up in the driveway, Murray swiftly appeared to greet the women. "If you want to take the baby inside, I'll bring in the last of these things. I've already put the boxes in the spare room."

"Thank you, darling," Louise smiled, while Dale lifted Joshua from his car seat.

Entering the house, Dale gasped as Louise led her down the hallway and into the kitchen. "This is such a beautiful home," she commented. "Oh, look Josh! There's even a high chair," she added, pointing to the end of the kitchen bench. "You've never seen one of those before, have you?"

With Barney the bear tightly clutched to his chest, Joshua returned a few garbled sounds whilst swinging his legs excitedly.

After placing her handbag down on the countertop, Louise said, "I thought I'd make us an early lunch, so come and I'll show you your bedroom." The door to the Corbet's new nursery remained closed as they headed back down the hall. "Murray will assemble the cot, ready for when Joshua needs a nap and you can just unpack the necessities for now. Will the baby have something to eat when we do? I bought some stewed apples, fresh apples, and I have a packet of rusks. I didn't really know what else to get. When we go out later, we'll grab whatever you both need at the supermarket on our way home."

"He'll be content with an apple, thanks Louise," Dale smiled. "I'll change his nappy then I'll come back and make up a bottle of formula and give you a hand."

"No need, I'm all set here," Louise smiled. "You just do whatever you need to do."

Mother and child entered their temporary haven and as Louise prepared the quiche and salad, she could faintly overhear the conversation taking place inside the room. Murray was setting up the cot whilst Dale changed Joshua's nappy.

"Do you mind if I watch you do that?" Murray asked. "It's not something I've ever done before, so I think I need a crash course."

"By all means," Dale replied, "and you can apply the new one. You'll learn much faster from a hands-on lesson."

Louise smiled at their friendly interaction…and her husband's eagerness to get involved. *'Just as well it was only a wet one this time around,'* she snickered to herself.

During lunch on the back deck, Joshua happily sat in his highchair kicking his legs and gnawing on a piece of apple. Every few minutes he'd point at birds in the yard and in his own language, notify the adults that they should look at them too. While the Corbets finished their lunch, Dale gave her son his bottle. As Joshua sucked away, his eyes grew heavy and it was time for a nap.

Dale returned to the deck after she put the baby down, drew the curtains and closed the door. "Thank you so much for the quiche, Louise. It was lovely. He'll probably sleep for about an hour and a half." Looking at Murray, she added, "Are you sure you don't mind looking after him when he wakes up? He's likely to need another nappy change by then, and just a warning…it could be a number two next time," she half-grinned.

"I'm sure I'll cope," he smiled back at her. "Honestly, I'm more than happy to spend some man-to-man time with Josh. Kissing Louise on the cheek he began clearing the table and encouraged, "You two go off and have fun. I'll clear away the dishes."

Within ten minutes the women were underway, headed for the

huge Lifeline warehouse in an industrial estate on the outskirts of Manly. As they drew up outside the premises, Louise handed Dale $300 and said, "There you go. Spend up big, my girl."

Dale's eyes sparkled with exhilaration as she reached over to squeeze Louise's hand. "I'll make sure you don't regret all these kindnesses, Louise. I sincerely mean that."

"I know you do, Dale. Now I'll leave you to your own devices while I fossick through the manchester section. Take your time, there's no rush."

The hour passed quickly and by the time Dale had completed her shopping, Louise was chuffed to have purchased two sets of cot sheets, a blanket and a padded baby-blue cot cover. All of the linen was brand new…its packaging had never been opened. She also found some educational toys and baby books.

Before slipping into the supermarket on their way home, Louise stopped at a local café for some cold beverages. The two women sat inside the quaint shop, sipping their iced coffees and thoroughly enjoying one another's company. Louise was hoping that this was the first of many enjoyable outings they'd share.

Reaching into her pocket, Dale produced the remaining cash she hadn't spent and handed it to Louise. "Thank you for everything Louise," she whispered, filled with emotion.

"No, Dale. That's your money. You keep it," she smiled, gently pushing Dale's hand back.

Arriving home later that afternoon, the women were pleasantly surprised to find Murray and Joshua in the spa bath. They appeared to be having the time of their lives. Surrounded by an abundance of bubbles, both were giggling as the baby gleefully splashed his little hands on the water.

Not wanting to prematurely interrupt their fun, the women remained inside and began sorting through Dale's purchases. Louise was more than impressed by her practical choices. She'd bought a cute dress, three shirts and a pair of jeans for herself, along with a large bag to carry all the necessities for mother and child. For Joshua there were two new jumpsuits, two t-shirts and three pairs of shorts. At the supermarket, they also managed to find some little plastic pants to cover his nappies.

"Oh, this looks like fun," Louise remarked as the women stepped out onto the back deck.

Dale tenderly ran her hand over Joshua's wet hair and enquired, "I hope he hasn't been any trouble for you, Murray?"

Looking down at the baby in his arms, he smiled and returned, "We've had a hoot! He was a bit scared when he first woke up and realised you weren't here, but as soon as I brought them out into the yard for a walk, he was as happy as Larry…and has been ever since."

"Who's 'them'?" Louise enquired.

"Barney came too. Didn't he mate?" Murray replied, smiling at Joshua. "We weren't going to leave his best friend inside all by himself."

Dale suddenly had a beaming expression on her face. "That's so sweet Murray. I'm glad you've enjoyed yourselves. I'll take him for a quick bath now, before dinner, if that's okay?"

"Sure," Murray answered, quite perplexed, "but isn't he already clean?"

After handing the baby to Dale, who immediately wrapped her son in a towel, she grinned and said, "It's just to wash the chemicals off. Their skin's pretty sensitive when they're this age."

"Oh, yes, of course," Murray replied, rather embarrassed. "I wouldn't have thought about that. Geez, I've got a lot to learn about babies before we start a family, Lou."

"It's alright darling," his wife smiled. "That makes two of us."

While the Corbet's started preparing dinner, Louise reflected on the fulfilling day and felt at peace with the world. Midway through, Dale entered the kitchen carrying her son. He was dressed in one of his new jumpsuits.

"What can I do to help?" she asked the couple.

"Nothing really," Louise smiled, "we're under control here, so you can feed Joshua whenever you want to."

After tickling the baby's foot and patting Barney on the head, Murray asked, "I'm just about to pour Lou a pre-dinner G & T Dale, would you like one? Or we have wine if you'd prefer."

"Just a cold water would be nice, thanks Murray. I don't drink."

"I can certainly arrange that," he smiled back at her.

At the end of the countertop, Dale placed Joshua in the high chair whilst preparing his meal. He patiently sat playing with Barney and watched the adults until it was time for Dale to apply his bib. That's when he became vocal, excitedly gibbering in his own lingo.

"Does that boy ever cry?" Murray asked her. "He's such a happy little chap."

"Yes, he's pretty good," Dale admitted, "but when he does get going, trust me…those little lungs kick into full gear. It's only when his teeth are coming through and he's utterly miserable. Other than that, he just grizzles when he's tired."

Gobbling down some lukewarm pureed vegetables without much mess, Joshua then sat on his mother's knee to suck on a bottle. Battling to remain focused on her face, within a minute his heavy eyelids closed and he was asleep.

Dale tucked Joshua up in the cot and swiftly returned to clean up the remnants of her son's dinner and set the table for three. Murray lit the fire while Louise plated the satay beef stir-fry and hokkien noodles they'd prepared.

Over dinner, the Corbets revealed a bit about themselves. Dale was surprised to learn that Murray was a pilot and admitted to having never set foot in a plane. Louise provided a brief overview of her I.T. business, including the recruitment arm, along with a comprehensive brief on the courses they provided. It had crossed her mind that perhaps Dale could benefit from the classes, should she choose to advance herself.

Listening with interest as she learned about the busy lives of her new-found family, Dale remarked, "Between work and your properties, I don't know how you find time to do anything else…let alone have Josh and me here under your feet as well. I so appreciate everything you're doing for us."

The couple smiled at her and Louise said, "We're unable to have children of our own, Dale, so having you both here is truly a pleasure for us…and an educational experience. We've applied to adopt a baby boy."

"Oh, that's wonderful. You'll be incredible parents. Sure, they're a lot of work, but they bring so much joy that you can't imagine your life without them."

"It could be another year off yet, but we've passed all the initial stages and had our interview...so the wheels are in motion," Louise smiled as she took her husband's hand.

Taking the plates and cutlery to the kitchen sink, Dale said, "Thank you for such a lovely dinner. I'll wash up before I take myself off for a shower, is that okay?"

Murray turned on the kettle and replied, "We have a dishwasher and I'm the packing master around here, so I'll show you how it's done."

As they did so, Louise added, "I'll give you a rundown on the washing machine and dryer in the morning...and if there's anything else you need, just let us know."

"Yes," Murray started, "we want you to treat this as your home, Dale...and not just now, but when you're settled in your own place. We're family, so if there's anything you need or if you have any concerns, please feel free to come to us. Would you like a coffee before your shower?"

Dale warmly smiled at him and said, "I think I'll pass tonight, if you don't mind. This has been a long and exciting day, so after I clean myself up, I'll toddle off to bed. Josh usually doesn't wake before six, so I hope he sleeps right through and doesn't disturb you during the night."

With the kitchen clean-up complete, Dale then hugged Murray and Louise in turn before heading down the hallway. Again, her heartfelt appreciation for their kindness brought tears close to the surface.

An hour and a half later, having also showered, the Corbets gratefully climbed into bed and quietly began chatting about their day. "I'm impressed by her gratitude and resilience," Murray commented. "I'd say she's done it tough for a long time, not just since becoming a mother. I really like her, Lou...and Josh is such a cute kid."

Louise closely cuddled into her husband and returned, "I'm pleased you feel that way, darling, and Dale's very intelligent too. I was only thinking a few months ago that I need a new home computer, now the interior decorating side of things has really taken off. One with a bigger hard drive and a much faster processor. When

I upgrade, I could give the old one to Dale so that she can do our I.T. course. Obviously, I wouldn't charge her for tuition. It gives her more opportunity for advancement, which could then lead to a steady career."

"Sounds like a feasible plan, Lou, as long as we don't appear to be organising her life for her. She's an independent young woman and pushing her too hard, too soon, could all be a bit overwhelming right now."

"I know exactly what you mean, my love," Louise admitted. "I'd just like to plant the seed. After that, it's up to her what she chooses to do with it."

Murray yawned and replied, "There's no harm putting forward the idea to see what she thinks. Night classes would be a great option, that way she could spend the days with Josh or perhaps find work somewhere."

The words were wasted on his wife, as she'd blissfully fallen asleep in his arms.

CHAPTER THIRTY-THREE

Just on daybreak, amidst a chorus of birds competing with the laughter of Kookaburras, Murray and Louise could hear Joshua gurgling in his room. Thankfully, he'd slept through the night.

The Corbets poured themselves a cup of tea and still in their dressing gowns, wandered out into the back garden. All the flowering plants appeared to be pest-free for the time being and shrubs that were pruned only a month prior, were already showing signs of new life. Louise smiled as dragonflies fluttered above her head and thoughts of her parents filled her heart.

"I think I'll take Dale over to see the little cottage this morning, if you don't have any plans," she informed Murray as they strolled the boundary fence. "I need to start to get an idea of the furniture she needs and the size of each space. You know how quickly a week passes."

"Mind if I tag along? Have to be at work around three, and I won't be back 'til Wednesday, so I'd love to see it before I go," he smiled.

"That'd be great. A family affair," she replied, kissing him. "I'll have to call Sara first, find out if we can collect the keys…and even though it's a Sunday, the landlord could well be painting. I suppose either way, at least she can still view the property from outside."

Suddenly a shrieking chuckle emanated from the deck when Joshua emerged on his mother's hip. He'd spotted the Corbets in the yard and couldn't contain his excitement. Little arms flapped in the air like a chicken, which in turn sent Barney flying down the steps.

"Good morning to you too, handsome," Murray laughed, waving at him.

Louise ascended the stairs, collecting the bear on her way up, then planted a kiss on Joshua's cheek before hugging Dale. "I'm about to make some scrambled eggs, would you like some?"

"That'd be lovely, yes please, I'll help," Dale smiled.

Whilst the women prepared breakfast, Murray played with Joshua in the lounge room. One of the toys Louise purchased at Lifeline the day before; a colourful, plastic shape sorter, managed to keep the baby totally occupied. As Murray placed each piece through a hole matching its correct shape and colour, Joshua attempted to do the same. The pieces would then disappear into the circular holder with a clunking sound that bemused him no end.

Breakfast ready, all sat at the dining table with Joshua close to Dale in his high chair. In between feeding him small spoonfuls of egg from her plate, he happily sucked on some toast with a dash of butter and Vegemite.

Louise observed the baby closely before commenting to Dale, "He has large hands and feet for his age, I think he's going to be a big boy."

"It was only the other day that Mum said exactly the same thing. I went to see her on Thursday to let her know what was happening. She was a bit worried that we wouldn't go and see her any more… but I assured her that we would. I've even looked up the train timetable and I can…"

Joshua's eyes suddenly lit up whilst blurting, "Doo doo way!"

Slowly shaking her head at her son, Dale said, "Not today buddy."

His little eyes briefly sunk before returning to lick his toast. Dale quietly whispered to the Corbets, "He's trying to say 'toot toot train'." Quickly returning to her previous volume, she continued. "He loves them…anyway, I found out that I can get to Parramatta with only one interchange."

"Terrific," Louise returned. "So…how does your mother feel about our arrangement?"

"Couldn't be happier," Dale beamed. "She's looking very forward to meeting you both."

"That's reciprocal," Louise smiled back at her. "Listen, I thought we'd take you over to the cottage this morning and show you around. Are you up for that? I suppose it all depends on what time Josh needs a nap too."

Dale swallowed her last mouthful of coffee and replied, "Am I ever…I can't wait to see it! Josh turns one in about three weeks, so he only needs a nap around lunchtime now. He'll fall asleep just about anywhere; in the car, in his pram…he doesn't have to be in his cot."

"Okay, great," Louise replied. "We'll do a few loads of washing before we head off while Murray cleans up. Smiling in his direction, she asked, "Is that okay, darling?"

"Absolutely. And I'll phone Sara for you, after I wash this little Vegemite monster's hands and face."

A few hours later, after having collected the keys from the real estate agent, they drove only a short distance to arrive out the front of a cream-painted concrete wall with a heritage-green wrought iron gate. One of the keys unlocked the entry gate to allow them access to the house and there was no sign of the landlord on the property. It was a rendered brick residence, also painted in cream. Above the front door hung a small, green sign that read, 'The Cottage'. Murray inserted the key then stood back, gesturing for Dale and the baby to enter ahead of them.

They walked straight into a good-sized lounge room with a gas fireplace, above which was a wooden mantelpiece. Windows were covered by venetian blinds with plain drapes either side, and all walls had been freshly painted throughout. The polished timber floorboards were in excellent condition. Each of the three bedrooms contained built-in wardrobes and all had ample natural light flooding in through their large awning windows The worn carpet in each room was yet to be replaced.

The bathroom, complete with a separate bath and screened shower, appeared to have been recently fitted with new fixtures, as did the kitchen. There was a very reasonably-sized pantry at one end and a stone benchtop ran the length of the room. The kitchen included a gas stove, fridge and there was space for a dishwasher and microwave oven. The small laundry contained a washing machine and stainless-steel tub.

Murray opened the back door to the enclosed yard and was surprised to find a tidy shed located in the western corner. There was a clothesline attached to the side of the house and three garden beds, somewhat overgrown, but they could easily be tidied up. A huge shade tree above the well-kept lawn, featured two thirds of the way between the house and the back boundary.

The Corbets walked around the side of the house before returning to the backyard, where they found Dale in tears. Tightly cuddling her son, she announced to the couple, "This is just all too much." Sobbing openly as she hugged them in turn, she added, "It's perfect. How can I ever repay you for something like this?"

Louise held her close and replied, "You and Joshua are thanks enough for us."

Once the tears subsided, Murray offered Dale a handkerchief for her tear-stained face. "Okay," he smiled, "enough with the waterworks you two, or you'll get me started. Come on...I'm taking you out for lunch before I head off."

• • • • •

When the women were on their own, they settled into an easy routine. Dale and Joshua went for long, regular walks as they became acquainted with their new neighbourhood while Louise worked on projects in her upstairs office.

Having discussed the prospect of Dale starting one of her I.T. courses, Louise was delighted to learn that her niece was as keen as mustard. Wasting no time, she set about researching a new computer but ended up purchasing one at the same time. Before completing the deal, the salesman agreed to transfer all the information over from her existing device to the new one, ensuring that the old hard drive was clear of everything other than its basic programs. Knowing that Dale had no experience with computers whatsoever, Louise was more than prepared to teach her the basics. She also knew that being an intelligent and motivated young woman, Dale would quickly acquire the necessary skills.

On Tuesday afternoon, Sara phoned to confirm that new carpet would be laid in the house by Friday and all painting would be completed. Therefore, from Monday onwards, Dale and Joshua were welcome to move in whenever they were ready. Louise agreed to pay the bond of four weeks rent, plus rent for a month in advance, to commence on Saturday.

That evening Murray phoned from Singapore. "I only have about forty minutes before we depart for Hong Kong, so I thought I'd phone to tell you that I love you, Lou…and see what our little family's doing. I wasn't sure if you were teaching tonight. I forgot to ask before I left."

"That's very sweet of you, my handsome pilot," Louise returned. "I love you too. Grace is covering the class for me tonight. Dale and I are just having a drink while we write up a list of furniture we need to source for the cottage. Well, I'm having a wine…Dale's beside me enjoying a non-alcoholic lemon, lime and bitters. We're going furniture shopping tomorrow." She then brought him up to speed with the happenings of the past few days.

"I'm rostered-on for the weekend as well, Lou. Bali on Friday, Kuala Lumpur Saturday and back via Bali Monday afternoon. How's Joshy? Is he good?" Murray eagerly enquired.

"Oh yes, chirpier than ever. He said 'mum' about five times this morning while Dale was feeding him. It was so cute. Now we're teaching him how to blow kisses…"

"Sorry Lou," he cut in. "They've just finished refuelling, so I'd better go. I'll see you tomorrow night. Give them my love."

The call then disconnected, so the women returned to their furniture list. Once satisfied they'd completed the task, Louise said, "They probably won't deliver anything over the weekend but at least we can co-ordinate it for Monday or Tuesday. I'll have to get your phone connected too, so you can call us…and your Mum of course…whenever you need or want to. That can go on my 'to do' list for Friday."

"This is so exciting. Beyond my wildest dreams," Dale returned, holding her face in her hands. "You're like my real-life guardian angel, Louise…I've never felt so blessed in all my life." Taking her glass to the sink, she then blew Louise a kiss and dawdled off to bed.

After breakfast the following morning, with Joshua and Barney contentedly huddled in the pram, Louise and Dale entered the Salvation Army furniture outlet. Here they purchased a double bed and two single beds with new mattresses, three bedside tables and two bedside lamps, one for each room. Whilst lining up at the cash register, Louise spotted a round cane-framed, glass top dining table with six matching chairs. She couldn't resist them, so they too were added to the tally.

"I'll make you some cushions for the chairs if you want to select a fabric," Louise suggested. "Perhaps you could use the same material for the kitchen and laundry curtains. I'd be happy to run those up for you too, if you like."

Full of beans, Dale reluctantly asked, "Would it be possible for me to use your sewing machine? Please Louise? I love sewing and I'd like to do it myself."

Wrapped by her niece's initiative, Louise smiled and returned, "Of course you can. You can use it at any time."

Next stop was a reward for Joshua. He'd been so patient whilst the women attended to their shopping that Louise decided a treat was in order. After buying a whipped vanilla ice cream from a small corner shop nearby, the trio headed across the street to the park. Sitting under the shade of a Jacaranda tree, Dale shared the ice cream with her son while Louise strolled amongst the myriad of native shrubs. Before returning to the car, both women laughed at Joshua's squeals of joy as he played in the sandpit.

At the second store, with Joshua now fast asleep in his pram, they stumbled upon a cane lounge suite with four matching side tables. They'd be a perfect fit for the dining table and chairs. It was upholstered in an olive-green suede, and like the dining setting, in near-new condition.

Dale immediately loved it, but upon finding the price tag, her face fell. "Oh, no way. This is far too expensive."

Inspecting the label herself, Louise remarked, "I think it's pretty reasonable, all things considered. It'll certainly wear well and the dimensions are spot on for that room. If you like it, we're getting it."

"Are you sure?" Dale replied, frowning seriously at her aunt. "I can't get my head around the fact that only less than a week ago, I had nothing more than two wooden kitchen chairs, an awful table, a single bed and a cot."

"Ah, yes…but that was last week. This is a brand new beginning," Louise smiled.

Paying for their purchases and again organising a Monday delivery, the women decided to duck into the shopping centre next door while Joshua was still sleeping. Dale knew that lifting her son into the car would prematurely wake him, so they had time up their sleeves.

In the 'Macey and Klein' store, Dale selected bed linen, blankets, pillows and towels for her new home. By the time they indulged in a quick coffee, Joshua was wide awake and ready for his lunch.

Murray arrived home at around 4pm and after kissing his wife, couldn't wait to hold Joshua in his arms. As he did so, the women excitedly informed him of all the purchases they'd made that day. "I think I'll crack open a Heineken and soak in the spa for a while," he announced. "That return flight was a stressful one."

Donning his bathers, he emerged on the deck with a large beach towel and bottle of lager in hand. "Anyone care to join me?" he asked.

Both women politely declined. Louise needed a couple of hours in the office before dinner, as she had a major design project to start on; an ultra-modern home in Manly whose owners had requested a nautical theme as an extension of their superb coastal views. Dale intended to call her mother then cook enough strained meat and vegetable meals to last her son for the next five days.

Joshua however, couldn't wait to get in. As soon as Murray turned on the spa, he came crawling across the deck as fast as his little legs would permit. Murray picked him up, and looking at his mother asked, "Is it okay with you?"

Taking Joshua from Murray, Dale nodded and smiled before taking the baby inside to put some towelling pants on him. This was the first time that the Corbets had heard Joshua hollering from the bedroom. He thought he was going to miss out on the bubbles. When Dale finally returned, his sad little face was streaked with tears but within seconds he was beaming and giggling again.

Twenty minutes in the spa was more than enough. The chill of the afternoon air was setting in and Murray didn't want Joshua catching a cold, so after gaining permission from his mother, he gave the baby a bath then they played a game of crawling hide-and-seek. This kept them both occupied until it was time for Murray to whip up a barbecue dinner for the family.

On Thursday, Louise, Dale and Joshua were out and about for

the morning, while Murray and Gordon spent all day labouring at their new building site. In town, Louise dropped into the office and introduced her niece to Beth and Grace. Grace was the new teacher she'd hired earlier in the year.

"Dale will be undertaking a course with us at the beginning of next semester," Louise explained. As her colleagues took turns playing with Joshua, he relished the attention. "She's new to computers and having just acquired one this week, I'll start to teach her the fundamentals well before the course commences. Haven't decided whether it'll be the day or evening course at this stage, but we have plenty of time to sort that out. Even though Dale's a novice, she's keen to learn."

"That's what we like to hear, Dale," Beth smiled at her. "Being eager to apply yourself to the task is the most important starting point."

"We're looking forward to having you," Grace added.

She promptly returned to her students while Louise and Beth had a brief chat. More than happy to hear that Grace had found her feet and was thoroughly enjoying the teaching aspect of the business, Louise then left the office with Dale and Joshua in tow.

Down at The Coffee Club on the foreshore, she purchased cappuccinos and butterscotch muffins for Dale and herself while the baby happily consumed some pureed banana with a dash of honey that his mother had brought from home.

Admiring the spectacular view, Louise said, "The government assistance you receive each fortnight is nowhere near enough to support you both, so I'm going to automatically transfer funds into your account each Monday for living expenses...until you find a job. That way you can use the social security payments to save for something else you might want. I know they're always advertising for check-out staff at the supermarkets here in Narrabeen, so I don't think you'll have too much problem landing a part-time job. I'd look after Josh while you're at work, as often as I could, and I know that some of my past students are always looking for a little extra money, so they may be able to babysit for a much cheaper rate than the child-minding facilities. Either way Dale, I'll cover the cost of his care whenever I can't care for him myself."

Leaning back in her chair with arms crossed, Dale seriously studied her aunt. "You do know that you're making this far too easy for me, Louise. I have to take some responsibility for these expenses you're covering. I'm beginning to feel very guilty, knowing that it's all one way traffic."

Smiling back at her, Louise returned, "I'm so enjoying what we're doing, Dale. Please don't feel that way. Who knows…there may come a day when I need your help? Let's just take it step by step and see what evolves. I'm just delighted that you have the mindset to better yourself…and it gives me great pleasure to assist you in that endeavour." Grinning, she added, "Perhaps when our baby comes along, you can be chief babysitter. Now let's go and get some groceries then we'll take this little fellow home for a nap."

Walking the aisles of the supermarket, Dale proudly announced, "I'm cooking dinner tonight. I was thinking Chicken Maryland in herb and garlic butter with sweet potato and broad beans. Is that okay by you?"

Very pleasantly surprised, Louise smiled at her and said, "You bet kiddo…just the sound of it's making my mouth water. Grab whatever you need."

"I have a few great recipes up my sleeve," she admitted. "Obviously Dad was the head chef in our household but when he died, I had to learn to cook for Mum before she went into the home…and from what she tells me, I'm pretty good at it. I'll let you and Murray be the judge of that."

Entering the kitchenware aisle, Louise said, "Tonight, we'd better make up a list of everything you're going to need to cook with. I think that should be next on our agenda. Things like plates, cutlery, crockery, saucepans…and then we need to start another one for all the general household essentials; door mats, a bucket and mop, a washing basket, pegs…oh, and you'll need an iron and an ironing board, a dustpan, broom…"

"Does your mind every stop spinning?" Dale questioned, shaking her head. "I'm not kidding when I say that you're the most organised woman I've ever met in my life."

Laughing, Louise contently confessed, "I don't doubt that for one moment. Poor Murray, sometimes I drive him up the wall with my endless planning but he's a bit of a perfectionist himself, so I suppose we're a perfect match. By the way…did I mention that we have a spare television set and vacuum cleaner in the shed?"

Again, Dale smiled and shook her head before hugging Louise tightly. Joshua held out his arms, desperately wanting to participate in the cuddle. Both women obliged, smothering him in their arms before tickling him all over.

That evening at home, while Dale prepared dinner, Murray lit the fire for the first time since she and the baby moved in. Joshua was considerably more fascinated by the bright orange, flickering flames, than the picture book Murray was attempting to show him. Each time Murray pointed to an animal, in the hope that Josh would look at the drawing, the baby simply made a loud 'ohhh' sound and pointed at the fireplace.

When Dale insisted that she didn't require any help in the kitchen, Louise took the opportunity to phone Martha and Donna, to let them know what had transpired since Dale and her son first arrived on their doorstep almost a fortnight ago. Her friends were fascinated by the story and many questions were asked in return, which she happily answered. Both women could sense Louise's compassion and growing love for these new family members and couldn't wait to be introduced to them.

Unable to contain his growing obsession with the fire, just before Louise helped Dale plate up dinner, Joshua made a b-line for the fireplace. Murray quickly pulled him back from the glass as Dale sternly yelled, "Joshua. No. Hot."

Murray placed him back down on the floor where Joshua sat on his bottom, quickly looked at his mother and went straight for the fire again. She repeated the firm order. He stopped in his tracks, again sat on his bottom and glared at her. Within seconds, the enticing flames lured him back but this time he approached more slowly. Just as Murray was about to scoop him up for a second time, Dale reached for her son's hand and smacked it, repeating the words 'no' and 'hot'.

Joshua was startled and his bottom lip began to tremble, yet he made another attempt. This time, Dale slapped his hand even harder, repeating the two words loudly. He flopped onto his stomach and cried. Gently picking him up, she cuddled him and said, "It's never too early to learn the words 'no' and 'hot', little man."

Placing him in his high chair facing the fire, all was forgotten when Dale set the picture book down on the tray in front of him and returned to the kitchen. "Good boy, Josh," she praised him, as the tears settled and he began looking at the drawings.

Louise considered what she'd just witnessed and thought to herself, *'That's good parenting, Dale. Well done.'*

"Nicely handled, Mum," Murray remarked before taking their plates to the dining table, "and this looks…and smells incredible. Thank you."

Joshua was happy to share some chicken and sweet potato with his mother while the Corbets also devoured their flavoursome meals. With plates looking like they were almost licked clean and dinner done, Murray offered to bottle feed Joshua once Dale had made up his formula. She was more than happy to oblige and with Louise determined to clean up the kitchen on her own, Dale toddled off down the hallway for a well-earned shower.

Lukewarm bottle in hand, Murray made his way to the lounge and sat down while Louise placed Joshua on the floor next to his high chair. She was eager to see if he'd head down the hall to look for his mother, or go straight to Murray. The couple watched on as the baby quickly crawled towards the fireplace, stopping about three metres shy of it.

"No. Hot," Louise said with an unsmiling face as he turned to look at her.

Shaking his little head profusely, he mumbled "Ho, ho," before changing direction and crawling to Murray.

"Good boy," she smiled, as the baby pulled himself up to a standing position in between Murray's knees and greedily grabbed for his bottle.

Cradled in Murray's arms, Joshua closed his eyes and scoffed down the formula until his weary body became limp. He was out to the world. Staring at the baby's delicate facial features while gently caressing his tiny fingers, Murray smiled and said, "I can't wait to be a Dad, Lou."

The phone rang at 8:30am the next morning, just as Louise was getting dressed. Cupping the receiver with his hand, Murray called out to her, "It's Martha. Do you want me to tell her you'll call back?"

"No, I'm here, thanks darling," she returned, emerging from the bedroom. Kissing her husband on the cheek as she took the handset from him, Louise said, "Hi Martha. Miss me already?"

"Hah…haa," came her friend's playful reply. "Listen Lou, I was thinking about our conversation last night and something occurred to me when you mentioned that your niece was moving into a new house. Does she have everything she needs in the way of furniture, kitchen stuff…all that sort of thing?"

"We've sorted most of the furniture but we haven't bought any kitchenware or cleaning items at this stage. That's on our 'to do' list for tomorrow morning. Why do you ask?"

Martha sighed and said, "Beryl, our elderly neighbour next door on the left, passed away last week…"

"Oh, I'm very sorry to hear that," Louise replied.

"Yes, she was a dear old thing. Ninety-one…and still lived a totally independent life. Anyway, Peter's helping her son move everything out of the house tomorrow and other than a few of his mother's keepsakes, Luke doesn't want anything else. He and his wife are in a new house and have everything they need, so the boys will be taking the lot to the Salvos. I just thought if there are any bits and pieces that she may want, you're most welcome to come over and grab them. Beryl loved to cook, so in the kitchen alone there are crockpots, every size of saucepan and casserole dish you can think of, a wok, milk shake maker, sandwich toaster…you name it! The only thing I'm taking is the fondue set. I've always wanted one of those."

Louise's eyes bulged with excitement. "Oh, Martha, yes…that'll save me a small fortune," she beamed. "You nominate a time and we'll be there. Murray flies out again this afternoon, so Dale and I might have to make a few trips from there to the house but that's okay, we're in no hurry."

"Great," Martha smiled. "I'd give you a hand but I promised to take Mum shopping. I know the boys will be making an early start, so how about I tell Peter that you'll be here around 9am. How does that work for you?"

"Perfect. Thank you so much my friend. We'll catch up for a coffee some time next week."

Hanging up, Louise relayed the balance of their conversation with her family. Dale was literally jumping out of her skin. As far as she was concerned, tomorrow couldn't come quickly enough.

Once the kitchen was cleaned up from breakfast, Dale smiled at Louise and said, "Okay, we're ready to head off now." Mother, son and his little bear were catching the train in to see her mother. Louise had offered to drop them down at the station, but being a glorious winter morning, Dale decided to walk. "We'll be back at 5:10pm according to the timetable."

"Excellent. I'll be at the station to pick you up. Have a safe trip and say 'hello' to your Mum for me."

Loaded up with Joshua and Barney on one hip and her carry bag on the opposite shoulder, Dale asked, "Would you mind getting the pram out of the boot while we say 'bye' to Murray? I know he's here somewhere."

"Out the back, I think," Louise smiled, making her way to the garage. "Said he was going to mow the lawns."

Dale found Murray in the garden shed and reaching her arms out to hug him, said, "Have a safe flight to Bali and we'll see you on Monday."

Murray embraced mother and son and said, "I love you both." Smiling at Joshua he added, "Toot, toot train!"

The baby kicked his legs and gurgled, "Doo doo way," before blowing Murray a kiss, which was promptly returned to him.

For the next few hours, Louise attended to general household duties and arranged to have Dale's phone connected before the Corbet's joined Gordon on the golf course. Sadly, within an hour of play, heavy rain set in and they were forced to abandon the game.

"We'll try again next week, Muzz," Gordon remarked as they all made haste for their cars. He beeped the horn and waved at the Corbets while slowly driving out of the carpark.

Murray gazed at his wet wife in the passenger seat and said, "Oh, that's a shame. Now I'll have to take you back to our empty house and make loud, unrestrained love to you."

Passionately kissing her, Louise immediately felt stimulated.

She began to gently stroke his crotch while Murray fondled her right breast. The rain now pelting down on the roof of the car only increased their insatiable desire for one another.

"We have to get out of here," Louise quickly murmured, their lips barely separating.

The drive home, given their sexually aroused state, wasn't easy. After parking in the garage and remotely closing the door behind them, a frenzied lovemaking session initiated. Ten short minutes later, the Corbets' drained but highly satisfied bodies finally emerged from the vehicle.

CHAPTER THIRTY-FOUR

Greeting Dale with a small gift-wrapped box as she entered the kitchen on Saturday morning, Louise handed it to her then scooped up Joshua and smothered him in kisses.

"What's this?" Dale asked, gazing at her aunt inquisitively.

"Just something you're going to need today," Louise smiled. "Open it up. I'll make us pancakes before we head off."

Placing the box on the countertop, Dale untied the white satin ribbon then opened the lid. Inside was a keyring with a sterling silver filigree heart hanging on it. Smiling back at Louise, she slowly removed the keyring from its box and discovered the words 'Home Sweet Home' etched on the front. Clasping it tightly against her chest, Dale remarked, "This is such a thoughtful gift. I love it Louise…and I'll treasure it always. Thank you."

"I'm glad," her aunt returned, "but what good is a keyring without keys?" Reaching into her dressing gown pocket, she produced a set of keys before jingling them high in the air and passing them to her niece. "Your cottage awaits, madam," she smiled.

Dale's firm hug as she squeezed her aunt almost constricted Louise's breathing. "Okay, okay…now I have to get this mixture in the pan while it's hot. What will it be? Golden syrup or maple syrup?"

"Whatever you're having," Dale returned whilst placing Joshua in his high chair.

After breakfast they all set off for the Dean's residence. There was a large removalist truck parked on the curb and Louise could see Peter, Luke and another fellow lifting a floral sofa into the back of it. She pulled up in the Dean's driveway and called out to Peter.

"Good morning, Peter. Have Martha and Skye left yet? I don't want to park her in."

"No, you're right Lou. She left about an hour ago. Come on over when you're ready."

After releasing Joshua from his car seat, they made their way next door. Introductions complete, Peter advised, "We've started in the lounge room, so if there's anything you want in there, take it, then you can move onto the other rooms. Truck's here for about four hours, so no rush, we won't be done for a while yet. Luke put a trolley in the kitchen, that'll make it much easier to get things to your car. Any heavy stuff, just give me a holler and I'll help you."

"Thanks so much. We really appreciate this," Louise replied.

"I'm just happy to see Mum's things going to another good home," Luke smiled. "Knock yourselves out!"

An hour and two carloads later, Louise and Dale had managed to acquire most of the kitchen cupboards' contents, plus some blankets and doonas, vases, a heater, fan, clock, laundry hamper, a small table for the television, a wheelbarrow and even a stack of gardening utensils. During their final trip back to the cottage, they stopped at Narrabeen bakery to purchase some savoury muffins which they'd consume a little later in the day.

The women began to unpack and stow away all their salvaged items, whilst Joshua crawled around familiarising himself with yet another new house. In the bedrooms, he seemed to enjoy the feel of the new cut-pile carpet under his hands and knees. Playing with some plastic spoons and Tupperware cups on the kitchen floor kept him occupied for the remainder of the time and allowed his mother to keep a close eye on him.

With lunch quickly gobbled up, Joshua then soundly slept in his pram on the back veranda. Louise and Dale decided to venture into the garden to do some weeding. With their acquired tools and a large bucket at the ready, the task wouldn't be too arduous.

"I used to do all the gardening when I lived at home," Dale remarked, pulling at the clover and dock weeds. "I find it really soothing. Dad worked six days a week and my older sister had no interest in outdoor activities at all, so it landed on me…but honestly, I didn't mind. Mum loves flowers and as you can imagine, her sense of smell is extremely strong. Whenever I used to plant something, I tried to make sure it had a pleasant scent. I want to encourage

Josh to enjoy the outdoors too, as he grows up. Whether it be sport, gardening…who knows. He gets so excited when he sees butterflies and dragonflies, even little lizards. I really want to foster those interests."

"And birds," Louise added. "He's crazy about them." Aiming for the next weed patch, she asked, "I've noticed that you haven't mentioned your sister, Dale? Where does she live?"

Without making eye contact with her aunt, she replied, "Nowhere, now, but she went to Melbourne when Mum was admitted to care. She was killed in a car driven by her boyfriend. That was two years ago. They charged him with 'drink driving causing death' so he's doing time in Pentridge Prison. Fifteen-year sentence, I think. I've never met him."

Shocked, Louise immediately ceased what she was doing. "Oh, Dale. I'm so sorry. Were the two of you close?"

"As children we were, but after she went to Victoria I didn't hear from her much. Mum said she'd sometimes phone the nursing home but rarely have much to say."

"You sure haven't had it easy, Dale," Louise admitted. "Thank you for having the courage to tell me that."

Gazing lovingly at her aunt, she replied, "Well, I'm not one to keep secrets…especially from family. I was going to tell you earlier but I knew you'd ask me sooner or later."

"That's very admirable for such a young woman…and I agree, keeping secrets destroys the soul," Louise smiled back at her. "I'm glad we can be openly honest with one another. Is there anything you'd like to know from me…that you haven't already asked?" The moment this question left her mouth, she suddenly felt extremely exposed.

"There is, actually," Dale replied in a serious tone, "though I don't know if you'll want to discuss it. I've been wondering why you and Murray can't have children of your own."

Louise's eyes saddened as she solemnly contemplated her response. A few moments later, returning to weeding, she said, "I suppose it's better you hear it from me, rather than someone else, but it isn't a short answer…and I'm just going to warn you that it involves your Uncle Ross. Did you ever meet him?"

Concerned, Dale looked at her aunt and replied, "Not that I can recall. He and Mum didn't stay in regular contact to my knowledge. Are you sure you want to tell me Louise? You look a bit pale."

"There aren't a lot of people in my life who know this story, but you'll end up meeting those who do, so yes, I think now's the right time. Before I start, I just need you to understand that he suffered from occasional bouts of depression and I think he may have been on the verge of becoming an alcoholic, if he wasn't one already."

Louise began by conveying how she and Ross had met on the Gold Coast, moved to Perth, married, worked in New Guinea and returned to build a life in Sydney. She then informed Dale of her uncle's weakness for rum and how it appeared to change his personality when he over-imbibed. Revealing that she'd tried to dismiss the indicators on numerous occasions, she then went on to explain why her uncle didn't want children.

Dale was rather surprised. "I've seen pictures of him, but I didn't know that he was literally blind in one eye," she admitted. "I'd better get Josh's eyes checked, just in case. Sorry to interrupt…please go on."

Relating more of the story, Louise included how she and Murray met, along with all the sordid details of events that occurred after Ross phoned the week her brother-in-law was staying over.

Whist recalling the details of their final, almost fatal encounter, and her subsequent injuries, Louise inhaled long, deep breaths.

"His boot into my stomach caused massive internal haemorrhaging which resulted in a hysterectomy. I'm guessing that because your uncle thought he'd killed me, he then committed suicide; blind drunk, jumped over the cliff at Dover Heights. So, there you have it, my friend. The whole ghastly story."

Shaking her head, Dale stood up and placed her arms around Louise's back. With her head nestled in the nape of her aunt's neck, she said, "That's absolutely dreadful. I don't know how anyone could possibly want to harm you, let alone my own uncle. Now I'm glad to know he's gone. Mum's such a placid, even-tempered woman. She wouldn't hurt a fly."

"For a while I hated him, Louise confessed, "but hatred turns to bitterness and the only person you end up hurting is yourself. I'm so lucky to have some wonderful, caring friends and of course I have Murray…he's my rock."

"Yes, he's a lovely man, Louise. I hope I can meet someone like him one day. I'm not in any hurry though…the very thought of a man in my life right now, scares the heck out of me."

"That's exactly how I felt until Murray entered mine," Louise smiled. "You can never rule out the possibility of true love, no matter when it comes, Dale."

During the next ten minutes, with two of the garden beds now clear of noxious weeds, Louise and her niece didn't do much chatting. There was a comfortable silence between them, each absorbed in their own thoughts.

• • • • •

Early Monday morning, Louise fossicked through the back shed and found the television and vacuum cleaner she was looking for. "We've got enough room for the sewing machine as well, so I suppose we should take that now," she suggested to her niece. "You'll be wanting your privacy in the kitchen, so at least it's there whenever you're ready to whip up those curtains."

After hastily loading the items into the boot of her car, they made their way to the cottage in order to arrive for a 9am scheduled furniture delivery. Dale was so excited that she almost forgot to bring the house keys with her. Joshua could sense his mother's joy and from his car seat, shouted, "Mum, Mum, Mum," several times over during the short drive.

Once the delivery guys had unloaded the truck and placed each piece of furniture in its designated position in the house, Dale and Louise set about making up the beds with their new linen. "We'll bring the cot over tomorrow after Murray disassembles it," Louise advised, "and I'd better get another one for home. I'm hoping Josh will have plenty of sleepovers, so we're going to need it."

"Oh, he'll love that Louise," Dale admitted, still beaming. "As long as Barney can stay too, I don't envisage you'll have any problems with him." Running her hand along the top of the lounge, she blurted, "I still can't believe that we're going to live here…in

Narrabeen…in this house! It looks incredible."

"Yeah, not too shabby if I do say so myself," Louise replied, hugging her niece. "Now the Telstra technician will be here at around 2pm, so do you want to head down to Spotlight and grab a few cushions and some fabric? We've got plenty of time…and when we get back, I'll give you a quick rundown on how to operate this high-tech sewing machine."

"Love to," came Dale's prompt reply. "Josh can have his bottle in the pram and I brought a few rusks for him to munch on as well."

Spending only twenty minutes in-store, they emerged with the fabric that Dale had selected, along with six decent-sized cushions and a non-slip rubber mat for the bottom of the bathtub. With still oodles of time to spare, they decided to do a shop for all the bathroom, laundry and pantry essentials.

Landing back at the cottage, Louise showed Dale how to use the sewing machine whilst the telephone was being reconnected. The technician picked up the receiver and upon hearing a dial tone, called out, "It's up and running girls. By tomorrow morning, the exchange will also have it connected on their end. Any issues, just let us know. The new number's written on the front of the handset. Gotta fly." And with that, he was gone.

"I have a few errands to run, Dale," Louise informed her, "so will you be right here if I'm away for a couple of hours?"

"Of course. Take your time. Heaven knows, you've given us so much of yours. We'll be fine, won't we Joshy?"

He mumbled something completely incomprehensible, using elaborate arm gestures to accompany what he was attempting to convey. Both women burst into laughter. Louise simply blew him a kiss and said, "I love you too. Be a good boy for Mummy."

In the hope that it was still there, Louise returned to the shop where she'd purchased her niece's linen. At the time, a painting caught her eye on the back wall and she knew by the large, red sticker in the corner of the frame, that it was on sale. Depicting a tranquil beach scene in earthy hues, she knew it would be perfect for the large blank wall behind Dale's lounge suite.

The timber frame was quite large but it just managed to fit into the back of her vehicle. A quick stop at the nursery then Louise returned home to prepare some lamb shanks in the crockpot for dinner and collect her tin of picture hanging bits and pieces.

Arriving back at the cottage around 3:30pm, she found Dale already cutting and pinning fabric, while Joshua was sitting on the lounge room floor, noisily banging pots and pans with a wooden spoon.

Absolutely thrilled with the picture, Dale stood back, clapping her hands and admiring it as Louise set about with hooks and hammer to hang the frame. Content with its position and levelling, Dale planted a kiss on her aunt's cheek and said, "Thank you. Now you're just spoiling me rotten."

At the Corbet's house that evening, Murray's return provided a warm welcome, as did the aroma exuding from the crockpot. It was wonderful to have the family all together again for dinner. They cheerfully conversed, discussing Murray's recent jaunts, the cottage, and a major milestone for Josh; he'd taken seven consecutive, wobbly steps earlier in the day.

With plans for Tuesday sorted, Dale kissed the couple before excusing herself to shower then retire to bed early. Over a glass of wine, Murray took his wife's hand, stroking her palm with his finger.

"She's so lucky to have you, Lou, as am I...and that's why I'm taking you away for a couple of weeks to celebrate our first wedding anniversary. I was thinking from August 12-28. Dale will be settled in her new place and the course won't start until September, so it's the perfect window. Would you be able to fit us in with those dates?"

"Really?" Louise beamed with enthusiasm, clutching his hand tightly. "Nothing will stop me. You're the best husband any women could ever ask for, Murray Corbet." Leaning in to gratefully kiss him, she asked, "Where are you taking me?"

"Singapore for the first week then Hong Kong for the second," he smiled.

"Wowee! That's so exciting, darling. All that warm weather in the middle of a Sydney winter...I can't wait!" Louise's eyes glimmered at the very thought.

"I still need to confirm the flights and accommodation, but now that I know you're keen, I can do that anytime this week. Only rostered-on for the Darwin route on Friday and I'll be back by lunchtime Saturday."

•••••

"It'll be great only having a ten-minute bus ride to the supermarket," Dale commented as she and her aunt shopped for groceries. In St. Mary's, I had to walk…and it took about twenty minutes each way."

Louise surprisingly looked at her niece and replied, "Unless I'm not here for some reason, I'll be driving you to do your groceries each week. There's no need to lug those heavy shopping bags onto a bus, along with the baby and a pram, when you don't have to. Besides, I'm always popping in here to grab a few things I've forgotten on my list."

"You're too busy to be carting us all over the countryside, Louise," Dale returned sternly. "I'm more than capable of taking care of that myself."

"I know. And I know you want to be independent…but it's for my benefit as well. I find grocery shopping on my own utterly boring but with great company, it's actually quite fun."

Dale shook her head. "Okay, you win…but only if you have the time, other than that, we're on the bus. Deal?"

"Deal," Louise smiled. "Well, I think that's everything, so let's get back to your place and unpack. I wonder what those boys are up to?"

Joshua and Murray were already at the cottage. Earlier that morning, the Corbets had decided to swap vehicles. Whilst Murray and the baby did two trips, one transporting the baby's dismantled cot over to Dale's house, and the other to relocate all of her belongings, the women went shopping in Murray's car.

Opening the front door, Murray winked at his wife and smiled as he loudly declared, "I can't seem to find Josh anywhere." He then quietly whispered, "He's hiding behind the lounge." Raising his voice once more he added, "I have no idea where Barney is either." After kissing her on the cheek and returning to a whisper, he said, "I'll give Dale a hand with the bags."

Entering the kitchen, Dale's face lit up when she saw a beautiful bunch of flowers in a vase on the countertop. Louise had cut the blooms from her back garden when she first got up that morning and asked Murray to bring them over. They were still wrapped in silver florist paper, complete with a wide, pink bow tied around the stems.

Tears flowed as Dale hugged the couple. "They're so lovely… and from your own garden. Thank you so much, both of you, for everything. As more tears threatened, she added, "This is the first time anyone has ever given me flowers. Now the cottage feels like a real home."

"That reminds me," Louise piped up, making a quick dash for her handbag. Producing an envelope with a hand written quote on the front that read, 'To plant a garden, is to dream of tomorrow', she handed it to her niece. "Consider it a house-warming present from us."

"Almost every single thing in this house is a gift, Louise, including the clothes on our back and the food in our cupboards. I don't think I can take much more. You have to stop buying things that aren't absolutely necessary."

"It's only something small…but it'll give you and Josh a great deal of pleasure for years to come. Go on," Louise urged, "open it."

Reluctantly Dale peeled open the backing, all the while keeping her eyes firmly focused on her aunt. Revealing a $100 gift voucher from a local nursery, again her niece's eyes welled up.

A group hug was in order then Dale placed her cold groceries in the fridge and freezer whilst Louise packed the pantry. With hands on hips, her aunt declared, "Well, I guess that's it. You've officially moved in."

"The place looks terrific girls, you've done a great job," Murray remarked. Looking at Dale he added, "The cot's back together in Josh's room. I put the sheets and his blanket on it…and I put all of your other stuff in the spare room. Do you want me to give this little guy some lunch before we head over to the building site? I told Gordy we'd all meet him there at 1pm."

"For sure," Dale smiled. "If you want to mash up a banana in his bowl, I'll chop up one of these beautiful peaches. We won't worry about putting him down for a nap, he's bound to sleep in the car anyway."

Gordon was there ahead of them, deeply involved in a discussion with the builder. Casually turning to greet the Corbets, he then suddenly became spellbound upon being introduced to Dale. Knowing Gordon as he did, Murray was surprised to note his friend's immediate interest in her.

As a group, they meandered through each of the units. Joshua fell asleep on his mother's shoulder within minutes. Much had been achieved since Louise last set foot onsite. The bricklayers had completed their work, the aluminium roof and guttering was in place, windows installed, and the majority of interior walls and ceilings were up. This enabled them to get a good perspective of the room dimensions. The electricians had even completed all the wiring work for power points and light switches.

Murray was aware that Dale would appreciate a break from carrying her sleeping son, so he carefully took the baby from her without disturbing him.

"Have you eaten yet, Gordon?" Louise asked. "While Murray has Josh, Dale and I thought we'd drive down to the little bakery at the end of the street and buy us all some roast beef and salad rolls."

"Yes, I have, well…sort of, but if you're offering, I certainly won't say 'no'. Thanks Louise."

The moment the women were out of sight, Gordon began to quiz Murray. "How does Dale fit into the picture, Muzz? The little bloke's adorable. Is his father at work today?"

"She's Lou's niece," Murray smiled. "We've just relocated her from St. Mary's and set her up in a cottage not far from here. She's had a tough life up to this point, so Lou decided to take her under her wing. What was your other question?"

"Joshua's Dad?" Gordon prompted him.

"Oh, yeah. Don't know. He took off way before Josh was born." Attempting to keep his mate's mind on the job, Murray asked, "Do you know when the guys are coming to seal all the wet areas Gordy?"

"Next Tuesday, I think. They have to do two coats and in this cold weather it's going to take ages to dry. That means the tilers might not be able to make a start until the following week."

"That's okay. Lou's already picked out the tiles and chosen the vanities, so she'll want to run all that past you way beforehand."

When the women returned, Joshua began to stir from his asleep. Seated on a large timber plank supported underneath by numerous plastering buckets, the group began conversing whilst eating their lunch. Joshua happily perched on Louise's lap to share a slice of tomato.

Gordon had managed to snavel a prime position next to Dale. Murray found his friend's behaviour rather amusing. As he observed Gordon and Dale's interaction, he looked at his wife and gave her a wink, tilting his head in Gordon's direction. She gazed over at them and noticed their playful banter. With raised eyebrows she grinned back at her husband whilst he returned a nod, causing Louise's eyebrows to shoot up even further.

Shortly thereafter, Joshua became restless and wanted to be put down. The slab surrounding them was covered in fine concrete dust and building debris, certainly not a place to allow a baby to crawl around. "Okay, little man," Louise conceded. "Let's take you home for some play time."

Bidding Gordon farewell, the Corbets then returned Dale and Joshua to their cottage. "We'll take off now and leave you both to settle in," Louise smiled. "I need to work on the balance of these design concepts for the units. The tradies are far more advanced than I anticipated, so I'd best get cracking."

Warmly hugging the couple, Dale said, "I can't thank you enough for everything you've done for us. I love you both. We'll see you soon. Do you have my number?"

"Yep, wrote it down in my teledex yesterday," Louise smiled. "If you need anything at all, just call us…and I'll pick you up at 10am on Thursday morning. Martha's looking so forward to meeting you and I know that Josh and Skye will be great playmates."

After each receiving a sloppy kiss on the cheek from Joshua, the Corbets waved to mother and son as they pulled out of the driveway. Arriving home, Louise's emotions stirred as she peered into the room where her niece and the baby had spent the last nine nights. It looked as though they were never there, yet the Corbet's lives had been so enriched by their presence.

Pouring themselves a coffee, Murray then went outside to

routinely clean the barbecue and spa while Louise headed up to her office to nut-out kitchen plans for the apartments. Given that they were all high end, north-facing, three-bedroom, two-bathroom residences, it was imperative that the design, finishings and furnishings met with the expected standard of quality.

Each unit's layout would be the same, though different materials and textures would be utilised. Determined to be adventurous with colour schemes and finishes, Louise proposed that each apartment have a feature wall of some kind in the living room which opened out onto a generous, semi-covered patio. Large wrap-around lounges would perfectly meld the interior with its exterior.

Terrazzo kitchen benchtops were an option that really appealed to her. The flecks of various natural colours would tie in nicely with the blonde oak timber floors and add an understated sense of sophistication to the space. High gloss, two-pack white cupboards contrasting against a matt, earthy-brown granite splash-back would combine every texture harmoniously. More than pleased with her choices, Louise was hoping that Murray and Gordon would feel the same way.

Seated for dinner that evening, Louise ran her concept sketches and ideas past her husband. "If you're aiming for the type of rental return you've mentioned, we'll need to up the ante when it comes to interior design. I know that you boys tend to be fairly conservative but I think these apartments require a more 'expressive' approach, if you know what I mean."

As Murray perused the plans, as well as Louise's colour palette and texture swatches, she added, "In each unit, I'd also like to see white plantation shutters on the windows and patio doors, instead of traditional curtains."

"It looks amazing, my sweet...so classy...and it's clean and bright. The shape of that expansive lounge gives the illusion that the kitchen and living space are twice as big as they actually are. So does that mirror feature wall. It's a brilliant concept."

At that precise moment, the Corbet's phone rang and Louise left the table to answer it.

"Hi there, it's me...already!" Dale grinned. "I'm about to put Josh to bed but we wanted to say goodnight first."

Louise smiled and said, "Okay, just hold on while I pick up the other phone and give this one to Murray, then we can both talk to you." A few seconds later she added, "Alright, we're listening."

"Say goodnight to Murray and Louise, Josh," Dale encouraged her son. "Blow them a kiss."

Holding the receiver up to the baby's ear, he heard the couple's voices and immediately released a smacking sound from his lips, followed by a round of giggling.

"Good boy Joshy," Murray and Louise returned, each blowing kisses back to him. He giggled again before joyously shrieking.

"Sleep tight beautiful people. We love you," Dale signed off.

CHAPTER THIRTY-FIVE

At the Corbet's thoughtful suggestion, Dale was excited to have her mother stay in the cottage whilst they were overseas celebrating their first wedding anniversary. For Louise, it ensured that her niece didn't feel isolated in their absence and allowed the Burns family to spend some quality time together.

Two days before the couple were due to depart, Louise, Dale and Joshua arrived at the nursing home in Parramatta. As prearranged, they found Dale's mother dressed and patiently waiting for them in her room.

"Hi, Mum," Dale said as she warmly hugged her. "I have Louise and Josh here with me." Smiling back at her aunt, she added, "Louise, this is my mother, Emily."

Louise nodded and returned, "Hello, Emily. It's lovely to finally meet you."

"Likewise," she concurred, smiling broadly. "Ross and I were estranged after our parents passed and he didn't contact me for many years. To be completely honest, I didn't even know he was married."

"That's a real shame," Louise empathised, "but now, thanks to your lovely daughter, here we are."

Joshua was squirming in Dale's arms. He desperately wanted a cuddle from his grandmother.

"Are you ready for a big hug, Nan? Here he comes," Dale declared.

"You bet," Emily replied, as the baby flung his arms around her neck. Holding Joshua under his bottom, she said, "You're getting so big, Joshy. I'll bet it's all that Vegemite Mum's feeding you."

Placing his tiny hands on Emily's cheeks, Joshua then gently leant forward and kissed her on the lips. Watching their physical interaction melted Louise's heart. As Emily slowly swept her fingertips over Joshua's delicate facial features, the baby closed his eyes and remained still for the duration. It was clearly a routine to which he'd become accustomed and her tender touch had a trance-like effect on him. Knowing that Emily had never actually seen her daughter or grandson, and never would, saddened Louise immensely.

"I'll pack this suitcase for you, Mum," Dale smiled. "Is there anything in particular you want to take? Do you want your pillow?"

"Yes, please sweetheart…and my slippers. Toiletries are done. They're in a bag in the ensuite. From the wardrobe, could you just grab my four pairs of shoes, the dresses and a few cardigans. I'll take all the underwear in the third drawer, oh…and just a few pairs of stockings."

Within ten minutes packing was complete and they all left the room. Dale took her mother by the arm while Louise pushed Joshua in his stroller. After signing out at reception they slowly ventured out to the car, where Emily was assisted into the passenger seat.

Driving back to the cottage, Joshua was asleep within minutes so Dale decided to take on the role of tour guide. Passing each location or point of interest, she described to her mother exactly what she was seeing in precise detail, much to Emily's delight.

Meanwhile, Louise considered the woman and realised that her appearance was much as she had envisaged. The shape of her face and olive complexion was the same as Ross's. Emily was more slightly built with straight, short grey hair. She possessed a ready smile and hazy blue, unseeing eyes.

Once at home, Dale took her mother around the house. With Emily's all-white cane, which had a sensor ball on the end, she counted steps between one point and another to generally familiarise herself with the new surroundings.

"Louise, I must thank you for being so kind to Dale and my grandson," Emily remarked. "This is an incredible thing you've done for them both."

"My husband and I have grown very fond of your family, Emily. I know it wouldn't have been easy, but you've managed to impart wonderful values in her. As a mother, you should be commended."

Emily smiled and returned, "We certainly tried, Louise. I'd like to think we were successful."

"Okay, well I guess I'll leave you to it," Louise announced. "There are a few designs I have to finish off this afternoon and then I suppose I'd best get packing myself." Hugging Joshua and Dale, she then added, "If there's anything else you need, don't hesitate to call me."

•••••

Day one on the small island of Sentosa in Singapore was a blissful start to Murray and Louise's week-long stay. Their luxuriously appointed hotel room surrounded by impeccable, tropical gardens, instantly washed away the southern winter chill.

Casually exploring the island, they were more than impressed by her natural, abundant beauty. Fine dining in the hotel's restaurant that evening saw the couple indulge in two bottles of Chardonnay before retiring to their room to make passionate love for well over an hour.

On the second afternoon they took the cable car over to the mainland. Views from high above the water were simply spectacular. From here they caught the speedy subway into the city's bustling centre. Alighting near Raffles Hotel, the Corbets crossed the road and browsed the exclusive retail shops surrounding its courtyard.

Finding seats in the sun, Murray ordered two 'Singapore Sling' cocktails, which Raffles was famous for creating. The blend of gin, cherry brandy, Benedictine liqueur and chilled pineapple juice was served in a very tall glass, garnished with lime and a tiny purple orchid bloom.

"Wow! This is without doubt the most exotic drink I've ever had Lou," Murray commented, savouring each flavour as he sipped away. "Hang the expense…worth every penny, I'd say."

His wife totally agreed. "I'd love another one, but I don't think we'd be capable of doing much sightseeing after that." Cheekily smiling at her husband, she then kissed him on the lips and said, "Thank you so much for this extraordinary anniversary getaway, my darling. Here's to us…and the happiest year of my life."

"Touché, my love," Murray grinned, raising his glass to her.

Visiting the 'Gardens by the Sea', a spectacular architectural piece set in parklands nearby, was something Louise had waited to experience for a long time. As the couple wandered along the enclosed walkway, spiralling upwards through a fine mist, they revelled in the breathtaking displays of colourful tropical plants surrounding them. There were many unusual species that they'd never seen before and the orchids alone were a sight to behold.

Some hours later, strolling along the waterside promenade, Murray and Louise chose to dine in a restaurant where patrons cooked their own food, at their own table. They thought it would be a novel experience and decided to give it a go. After being directed to an outdoor table beside a group of six young Canadians who were having fun cooking their meat, the Corbets struck up conversation with them. Louise suggested that she and her husband order the same as the Canadians were having, including two glasses of chilled, 'Tiger' beer.

Following this unique eating-out experience, the Corbets then accompanied their new-found friends into the city where they all engaged in a little of Singapore's night life before parting ways at around 9pm. Catching the local bus back to Sentosa, Murray and Louise were almost asleep on arrival.

The balance of their week was spent lapping up numerous activities available to resort guests on the island; two days lazing around each of the swimming pools and soaking up the sun, three hour-long massage sessions, window shopping on Orchard Road, a round of golf on the magnificent Laguna Bay course and numerous meals divided between the hotel's restaurant and the Golf Club.

By Sunday it was time to move on. Transferring to Changi Airport was a swift process and whilst boarding their flight to Hong Kong, Murray discovered that Bruce, a close colleague, was captaining the aircraft. Bruce invited Louise into the cockpit shortly after take-off, as they flew high over the South China Sea.

Returning to the seat beside her husband, Louise was exhilarated. "What an experience! I had no idea what was involved in flying one of these things…it's far more complex than I expected. No wonder there's so much training involved."

Murray smiled and returned, "Wait 'til you see the landing strip at Kai Tak…it's a doozy. That's when we really have to have our wits about us."

Coming in to land some four hours after take-off, Louise was astonished to see the plane's close proximity to surrounding buildings. Holding her breath, she could actually see into hotel rooms and apartments as they prepared for touchdown.

Turning to her husband with wide eyes, she declared, "That was positively frightening, Murray. Knowing what I do now, the mere thought of you flying the Hong Kong route scares the heck out of me!"

Softly laughing, Murray took her hand and said, "Well, you won't have to worry for much longer, Lou. Construction's well underway for a new airport."

Safely on the tarmac, Louise was more than relieved. Making their way to the Marriott Hotel in the Admiralty district via taxi, was also an eye-opening experience for her. Looking up at the light poles she couldn't help but notice a huge mingle-mangle of electrical wires. It was like spaghetti strewn from one pole to the next. *'How on earth do they knew what's what if they need repairing?'* she curiously thought.

Pulling up outside the hotel's entrance, the driver helped unload their luggage then the couple were escorted to the forty-sixth floor; a room overlooking Victoria Harbour. From the expansive windows they marvelled at the building under construction across the street. Its thirty-two floors were suspended on bamboo scaffolding with workers climbing around the structure like monkeys.

Attached to the Marriott was a large shopping mall and approaching lunchtime, the Corbets ventured down for a bite to eat in a café at the centre's junction. They enjoyed watching avid shoppers whilst consuming a variety of breads dipped in olive oil.

"We're on the Kowloon side," Murray explained. "When we're done here, let's catch the ferry across to the other side and take a look around."

Louise was more than happy to be directed by her husband, after all, he knew this part of the city quite well.

Alighting from the ferry, they purchased tickets for a 'Hop

on-Hop off' bus tour, collected a tourist map and earphones then climbed up to the top deck. The route took them to Discovery Bay, past the Hong Kong Racing Club and the stadium where the Cathay Rugby 7's Tournament took place in March each year. Back down on the waterfront they enjoyed a strong brew of coffee before taking in all the major sites.

"It's such an exciting city, Murray," Louise smiled, "dirty compared to pristine Singapore but being far more densely populated, I love the hustle and bustle of it. Fragrant aromas are filling my nostrils everywhere we go."

"So do I, Lou. It's a lively place. Never a dull moment. Even though I've seen a lot of things in this city, we really don't get enough time to absorb the atmosphere. We're always rushing in and hurrying out again. It's nice to be able to enjoy the experience for a change."

During their stay in Hong Kong the Corbets took a second 'Hop on-Hop off' tour around Kowloon, disembarking to ride the cable car up to Victoria peak. Returning to the base they then re-boarded the bus, stopping for lunch at the exclusive Sandringham Yacht Club, who provided honorary membership to Qantas pilots.

They joined a day trip to Macao and had lunch in the casino. Here, the couple were astonished to discover just how much Asian folk loved to gamble…and the sums they were prepared to wager.

An entire day was spent at Stanley Markets, where Louise couldn't resist buying all manner of gifts for Dale and Joshua. She even purchased a few baby items for their own son-to-be. When collecting Emily from the nursing home before they left Sydney, Louise noticed a small radio/cassette player on the table beside Emily's chair. The majority of cassettes appeared to be based on the sounds of nature; bush, water, ocean, and even bird songs. In a music shop opposite the markets, Louise selected half a dozen tapes that she hoped Emily would enjoy and purchased a new cassette deck for Dale to keep at the cottage.

Knowing they'd now be well in excess of their luggage weight limit, Murray purchased another suitcase, which they filled to the brim. A fellow pilot kindly offered to declare the luggage as his own, in order to return it to Sydney along with the balance of the couple's bags. The Corbets had bought very little for themselves but they'd so enjoyed their shopping spree and couldn't wait to hand the goodies over to the Burns family.

• • • • •

"Good heavens…that was like four Christmas Days rolled into one hour!" Dale beamed as she opened Murray and Louise's final gift. "I can't believe you were shopping for us on your holiday. That's so thoughtful and generous. We sincerely appreciate it."

"Absolutely. Thank you, from the bottom of our hearts," Emily concluded. "Can I give you both a hug?"

Naturally, the Corbets were only too happy to oblige.

Joshua was clearly very excited to have the couple home. As Murray tossed him in the air, he noticed a new tooth. Standing the baby down on his feet, he asked, "Are you walking yet Josh? Can you show me how you walk?"

Slowly releasing his grip from Murray's fingers, Joshua was all giggles and dribble as he tottered towards Louise. She scooped him up, hugged him tightly, smothered him in kisses and said, "You've grown so much in a few weeks."

Placing him back on his feet, the baby immediately staggered to the lounge, snuggled his face into Barney then grabbed the bear by one ear. Directly returning to Louise and pushing the bear into her chest, he giggled again. Louise knew exactly what she was being asked to do. After kissing the bear several times, she declared, "Yes, of course I missed you too, Barney."

"How great is the playpen?" Dale smiled at Louise. "Mum and I met Katie, the neighbour a few doors down last week, and she was giving it away. Her daughter, Monique, is three now, so she's outgrown it."

"It's fabulous, Dale" Louise replied, "and still in really good condition too. I bet that'll come in handy."

"Honestly, it already has. I haven't once had to worry about Mum tripping over Josh, or his toys…and he loves playing in it." Smiling at her son, she then turned to Louise and asked, "Will you please stay for dinner? I'd really love to cook for you both."

"We'd love that to, and thank you for offering…but I'm afraid we'll have to decline. Murray's flying to Darwin in a few hours and I haven't even ironed his shirts yet, so we'd best get home. I'll catch up with you again in a few days."

Saying their goodbyes at the front door, an emotional Emily said, "I'm planning to leave on Wednesday, so if I don't see you before then, thank you both for everything."

"Is Dale taking you back on the train?" Louise queried.

"Yes," her niece swiftly replied. "It doesn't take long…and then we'll be straight back."

"Nonsense," Louise blurted. "Let me know what time and I'll be here to pick you all up. I have to check out some plantation shutters at the showroom in North Ryde anyway, so we can kill two birds with the one stone."

After seeing Murray off to work later that afternoon, Louise began to assess her priorities. She knew that the next four weeks were going to be somewhat of a scramble, so her organisational skills would be paramount.

Opening a notepad, she compiled two lists; one for work, the other titled 'Personal'. The entries included completing the two design jobs she currently had on the run, ordering window coverings for the units, choosing the carpet then hunting down the furniture and décor items, plus phoning Janet and Katherine to ensure all was well with the business in Perth.

For the 'Personal' column, only one particular entry was important at this point in time…and that was to source a babysitter for Joshua. Her niece had opted to take the daytime classes for the I.T. course, which commenced in three weeks. Dale figured that it was best to apply herself full-time over one semester, as opposed to dragging out the night class alternative over two semesters. Louise would be minding Joshua for most of the time but in cases when work commitments became a priority, a sitter would be required.

'That reminds me…' she silently prompted herself. Returning pen to paper she wrote down the words, 'cot' and 'playpen'. *'I'll be able to sneak in a bit of work when he's napping… and if I had the playpen up in the office, I might even be able to grab another hour. We'll just have to wait and see.'*

At 9pm she phoned Janet in Western Australia and the women happily spoke about business, babies, marriage, and life in general, for well over an hour. Tomorrow night would be Julie's turn for a catch-up call. Louise was eager to tell her sister all about their overseas trip and hoped to speak with her niece and nephew at the same time. For some reason, Louise was dearly missing her New Zealand family.

Crossing Janet's name off the list, Louise yawned as she perused the balance of her detailed entries. "Well, that's one down…only about fifty to go."

The following morning, having promised Murray that she'd check on the build while he was away, Louise arrived onsite. Gordon had purchased her chosen tiles for the bathrooms while the Corbets were overseas and the tilers had almost finished laying them. In the kitchen, all cupboards and doors had been installed and the terrazzo benchtops were due to arrive next week. The fireplaces, set on sandstone hearths with a similar sandstone cladding on the walls behind them, were an outstanding feature in the living rooms. Louise was ecstatic with the result. Painters were due to commence work as soon as the tilers were done, and after that, the only jobs remaining were to lay the carpets and attend to the landscaping.

CHAPTER THIRTY-SIX

Without question, mid-Spring was Louise's favourite time of year. The season rejuvenated her senses and with that came a fresh appreciation for all that she held so dear to her heart; particularly in regard to family and friends.

Since Emily's first stay at her daughter's house, she'd returned for a week each month, much to everyone's delight. The new semester for Dale's I.T. course was in full swing and she was thriving in the learning environment, as well as doing plenty of additional work at home. Louise was aware that her niece had wanted to apply for a part-time job from the moment she arrived in Narrabeen, but after much discussion, her aunt gently persuaded her to solely focus on her studies.

Louise now considered herself Joshua's part-time carer, a role that she seriously cherished, as did her husband whenever he was home. The only challenge the Corbets had with Joshua, was catching him. No longer did he walk here and there, he broke into a run at any given opportunity. On the rare days that they were unable to look after him, Joshua went to the Dean's house. Martha was more than happy for her daughter to have a playmate and besides a few minor squabbles here and there, usually over toys, Joshua and Skye loved being together. Louise often returned the favour by having both children at her house whenever Martha needed a helping hand. Of late, a supplementary volunteer had raised their hand to babysit Joshua. That was none other than Gordon Perry, much to the Corbet's surprise.

On Monday, when Louise dropped Joshua home after minding him for the day, she said to Dale, "The apartments have all been leased for a year. We can't believe they were snapped-up within days of placing the advertisement in the newspaper. Isn't that great?"

"Yes, I know, it sure is," Dale smiled, "and even better that they managed to get the rental price they were asking."

Curiously looking at her niece, Louise queried, "Did Murray already tell you?"

"No, Gordon did," she returned. "On Saturday he brought over some timber he had lying around and we made a frame for my bean runners. Then he grabbed a few bags of cane mulch, some potting mix and four beautiful ceramic pots from the nursery, so we spent the afternoon preparing the garden beds for the other punnets of seedlings I'm planning to buy next weekend. He's a lovely guy and he's wonderful with Josh. If we're ever stuck for a babysitter, Gordon said he'd be happy to do it...if he isn't working of course."

Louise's eyebrows almost hit her hairline. "Really?"

Shyly looking at her aunt, Dale replied, "Yes, really...and last night he bought us takeaway Thai for dinner. When he gets back on Thursday, he's going to bring over some Vietnamese food."

"Oh, that's very sweet of him," Louise smiled, whilst attempting to process this revelation. Strangely, the Corbets had only just played golf with Gordon yesterday morning and he didn't mention anything about seeing Dale. *'Must be keeping his cards close to his chest,'* she deduced.

Kissing Joshua on the cheek and hugging her niece, Louise said, "I'm off. See you both in the morning. I'll have a quick look at what you've done in the garden tomorrow."

Moments after pulling up in the garage, she rushed inside to answer the phone.

"Sorry to bother you, Louise," Sara started, "but I've just had a meeting with the owners of the house you're renting for your niece. They've decided to build a new home in the Blue Mountains... therefore they have to put the place on the market. We have two choices; we can either sell it as a tenanted property, which would restrict options for any potential buyer, or we can find somewhere else for your niece to live."

Louise let out a heavy sigh. "Oh, I see. That's a real shame. Dale and her son are so happy there. She's planted a vegetable garden and flower beds...and the place is so secure for the baby. It'd be very disappointing if she had to move." Hearing herself speak, the wheels began to turn in Louise's head. She added, "Can I have just a couple of days to ponder on that, Sara?"

"Of course. Let me know what you decide by the end of the week. Have a good night."

After a long bubble bath and some leisurely personal grooming, Louise poured herself a glass of wine just before Murray phoned from Cairns.

"How's beautiful Queensland, my darling?" she asked. "I saw on the news that you could be in for some harrowing weather."

"Yeah, it's not too great at the moment, Lou," he admitted, "absolutely bucketing down. We just caught the tail end of Cyclone Alice coming in last night. The hammering winds had passed, but the remainder of the deluge is pretty intense. Apparently, she's heading further north-east now and they say it'll fizzle out pretty quickly over the next five hours."

"Well, I'm glad to hear it's almost gone, love. What else is news?"

Murray scratched the back of his neck and replied, "Nothing much really. Had a game of squash here at the hotel with Jerry this morning. Talk about rusty! It was more like a 'hit and giggle' than an actual game. Jerry hadn't played in a while either. Was Josh good for you today?"

"Oh yes, he was terrific. I think he might be getting a bit of a cold but it doesn't seem to faze him. We had to perform some minor 'sewing surgery' on Barney too, his little ear was just about hanging off. I do have one very interesting news flash for you… apparently Gordon spent the entire day at Dale's on Saturday. Built some things in the garden, bought some stuff for her at the nursery, shouted takeout dinner…and even offered to mind Josh once in a while."

Silence prevailed for a few seconds before her husband responded. "Wow! Okay. I don't really know why I'm surprised because I could tell straight away that he liked her…just funny that he didn't say anything about it yesterday."

"I know," Louise concurred, "but then I thought, well it's not like he's trying to keep it a secret. He knows that Dale would mention it sooner or later."

"That's right," Murray acknowledged, "and I know Gordy. He wouldn't be trying to hide it from us, he's just really shy when it comes to talking about his relationships. He'd prefer to dodge the topic altogether. It's obviously very early days but for the time being, I think it's good for them both. How do you feel about it?"

"I'd probably have to agree. Admittedly, eight years is a decent age gap…but if they're happy, then I am too," she smiled. "Gordon's a genuinely decent, mature man with a level head on his shoulders." Taking a small sip of wine she added, "Speaking of Dale, there's something else I'd like to talk to you about but it can wait until you get home."

Murray gazed at the water streaming down his hotel window and said, "We can't go anywhere in this rain, and I've already had dinner…so I'm more than happy to keep chatting my love."

"Okay." After taking another sip she told her husband what had transpired in regards to Sara's call earlier. "I did some brainstorming and came up with a possible solution…but obviously I want to pass it by you first. A few years ago, I promised Janet that if I ever sold the Perth business, I'd give her first crack at buying it. So, I was thinking…why don't we sell it off, if she still wants to purchase it of course, and with that money we can buy Dale's house. The place is perfect for them and I figure we might as well own the house, instead of having to pay rent on it. Do you think that's a good plan, or am I losing my marbles?"

"It's an excellent strategy and no…you're definitely not going crazy, Lou. We're settled here on the east coast so it makes sense for 'you' to let go of the Perth branch. Note my emphasis on the word 'you' my sweet. It's your business, Lou, therefore 'you' would be buying the house, not me. And I think the timings right too. With the baby coming in the very near future, it's just one less obligation to contend with."

"Clearly you still don't agree with my 'bucket' concept when it comes to our finances. But anyway, I'm not going to argue about it now, I appreciate your opinion and it backs up exactly where my mind's headed. It's only 7pm over there, so I might call the Wilsons now and sound them out. Before I go, I was wondering how you'd feel about inviting them over for Christmas and New Year?"

"I'm all for it. The more, the merrier. Yep…that'd be great, Lou."

Immediately following the conversation with her husband, Louise phoned the Wilsons in Perth. Ken informed her that Janet was available, so she asked them both to remain on the line whilst she delivered her proposal.

After discovering Janet was extremely keen to buy the branch, much discussion took place in regards to financing the purchase. It was decided that once a valuation had been obtained, Louise would sell it to the couple at a discounted price then provide them with a low-interest business loan for approximately fifty percent of the total asset cost. Naturally, this arrangement completely rested on the outcome of the business's saleable worth.

The next morning, having spoken with a valuer in Scarborough, Louise emailed the firm with all relevant details including Janet's contact information. He pointed out that being a unique operation, given the fact that it was a teaching facility as well as an employment agency, it would take approximately three days to complete the valuation.

Friday morning rolled around and the firm had yet to advise Louise on a price. Knowing that Sara was waiting to hear from her that day, she phoned the real estate office to explain the developing situation. Informing her client that she could hold the owners off until Tuesday, Louise thanked her and within half an hour an email arrived from the valuer.

Printing it off, she walked downstairs to show Murray the document. "It's a reasonable appraisal…not too far away from what I was anticipating…so, I'll deduct 10% off this price and finance them as agreed over five years. I'll first run it past them verbally then I'll have the agreement legally drawn up. Do you think that's fair?"

"Which part?" he questioned, curiously observing his wife.

She returned a smile and said, "The discount and financing arrangement."

"Oh, good. I'm out when it comes to estimating a company's worth, wouldn't have a clue…but what you're offering the Wilsons is more than reasonable in anyone's language."

While Murray and Joshua kept themselves amused with a

wooden jigsaw puzzle, Louise phoned Janet and ran the figures past her. The Wilsons had already discussed a maximum price that they were prepared to pay, so discovering the final sum was way under their expectations, Janet asked her friend to commence with their contract arrangement. This included Louise's business loan for half of the total amount.

"Now, business aside," Louise began, "Murray and I were wondering if you could possibly fly over for the festive season. With most of your family abroad until January, we'd love to have you all here. Please don't feel like we're putting the financial squeeze on you with airfares, we just thought we'd run the idea by you."

"That would be really lovely, Lou," Janet admitted. "I'll discuss it with Ken and see what we can do. Leave it with us 'til next week."

• • • • •

Five weeks shy of Christmas, Dale's cottage was purchased in both of the Corbet's names. Louise had won that argument, if indeed there ever was one. In fact, the couple hadn't had a serious disagreement to date. They concluded that Dale needn't be aware of their ownership at this point in time, so managed to keep it all under wraps.

Meanwhile, all the babysitters continued to rally behind Dale, minding Joshua while she attended classes and earnestly studied. Her tutor, Grace, reported to Louise that her niece was grasping the concepts extremely well, her homework was always on time, as was she, and her attendance record was impeccable.

Qantas had just published the December/January rosters much earlier than usual, so Louise began planning their Christmas celebrations. Both Murray and Gordon would be at home for Christmas and Boxing Day then both were rostered-on for New Year's Eve. As all of their invited guests, bar two, would be at the Corbet's house for Christmas lunch; the Deans, Dale and her mother, Gordon, and the Wilsons, Louise decided that a 'grab and go' barbecue along with a selection of fresh salads would be the optimal way to go. That would make nine adults and three children in total. The Hoffmans were unable to attend, due to visiting family in Switzerland over the break.

A fortnight into December, Dale's course drew to a conclusion. Grace was proud to announce to her boss that Dale had topped the class by a long shot and suggested that her niece was more than ready to seek employment within the I.T. industry framework.

Later that afternoon when Louise dropped Joshua home, she arrived with a beautiful bouquet of cream roses, purchased from a florist on her way over.

First handing over her niece's son then the flower arrangement, Louise hugged Dale tightly and said, "I'm so proud of you for topping your class, sweetheart. I knew you'd do well because you fully apply yourself to everything you do. And I'm well aware of how hard you worked for this."

Tearing-up, Dale replied, "I was so grateful for this opportunity, Louise…there was no way I was going to stuff it up. I owed you that much. All I need now is a job and my life will be on track."

Arriving home just in time to prepare dinner, Louise glanced at Joshua's toys then a niggling sadness washed over her. It almost felt like a sense of loss. The realisation that Dale's course had ended, meant that her babysitting duties would rarely be required. No longer having a toddler running around the house on a daily basis, was a prospect that daunted her.

Shaking the thought from her mind, she gave Martha a quick call to share the news of Dale's results. She also enquired about possible job vacancies that could be made available to her niece.

"I do have one that could be perfect for her, Lou," Martha suggested. "We have an electrical contractor looking for a computer operator three days a week. It's a work from home position, so that would really suit her. The job entails paying creditors, compiling invoices, keeping records, carrying out fortnightly bank reconciliations...all that kind of thing. The client's a local, in fact you might even know him. I'm positive I saw a sign for RAM Electrical at the last block of apartments Murray and Gordon constructed. His name's Rob St.Clair."

"Yes, you're right Martha, I do know him. We worked together on the lighting design for both of the boys' builds. He's a very nice fellow."

"I've recently sourced two electricians and a labourer for Rob, so I only spoke to him about a week ago. I'll call him in the morning, make some arrangements and we'll see where it goes from there."

An interview was arranged at the Narrabeen office for Tuesday. Dale was extremely nervous but Grace assured her that it was a futile emotion, as Louise and Beth would always be there to guide her, should she require any assistance.

Within half an hour, the job was hers. Rob informed Dale that his business would be closing between Christmas and New Year, resuming the first Monday in January. She was somewhat relieved to know that she had three weeks to familiarise herself with the boss's needs and expectations.

That evening Dale couldn't wait to phone her aunt. "I got the job, Louise! I'm really excited. Thank you so much…and please thank Martha on my behalf. I'm starting on January 5th. I just hope I don't mess it up."

"You won't," she smiled, "besides, I'm here if you need me. This is a huge achievement, congratulations Dale. I couldn't be happier for you…and Rob's a lovely guy to be working for."

"Gordon has just popped over and asked me out to dinner tomorrow night, to celebrate my graduation…and now, getting a job as well. I was wondering if I could please ask a favour…"

Louise swiftly interrupted her niece. "Of course, we'd love to mind Josh."

"Oh, thanks Louise. I was thinking we'll drop him over to your house then pick him up on our way home."

"Make it early, if you can. The three of us will have a spa together before we feed him. Are you sure you don't want Josh to stay here overnight?"

"No, honestly, it's okay," Dale smiled. "I'll bring him home. Do you want me to call you in the morning with a time?"

"Sure. Once you know your plans, just give us a tingle. Love you. Sleep tight."

At 9am the following morning when Dale called the Corbets, Murray declared, "Well, well…a dinner date, hey? That's very romantic. Where's he taking you? Is it somewhere local?"

Before she had an opportunity to answer, Louise quickly signalled for her husband to hand over the receiver. "Please excuse

Murray's third-degree grilling, Dale," she smiled. "Sometimes I think he needs to be reminded that you're not his daughter."

They both laughed before Dale replied, "It's sweet. Shows me how much he cares. Anyway, I am a little anxious but very excited at the same time. I've never been taken out to dinner by a man before. Thank you for minding Josh. We'll drop him over at around 4:30pm and won't be late picking him up."

"I want you both to have a great time," Louise admitted. "Gordon will treat you like a true gentleman should, so savour the experience."

•••••

A wonderful Christmas gathering at the Corbets was immensely enjoyed by all. Murray placed a small inflatable swimming pool on the back lawn and the children loved splashing in it. Of the three kids, Joshua was the youngest and although there were a few tiny spats, they had a lot of fun. Santa Claus had been particularly generous in his gift giving and aside from some blow-up pool toys, Murray and Louise presented each child two superbly illustrated picture books.

Holding her husband's hand as they sat at the table mingling with friends, Louise observed Gordon being extremely attentive towards Dale. He'd bought her a gold necklace for Christmas, which she was wearing, and as Louise watched her niece frequently run her hand over the chain, they'd look at one another and smile. *'She's obviously getting over her distaste for males,'* Louise thought, inwardly grinning. Gordon and Dale were always keeping a very close eye on Joshua, which she also found touching. It was obvious that Gordon Perry was smitten with both mother and her son.

Another notion immediately followed. This was the last Christmas that she and her husband would ever be childless. The anticipation of their own son playing in the yard sent Louise's emotions skyrocketing. She hugged Murray tightly, raised her wine glass and proposed a toast. "Here's to the best family and friends we could ever ask for. Merry Christmas everyone."

While the children napped, Murray produced the final plans for their pole home, as requested by Ken and Janet. He explained the advantages of such a structure to his interested audience then they discussed Louise's innovative design input on the project.

"As soon as the holiday season's over, our builder will lodge the plans with the Gold Coast City Council," Murray informed the group. "It'll take about six weeks or so, before we hear anything back. As long as they're approved well before Easter, I'll be a happy man. That's when we intend to start building."

"Maybe by this time next year, we can all have Christmas in the mountains behind the Gold Coast," Louise suggested.

When Dale escorted her mother to the bathroom, Martha quietly said to Louise, "Emily's an incredible woman, Lou. Just watching her sheer determination to serve herself lunch...almost blew my mind. Now I can see where her daughter gets it from."

"Yes, I know. And the fact that she raised two children makes her even more remarkable in my book. Sadly, her eldest daughter was killed in a car accident a few years back, only twelve months after her husband passed. She's a tough cookie alright. I have the utmost respect for her."

Janet quickly piped up. "Not only have you done an incredible thing for Dale and her son, you've also given Emily a new lease on life, Lou. I know you're hardly a saint, but I tell you what...you're pretty darn close."

Louise placed her arms around the shoulders of Martha and Janet then they both snuggled into her. "It's all thanks to the great friends who support me," she smiled back at them through teary, blurred vision.

CHAPTER THIRTY-SEVEN

Murray got the shock of his life when a barrage of voices yelled, "Surprise!" Dale had just ushered the Corbets through her front door and unbeknown to Murray, inside Gordon and the Deans were awaiting his arrival. Everyone laughed at the stunned expression on the birthday boy's face.

"Wow! Thank you all," Murray beamed. Looking straight at Louise, he said, "I take it we're not going out to dinner?"

She smiled up at him and replied, "That was just a decoy, my love. Dale's cooking for us all tonight and we're going to celebrate here."

"Fabulous! Very sneaky…but I love it!" he returned, while Joshua attempted to tackle him around the legs. Swooping the toddler up in his arms, Murray then shook hands with Gordon and Peter before hugging Dale and Martha.

"A Heineken to start you off Muzz?" Gordon queried.

"Yeah, sure. Thanks Gordy…and a G&T for Louise if you're playing barman."

Patting his friend on the back, Gordon said, "I am 'old' pal. Tonight, your wish is my command."

Half an hour later, Joshua gave everyone goodnight kisses before his mother put him to bed. The women then helped Dale serve up dinner and deliver it to her beautifully decorated dining table. Louise was markedly impressed to hear that her niece had been preparing and cooking for much of the afternoon. Pastry parcels of chicken and banana, asparagus, julienne carrots and potatoes in their jackets with sour cream, were devoured in no time.

Gordon continued attending to drink duties and generally proved to be a worthy co-host. Once he'd cleared the dinner plates from the table, all non-essential lighting was switched off whilst Dale emerged from the kitchen with a huge, cream-filled chocolate cake. It's rich icing glistened in the dazzle of the sparklers perched atop.

The group's 'Happy Birthday to You' song was followed by a short, heartfelt speech from Dale. As Louise lovingly observed her niece, she recognised the great strides that Dale had made over the past five months. Not only was she poised and attractive, her confidence had grown ten-fold.

Murray delivered his unfeigned response. "Thank you so much, Dale. Dinner was absolutely amazing...and I know that Lou would agree when I say we so enjoy having you and Joshua in our lives." Turning to look at each guest individually as he raised his glass, he added, "Thank you everyone."

Coffee, liqueurs and joyful banter followed for well over an hour before the group dispersed. Murray and Louise concurred that celebrating a birthday with family and friends, beat dining in even the finest of establishments any day of the week.

• • • • •

Construction on the Corbet's Wongawallan pole home began without any delays, therefore the couple quickly found themselves engrossed in the project. Murray was thrilled to be onsite when the first of the enormous poles was being erected. Michael, the foreman overseeing the base construction, informed him that the concrete footings would take almost a week to fully cure before any of the cedar beams could start being attached.

Due to roster rescheduling, it was another month before Murray could return. When he did so, he was quite astonished to see the rapid progress that had been made in his absence. "This is incredible, Brian," he remarked as they tentatively walked a plank from the street to the top floor of the house.

"Yeah, we're pleased with it," Brian smiled. "All the beams are bolted on and we're just about to start on the framework. The cladding's here. Come over and meet young Tim, one of my apprentices. He's staining it now."

After a brief introduction, Brian asked Murray, "Are you happy with the colour?"

"Absolutely. It shows up the timber-grain pattern really well."

Brian scratched his head as though deep in thought then turned to face the street. "We're replacing the plank with some industrial ply tomorrow. That has to be done before we can put the front cladding up…and the windows and sliding doors should be here by next week."

"Wow, so it's all systems go then," Murray beamed. "I won't hold you up any longer Brian, I just want to grab some more photos for Lou before I leave. Is that okay?"

"Be my guest mate. Take your time and I'll see you again in about a fortnight."

Back in Sydney, the pictures really excited Louise. "Gee…the two concrete water tanks look like they're in a precarious position."

"They're perfectly stable, Lou," he assured her. "There's twice as much concrete below ground as there is above it, so they're not going anywhere. Do you still want to meet me up there on the 8th? If so, I'll book you a flight."

"Sure do…can hardly wait," she smiled before kissing him. "I'm really looking forward to taking Josh to the circus in the morning too. What time did you say the show starts?"

"10am. When I bought the tickets on Friday, the guy told me that there's a petting zoo and some rides for the kids as well…he'll love it. I thought we might do that part before the show commences. What do you think? Gates open at 8:30am."

"Yep, I agree. Dale said she has a lot of work to cram into tomorrow, so it should suit everyone. I'll give her a call…sound her out."

Next morning the Corbets arrived at the cottage to collect Joshua, Barney, and his push-chair before heading off to Manly Showgrounds. Approaching the carpark, the famous Ashton's Circus big-top tent dominated the sky like a beacon.

A sense of blissful nostalgia swept over Louise as she peered up at the bright red and yellow triangular flags adorning the tent's perimeter. Every summer for almost a decade, her family would attend the travelling circus show when it came to town.

Inside the petting zoo enclosure, while Murray hand-fed baby lambs, goats, guinea pigs and ducklings, Joshua gently patted each animal. Gaining confidence by the minute, one lamb wasn't overly impressed when he grabbed its coat a little too tightly. The animal took a few steps back and began bleating at him. Much to Joshua's delight he clapped his hands with a loud "bah, bah, bah," reply. Murray and Louise had never seen the toddler so excited, nor had they laughed this much in a long time.

The carousel was Louise's favourite ride when she was a child. Mounting their chosen horse with Joshua seated in front, her hands firmly around his little waist, she admired all the elaborately painted prancing ponies as they rotated around a mirrored hub. Murray and Barney waved to them from the gate each time they passed by. Joshua would laugh and wave back with one hand, whilst gripping the pony's horse-hair mane in the other.

A ride on the miniature steam train, whose track circled a snowy mountain scene, saw the toddler in his element. It was a slow ride and one that he could take unassisted, thanks to a metal locking system to keep children securely in their seats. As the train tooted its whistle, the locomotive driver would then call out "all aboard" and tip his cap to onlookers. Joshua imitated the driver's words and movements numerous times over with a roaring giggle.

Seated in the twelfth row inside the giant big-top tent, the view to centre ring was superb. Jugglers, clowns and trapeze artists were the first to perform, receiving a standing ovation from the crowd at the end of their segment. Oddly, Joshua didn't find the clowns funny at all. He cautiously observed them while remaining completely still. The Corbets wondered what his little mind was thinking.

Suddenly lights dimmed and the music's volume increased. Audience anticipation escalated when a spotlight was thrown on the red velvet curtain at the back of the tent. An enormous elephant emerged with a stunningly costumed female performer side-saddled on its back. The crowd erupted, clapping and hollering as the huge beast slowly made its way to the centre of the ring.

Joshua's eyes bulged at the sight of it and joined in with the applause. Clearly, he wasn't the least bit frightened by all the clamour. "Efant, efant!" he yelled at Louise, quickly glancing at her before looking back at the animal. "Oooh…bi, bi, efant!"

"Yes, he's a very big, beautiful elephant, isn't he?" she smiled.

"Booful," Joshua nodded as his body began to sway in time with the mammal's trunk.

On the ringmaster's command, the audience watched on in awe as the elephant stood up on its hind legs, spraying water high into the air. It then performed numerous other tricks before trumpeting a loud farewell to the crowd.

This act was followed up by a skit involving some cheeky monkeys who stole and dressed-up in all the queen's outfits and jewels while she was out shopping; a routine that had everyone in fits of laughter. Poodles then rode pink bicycles around the arena while three fur seals performed an incredible acrobatic show. For the grand finale, a Bengal tiger leapt up onto various elevated platforms then using a key in its mouth, unlocked the latch to a cage that released ten white doves. The applause was almost ear-piercing from a crowd who'd thoroughly enjoyed the entire spectacle.

Heading back to the Corbet's house, the little chatterbox in the back seat hardly took a breather. Louise laughed and placing her hand on Murray's thigh said, "I'd love to be a fly on the wall when he tells his mother about everything he saw this morning."

Louise was grateful to be minding Joshua on Mondays and it was a pleasure that she looked forward to each week. Meanwhile, this allowed Dale to entirely focus on her job. Working Mondays, Wednesdays and Fridays still afforded her plenty of quality time with her son and she was elated to be able to start paying her own way. From what she'd told Louise, her relationship with Gordon was also gaining momentum and they now officially considered themselves 'boyfriend and girlfriend'.

The 8th of April was upon the Corbets in no time and when Louise landed in Brisbane, Murray met her at the airport. He'd already flown in the evening before. Hiring a sedan at the Hertz counter, the couple then headed south along the M1 towards the Gold Coast.

Pulling up at their partially completed Wongawallan home, Murray was pleasantly surprised to find it almost at lock-up stage. The exterior was virtually completed, the suspended ramp from the street to the house was built and fenced, a temporary front door had been installed and all windows were fitted.

Inside, sliding doors were in place, internal walls gyprocked and the imposing raked ceiling was nearing completion. As the couple surveyed the carpentry work, Brian said, "It's lovely to see you again Louise. Murray tells me you want to design the kitchen and bathroom so let's have a gander and take some measurements. I can recommend a local cabinetmaker if you like, he's a true craftsman. And then there's the front door design. I have a few pictures to show you which may assist in your decision making. Do you want flyscreens fitted as well?"

Smiling, Louise returned, "We hadn't really thought about that, but being Queensland, with her umpteen strains of mosquitoes, I think they're a must. So, yes please, can you organise them?"

"No problem at all," Brian replied. "I can also suggest a tiler if you don't want to source one yourself. He does most of my wet area work. If you could choose the tiles and the interior paint colours you'd like fairly quickly, we're almost ready for the tradies to come in."

Looking at her husband, Louise suggested, "I'm going to need to stay overnight and attend to all of this tomorrow. I think we should get you back to Brisbane ready for work in the morning then I'll come back down and do what I have to do here."

"Good plan. We don't want to hold Brian up any more than need be. I know between the two of you, you're more than capable of sourcing everything and when it comes to design and colour choices…you know I trust your judgement implicitly, Lou. Let's drive up to Romano's and give Bill and Robyn a call. You're going to need somewhere to sleep the night."

"Yes, of course. I hope they're home. If not, I'm sure Romano wouldn't mind putting me up."

"If you get stuck, just let me know," Brian interrupted. "We've got a spare bed at home and we'd be more than happy to have you."

Fortunately, Romano was home, as were the Johnsons. It was arranged that Louise would arrive at Bill and Robyn's around 7pm that evening after dropping Murray back at the Ibis Hotel adjacent to Brisbane Airport.

With the balance of the afternoon up their sleeves, the Corbets sought out a few suppliers and collected samples for the kitchen cupboards and benchtop. They then visited the massive Tile Warehouse in Ormeau where they chose and purchased all the travertine-look tiles for the hallway, bathroom, laundry and toilet. The store sold all sorts of flooring, which was extremely handy, so they also ordered rustic cork tiles for the kitchen.

Murray prepared for his Asian route early that night while Louise returned to the Gold Coast. Even though the couple often spoke to the Johnsons over the phone, Bill and Robyn were extremely happy to see Louise again after almost eighteen months. By 8pm Murray called his wife to confirm that her return flight had been rescheduled for 6:45pm the following evening. After enjoying a late dinner with the Johnsons, Louise then shared a few glasses of wine with them before retiring to bed.

Aware that the crew would be onsite by 7am, Louise arrived shortly thereafter and began to nut out the kitchen design before discussing it with Brian. A few rough sketches later, she handed him the chosen samples and advised that she'd also like to see a shelf outside, under the kitchen window, facing the northern deck.

How to tackle the entry area was next on the agenda. It was decided that angled stairs would be built from the ramp up to a solid entry door constructed from rough, vertical timbers. All exterior woodwork, including the front door would be painted an olive colour, similar to that of the treated poles.

Southport was filled with just about every retail outlet a home builder or renovator could possibly need, so by lunchtime, after grabbing a bite to eat at Helensvale, Louise ventured in to Solomons Flooring. With a sample in hand of the travertine-look tiles they'd sourced the day before, she chose a hard-wearing creamy coloured carpet that accompanied the tiles superbly. At Perry's Paint Place the interior wall and exterior woodwork colours were selected; a very light shade of cream inside and an olive-grey hue for the timber.

Returning to the house she delivered the paint swatches and a sample carpet square to Brian. "I'm happy with these paint colours, so that's finalised…and Solomons want to come and measure up themselves to confirm the price with us before they lay anything." Passing Brian a business card, she added, "Here's Rodney's number. Just let them know when they can gain access to do that. Is there anything else you need me to do at this point in time?"

"No, that's pretty much everything," Brian returned in amazement. Crikey! You don't muck around when it comes to making quick decisions, do you Louise? I can't believe you've done all of this in literally twenty-four hours. Wish all my clients were this decisive."

Appreciating his compliment, Louise smiled and said, "Well, to be fair Brian…with the units and townhouses Murray and Gordon have built in the past year, I've become accustomed to making hasty choices. And truth be told, we had a fair idea of what we wanted for this house during the design stage…so that certainly helped. Thank you for everything. We couldn't be happier with how it's all coming together. I'm going to slowly make my way to the airport now, so if there's anything else you need, just give us a call or shoot me an email."

•　•　•　•　•

Towards the end of May, Murray and Louise received a call from their builder informing the couple that final inspections would take place the following day and if all approved, power was ready to be connected.

Having the weekend plus Monday off, Murray advised that he and his wife would fly up on Sunday. With an arrival time of 8am into Coolangatta, Brian agreed to meet the Corbets at the house around 10:30am.

Louise was yearning for a cappuccino after such an early start so the couple stopped at a coffee shop right on the beach in Miami and admired the glorious morning scenery. From there a leisurely forty-five minute trip up the highway saw them ascending Wongawallan Drive.

The Corbets gasped as they pulled up outside their new home. "It's beautiful," Louise remarked, "and it captures all of that incredible view so well."

Brian emerged from the house, smiling and waving as the couple made their way up the ramp to the front door. "What do you think of the steps?" he asked.

"I love them," Murray replied. "Lou described them to me but I have to admit they look twice as good as I expected. Just fabulous, as is that feature door."

Inside was just as they'd envisaged. The angled, cedar-lined walls in the bathroom were a beautiful design touch, matching the vanity doors. A sliding door from the bathroom led onto a small wooden deck with a view through the trees to the mountains in the background. The white shutters in each bedroom added to the sophisticated charm.

Near the entry is where the two-step split level came into play. The lower level contained the dining area, living room, bar and kitchen. A glassed-front fireplace set on rustic bricks immediately jumped out as the primary feature in the living room. Romano had done a brilliant job of laying the brickwork. The exposed flu would add warmth to the area during cool, winter months. Views from the expansive timber deck were nothing short of breathtaking.

"Now," Brian started, rubbing his hands together, "onto the kitchen. It's my favourite part of the house. Love the flow and practicality of it, coupled with brilliant texture combinations. I should get you to do some designing for me, Louise."

The laminated cupboard door fronts and drawers were a natural linen-look with light Tasmanian Oak handles and matching trim around the edge of the benchtop. The bench itself was a textured watermelon shade which lifted the colour pallet of the entire area.

"I'm pleased as punch with the kitchen," Louise remarked. "The cork floor just seamlessly ties the whole interior together."

Her husband completely agreed. "It just feels like home…and it isn't even furnished yet. Imagine how incredible it will be once you weave your interior design magic into it, Lou."

"Yes, but we need to get the appliances in here first. That's our starting point."

Murray began measuring the recess for the fridge when Brian said, "Well, my work here's done and my daughter's netball gala starts in about an hour, so I'd best choof off. The security code for the alarm system and the house keys are on the end of the bench over there…so I guess that's a wrap."

As they saw Brian off at the front door, Murray shook his hand

and said, "Thank you for an incredible job, mate, I hope we can get you back to do the next part of the build, underneath, in the not-too-distant future."

"More than happy to," he returned. "Give me a tingle any time."

For the majority of the day, Murray and Louise spent their time purchasing an upright fridge, bar fridge, washing machine, oven, microwave, three beds, a couple of lamps and some linen. All of the large items would be delivered first thing in the morning.

They'd arranged to meet Romano and the Johnsons at their new home by 6pm. All were keen to see the finished product. Bill and Robyn told the Corbets they'd bring fold-up chairs and pick up a few pizzas on the way and naturally, Romano offered to bring down a bottle of red wine and some glasses.

Relaxing out on the back deck, Romano asked, "When do you think you two will be back up?"

"As soon as we can," Murray replied. "We were talking about it this afternoon and decided to get it all fitted out so that we can just come and go as we please. If we leave a key and the security code with you, would you mind checking it out now and again for us, please? I know it's fairly isolated up here so we bought some lamps and tomorrow I'll grab some timer switches for them. That way we can stagger the lamps to come on intermittently throughout the night."

"Great thinking," Romano smiled. "There isn't much traffic up here, well at least not until the proposed development starts. Yes, of course I'll keep an eye on it.

The group then thoroughly perused the dwelling, sipping their wine and chatting before Murray locked up the house and they all parted ways. After sleeping soundly at the Surfers Paradise Motel that evening, the Corbets were up early. They purchased some timer switches at a hardware store then by 8:30am they were back at Wongawallan awaiting their deliveries.

Beds were the first to arrive; a queen and two singles, quickly followed by the washing machine and fridges. Both delivery drivers commented on the sixteen-degree gradient of the climb up Wongawallan Drive. The fellow from Harvey Norman said, "Must have been a mission getting all those poles up here, my little two-toner could hardly make it! But how's that view, hey. Feels like I'm on top of the world."

While Murray was setting up the plumbing for the washing machine, ensuring water intake and outlet hoses were firmly fastened, the oven turned up. Two men, one a licensed electrician, had it installed and working within fifteen minutes.

"That's all of it, my love," Louise smiled as she kissed him. "A great start for when we next return."

Closing the shutters, locking up the house and setting the security alarm, the couple then slowly made their way back to Coolangatta in readiness for the flight home.

Stopping at a service station in Burleigh Heads to refuel the car and deliver it back to Hertz with a full tank, Louise noticed a small indigenous sign on the footpath across the road. It read, 'MIRIKAI – Place of Peace'. Immediately she'd stumbled upon the perfect name for their new holiday house.

CHAPTER THIRTY-EIGHT

Sydney was in the grip of a major flu epidemic by the start of winter, which saw many of Qantas' pilots struck down by the horrid disease. Murray had managed to evade it thus far but unfortunately that meant his workload almost doubled. He was either interstate or overseas for much of June.

One Wednesday evening, about halfway through the month, Louise invited Dale and Gordon over for dinner. It was one of the rare occasions her husband would be home and she knew that he'd want to catch up with his family.

Casually seated in front of the fire late that afternoon, the adults conversed while Joshua played on the floor with his toys. Murray sensed that something was off with Gordon. His friend had been unusually quiet since his arrival.

Dale was adjusting her cardigan sleeves when tiny sparkles of refracting light caught Louise's attention. Looking down at her niece's hand, a gleaming gold diamond ring revealed itself. "What's this?" she shouted, grabbing Dale's wrist and pulling it towards her.

Quickly looking up at her niece then immediately across at Gordon, a broad, involuntary smile covered Louise's face. "Is this what I think it is?" she asked, gazing into Dale's eyes.

"It is. Gordon asked me to marry him and I said 'yes'."

"Oh, wow! This is wonderful. I'm almost speechless," Louise confessed as she tightly embraced Dale. "When did this happen?"

"Last night. We wanted you to know first, before I tell Mum."

Meanwhile, Murray was struck dumb. He hadn't said a word until finally reaching for Gordon's hand, firmly shaking it then giving him a strong hug. "Well, I'll be darned…congratulations, mate. I couldn't be more surprised, or more pleased."

Rising from the lounge he made his way over to Dale. She stood up, threw her arms around his chest and they squeezed one another tightly. Kissing her on the cheek he smiled and said "Congratulations, sweetheart. This calls for champagne. What would you like to drink?"

"A lemon squash, please Murray…and I'll just have a tiny sip of Gordon's champers."

"Why don't you call your Mum now, Dale?" Louise excitedly suggested. "She's going to be over the moon! Dinner's a while off yet."

"Alright, thanks Louise, I will."

Over the phone with Gordon by her side, Dale delivered the news of their engagement to her mother. Everyone in the room could hear the squeal of glee Emily returned. Describing the ring, Dale explained that it was a solitaire diamond set on a white gold band shaped like the end of a ribbon. "You'll know exactly what I mean when you feel it, Mum. It's just gorgeous." A short while later, her mother asked to speak with Gordon.

"Hello Emily. I hope we haven't shocked you too much?" he enquired.

"Well, I am a bit stunned…but it's a feeling of sheer jubilation, I can assure you. I'm so happy for you both. You're a kind and gentle man, Gordon…and I'll be very proud to have you as my son-in-law."

"Thank you, Emily, that's very sweet of you to say. I'll just put Louise on. She'd like a word."

Louise couldn't get her hands on the receiver quickly enough. The women exuberantly spoke for almost half an hour. Meanwhile, Murray and Dale took it upon themselves to assume control in the kitchen while Gordon and Joshua playfully wrestled on the lounge room floor.

• • • • •

On June 29, Murray was rostered-off for three days when an official 'Priority mail' envelope arrived at the house. Inside, the letter read: 'To Mr and Mrs Murray Corbet, you are hereby notified that an infant has been selected for adoption. Please arrange your attendance at the Child Services Department office in order to complete final paperwork. On sign-off approval, you will be requested to present yourselves at the Sydney Children's Hospital in Randwick to view the infant. Should you feel that this particular infant does not meet your adoption requirements, there will be others up for your consideration in the near future.'

Murray was so elated, with letter in hand, he practically ran to the backyard to find his wife. "Lou, where are you?" he called out with urgency.

"Behind the garden shed," she shouted back at him. "Is everything okay?" Peeling off her gardening gloves, she quickly made her way towards him.

"Everything's far better than okay," he smiled with teary eyes. "Look. Our baby's here!" Sweeping her up off her feet, he then twirled her in the air while she attempted to read the letter aloud.

Once firmly back on the ground, Louise pulled the piece of paper to her chest and said, "Oh, Murray...I don't know whether to laugh or cry. This is the best letter ever!"

They embraced for a solid minute before Louise declared, "I'll just lock up the shed before I come inside for a shower. Do you want to give them a call and organise a time for tomorrow?"

"You bet," he smiled, kissing her.

After a restless night, tossing and turning in anticipation of finally becoming parents, Murray and Louise arrived at the office half an hour earlier than their scheduled meeting time. They were far too excited to stay at home any longer.

Their adoption agent informed them that the baby boy was born sixteen days ago, on June 14. His parents were both New Zealanders; the father a house painter and his mother a trainee laboratory technician. They'd decided to put their baby up for adoption because they felt far too young to raise a child. They were literally still children themselves. None of the grandparents were aware of the pregnancy, which is why the baby's mother temporarily moved to Sydney. The baby's father was present for the birth but both had since returned to Auckland.

Attending to the rigorous paperwork, Louise saw a note paper-clipped to the top of the file that simply read, 'Cute Kid'. She inconspicuously pointed it out to Murray and immediately they grinned at each another.

"Well...that's everything from this end," the agent declared, taking off her reading glasses and smiling up at them both. If you want to make your way over to the hospital, I'll meet you out the front of the maternity ward in say...45 minutes. That should give us all plenty of time to commute in the afternoon traffic and find a parking spot."

The Sydney Children's Hospital was a huge complex, made up of several large buildings plus numerous wings which sprawled across the entire site. At the main reception area, Murray and Louise were escorted to the maternity ward by a chirpy eldery woman. She was a volunteer Uniting Care worker who assisted at the hospital three days a week.

"Thank you, Esmay," the agent smiled, as the couple entered the waiting area. "This place would be lost without you."

"Yes, yes...so they keep telling me dear," the woman jested before returning to the corridor.

Taking the Corbets into a small, isolated room, the agent then asked them to be seated. "I'll only be a few minutes. Just have to let the matron know that you're here and a nurse will bring the baby in. Please, make yourselves comfortable."

After she left, Louise said, "I'm so nervous Murray. My heart's pounding like crazy...and I'm warming up at a rate of knots. Do you think it's hot in here?"

Reaching for her hand, he replied, "No, it's actually quite cool. I'm sure it's only nerves, Lou. After all, this is a really big deal. We're about to meet our son for the..."

"Really?" she glared at him. "That's not helping, honey. I'm just going to close my eyes and focus on my breathing."

"Good idea, I'll join you," he concurred.

As they began to breathe in rhythm, their eyes sprung wide open at the click of the door handle. A nurse entered, pushing something that resembled a shopping trolley. At first it appeared to be filled with blankets, but when she partially peeled back the top layer, a tiny, angelic face was revealed.

The Corbets instantly fell in love. While the nurse lifted the baby from his cozy crib, she smiled at Louise, nodded then gently placed the precious bundle in Louise's arms. Tears began to stream down her face as she gently brushed his delicate cheek.

On passing the sleeping infant to her husband, silence prevailed whilst the couple exchanged a knowing glance. Murray stroked the baby's soft head before caressing his teeny fingers.

A short while later, the nurse quietly asked, "Is this the child you'd like to take home?"

No consulting was necessary. Both looked up at her through misty eyes and nodded vigorously.

• • • • •

It wasn't long before baby Martin William Corbet fondly became known as 'Marty'. He grew like a happy little weed with an infectious smile and brilliant green eyes. Marty giggled at just about anything but his favourite source of amusement was a crocheted green and yellow clown named 'Wee Cloony'. The toy hung from a piece of elastic tied to the hood of his stroller.

Frequently, Louise would defer to Dale for parenting advice and guidance. Her niece was more than happy to oblige and Dale felt that in some small way, she was helping to repay the Corbets for all their kindnesses. Joshua was infatuated with Marty from the moment he laid eyes on him.

Almost a year after Marty's arrival, the top level of 'Mirikai' was completely finished. Louise had done a superb job of the furnishings during their three visits. Bill made a beautiful cedar toy box to house all of Marty's playthings, which was proudly positioned in the corner of the lounge room. As the baby seldom saw these toys, it was like Christmas every time the Corbets flew up to their family holiday home.

Murray and Louise cared for Joshua while Dale and Gordon took a so-called 'holiday' to Fiji. Truth is…they'd eloped, and returned to Sydney as a married couple. They told the Corbets that neither of them wanted any fuss and Dale knew that a wedding would have been difficult for her mother.

Together the newly-weds designed and built a home, not very

far from Murray and Louise. The cottage was then leased to one of Louise's former students. Dale had always shown great interest in interior design, so upon completion of the same home decorating course that Louise had done, she began working part-time for her aunt. In conjunction with her existing job, Dale now found herself earning a rather handsome wage each week.

Marty loved bedtime stories so between them, Murray and Louise made up a special tale about their treasured son:

One day the postman came along on his motorbike. Brrrrrrm, brrrrrrrm. Mummy and Daddy saw him put a letter in the letterbox, so they went out and got it. When Daddy opened it up, he read that there was a little baby boy in the Sydney hospital for them to go and see. It said that if Mummy and Daddy loved the baby, they could bring him home.

Next day, very early, Mummy and Daddy got up, had a shower and drove over the big bridge to see this tiny baby in the hospital.

A nurse took Mummy and Daddy into a little room then went away. When she came back, she was pushing a trolley just like the one we put our groceries in at the supermarket. In the trolley there was a pile of blankets and when Mummy and Daddy lifted them up, there was a tiny, tiny baby boy underneath.

"Oh!" Mummy and Daddy cried. "What a beautiful baby."

The nurse asked them, "Do you love this little person?"

"Oh, yes, we do!" Mummy and Daddy said.

"Well, you can take him home to live with you," the nurse smiled.

The nurse then took the baby away and dressed him in the clothes that Mummy had made for him. When the nurse came back, she gave the tiny baby to Mummy to cuddle.

"What name will you call this bouncing baby boy?" the nurse asked.

And Daddy said, "Martin William Corbet."

This story quickly became Marty's favourite and the couple knew that when he was old enough to understand, they'd tell their son that he was adopted.

One Tuesday while assisting Louise on a design project in her office, Dale proudly announced that she was pregnant.

"That's wonderful news," her aunt beamed. Immediately standing to hug her niece, she added, "Oh, Dale. Gordon must be tickled pink!"

"I haven't told him yet," she admitted, gently biting her lower lip. "The doctor only confirmed it yesterday and I'm about eight weeks. Gordon gets back tomorrow night, so I'll tell him then. You're the first to know and after I tell him, we'll invite Mum over and break the news together. I know she'll be happy for us too…and it'll be great for Josh to have a sibling."

Smiling, Louise remarked, "Will it ever! Do you want to know the sex of the baby?"

"I'm not sure. I didn't last time. If Gordon wants to know, I'll run with it, otherwise I'm happy to wait and see. Josh will just be starting preschool when the baby's due."

The following evening, Gordon was ecstatic when Dale revealed her pregnancy. Like his wife, he agreed that not knowing the sex of their baby was all part of the mystery. Immediately phoning Murray he said, "Muzz, I think we need to plan for another build. If I don't keep myself busy for the next seven months, the wait for this baby of ours will kill me."

"Are you serious, Gordy?" his mate laughed. "We had to wait eighteen months! You'll be right pal. But we could do another one… the timings perfect for me, and I want to build the bottom floor at 'Mirikai' by this time next year."

Over the course of summer and half way into autumn, Murray and Gordon built another four townhouses. Louise and Dale played their part in the decorating, only this time, Dale did the vast majority of work. Again, they went to auction, selling three villas and keeping one as their own investment property.

● ● ● ● ●

"Lou, Dale's waters have just broken," Gordon declared in a panicked state. "She needs to get to hospital immediately. Can you come over and get Josh?"

Dale could be heard in the background saying, "Stop getting in a tizz, Gordy, there's plenty of time. We'll drop him off on the way to the hospital. She can't leave Marty at home on his own."

"Okay, okay," he surrendered to his wife. "Sorry Lou. Change of plans. We're leaving right now and we'll bring Josh over."

"Alright, Gordy. Dale knows what she's doing, so just stay calm and follow her lead." With that, she hung up the phone at 11:45pm, prepared Joshua's bed and switched on the porch light.

Within minutes Louise heard their car pull up. Unlocking the front door, she then dashed outside. As Gordon extracted the sleeping child from his seat, Louise leaned through the passenger door and gave her niece a warm hug. "All the best, sweetheart. We'll see you soon."

Gordon swiftly carried Joshua into the house and placed him in bed while Louise retrieved his little suitcase from the back seat. From the door of the spare room, she could sense Gordon's hesitation.

"He'll be fine," she assured him. "He knows this place inside out, so he won't be the least bit frightened when he wakes up. Off you go, your wife needs you."

Morning came and Louise was up early preparing breakfast. Rubbing his sleepy eyes, somewhat confused as he entered the kitchen, Joshua asked, "Aunty Lou, where is evybody?"

Cuddling him, she replied, "Mummy's gone to hospital to have your baby brother or sister, so Daddy brought you over here last night on the way…for me to look after you. You were fast asleep and they didn't want to wake you up."

Satisfied with her answer, Joshua smiled and said, "Okay," before laying down on the lounge room floor to play with Marty. Within seconds he asked, "Where's Uncle Murray? Am I going to preschool today?"

"Not unless you want to," Louise smiled at him. "I thought you might like to stay here today. Murray's at work, but he'll be home around lunchtime. By then we might know if you have a brother or sister. Isn't that exciting?"

Screwing up his forehead, Joshua gazed at her and posed another query. "Will they cut Mummy's tummy open to get the baby out?"

This particular question threw Louise, so for a brief moment she considered how to answer it. Believing 'the truth' was generally the best approach, she said, "Well…if the baby comes out of the hole head first, then no. But if the baby's legs come first, they might have to cut Mummy's tummy. If they do, it won't hurt her, Joshy. They're very clever doctors."

"What's the hole?" he asked immediately. "Do you mean Mummy's mouth?"

'Oh gosh…good on you Louise', she silently reprimanded herself. *'Now you've opened a can of worms!'* Thinking on her feet for a moment, she slowly replied, "No. It's a different hole. When a Mummy wants to have a baby, the angels give her a little hole at the top of her legs. While the baby grows inside Mummy's tummy, the hole gets bigger and when the baby's ready, it comes down through the tunnel and out of the hole." Quickly changing the subject, she added, "Come and eat your breakfast little man…then you can get dressed while I change Marty."

Joshua remained very quiet whilst he hoed into his cereal. Meanwhile, Louise could almost see the cogs turning in his little brain when another doozy question followed.

"Aunty Lou…how did the baby get to Mummy's tummy?"

'That's it. I'm out,' she secretly concluded whilst smiling at him. "That's a question I think you should leave for Mummy, Josh. I'm sure she'd like you to ask her that one."

Louise then made a mental note to relay this conversation to his parents. Could be helpful information if their son was to ask any further questions about the birds and the bees.

While the boys were playing out on the back lawn, Gordon phoned from the hospital. "We have a beautiful daughter, Lou. Everything went well. Dale's fine and the baby's really healthy. They're both sleeping now, so I'm going to try to catch some shut-eye in the chair beside Dale's bed. How's Josh?"

"He's great…and congratulations. Josh will be stoked to have a baby sister. Murray should be home shortly, so we'll all come over to the hospital when he arrives."

"Terrific," Gordon replied. "We can't wait to introduce you to Wendy Emily Louise Perry."

"Wow, that's some handle!" Louise smiled. "I'm absolutely flattered. Thank you."

"It was a no-brainer, Lou, you're like a second mother to Dale. See you when you get here."

When Murray walked through the front door, he was thrilled to hear the fabulous news. After a quick shower, they all piled into the car and stopping at a florist along the way, Louise purchased a magnificent bunch of native flowers for her niece.

"Can I please give them to Mummy, Aunty Lou?" Josh excitedly asked.

"Of course, you can. That's very sweet Josh. I'll carry them until we get to the door of Mummy's room then you can take them in. How does that sound?"

He simply nodded with a big grin and returned to playing with Marty in the back seat.

Murray, Louise and the boys found Dale looking surprisingly rested while her husband carried a proud smile. A lot of hand shaking, back slapping and kissing went on, as Joshua presented the floral arrangement to his mother. He then looked around the room and under Dale's bed before asking, "Where is she Mummy?"

Hugging her son tightly and kissing him on the forehead, Dale replied, "Your sister's asleep in the nursery. We'll go and see her in a minute. Where's Barney?"

"He's sleeping too, in the car. Did they chop open your tummy to get the baby out, Mummy?"

Looking quite amused, Dale returned, "No, they didn't have to do that, darling."

Gently placing the side of his head on Dale's stomach, Joshua then blurted, "Where's the angel hole she came out from?"

Dale gazed at Gordon surprisingly and they both grinned. "Perhaps some other time, Josh," she advised him. "For now, let's go and see Wendy. Do you want to see her?"

"Yes, yes, yes," he shouted, jumping up and down on the spot.

Donning a robe, Dale held her son's hand while the group paraded along the corridor to the nursery. An attending nurse smiled at the Perrys before bringing the bassinet over to the window. Murray and Gordon picked up the boys for a good view of the baby.

"Oh…I want to cuddle her," Josh sighed.

"Okay," his mother started, "We'll get Daddy to ask the nurse if we can take her back to our room. That way you can give her a cuddle in the big chair."

Looking proudly up at Gordon, whom Joshua considered as his father, he said, "You can cuddle her too Daddy, but you have to be very, very, very gentle, okay?"

Gordon kissed him on the cheek and said, "Love you, Joshy. I promise I will."

Shortly after the Perrys married, Gordon looked into the process of adopting the boy. He was informed that Joshua must remain a step-son for a minimum of three years before an application could be submitted. In the meantime, Gordon and Dale decided to handle the situation as though it had already been carried out. When the waiting period had been fulfilled, the couple would then make it official.

Back in the room, Gordon sat Joshua in the chair while Dale placed her daughter gently into her son's arms. He lovingly gazed down at her in awe. "She's tiny, tiny, isn't she Mummy? So is her nose…but her eyes won't open…I can't see her proply."

"You'll see them when she wakes up Josh, but for now she needs her sleep. Brand new babies need a lot of sleep. And we'll have to wait for her to get a bit bigger before she can play with you. Until then, I hope you'll help me and Daddy look after her."

"Yes, cause she's very, very special," Joshua smiled. "Can I take her to preschool tomorrow?"

Murray and Louise burst out laughing, closely followed by little Marty. Dale explained that they would take his new baby sister in to show the class one day, but Wendy would have to return home with her straight afterwards. Joshua was less than impressed by his mother's answer.

The Corbets finally had their opportunity to take turns nursing the newborn. Murray and Louise agreed that Wendy's delicate facial features were a perfect combination of both parents. Marty was simply content with snuggling into the baby's pink bunny rug.

As Louise peered down the lens of her camera to snap some family photographs, tears of joy began to blur her vision. She truly felt like the luckiest woman on earth, with a depth of love and devotion that was almost indescribable.

CHAPTER THIRTY-NINE

One superb Saturday afternoon in March, when Marty was twenty-one months old, neighbours James and Belinda Black invited the Corbet family over for barbecue to celebrate their daughter's tenth birthday. Numerous other guests were in attendance and even though little Marty was by far the youngest of all the children, the older kids were happy to keep watch over him whilst they played on the vacant allotment next door.

Jasmine and Oliver Black would often come across the street and play with Marty after school, if they saw Louise and her son pottering around in the front yard. They were great kids and Marty relished the opportunity to join in whatever game they wished to play...which was usually handball. On several blistering days during summer, Louise and Marty had jumped at the invitation to join the children in their pool for a swim.

Imbibing in a few celebratory drinks at the barbecue, as adult guests mingled on the north-facing deck outside, every few minutes the Corbets would pop their heads over the timber fence to check on their son. Just before 1pm, one of the mothers went to round up the kids for lunch and discovered that Marty wasn't with the group.

"Where's the little boy?" she quickly asked Jasmine.

"I don't know." Calling to her brother, she shouted, "Oliver. Where's Marty?"

"I haven't seen him for a while. He must have gone back to his Mum."

With that, the woman urgently bellowed over the fence, "Louise! Is Marty with you?"

"No," came her bewildered reply.

A mad scramble then ensued. Adults and children darted in every direction looking for the toddler. Louise and the kids called Marty's name as they checked the street, whilst the balance of the group scoured the inside of the house. Meanwhile, Murray ran around to the fenced pool area on the southern side of the yard. His heart sunk when he saw the gate ajar.

Rushing through it, he discovered his son face down on the bottom of the pool in the deep end. "He's in the pool!" Murray yelled, before diving in and hauling Marty's pallid, lifeless body up to the surface.

James was already in position, kneeling on the pavers when the toddler was passed to him. Barely touching the sides as he leapt out of the water, Murray began to resuscitate Marty. Louise and some of the other adults watched on in horror while Belinda kept all the remaining children inside the house.

"I'll call an ambulance," one woman declared as she bolted off.

James turned to the onlookers and said, "Someone go and get Alex. He's a doctor, lives six doors down, number 38. Hurry!"

Within three minutes Alex arrived on the scene and during that time, Murray had managed to get his son breathing again. Shortly thereafter two ambulance paramedics appeared, asking the Corbets to dry Marty off before taking the family to hospital. The toddler would need to have his lungs assessed.

Everyone present was clearly shocked and shaken to the core. Investigation into how the pool gate was left open, revealed that one of the older children had gone into the area to retrieve Jasmine's bike but failed to close the gate on his way out. Marty must have wandered in, seen Oliver's sailing boat bobbing on the water and tried to reach over and get it.

At the hospital, x-rays detected water in both lungs and in Marty's stomach. While Louise sat in a chair with her son straddled across her legs, facing her, she hugged and comforted him. Suddenly, a wave of chlorinated fluid spewed all over her chest. Relieved and smiling with tears in her eyes, she looked up at her husband and said, "I've never been so happy to be vomited on!"

The next morning, quite early, Murray and Louise had just brought Marty into bed with them when they heard a knock on the front door. It was Jasmine and Oliver Black.

"How's Marty, Mr Corbet?" Jasmine anxiously asked whilst

holding a colourful bunch of gerberas from her mother's garden.

"He's fine kids," Murray smiled. "Come on in and see for yourself."

Climbing up onto the end of the Corbet's bed, the two children were so happy to see Marty. They hugged and tickled him while Louise went to place the flowers in a vase of water.

"I sleeps in da pool yesday," Marty told Oliver.

Murray was shocked by his son's memory of the event. Immediately he realised that getting Marty back into the water as soon as possible, was paramount.

"We know," the eight-year-old smiled back at Marty, "but you can't go near the water by yourself, you're too little. Mummy or Daddy have to be there too." Turning to Murray he hesitantly added, "We're sorry, Mr Corbet..."

"Yes, we are," his sister interrupted. "We told you and Louise... and Mum and Dad, that we'd look after him. But we didn't. We were too busy playing with all the other kids and we forgot about Marty for a little while. We're very sorry and we'll never let it happen again, ever! We promise."

"I'm sure you won't," Murray smiled at them both, "and thank you for your apologies. That's a very grown-up thing to do."

Tuesday of the following week, after school, Belinda, Louise and their children enjoyed a dip in the swimming pool. Marty was slightly hesitant to get in the water with his mother at first, but after some gentle encouragement from Jasmine and Oliver, he splashed about and played with them for well over an hour.

Shortly thereafter, Louise enrolled her son in swimming lessons. Informing the instructor about Marty's prior mishap, he approached the toddler with a gentle yet firm teaching method. Marty was enjoying the experience and gaining confidence with each lesson, however, it was a good two years before he'd hold his breath and put his face underwater.

• • • • •

The Corbets decided that by the time Marty turned three, adopting a little sister for him would complete their loving family unit. The procedure was the same as previously, though the waiting time far less. By the end of October, Murray and Louise were blessed with a tiny daughter they named Annie. In the beginning she had blue eyes and very little hair but within the span of a few months, penetrating green eyes had manifested beneath her dark curls. Many people remarked on the resemblance between mother and daughter.

Marty loved Annie to bits and he was very gentle and protective of her. His happy-go-lucky nature was a characteristic that Murray and Louise had always admired, and as Annie's personality developed, it appeared she'd carry similar traits. From the moment she could crawl, Annie followed her big brother everywhere.

Yet another year behind schedule, the Corbets were now ultra-keen to add the lower floor to their Queensland holiday home. The family had been spending more time up there of late and as plans for the self-contained ground level were already approved, they asked Brian Clarke when he'd be able to make a start on it. He advised the couple that after completing a home on Mt Tamborine in approximately three weeks time, he'd be available to commence work. They discussed timelines and Brian confirmed that it would be completed by early December.

Arrangements for Christmas at 'Mirikai' with John, Julie, Gordon, Dale and all the children were put in place. This meant that Murray and Louise would only have three short months to organise everything from its initial colour scheme right through to being fully furnished.

They decided to tackle each step, in advance, to alleviate the pressure of completing everything in December. Murray's roster would likely only allow one trip during the construction period but Louise was happy to take the reins.

At the beginning of November, she bundled up Annie, along with her daughter's car seat and they flew to Queensland. Gordon was rostered-off for the next three days, so the Perry's kindly offered to take care of Marty while his father was at work. Joshua couldn't wait to have his little friend stay with them.

Brian Clarke was well into the build when Louise and Annie arrived at the house. The outer walls had been erected, the floor was down, and the separate entry door and windows were all in place to secure the lower level. Louise was absolutely thrilled with the builder's swift progress.

After putting the baby to sleep in Marty's cot, Louise went back downstairs to discuss the configuration of the interior with Brian. Insulation was to be installed between the upstairs floor and the ceiling below to alleviate foot traffic noise but little else had been decided. They paced around for quite some time, measuring out where internal walls should be built and choosing a location for the fireplace that would be installed next winter.

Brett, the cabinetmaker, arrived at around 2pm and Louise showed him sketches and sample materials of what she'd envisaged. He measured it all up and advised that he could have the kitchenette and all of its cupboards, as well as the built-in robes in all three bedrooms finished within a fortnight.

"The bathroom plan's perfect Brian," Louise told him. "Plenty of room for everything we need. I'm going to buy a modular shower for down here and I'll try to get the same tiles as upstairs. What else? Oh yes, the toilet, I'll organise that tomorrow too. When do you want everything delivered? That could be the tricky part."

"If you schedule everything for next week, we'll be able to work around that. The framework for the walls can be started now I know where you want them…then I'll call the plasterers in."

"Okay," Louise concurred. "By the time I leave, I will have ordered the vanity as well. We'll carpet the lounge room and bedrooms the same as upstairs and I'll order the shutters too…but only for the bedrooms down here. You'd need a sky hook to see into any of the other rooms. I'll attend to the bathroom side of things first, so that you have all the measurements for the plumbing. Can you arrange all the flyscreens again?"

"Yep, sure can," Brian smiled at her.

"I'm hoping Murray can join me for the next trip up, but either way, I'll be choosing all the furniture before December. We're having six adults and six kids here for Christmas, so I need to get the place fitted out before everyone arrives."

At that moment, they heard Annie cry upstairs. Excusing herself, Louise called back to Brian, "Holler if there's anything else you need. We're just ducking down to the supermarket for some supplies."

"We're out of here anyway, Louise. See you tomorrow."

Annie broke into a huge grin, kicking her legs around with excitement as Louise entered the room. Changing her nappy, Louise then grabbed the keys and they headed off for some menial grocery items.

Inside ten minutes of arriving back home, the front door chime rang.

"Hello Romano, it's lovely to see you," Louise beamed.

"Hi Louise, how have you been? I just saw the rental car in the driveway and thought I'd pop in. Hope you don't mind? Who's this adorable little cherub?" he asked, gently reaching for the baby's foot.

"This is Annie," she replied. "Our latest addition to the Corbet family."

"Congratulations…what a cutie pie." Smiling at the baby, Romano declared, "Her curly hair's almost as beautiful as mine. I'll bet Marty adores her."

"Oh, yes," Louise returned. "Her big brother's pretty besotted. Have you had a sneak peek at the additional floor downstairs?"

"No, but I must say, it looks like you're almost doubling the size of the house, Louise."

"Well, yes, I suppose we are. The family's coming for Christmas this year so that kind of pushed the agenda. We'll be chock-a-block when they all arrive. Would you like to come down and see it?"

Romano scratched his chin before replying, "I'd love to, but maybe next time you're up. I really do have to run. If you need anything just let me know. Addio amica."

"Thanks Romano, addio," she returned, waving him off.

Out on the back deck with Annie, Louise scattered some bird seed in the hope of attracting a few feathered friends. Several brightly coloured lorikeets chirped to one another as they gathered nectar from the native trees nearby and two butcher birds flew down beside them, but showed little interest in the food on offer. They much preferred meat. Mother bird was black and white, whilst her youngster was a light shade of brown. Cunning magpies however, weren't so fussy. Annie squealed with delight as they pecked away at the seed. Her outburst didn't appear to faze them one bit. Three kookaburras suddenly joined the party, swooping onto the rail and chorusing their laugh, much to Annie's great enjoyment.

Putting her daughter to bed early that evening, Louise returned to the kitchen and noticed movement on the shelf outside the kitchen window. It was a possum, though she'd never seen one up this close before. Taking pieces of diced carrot from her salad and placing them in her hand, she then gently slid the window open just enough to fit her hand through. The possum, without hesitation, took a piece of carrot from Louise in its delicate fingers and began munching. This was a thrilling and unexpected wildlife encounter, given the fact that in New Zealand, possums were considered pests…and there was a hefty bounty on their heads. After observing the small marsupial for quite some time, Louise named it 'Blossom'.

Whilst quietly reading a book in the living room, Louise then heard a noise out on the deck that sounded like a baby crying. Next thing, there was a huge kerfuffle. She jumped up to investigate and discovered that another possum had arrived. The two were fighting and though it was only short lived, Louise wondered if the squabble was over the other pieces of carrot or perhaps a territorial dispute. Either way, the altercation intrigued her.

Kookaburras woke Annie and her mother early the following morning. After Louise prepared breakfast she took the highchair out onto the deck and they captured the rising sun. It was so peaceful with only the faint hum of chirping crickets and birdsong in the background. But the tranquillity was short-lived, as Brian and his team arrived to commence their working day.

By 9am, Louise and Annie were on their way down to the Gold Coast to source and purchase all the items on Louise's extensive list. They were gone for the entire day and with everything finally accomplished, heading home to the hills was a much-welcomed respite. That evening Louise wearily flopped into bed within an hour of putting her daughter down.

Back in Sydney by 3:30pm on Wednesday, Dale was super excited to pick up Annie and her aunt from the airport. She'd obtained her driver's license and purchased a second-hand sedan only a month prior. For Dale, it was a newfound freedom and she jumped at the opportunity to drive anyone anywhere. On the way home, Louise told her niece about everything she'd managed to achieve in Queensland.

"I can hardly wait for Christmas," Dale enthusiastically admitted. "Gordon and I were thinking that we might actually drive up in the station wagon and stop for a night somewhere along the way. Josh would love the road trip and I've always wanted to see 'The Big Banana' in Coffs Harbour, ever since I was a kid. Apparently, there's a giant fun park there too."

"Oh, yes," Louise smiled. "I've seen pictures of the giant slide on the hill…he'd be in his element. And Wendy would sleep most of the way, so it's a great opportunity to spend some quality time with him. He's growing up so fast."

Gordon was already at the Corbet's house with Joshua, Marty and Wendy when they arrived.

The two boys raced out to the car and gave Louise and Annie hugs before breaking all their exciting news of the past two days.

"Mummy, guess what?" Marty started with bulging eyes. "Uncle Gordon and me and Joshy builded a huge, huge, Lego dragon! He's green and he has big fire coming out of he's mouth…and Aunty Dale maked us a big chocolate cake…wiv rainbow sprinkles. It was so, so yummy."

Smiling into her son's eyes as she hugged him, Louise replied, "Sounds like you've had a wonderful time, darling."

"Yeah…and Aunty Dale buyed us a new soccer ball too. The uver one got a hole in it."

Poor Joshua quickly realised that he wouldn't get a word in edgeways, so instead decided to carefully carry Annie inside with his father's permission, and place her in the bouncer.

"He's been such a good boy, Lou," Gordon declared as they entered the lounge room. "We've all really enjoyed having him."

"That's wonderful to hear," she smiled, hugging the couple. "Thank you both, so much. Murray and I sincerely appreciate it."

"We know you do, Louise. More than happy to have Marty any time," Dale professed. "What time does Murray get in?"

"He should be home around 7pm."

Marty's little ears pricked up then he bolted towards his mother. "Is Daddy coming home?"

"He sure is," Louise smiled, bending down to pick up her son. "Hopefully he'll be here to tuck you into bed tonight."

Throwing his arms around her neck, Marty yelled, "Yippee!" Holding up his fingers, he began counting. "Mummy…and Daddy…and Annie…and me. That's four. Same as me, Mummy!"

CHAPTER FORTY

All of the Corbet's groundwork fell into place and within five weeks, 'Mirikai' was ready for their family's Christmas invasion. Murray and Louise would catch an early flight on the 22nd to prepare for their guests' arrival, collecting a hired people-mover van at Brisbane airport for the duration of their stay, along with a fitted car seat for Annie. The Perry family were scheduled to arrive by vehicle the following morning and the Keanes would be flying in that afternoon.

Attending to the vast majority of grocery shopping before landing at the house, Murray and Louise then stowed it all away. The three fridges were full to the brim and there was little remaining cupboard space in either kitchen. Meanwhile, a hire company delivered the additional cot and highchair that would be required, as well as numerous toys suitable for children of all ages.

Later that day, after Annie's nap, Murray bundled his children into the people mover and headed down to the coast while Louise cleaned floors, countertops and did a bit of last-minute dusting.

Downstairs, whilst laying out some fresh towels in the bathroom, she could hear a scraping sound in a tree immediately outside the window. Peeking through the flyscreen, a massive yellow-spotted monitor came into view. He was slowly clawing his way up the bark of a scribbly gum. The lizard, at least a metre long, had also caught the attention of a butcher bird higher up in the tree. As it began to squawk an ear-piercing alert to the other birds, within seconds a squadron of them appeared from nowhere, darting at the monitor in great numbers. Louise could only assume they were trying to ward off the enemy in order to defend a nest. Fed up with their onslaught, the lizard turned and commenced his descent back down the tree. *'Oh, the children are going to love having all these critters around,'* she thought to herself.

Murray arrived home with all the final items on his wife's Christmas list, including a beautiful Christmas tree. Together, father and son set it up in a bucket of sand downstairs on the hearth. Tomorrow the tree's decorations would arrive, as they were already onboard with the Perrys.

A very full day saw the Corbet children in bed early while Murray and Louise relaxed with red wine in hand, out on the back deck.

"Shhh," Louise quickly signalled to her husband, covering her lips with her pointer finger.

A familiar squeaking sound could be heard coming from behind the couple. Within seconds, Blossom jumped up onto the railing and strode towards them. Breaking off a tiny piece of pizza, Louise stretched her hand out towards the assertive possum. It held onto her pinky finger with one hand, whilst taking the food offering in the other. Murray was fascinated by the critter's lack of trepidation.

"I think Blossom's become our resident pet," she smiled. "We'll have to remind everyone to keep the flyscreen sliders closed at all times, otherwise it could eat us out of house and home!"

"True, it looks like a highly intelligent animal, Lou." Murray concurred. "Well, I suppose we should call it a night, my love. Big day tomorrow. Do you want that last slice of pizza?"

"No, thank you darling, we'll put it in the fridge if you don't want it. The kids would love to see this…if the poor thing's game enough to hang around here for the next week." Watching Blossom slowly dawdle off, Louise then took their rubbish to the bin while Murray locked up.

Next morning, Murray entertained his children while Louise performed her culinary artistry in preparation for Christmas lunch. The Perrys arrived just before noon and as Louise opened the door to greet them, Joshua hugged her tightly before giving a full, running commentary on their long trip north.

Inside, the adults stood gazing out at the panoramic coastline then the Corbets showed them through the house. There was much 'oooing' and 'aaahing' from the Perrys. Neither Gordon nor Dale had ever been inside a pole home. They were astounded by the spaciousness of the structure. Marty was more than excited to have Joshua at his holiday house and immediately took his friend downstairs to show him the 'passion pit'.

Together the men unloaded the station wagon while Louise and Dale fed their daughters. By the time everyone got settled, Murray and Louise were preparing to leave for the airport. Dale suggested that Marty and Annie remain at home with her and Gordon, to allow the couple some time alone with their New Zealand family.

The Keane's flight was half an hour overdue but this allowed the Corbets to enjoy a leisurely coffee while waiting for them to touch down. John, Julie and the children were among the first passengers through customs and immigration. Louise's niece and nephew bounded up to the couple, followed more sedately by their smiling parents, dragging suitcases behind them.

Exiting the terminal, the Keanes were immediately hit by Queensland's steamy humidity. This was in part due to a major storm brewing out west which appeared to be tracking towards the ocean. After piling their luggage into the back of the people mover, the group slowly headed south from Brisbane to the Gold Coast.

Bringing their suitcases into the house, introductions took place all round. Louise found it uncanny that the Kiwi contingent had never met Dale or Joshua, let alone her own children. John and Julie were first introduced to Gordon at Louise's Citizenship party, though very little conversation was exchanged between them.

As the increasingly tempestuous weather gained momentum, Louise gathered up Lucy, Mark, Joshua and her son. Taking them to the large living room windows, she began to explain what occurs during a tropical storm.

"See how dark those clouds are?" Louise pointed out. "If you keep watching, you'll see flashes of lightning come out of the clouds. When the storm gets even closer, you'll be able to hear cracks of thunder after each lightning strike. The closer and closer it gets, the amount of time between seeing the lightning and hearing the thunder will get shorter. And then the whole storm will blow out over the ocean. I love storms. I think they're really exciting."

"Will you stay with us, Aunty Lou?" Josh asked.

"Yes, of course. We'll all be here Josh, so we can watch it together. Now when the storm moves over the top of us, it's going to drop a lot of rain…and it might get pretty windy because we're up so high off the ground. If you feel the house shake a little bit, I promise you, it's nothing to worry about."

"It's getting darker and darker," Lucy declared, her eyes as big as saucers.

"Yes, sweetheart, it is," her aunt smiled. "That's because the clouds have blocked out the sun."

During Louise's meteorology lesson, the remainder of the household had quietly entered the room and were seated on the lounge suite. "What should we do if we ever get caught outside in a storm, Aunty Lou?" her husband asked.

Grinning back at him, she replied, "That's a very good question, Uncle Murray. Well, it's important not to take shelter under any trees, because they might blow over in the wind. You should try to find somewhere safer to stay…like inside a house or a building of some sort. And just like now, when you can see the storm's really close, you should stay away from glass windows and doors, just in case they break. That's why we're all going to move back to the lounge, until it passes over."

Inside a minute, gusty, swirling wind ripped through the trees, tossing them back and forth like ocean waves. Heavy rain droplets on the deck were a cue for the deluge of rain that was soon to come. A huge flash of lightning, followed shortly thereafter by an echoing clap of thunder, saw everyone grimace.

"Ooooh…that was a big, big one, Mummy," Marty shouted, snuggling into her.

Annie and Wendy, who were perched on their fathers' laps, immediately began whimpering. Lucy reached into the nearby toy box and pulled out a plush animal to give each baby, in the hope she could alleviate their tears. Her plan appeared to be working until a second crack of thunder boomed across the hinterland, but this one wasn't quite as loud as the first.

Just as the rain began to ease, out west, pinkish hues of the setting sun appeared below the cloud line. Joshua and Marty returned to their Lego construction, inviting Mark and Lucy to join them.

"Well, that was quite the spectacle," Julie remarked to her sister. "Glad it hit after we landed. I don't think I've ever seen that amount of rainfall in such a short period."

"I know. Welcome to Queensland!" Louise replied. "That reminds me…while I have you all together, Murray and I just want to let you know that we're not connected to the city's water supply here. We have two big tanks down in the garden and I'm guessing they'll be pretty full after that downpour, but it's important for everyone to check that each tap is turned off tightly after you've used it. Okay?"

"Yeees," the children chorused.

The Perrys had bathed the babies earlier and dressed them in their pyjamas while Murray and Louise were at the airport, so they were ready for dinner and sleep. While Julie fed Annie, her sister poured the children a drink and prepared their spaghetti bolognese for dinner.

With the kids quietly seated at the dining table, Louise delivered their meals and said, "If you finish everything in your bowls, there's red jelly and ice cream for dessert. But remember the rule…no empty bowl, no dessert."

Four beaming faces eagerly nodded back at her.

Mark declared, "We have that rule at home, Aunty Lou…don't we Mum?"

"Yes buddy, we do," Julie replied, as a smile passed between the sisters.

Annie and Wendy were now tucked up in their cots, so Gordon watched over the children as they gobbled up their dinner. Dale and Julie helped Louise prepare some vegetables to accompany the garlic lamb shanks that had been slowly cooking in her crockpot all day. Meanwhile, Murray and John took all the Keane's luggage downstairs then the host gave his brother-in-law a quick rundown on everything he needed to know.

Returning to the top floor, Murray clapped his hands together and said, "Righteo…now it's our turn. What would the adults like to drink?"

Furnishing them with a beverage of their choice, he then raised a toast. "Here's to our first official guests and a great holiday. To the Keanes, and the Perrys, Lou and I are absolutely chuffed to have you all here together. Good health everyone."

• • • • •

Christmas Eve at 'Mirikai' wasn't exactly serene with a house full of twelve people. It was in stark contrast to what the Corbets were accustomed to in their Wongawallan home, but Murray and Louise couldn't be happier. The sound of babies giggling, children laughing and adults conversing, echoed through the open spaces like a breath of fresh air.

The older children made their haven downstairs, carting with them almost every toy in the house. From time to time during the course of the morning, one of the adults would check on them but for the most part, they were happy to be alone. All appeared to be getting along very nicely. Lucy, Mark and Joshua did their best to include Marty in every game they played, so even the youngest member of the group was having a blast. It was evident that Marty was becoming particularly fond of Lucy, probably because she took it upon herself to play a motherly role.

Louise phoned the Johnsons that morning to invite them over for mid-afternoon drinks on the deck. Robyn told her that she and her husband were looking forward to meeting the entire clan whom they'd heard so much about. Sadly, Romano wouldn't be able to attend as he was in Noosa visiting his sister, but Bill assured Louise that he'd be back on Boxing Day.

Just after lunch, Julie and Louise took all the Christmas decorations downstairs and watched their excited children adorn the tree. Both sisters recalled fond memories of this special occasion in their own house and it was wonderful to witness the cousins happily interacting with one another.

"Well…you've all done such a superb job," Louise smiled at the kids, "I think you should be rewarded. Just wait here and I'll be back in a moment."

"What is it, Mum? What's our reward?" Mark pleaded with her.

"I have no idea buddy," Julie confessed. "You'll just have to wait and see."

Returning with a large bucket of multi-coloured Playdough and a plastic felt-backed tablecloth, Louise said, "I think this should keep you all occupied for the afternoon."

Jumping for joy, the children first let out a simultaneous round of excitement before expressing their gratitude. Louise laid out the large tablecloth on the floor and said, "Now just make sure that all the Playdough stays on this mat, okay? That'll make it much easier for Julie and I to clean up."

All heads briskly started nodding as the sisters made their way back upstairs.

Bill and Robyn turned up shortly thereafter with two bottles of sparkling wine and a gift for the Corbets; an international cuisine recipe book and some unusual spices for the pantry. After heading downstairs to meet Joshua, Mark and Lucy for the first time, the Johnsons then joined the adult gathering out on the deck. Dale had placed Wendy and Annie side by side in their bouncinettes and as the balmy afternoon progressed, both fell asleep despite all the chatter and laughter surrounding them.

The Perrys and the Keanes were taking care of all household and parental duties this evening, allowing Murray and Louise a night off to enjoy the Johnson's company. Dale and Gordon volunteered to attend to dinner while Julie and John bathed the babies, ensured that the older children had showered and donned pyjamas, and all were ready for bed when the time came.

Sausages and salad were on the menu for the kids while the adults were being served satay chicken curry, accompanied by coconut rice and papadams. By very early that evening, Louise almost felt as though she was back in New Guinea with her house girl, Maria, on hand. It had turned out to be a very relaxing day, though she knew tomorrow would be vastly different.

As darkness set in, Murray draped a string of Christmas lights on the tree and the older children turned them on before going to bed. They were delighted with the bright, twinkling glow.

"Uncle Murray," Joshua started, "how will Santa know where to find us?"

"On Christmas Eve, he knows where every child in the world is, Joshy. And I'll bet he's writing his 'naughty or nice' list right now. Okay, time for bed you lot. Remember…he won't come if you're not asleep. Go and give everyone a goodnight hug and one final thing. No going near the presents under the tree until after breakfast."

The eight adults enjoyed their delicious meal whilst imbibing on the deck, overlooking the sparkling lights of the Gold Coast. At 7:30pm when the Johnsons left, Murray and Gordon placed a plate of cookies out the front for Santa and some carrots for the reindeer, as they promised the children they would.

After a quick clean-up and a few quiet card games, the couples dispersed to organise their children's gifts then retired to bed. Louise quickly checked that Marty was asleep before her husband crept outside to dispose of the cookies and carrots, leaving only a few crumbs and one chunk of carrot on the footpath.

The older children were up so early the next morning, they practically rose with the sun. Even the babies hadn't stirred up to this point. Anxious to get breakfast done, Murray prepared pancakes for ten while Annie and Wendy sucked on their bottles.

Downstairs, the kids' excitement was palpable. They grabbed for their stockings and began raking through them with mouths wide open. The adults had collectively decided to give the children gifts in the form of entry passes to two theme parks and some McDonald's vouchers. Inside each stocking they also found a Lego set, a variety of tasty treats and a note from Santa which read, 'Your special present will be waiting for you when you get home'. Gift-wrapped under the tree they each received a beach towel and there was a beach-ball and a cricket set for all to share.

Santa gave Annie and Wendy matching plush mermaids, one pink and one purple, with shiny tails, long braided hair and tiaras. They were also given various 'touch and feel' vinyl books. Annie was mesmerised by her mermaid, though Wendy seemed far more interested in the books. Touching the fluffy wool on the sheep's back and the fish's silky scales, she let out a shrieking giggle that bemused everyone.

More than satisfied with their gifts, by 9am the fathers piled their children into the people-mover and headed for Main Beach at Southport. This left the women at home to prepare Christmas lunch and look after the babies.

Louise had pre-glazed a ham and made two trifles the day after they arrived; one with no alcohol for the kids, so that was a great head start. Dale and her sister were now helping baste and cook the turkey, plus make up a potato and a fresh, tossed salad. Julie was also planning to assemble a fruit punch for the children.

When the remaining family members returned from Southport, lunch was ready to serve and two tables were set up, end to end, out on the deck. Each was beautifully decorated with centrepieces consisting of four Playdough creations that the children had made the previous day: a gingerbread house, snowman, candy cane...and Marty's comical one-armed elf.

Throughout lunch, everyone enjoyed themselves immensely. Lucy took it upon herself to supervise the younger ones and became Louise's ultimate little co-hostess, helping out wherever she could. The Christmas crackers proved a hit. Inside, each one contained a small toy with an accompanying joke. After a great deal of laughter, the group agreed that the following were their favourites; 'What do you call a reindeer with bad manners? RUDE-olph!' and 'What do you call a reindeer who wears earmuffs? Anything you want! He can't hear you!'

With lunch over and stomachs almost bursting at the seams, Lucy, Mark, Joshua and Marty went downstairs to play with their new Lego sets while Annie and Wendy had a nap. Gordon poured the adults a second glass of wine, lemon squash for Dale, then the couples continued their conversation for well over an hour before the babies woke.

Murray smiled at Louise and kissed her on the cheek. "Bubs are up...so that means clean up time, chaps. Thank you so much ladies...a truly fabulous meal!"

John and Gordon shared his sentiment wholeheartedly. As Gordon left the table to change nappies and prepare the babies' bottles, Louise declared, "A siesta would be great, but that's not going to happen. We'll feed the girls downstairs and watch the kids work on their Lego creations for a while."

Mid-afternoon saw the Corbet's kitchen squeaky clean and the fathers had also tidied up the house, disposed of all the rubbish and vacuumed the floors. Murray then proposed they take all the children down to the park at the end of the street for a play on the swings and a game of cricket. "I think they'll all be in bed by 7pm, so we'll go now before they get too tired," he told Louise.

"Great idea. I'll just do them some toasties for dinner...and we'll have left-overs. There's still plenty of ham in the fridge and we hardly put a hole in the potato salad."

The three women thoroughly enjoyed their peace and quiet over the next few hours. Flicking through some Woman's Day and Women's Weekly magazines they chatted about celebrity gossip, entertainment news and fashion trends before settling into a comfortable silence to complete some crossword puzzles.

When the exhausted troops finally returned home, Murray, Gordon and John oversaw the showering of the older children while Louise and Dale attended to bathing the babies. As the children were hardly hungry, a final treat of trifle and custard for dinner would suffice. All the adults agreed to forego dinner entirely and signed off Christmas night with coffee and a few shortbread biscuits.

Boxing day saw the entire family refreshed and just after lunch, 'Mirikai' was bustling with even more invited guests. Brian Clarke and his wife, Jane, dropped in for a visit that afternoon, as did Romano and three other neighbouring couples. All the children kept busy downstairs in the 'passion pit'. They'd turned it into a makeshift cubby-house using Louise's spare sheets and blankets.

The remainder of the family's holiday was spent at Sea World, Dreamworld, the beach, and a day trip to the zoo in Brisbane. Their time together literally flew by and before they knew it, a New Year was born. Gordon had to commence work on the 3rd, so the Perry family departed two days before the Kiwis returned to Auckland. During that time, the Keanes explored the hinterland with Murray, Louise and Marty as their guides. They walked forest trails, visited the waterfalls and strolled through Mt Tamborine's arts and crafts market.

All too soon, both families arrived at Brisbane Airport for the Keane's early departure. With hugs and kisses for everyone, the Corbets then waved them goodbye and sadly watched on as John, Julie, Lucy and Mark made their way to the boarding gate. It had been a wonderful holiday...one they'd remember forever.

CHAPTER FORTY-ONE

Like a tiny yacht in a boundless ocean, Murray and Louise continued to capture the wind in their sails and make the most of any opportunity the currents sent their way. It wasn't always smooth sailing but for the most part, their lives drifted along, happily intertwined with family, work and friends.

Twenty-three years had passed so quickly, the couple could hardly fathom their son turning twenty-one next week. Even Annie was only six months shy of eighteen years of age.

As Marty grew, his caring, charismatic personality flourished. He followed in Joshua Perry's footsteps, first joining the nippers at Narrabeen Surf Life Saving Club then graduating to senior cadet by age fourteen. Marty just loved to swim and was proud to represent his high school at State level. He'd come a very long way since almost drowning as a toddler.

Joshua and Marty attended the same school, though Joshua was three grades ahead, meaning their friendship circles were years apart. Nevertheless, Joshua always kept a keen eye on his 'cousin'. Marty also became a valued member of the school's rowing team, while Joshua played cricket and enjoyed sailing. During the winter months, both boys played rugby union.

By the time Joshua completed Grade 12, he left Sydney to obtain a degree in architecture at the New England University in Armidale, New South Wales. This meant living on campus, which was quite the conundrum for Marty, so upon completing the final school year himself, he enrolled at the same university. With good grades under his belt, particularly in mathematics, he chose to pursue an electrical engineering degree.

During her younger years, Annie was always a confident, highly intelligent, quiet achiever…and little had changed as she approached adulthood. At around the age of six, Murray and Louise told their daughter she was adopted by way of a special bedtime story, just as they had done with Marty. Her passion for the natural world was unwavering, so Annie's eyes were already firmly set on studying marine biology or environmental sciences.

Wendy Perry, on the other hand, was far more of a social butterfly. She oozed self-assurance and when it came to considering her future, by mid-way through the final year of high school, she was more than happy to leave it 'in the lap of the career Gods' to guide her forward.

Though the girls' personas were worlds apart, Annie and Wendy remained the closest of friends. Like their older brothers, both excelled in their chosen sports. They played competition netball on the same team and also enjoyed competing in swimming events. Since they were babies, Joshua and Marty always looked out for their younger sisters and together, all four were a very tightly-knit group.

Gordon and Dale had managed to cram some international travel into their busy lives, visiting Europe and doing an African safari adventure some two years later. Their marriage was strong, with Joshua and Wendy still being the most treasured assets in their lives. Contemplating a third child within a few years of Wendy being born, Dale fell pregnant but sadly lost the baby at around fourteen weeks gestation. After that, the couple decided not to try again. They were extremely grateful for the son and daughter they already had…and Dale confessed that it wasn't a scenario she could ever face again. Instead, they adopted a playful, cream-coloured puppy named Lacy; a French poodle from the local pound.

Dale's mother was now facing some serious health issues and with age no longer on her side, Emily rarely visited her family. She became reclusive and was determined to remain at the nursing home where doctors were readily available around the clock. Obviously, her daughter, son-in-law and grandchildren visited frequently, but Dale admitted to Louise that her mother had lost the strength and the will to fight for life.

Murray and Gordon continued in their rewarding careers with Qantas. 'The flying kangaroo', though still a relatively young company on the global stage, was now beginning to make its mark. Planning included doubling their international fleet to extend to destinations such as the United Kingdom, the United States and the United Emirates.

Together, the men built, sold and retained another four properties over a nine-year span, including a condominium of ten units. Thanks to a great deal of hard work, their real estate portfolio accrued to a balance they'd never imagined possible.

Louise and Dale formed a business partnership, consulting on their husbands' various projects and those of numerous others. After being interviewed by the media, an article on the dynamic duo appeared in the Sydney Morning Herald newspaper and the request for their services skyrocketed. The aunty-niece collaboration became the talk of Sydney's northern suburbs.

Computer software development and information technology had boomed during the last decade, so much so, that computers were practically running the world. It took Louise and her business's staff, now totalling ten, a great deal of time and effort to keep up with all the advancements. Martha Dean described it as, 'forgetting everything you learned yesterday, because it's no longer relevant tomorrow'. As of six years ago, Martha became co-owner of the business and took over as full-time manager, much to her mentor's delight.

At any given chance to escape the city's hustle and routine of daily life, Murray and Louise could be found taking solace at 'Mirikai'…their 'place of peace'. It was also a haven they shared with many friends, both old and new. Over the years, the Victorian Corbet family, the Perrys, the Hoffmans and the Deans had stayed at the holiday house. The Keane family were also regular visitors, flying over at least once a year to meet up with their Australian family. The Corbets weren't always present, they were more than happy to allow family and close friends to utilise the home in their absence. The Evans family from Brisbane had stayed for a week, as had the Wilsons from Perth and on more than one occasion, Jillian and her family, now consisting of her husband and two daughters, met up with mutual friends from the Sunshine Coast and travelled down to stay for some fun in the sun.

Just over a year ago, Murray and Louise befriended Eleanor and Dirk McGrady, a Bundaberg couple. They were keen golfers and Dirk was a still-life artist. In oils, he painted the Corbets a huge canvas of two hybrid hibiscus flowers which hung in pride of place; the upstairs living room in their holiday home.

As Murray and Louise sat in front of the cosy fire at 'Mirikai' one evening, Murray began to nod off. His eyelids grew heavy, refusing to stay open. Seated on the lounge, his head fell back and he was out to the world.

Intermittently sipping on white wine, Louise studied her husband's profile in the glow of the flickering flames. He looked so utterly content. Murray was still a handsome, youthful man, despite greying a little around the temples. "I love you even more than the day we married," Louise whispered.

Before waking him, she gazed back at the fire, contemplating her life thus far. It had been twenty-four years, to the day, since Ross Green took his own life. Thinking about that pivotal event provoked a truth which she acknowledged with an open heart. His death was in fact, Louise's rebirth. *'To life, love and second chances,'* she inwardly smiled, raising her glass to take the final sip.

Whilst many aspects of this novel are based on my own life, some pseudonyms apply. Several characters may recognise themselves or relate to events described, many of which have been altered by means of 'poetic license'.

I've never personally experienced any form of domestic violence but sadly, the same can't be said for a very close friend of mine whose life was taken back in 2002. Pronouns have been used in the following account to conceal the couple's true identity, though the investigation was widely covered by The Gold Coast Bulletin newspaper and other media organisations at the time.

TRUTH

The couple purchased a home opposite ours and after introducing themselves, invited me in for coffee. They expressed a wish to meet some of the residents of our rural community by way of a barbeque at their home, so left it to me to invite a dozen or so neighbours.

A delightful afternoon was spent overlooking the eastern hinterland and coastal stretch of the Gold Coast, from Jacobs Well to the New South Wales border and inland to Binna Burra.

Nine of us locals formed solid friendships, sharing meals in one another's homes and occasionally enjoying weekends away on camping trips.

After two years in the house, the couple discovered that it had been entirely infested by termites. Access was gained through a power conduit, an afterthought of the previous owner, which hadn't been treated for white ants at the time of installation. In order to replace all the timber framework, stripping the interior wall linings and replacing the frames within the exterior brickwork would be an onerous task, but one which the owner was capable of carrying out.

This setback caused him great distress and I believe that it severely impacted his mental health. He wanted to fix the house and sell-up but his wife, having formed valued friendships in their new location, wanted to complete the reconstruction and stay put. These opposing views caused much disharmony between the couple.

Seven members of our group shared a still, which was located in a room underneath the couple's pool. It was the perfect place to make our own whiskey, gin, rum and liqueurs. During the house repairs, he began consuming rum in copious quantities and became quite aggressive after two or more rounds, as was often the case.

One weekend, on the Sunday, all nine of us were returning from a camping trip to Lake Catharaba when we stopped for ice-creams. This was the last time I ever saw my friend.

He called my husband the following Tuesday to cancel an appointment that his wife and I had made for that afternoon when I returned from work. He informed Bob that she'd been urgently called to Sydney. Bob expressed his concerns and enquired if she was alright. He was abruptly told that her trip was 'a family matter', putting paid to any further discussion. We both knew that they didn't have any relatives in Sydney.

We'd received an email from her around 4.30pm the previous day and this was the last known contact that she'd had with anyone. Given the fact that my friend and I spoke daily on the phone, or emailed one another, it appeared very odd that her communication suddenly became non-existent.

Eighteen days after our last contact, at around 10:30pm on a Thursday evening, I was woken by a phone call from her close friend in Sydney. I'd never met this woman but I'd certainly heard much about her. She informed me of her concerns after being told by her friend's husband that his wife had moved out while the renovations were being undertaken. Apparently, she was fed-up with all the noise and the mess. He even proposed that his wife may well fly to the U.K. to visit a friend who'd recently moved over there from Sydney. Immediately there was a haunted silence between the caller and myself. Somehow, we both knew that our friend was dead.

As I lived closest to the crime it was decided that I should be the one to announce it, so before work early the next morning, I called into the police station to file a Missing Persons report. By the end of my interview with the officer, he asked, "You don't think this is an actual missing person, do you?" To that I replied, "No officer, I believe this is a homicide." Before leaving the station, he arranged for detectives to meet me at my office later that day when they returned on duty.

Meanwhile, I phoned Bob to update him on the interview. He too believed that our friend was dead. After ending the call, Bob walked up to the couple's house to retrieve the still, ostensibly for our own use. He was surprised to find the homeowner had packed his car, ready to spend the weekend cycling in the Northern Rivers of New South Wales. Labourers were onsite, continuing to assist the owner with his reconstruction. Swiftly returning home with the still, Bob called me to suggest that if the police wished to interview our friend's husband, they should get there pronto…before he departed.

This they did and after asking him numerous questions, one that must have really 'rattled his cage', he ordered the police off his property. They then directly visited my husband and questioned his account of the facts. When Bob's answers failed to gel with the perpetrator's story, the police phoned me and asked if I'd make an official statement before accompanying them to inspect the house, in the hope we could find some solid answers.

Arriving at the property, the first thing I noticed was the pool. The couple had planned to have its walls raised but given the fact that it was far from a priority in the scheme of things, I was surprised to find the pool empty and the walls had indeed been elevated. Calling over the labourers for information, they explained that just over two weeks ago, after returning onsite that morning, the owner informed them that concrete was due for delivery and they'd be working on the pool that day. Between the afternoon of leaving the property only the day before, and arriving the next morning, rubble and mesh had already been laid down in the bottom of the pool, together with formwork for a new step and the raised sides.

Immediately it was assumed that my friend's body was buried amongst the rubble, now completely covered in concrete. Cautiously entering the home, which was a total mess, I discovered no sign of a woman's possessions anywhere in the house. The wardrobe in the spare bedroom which I knew was crammed with my friend's clothes, was now empty. Furniture had been disposed of and in their bedroom upstairs, not even a piece of her jewellery could be found. In the office, we managed to locate her passport, so she certainly wasn't travelling overseas. The police retrieved the computer which was later found to have been utilised for investments and the viewing of pornographic websites using her husband's own password.

To cut this very long saga abruptly short, his body was recovered at the base of a waterfall near Nimbin in New South Wales...wrists slashed and throat cut. At the top of the falls, an empty bottle of rum; the only evidence behind his spiralling demise.

My dear friend was officially declared deceased after three years. Her bank account remained untouched since her disappearance and her body was never found.

www.ingramcontent.com/pod-product-compliance
Lightning Source LLC
Chambersburg PA
CBHW061052100726
47911CB00012B/197